The
Queen's
Faithful
Companion

The
Queen's
Faithful
Companion

A Novel of Queen Elizabeth II and
Her Beloved Corgi, Susan

Eliza Knight

WILLIAM MORROW

An Imprint of HarperCollinsPublishers

HarperCollins books may be purchased for educational, business, or sales promotional use. For information, please email the Special Markets Department at SPsales@harpercollins.com.

FIRST EDITION

Designed by Diahann Sturge

Interstitial illustration © Caelestiss / Shutterstock
Title page and part opener image © chrisbrignell / Shutterstock

Library of Congress Cataloging-in-Publication Data has been applied for.

ISBN 978-0-06-328101-1

24 25 26 27 28 LBC 5 4 3 2 1

To my beloved faithful companions, Lady Belle and Merida, the sweetest loves, the quirkiest personalities, who inspired me to write a story about the love between a dog and her best friend

PART I

THE
PRINCESS

·୦ঙ৩·

PROLOGUE

$\mathcal{P}$RINCESS $\mathcal{L}$ILIBET

Late December 1939

$\mathcal{T}$here comes a time in every princess's life when she must set aside the nuances of childhood and preexisting ideals, because the reality of her future is most formidably laid at her feet.

Although she didn't realize it at the time, for thirteen-year-old Princess Lilibet, first in line to the throne after her father, King George VI, that moment came in the fall of 1939 when her country, a land over which she would someday reign, declared war against Germany. It was also at this time that Lilibet's sense of betrayal by a formerly most favored uncle was solidified, because how could he have placed such a great burden on her father?

Lilibet thrilled at the sounds of London as she exited Buckingham Palace. Just beyond the massive gates, car horns blared in the morning traffic, and people who'd gathered to watch the royal family cheered. Dookie, her favorite of the family dogs—a corgi—stopped short on the leash she held, one short front paw lifted, as he stiffened, ears perked. She glanced toward the wrought iron gates, the marching King's Guard in their red and black uniforms, hats as tall as her sister, Margaret, whom they called Margot.

For as long as she could remember the people of London had been enamored of her, always wanting to take her picture. Lilibet was happy to oblige, waving to the growing crowd as flashes from the cameras blinked at her from between the faces.

"Come along, Lilibet, Margot," their governess, Crawfie, urged.

Lilibet turned, and watched as Margot led their other corgi, Jane, into the waiting automobile.

"Come on, Dookie." The corgi glanced up at Lilibet, mouth open in almost a smile. He took one last glance at the throngs beyond the iron bars and then trotted toward the car with Lilibet racing after him.

For more months than she cared to count, Lilibet and her younger sister had been sequestered in Balmoral, Scotland, separated from their parents who'd remained in London. Everyone said it was for their own safety. Most of the children in the city had been sent to the country, and her parents didn't want them to be the exception, even though Lilibet made the argument they were safe behind the walls of Buckingham Palace.

To keep the two of them busy and feeling as though they were contributing to the war efforts, Crawfie arranged for the princesses to sew with some of the women in the nearby village. Lilibet didn't particularly like sewing, but she did like being a part of the group.

Now, as she clambered into the black Lanchester limousine, sitting beside her sister, opposite their smiling mother, Lilibet was glad for a chance to be on holiday, reunited with her parents again. They were "us four." And "us four" wasn't a thing if it was only "us two."

Dookie hopped up on the seat beside her, his tiny claws clicking against the window as he pushed himself up on his hind legs to stare out. Jane joined him, their little fluffy bottoms wiggling with excitement.

Lilibet had never been more excited about the prospect of a holiday with their parents. But she was nervous as well—because on this holiday there was already the anticipation of an ending, of a moment when the pleasure would be yanked away and the family would be separated once more. For this reason, she found it maddening how slowly the driver pulled through the gates of Buckingham Palace. The car was moving at such a snail's pace the princess couldn't help fearing that any moment her papa would open the door, step out onto the pavement, and—holding out a hand to their mother, Queen Elizabeth— leave Lilibet and Margot to be whisked away. Their majesties had decided their daughters ought to be closer to them in case something catastrophic happened. So, after their Christmas holiday at Sandringham in Norfolk, Lilibet and Margot would be moved to Windsor Castle. Well, Lilibet thought, at least that was closer than Balmoral. But Lilibet pushed that eventuality momentarily away. A glorious few weeks with her parents at Sandringham lay ahead, a holiday that felt almost normal. If anyone had dared to change those plans last minute, Lilibet had decided she might just pull a Margot and let everyone know what she thought about it—loudly and with a stamping foot.

"Will there be a blackout at Sandringham?" Margot asked as they passed the scores of people who'd gathered to wave good-bye to the royal family.

"Of course there will," Lilibet answered with all authority. "Sandringham is still in England. All of the country is under blackout orders."

Margot stuck her tongue out at Lilibet, who just shook her head and stared out the window. They passed by shop fronts with large signs painted in bold: Order Your Xmas Game and Poultry Here and Now!

Father Christmas waved outside a toy shop, his traditional red hat replaced with a tin helmet, looking like he might be marching to the front soon. Lilibet nudged Margot and pointed. Her sister squealed and waved wildly, causing Dookie to start barking and Papa to begin shushing him.

Lilibet grinned, thinking of the wrapped packages in the boot of the car that she and Margot had purchased at Woolworths in Scotland. Gifts for their parents and select others. But the best Christmas gift they'd selected was not from Woolworths. With the help of their grandmother Queen Mary they'd picked a beautiful Fabergé fan, of cream silk, and silk gauze leaf, with mother-of-pearl and pink and white enameled gold, decorated with diamonds. A glorious gift for their mother.

Two tiny paws pressed on Lilibet's knee. Dookie had somehow gotten down on the car floor and was nudging her hands for a lift back up. Lilibet obliged, giving the corgi a kiss on the nose. Not to be left out, Jane gave a short yip, and Margot tucked the second dog onto her small lap. Dookie, originally named Duke, had been brought into their family about six years ago, and Jane a few years after that. Crackers and Carol, the newest additions, born last Christmas Eve, were on the seat between their majesties, busily tugging back and forth on a stick they'd somehow sneaked into the car.

There was such a difference in the London they passed through on their way to the roads that would take them north to the safety of the Sandringham estate. Despite the coming holiday and its cheer, there was no missing that the country was at war. The pre-Christmas liveliness felt muted. Perhaps it was the lack of children running through the streets. The absence of mothers shopping, pushing their prams. Despite the festive shop windows there was no one to draw inside; the streets were unnaturally empty.

Christmas was bound to be solemn with so many fathers, sons, grandsons missing. Because while some men had been able to get leave to come home, others were still stationed in France and elsewhere abroad. Lilibet glanced at her father, who sat stoically beside her mother, both of them gazing out their respective windows, their hands clasped on the seat between them. Her father had been marching through the halls of the palace since Lilibet and Margot had arrived, practicing the Christmas speech he would record when they reached Sandringham. A speech promoting perseverance despite the understandable feelings of desolation. If his message was meant to soothe the adults, perhaps a similar message from her would soothe the children separated from their parents.

Even at her age, Lilibet wasn't oblivious to the world, or to the emotions of her parents. She knew, of course, that her father remained angry with his brother for abdicating in 1936. Papa had told Lilibet of his feelings himself. Even if the royal family had striven to hide that fact from the world, even if the staff had whispered about King George's displeasure when they thought she and Margot weren't listening.

Her father had believed that as a future queen she had the right to know what a disappointment it was that her uncle David decided to abandon his duties for matters of the heart. The very idea of choosing selfishness over duty sat so thick in her belly that Lilibet could hardly breathe when she thought of such behavior. Behavior made more wrong in her eyes by the enormous pressure this put on her beloved father.

Lilibet glanced toward her younger sister, so innocent at nine years old and filled with as much fire as an unbroken, wild horse. She would never do to Margot what their uncle had done to her father. She would never fail her family, or her country, by passing the crown to her younger sibling. Not ever.

* * *

LILIBET UNCURLED HERSELF from around Dookie's body as he leaped toward the window, wagging tail hitting her in the nose. Crackers and Carol were yipping and clamping their teeth on Mummy's hem in their excitement, while Jane sat on Margot's lap, panting and wagging her nubby tail, trying to escape the young princess's tight hold.

"We're here," Margot cried excitedly, letting go of Jane who inadvertently leaped on top of poor Dookie in order to get a better view.

The dogs seemed to know when and where they'd arrived, their levels of excitement different. Always more so when they reached their country estate, perhaps hopeful to go out in pursuit of game. Though they weren't allowed to work like the hunting dogs in the kennels, they loved to pretend, and Lilibet enjoyed watching.

The Lanchester pulled to a stop in front of the great house originally bought by Queen Victoria for her son Prince Albert— later Edward VII—and used as a holiday retreat ever since. The servants were lined up in a row to greet the royal family in front of the redbrick building with its cream-colored stone trim. Sandringham always reminded Lilibet so much of Hampton Court Palace.

Dookie and Jane burst from the car at the first moment the footman opened the door, startling some members of the staff. A butler tossed them each a little biscuit to keep them from tasting the ankles of the various servants who were unloading the car and greeting the royal family.

"Your Highness," the butler said, bowing deeply—a bow that was mimicked by all those standing at attention behind him.

"A happy Christmas to you all," the king said.

Even as her father was speaking, Margot darted beneath the stone portico and through the wooden front doors. Lilibet wasn't far behind. Someone needed to keep an eye on Margot— Lilibet had learned that over the years—but this time it was also an excuse to get on with the fun. Inside, the grand house smelled sublimely of Christmas—like a combination of wishes, crisp fir trees, and freshly steamed Christmas puddings.

Lilibet followed Margot to the dining room, where two newly cut fir trees stood tall and proud on separate tables. One tree was for the royal family itself, while the other was for the household. Candles had been placed evenly on the branches, surrounded by decorations, including gilt gingerbread, golden eggs, and red and ivory ribbons. There was a third tree, tall and just as beautifully decorated, in the sitting room. Until that moment, Lilibet had feared the holiday would somehow be taken from her; but now she was filled to the brim with Christmas happiness, and a broad smile spread across her face. Wrapping her arms around Margot, she gave her sister a squeeze. Margot squeezed her back, before ducking out from under her arms and reaching for one of the gingerbread men.

"Well, this looks splendid," Mummy said as she breezed into the room.

"Quite." Papa nodded with satisfaction. In his military uniform, which he'd taken to wearing at all times now that they were at war, he looked as if he'd just come from a tour of duty abroad.

Suddenly, a lively, wriggling mass burst into the room as the corgis raced to the tree and began running around it. Taking a detour, Dookie jumped up and closed his mouth around the gingerbread man in Margot's hand, racing away with it as she shouted.

Dookie dashed out of the room once more with Jane, Crackers, and Carol in pursuit, their yips echoing, followed by a howl from one of the servants who likely got stuck in the middle of the canine horde.

"It's a good thing they are cute," Queen Elizabeth murmured.

Lilibet wholeheartedly agreed with that sentiment. "Their bums are so fluffy," she whispered to Margot, knowing it would coax a much needed laugh out of her sister, who was close to tears about the lost gingerbread man. It did the trick, and Margot was back to her old self.

* * *

LILIBET LEANED HER ear against the closed office door, listening to her father as he struggled to push out the words of his Christmas message. They were prerecording the speech rather than broadcasting it live both to accommodate her father's speech impediment and because Christmas seemed to be the one holiday the family could still largely claim for their own.

"The festival . . . which we all know . . . as Christmas . . . is . . .   ab-ab-ab-ab-above all, the festival of peace and of the home . . . Among all free . . . peoples . . . the love of peace . . . is profound . . . , for this alone . . . gives . . . security . . . to the home . . . But . . . true peace . . . is in the hearts of men . . . and it is . . . the tragedy of this time . . . that there are . . . powerful . . . countries . . . whose whole direction . . . and policy . . . are based on . . . ag-ggression . . . and the suppression . . . of all that we hold dear for mankind."

He always had the most trouble with his *A*s, Lilibet noted. If only it were possible to write a speech leaving out that dreaded letter.

"There you are." The sharp tones of her governess sounded behind the princess. Lilibet whirled to see Crawfie standing, hands folded in front, looking down at her. Her thin hair was neatly styled, her plain wool skirt and jacket almost uniform like.

"You oughtn't to be snooping." Crawfie pursed her lips in the way she did when she was disappointed.

"If I am to be queen, then shouldn't I know what is expected?" Lilibet straightened, trying to mimic the stance her grandmother Queen Mary used when addressing members of the staff.

Crawfie, while employed by the royal household, was more of a family member. So she wasn't in the least intimidated. Without so much as a twitch, she replied, "It is expected as queen you'll not be so base as to eavesdrop."

Lilibet pressed her lips together. The woman had a point she couldn't argue with.

"Besides, it's time for tea." Crawfie started to turn, clearly expecting Lilibet to follow her.

Ordinarily, the princess would have. Lilibet believed in rules and the following of them. After all, if there were no chain of command, whether in a family or an entire country, things would fall apart. This, however, was a hill she'd decided to die on. "Papa is not done."

Crawfie paused, the squint of her eyes the only hint of her surprise. "He'll be done soon enough. Your queen is waiting."

One of the footmen took that moment to arrive with the dogs who'd been out for a walk, and rather than the exercise having calmed them, they seemed only to be overexcited now.

Let off their leashes they joined Lilibet and Crawfie as they headed to the drawing room, their doggie heads high, their paws prancing. There was something so endearing in their short-legged trot, the wiggle of their bums, the elegant lift of their chins. And, oh, how they loved. Yes, Lilibet thought, there was no other word for it. When Dookie cuddled up to her, he actually smiled, his eyes closed, and the muscles in his little snout flexed as if he were trying with all his might to show her his joy at being with her.

Lilibet had tea with her sister and then the two joined their parents and their grandmother Queen Mary in the cozy fire-light of the small sitting room that the family favored when alone, where presents lay beneath the tree ready for the family exchange. But despite the piles of wrapped packages, what immediately caught Lilibet's eye as she entered were the small stockings dangling from her mother's fingers. Little red velvet things, each with the name of a dog embroidered on it in silver thread.

"Would you ladies like to do the honors?" The queen held out the stockings to Margot and Lilibet.

Margot plucked out a ball which she tossed in Jane's direction, only to be intercepted by Crackers, with Carol nipping at his heels. Lilibet took Dookie's stocking from her mother and made eye contact with the corgi. He came forward and sat down in front of her, his gaze concentrating so hard on her that it felt as if he were peering into her soul.

"You're a good boy, Dookie," she said quietly, pulling a biscuit from his stocking and holding it toward him. "Gentle."

Dookie understood. He gingerly parted his black lips and slowly clamped his tiny white teeth on the biscuit, waiting until she said, "Bon appétit," before tucking in to chew. They'd practiced this many times over the last six years, and Dookie had learned that Lilibet had infinite patience and was always willing to reward good behavior.

But even Lilibet's patience had its limits, and she was delighted that it was, at last, time to sit down to open her own Christmas presents and see how her parents liked the gifts she and Margot had selected for them. She dearly hoped her mother would love the Fabergé fan.

* * *

THE FOLLOWING MORNING, after attending church at St. Mary Magdalene, the family sat together in comfortable silence for the short ride back to Sandringham for their holiday feast and the broadcast of Papa's Christmas message—something they would listen to with the rest of the nation.

Lilibet stared out the car window at the cloud-riddled sky, and for a moment her mind left the lovely local scene with its scent of snow in the air. She found herself wondering what Prince Philip was doing this Christmas Day. Philip was the son of Prince Andrew of Greece and Denmark and Princess Alice of Battenberg and, through their mutual relation Queen Victoria, was Lilibet's third cousin. They'd first met at the wedding of her uncle Prince George to Philip's cousin Princess Marina in 1934. They'd become reacquainted earlier this year on her visit to the Royal Naval College at Dartmouth, where Philip had charmed her with his humor and his athleticism as he leaped over the tennis nets. Although he was nearly five years older than she, they'd exchanged a few letters since, a cordial correspondence in which Philip never made her feel like a little girl.

With her face heating up at the thought of Philip, Lilibet gave a sideways glance at her family to make sure they hadn't noticed.

Margot teased Lilibet whenever she spied her writing to Philip, calling it a crush and singing rubbish songs about it. Crawfie insisted Philip was too old for her. But Lilibet was four years older than Margot and they'd grown up dressing alike and playing together. What difference did a few short years make? Besides, he was lonely, and in a way, so was she now that Papa had become king.

Lilibet bit her lip, returning her attention to the overcast sky. Perhaps it *was* a crush, she conceded to herself. So what? Didn't every princess dream about a Prince Charming? It didn't mean she was going to marry Philip.

ROYAL REPORT

TRUSTED NEWS OF ALL THINGS ROYAL

There's been a new addition to the Royal Family. Fans of the Pembroke Welsh corgis, Their Majesties have procured for our beloved Princess Elizabeth on the occasion of her eighteenth birthday a corgi of her own. We've yet to learn the name of the newest royal pup, but we have heard from an anonymous source that a proper bed has been commissioned to match Princess Elizabeth's new suite of rooms in pink and flowered chintz. Coming of age, Princess Elizabeth, the heir presumptive, has been given a personal household at Buckingham Palace along with an official flag displaying her own royal coat of arms. Though she has been named counsellor of state, King George VI has yet to name his daughter heir apparent, as there is still a chance a son could be conceived, thus our princess has not been titled Princess of Wales.

·⁕·

CHAPTER ONE

SUSAN

February 1944

Memory is all anyone has left of the days they've lived, those they've loved, laughs shared, tears shed.

Memories are special gifts we take out and unwrap over and over again.

Without memory, we are lost. Who is to say we've really lived? Or how we find our way home?

Without remembrance, we vanish with the wind. Fade into the rhythmic ticktick of an earthly clock that signals the passing of a currency no one can quite grasp—*time*. But then there is a smell, a sound, a touch, and some elusive moment is snatched from the far reaches of a labyrinth inside our head and relived.

Moments good *and* bad.

The first memories I have are of being warm amid a heap of squirming furry bodies. The simple pleasure of a full belly and stretching as far as my paws would let me reach.

Have you ever noticed how good it feels to stretch? Take a moment, I'll wait.

I am stretching now. Feeling very at home as the squeaks of my brothers and sisters sound around me, the comforting tones of my mother's heavy panting. And then—magic. The delighted sound of human voices reaches me where I lie cozily. Not the humans who were raising me, different ones. They don't all sound the same, humans, but the vibrations inside their necks mix with the formations of their shortened tongues creating an enchanting noise: *words.*

The deeper voice belonging to a stranger mixes with the softer lilt of the woman who checks on us throughout the day. I like her voice, she is kindhearted; she rubs our tummies and loves our mother.

"I think she'll like that one." The low timbre vibrates in my ears, and I squirm deeper into the pile, trying to hide.

"The one on the left?" asks our keeper.

"No, no, the one in the middle."

"Ah, that's Pippa."

That's me. I'm Hickathrift Pippa, a Pembroke Welsh corgi.

"Pippa." I can hear the grin in his voice, and then he wraps me up in his large, five-fingered paws and lifts me into the air.

I startle, my stubby limbs straightening out, and I have that strange feeling of falling with no place good to land, only to realize I am still tucked safely in the stranger's grasp. The two humans laugh, a sound that makes me want to join them, but all that comes out is a minuscule yip.

I blink open my eyes, my vision blurry. The man is huge; his blue eyes look into mine. Everything in the world stills a little. There's a connection between us. How surprising. But I feel as if I can see straight into this human's soul. I may not fully understand the deep meaning behind what I can see, but I'm not afraid of this human. Instead, I feel at peace.

The flesh snout on him is not as long as Mother's, and I wonder what it would taste like if he were close enough to lick. He smiles. I squint my eyes, trying as hard as I can to smile back. I decide I like him, and I want him to know it.

"Hello, Pippa, a pleasure to meet you," he says. "I'm King George."

I am not sure what a king is. But even at my tender age I understand the pack system we dogs use. There's the alpha, the betas, the deltas, and the omegas. I'm pretty sure this man is used to being the alpha.

I open my mouth to ask, but all that happens is a massive yawn that ends on a short squeak. I keep forgetting that dogs can't speak in the same way as humans.

"Adorable," he croons, his voice changing into something that makes me wriggle deeper into his hands. I'd be happy if he held me longer.

"The princess will love her," my caretaker says.

The man's big hands stroke my head and rub my belly. "When can you bring her to Windsor?" he asks.

"On her highness's birthday if you'd like." My caretaker touches my nose with her finger, her hand that always smells slightly of biscuits.

"Brilliant." King George lowers me back into the nest of blankets with my brothers and sisters, the dull thud of his shoes echoing against the kennel floor and his voice fading as he and my caretaker drift away.

I didn't fully understand right then what was happening, but I soon learned that this chance meeting would change the course of my life, and those of the generations of corgis to come after me.

Today I became Lilibet's, but more important, a future queen became mine.

·ᴏᴥᴇ·

CHAPTER TWO

PRINCESS LILIBET

Windsor Castle
April 21, 1944

*T*oday was her eighteenth birthday.

Princess Lilibet bolted upright on the soft mattress, swung her feet over the side of her four-poster bed, and then, feeling the draft of the old medieval castle at Windsor, quickly tucked them back beneath the covers. She knew it was morning, but her room was still pitch-black. The windows were draped in thick curtains—blackout curtains—to prevent any light from shining out. A country at war had to protect itself from enemy pilots searching for any glow. Dropping their bombs when they spotted one.

Stifling a yawn, she slipped a hand beneath her silk pillow and pulled out the envelope she'd been saving for the perfect day—her birthday—to open. With a smile, Lilibet leaped out of bed. She hopped on tiptoe as her feet came off the rug and met the chill of the wood floor, as she moved toward the window.

Wrenching open the heavy curtains, she blinked rapidly, momentarily blinded. Mother Nature had, it seemed, listened to her royal request for a beautiful day. The upper ward was quiet; a few liveried guards stood at attention at their posts. Ravens perched and cawed on the castle walls, greeting the day. Unlike those at the Tower of London, these ravens were free to fly away. But otherwise, it was too early yet for anyone to be about. A glance over her shoulder at the clock on the mantel showed it was still a good thirty minutes before either her old governess, Crawfie, or Bobo—as she called her nursemaid turned dresser Margaret MacDonald—would come in to wake her.

"Perfect timing," Lilibet mused to herself, sitting down in the near window and curling her legs under her for warmth. Her moments of peace and solitude were limited—so she always cherished them. Today in particular they would be few.

She smoothed her hand over the envelope she'd laid in her lap. The familiar scrawl on the front was as welcome as the summer sun on the Scottish moors at Balmoral Castle. Every morning for a week now, she'd pinched the paper of the envelope and willed herself to put it back unopened until today. Yet now the moment had come she realized the anticipation had also been delightful, so she let her gaze wander out the window in front of her. In the distance a pack of family dogs yipped as a footman took them for their morning walk. Lilibet herself made a daily practice of walking the dogs after luncheon. But the morning walk belonged to a footman because the pups woke early, as early as the earliest rising servant.

Lilibet watched the footman throw a stick and all the dogs—Crackers, the only corgi left to them, Labradors, and a Tibetan lion—took off toward the Round Tower in what seemed a race for their lives. And she smiled, loving as she did the sheer joy and exuberance of animals at play. Animals were so blessedly clueless in those moments of life's larger trials. They didn't care about Hitler, his Nazi goons, or the Luftwaffe trying to bomb England into oblivion. They didn't worry about wearing and saying the right thing—something she worried about daily. Nor did they care for such things as state secrets and the hierarchical system. Particularly when they were at play, they lived in the moment. Right now, she thought, all they cared about was who was going to reach the bit of dead tree branch first.

Watching them cavort, she recalled the first time she'd ever seen a corgi. She'd been seven and begged her father for one. That was when Dookie had joined their family. And she had loved him like he was of her own blood. The pain of losing him at the start of the war had yet to wane. And more recently there'd been another loss: Dookie's playmate, Jane, had been run over by an estate worker. Lilibet flinched anytime a vehicle came near the dogs now.

Lilibet glanced at the clock again, her belly doing a little flip.

At any moment Margot was bound to burst through the door in song as she did every birthday. And Lilibet did not want her sister to snatch away this one secret gift she'd been saving for herself. The time had come to open the letter from Prince Philip.

Slipping a thumbnail beneath the flap of the envelope, she released it without tearing it. The scratch of his cursive bloomed on the paper folded inside. She drew the pages out, stopping only to listen for footsteps outside her bedroom door.

Papa had made it clear he didn't like the idea of Lilibet and Prince Philip as a couple. He thought she was too young for anything serious, and the prince too penniless to be a good match—though the king admitted he found Philip charming enough, and even liked hunting with him. Recently her father and mother had started to discourage Lilibet's contact with the prince, which seemed ridiculous, given it had been going on for five years.

At the wedding of Philip's cousin Princess Alexandra to King Peter of Yugoslavia, Papa had gone so far as to tell Philip's uncle that there should be no more thought given to a marriage between Philip and Lilibet. Of course, that statement, when leaked, though who knew how, had only fueled romantic speculation on the part of the public. Lilibet herself had never expressed her wishes out loud, and as far as she knew, Philip had not either. Her cheeks still heated with embarrassment at the thought that at someone else's wedding last month, her own marriage prospects had been debated.

But if Lilibet were honest—and she prided herself on being so unless discretion demanded she remain silent—Prince Philip was a man she'd been in love with since the moment she'd watched him leap over those tennis nets at Dartmouth years ago.

Those feelings had been cemented when he'd come several months ago to stay at Windsor during Christmas. He'd laughed the loudest at the *Aladdin* pantomime they put on in the Waterloo Chamber, the sound echoing from the walls stripped bare of artwork and the carpets removed. With every chuckle from his direction, Lilibet became more enthusiastic and animated in her performance as Aladdin himself. She was playacting for Philip more than for anyone else in the audience. At night, they'd turned the gramophone on and danced until nearly one in the morning. Only stopping regretfully and parting from each other when Crawfie made remarks about beauty sleep and the reputation of the princesses.

That had been one of the most memorable Christmases Lilibet could recall.

From beneath her bedroom door came the boisterous barks and trotting footfalls of the dogs. Very soon, Crawfie was likely to come knocking, wondering why Lilibet was still in her night-clothes, which of course was the result of her begging Bobo to come late so she could sleep in, a rarity even on a birthday.

Lilibet hurried to read the letter, prepared to tuck it safely beneath a cushion on her chair if anyone came in.

Dearest Princess,

How much I regret not being there in person to wish you the happiest of birthdays. I am certain you will be blessed with many beautiful gifts that will hold a special place in your heart for all time, and that the celebrations will be worthy of a woman as endearing as you are to so many.

A woman . . . Philip called her a woman.

One of her greatest fears was that he still thought of her as a girl and considered her someone entertaining to exchange letters with and to dance with when no one else was around. She worried that when he was living his larger life she was mostly out of his mind as he pursued more worldly women. There certainly had been gossip . . .

But in his opening lines Philip made clear he thought *her* a woman. So maybe there was hope yet that her affections might be returned.

If only he were here in person for her birthday. She'd never be brave enough to ask him how he felt about her, but perhaps she would be able to glean something just from his manners, his actions.

She was used to receiving praise, being a princess of England, and she'd been trained to accept it with polite graciousness. But when Philip bestowed admiration on her, she became flustered, as tongue-tied as Papa, and feeling as wild inside as Margot was on the outside.

Biting her lower lip, she continued reading.

My favorite time on this ship is in the earliest part of the morning, when the sun starts to rise, glistening on the open sea, and the water sparkles the same shade of blue as your eyes.

Lilibet blew out a long breath, leaning back against the chair. Over the years of their correspondence Philip had shared stories of his experience as a cadet in training and then as a midshipman all over the world—down to descriptions of countries he'd visited and the surprisingly equally interesting innerworkings of a ship. But this comment about the color of her eyes felt different.

With a sigh, she returned her attention to Philip's neat handwriting, letting herself be taken away by his details about the ocean. It was nice to experience the world through his eyes—at least the parts he could write about without the entire thing being redacted. His last line sent hope soaring through her.

I will endeavor to visit in July when given my promised shore leave.

"I will count the days," Lilibet said wistfully, staring out the window at the freshly budding trees in Windsor Great Park.

And hope nothing happened to prevent that leave . . . particularly the worst thing of all. Men were dying for Britain, including those brave men serving on the seas.

Lilibet felt certain Philip kept hidden most of what he saw of war, which she counted as a blessing. From the highest points of Windsor, she'd been able to see London burning during the Blitz. Many nights they'd slept in the castle's dungeon, now remade into a bomb shelter, with cots, blankets, books, and other necessities. On each of those nights, she and Margot had packed up their tiny suitcases and trudged down into the dark, unsure of how long they'd have to remain.

They were fortunate thus far not to have been hit. Lilibet heard some of the servants whisper about Hitler wanting to live at Windsor when he invaded, and she'd made up her mind to personally burn the place to the ground before she let that dictator set foot in the castle that held so much importance for British history.

Fortunately, Lilibet didn't believe Hitler's boots would ever stomp on the quadrangle. Her mother was fairly confident too. After the Luftwaffe had bombed Buckingham Palace—with her parents in residence—Papa declared it was God's will that Hitler would not defeat him. They'd started walking among the people at the bomb sites, talking to them. Mummy said she could look those in the East End in the eye now that her own home had also been bombed.

Lilibet was jealous of her parents' London walks. She wanted to move among the residents of the capital as well. Next month she would make her first public speech at the Queen Elizabeth Hospital in Hackney—bearing her mother's name—as its president. But while she was proud to be honored with such an important duty, she longed to do something to support the war effort.

So many girls her age had joined the Women's Auxiliary Territorial Service, including some from her own Girl Guide and Sea Ranger troops at Windsor. Lilibet longed to pull on the scratchy wool uniform and pin her hat in place. Mary Churchill had been allowed to join the ATS and was now serving in the antiaircraft batteries. It was a job that seemed compelling and important. What she wouldn't give to be able to shoot the Luftwaffe out of the sky.

Perhaps I ought to appeal to Winston Churchill to intercede with Papa, she thought, folding the letter on her lap and sliding it back into its envelope. As a father himself, Churchill might persuasively argue that a daughter's duty to country was not such a bad thing.

But even without an appeal to Churchill, Lilibet was determined to continue her fight to become a second subaltern in the ATS and then work her way up to junior commander like the prime minister's daughter. No other woman in the royal family had served on active duty, and Lilibet was determined to be the first.

If she wasn't a princess, her father's approval wouldn't matter much. Plenty of women had gone against their father's wishes and joined up—like Hanna Penwyck, one of her fellow Girl Guides and daughter of the head gamekeeper at Windsor.

When Hanna went missing one day, Mr. Penwyck had nearly every ARP warden on the estate on alert. Then she'd turned up later that evening, orders in hand, looking as proud as any of the male naval cadets at Dartmouth.

Lilibet wished she could do that, but she feared if the king arrived at the Labour office, they would simply cluck their tongues and shoo her away.

A quick knock sounded on the door and Bobo ducked inside. Lilibet shoved the letter in its envelope beneath her thigh and sat up straighter.

"Happy birthday, Princess," Bobo said, shutting the door and turning to face Lilibet with a brilliant smile. Her soft hair was styled, and she wore a sensible wool skirt and starched white blouse.

"Thank you, Bobo." Lilibet smiled back with genuine affection.

Bobo came deeper into the room, eyeing Lilibet in her nightgown. "Shall we dress? I thought I heard Crawfie shouting demands already. You know she can be heard clear across the castle. I think that's why she chose to have her rooms so far from yours, just so she could shout on her way here." The jest was good-natured. Bobo screwed up her face as Lilibet laughed. "Don't tell her I said that."

"We'll consider it a state secret." Lilibet gave her an exaggerated wink.

As Bobo went to the wardrobe to pull Lilibet's outfit for the day, the princess popped out of her chair. Pulling a key from a floral English bone china pillbox that used to belong to Queen Victoria, she unlocked the secretary box on top of her desk and placed Prince Philip's letter within, beside those that had come before it. She was replacing the key as Bobo returned, tactfully ignoring what Lilibet had been doing.

While Lilibet was dressing, Crawfie came in and immediately began reeling off the day's itinerary—as was her habit.

"During the changing of the guard in the quadrangle the colonel will hand you the standard, which will be used for future inspections. You'll have luncheon with the king and queen, Margot, and your grandmother Queen Mary, followed by a family portrait." Crawfie ticked the items off the imaginary list she kept in her head, while simultaneously inspecting Lilibet's clothes.

"I do hope I'll have time to go for a ride with Margot." Lilibet kept her voice pleasant, though she intended to make time. A day without riding was not a good day; and today was her birthday, so an exhilarating ride was in order.

Now that she was eighteen, she expected her duties to increase. Being the future queen involved a great deal of responsibility. It was an honor, yes, but this particular life was never supposed to be hers. And even as she made up her mind to live up to it, she did not feel that making time for a few things like riding was shirking her duty.

A mixture of emotions passed through Lilibet as she turned to inspect her clothes in the mirror. Her brown hair was swept away from her face in a bouffant wave and curled at the nape of her neck. She stopped to notice her eyes. Thanks to Philip's letter, they seemed particularly blue today. Turning slightly, she noticed with pleasure that her floral-print dress was flattering to her shape. A string of pearls and black heels with a delicate bow completed the look.

"You look lovely," Bobo murmured.

Lilibet smiled at herself in the mirror, but then the smile slipped just a little. An eighteenth birthday for most was a pivotal point in life—the threshold into adulthood. But for her, it was much more complicated. She was now of age to do state business—some of which she'd begun already, like the inspections of the guards. However, at eighteen it became more serious. As an adult she could now represent her father if he was ill or out of the country.

Lilibet touched the pearls at her neck, grateful to still be alive when so many of her countrymen and -women were not. The royals were among the lucky ones who'd lived thus far through the Blitz, war, and rations. And they'd embraced those hardships instead of trying to use their privilege to avoid them. Papa had made it clear it would be wrong to evade the rules: one boiled egg a week like everyone else.

Margot and Lilibet had joined Dig for Victory, their garden flourishing enough to fill the kitchen at Windsor with vegetables. Lilibet had taken up knitting in weekly circles with the other women on the estate. It was a task she did not enjoy and wasn't exceptionally good at, but she did it nonetheless because socks were needed by the soldiers on the front.

Five years had passed in this fashion. Five years of worrying another bomb would drop on Buckingham Palace or one on Windsor. Five years of watching her father's temper swell, as the hair at his temples grew grayer and the wrinkles at the corners of his eyes deepened. And Lilibet pinned the blame for every sign of age, or rage, firmly on her uncle.

But today Lilibet wanted to be happy, was determined to be happy. And, she thought as she turned from her mirror, there had been good memories in these war years as well. Among them the adventures she and her sister had crawling through the medieval castle they called home; Christmas pantomimes, tea parties, and of course time spent out-of-doors. Lilibet loved being able to continue riding and walking the dogs through the extensive acres of Windsor Great Park. These occasions were perhaps her happiest memories. She always felt particularly alive when a crisp wind was blowing, threatening to rip off the scarf wrapped around her head.

"Lilibet!" The singsong voice of Margot echoed through the door from down the corridor, followed by the deeper timbre of the king's laughter.

Lilibet was surprised to hear her father's voice so early.

Normally at this hour he was reading the papers and getting ready to open the red boxes that held all the official correspondence and reports each day for his immediate perusal.

The door swung open, and Margot bounced in, pretty as a picture as always, wearing one of Lilibet's older dresses refashioned, just as Lilibet was wearing one of the queen's.

"Happy birthday, Lilibet," Margot sang, throwing her arms about her sister.

Lilibet laughed, squeezing her sister back, and then her eyes alighted on her father and mother standing just inside the door, a squiggling, red, furry body in her father's arms.

"Who is that?" Lilibet rushed forward, holding out her hands to take the puppy.

"Hickathrift Pippa." Papa passed the wriggling pup to her. "And she's all yours."

Lilibet cradled the pup like a newborn babe, stroking her soft snout and behind her ears, running a hand over her silky, fat puppy belly. "She's adorable." Lilibet brought her close, smelling the delicious puppy scent that clung to all dogs for a little while. "But I do not think she looks like a Pippa."

"Oh?" Papa chuckled, and she glanced up at him, taking note of his ever-impeccable uniformed self.

Lilibet turned her gaze downward again to meet the dark brown eyes of the newest royal corgi—her dog, not one that belonged to the family. Just hers. "I think she may be a Sue. What do you think? Are you a Sue?"

The reddish head cocked to the side, lips parting, and a tiny pink tongue poked out between the tiniest teeth before she made an adorable yip.

"Ah, see, Bertie?" The queen linked her arm affectionately through the king's. "I told you Pippa didn't seem to fit."

The king laughed, and Margot came closer, giving Sue a kiss on the tip of her wet black nose.

"Sue seems so . . . I don't quite know." Margot wrinkled her nose.

"Hmm . . ." Lilibet nuzzled the puppy, who promptly clamped her teeth on one of the princess's curls. As she tugged her hair from the corgi's mouth, she said, "Maybe Susan?"

The corgi's nub of a tail went wild.

"She likes Susan," Lilibet declared, using the same excited tone as when she asked the other dogs if they wanted a biscuit or a cuddle.

"Princess Susan of Windsor." Margot used her theatrical voice and then gave a great bow.

Lilibet put the puppy down and knelt before her, bowing her head while the corgi looked up at her as if to say, *What in the world are you doing?*

"Princess Susan of Windsor." Lilibet picked up one of Susan's paws. "I, Princess Elizabeth, do hereby pledge my service to you until the end of our days together for however long or short that may be, with hopes they last forever."

"Oh, Lilibet." Mummy laughed. "Do get up. You'll spoil the poor thing."

Lilibet playfully rolled the puppy on her back, gently scratching her tummy. "Oh, Mummy, do say you have some of those homemade dog biscuits in your pocket?"

"I am never without them."

As the queen reached into her pocket, Lilibet shot a who-spoils-their-dogs-exactly smile in her mother's direction. Queen Elizabeth just shook her head and made a tsking sound as the king chuckled.

Mummy passed a biscuit, and Lilibet waved it below the

puppy's nose. Immediately Susan rolled to standing, wagging her little nub and trying to steal the treat.

"Now, don't be rude, Susan. A princess must always act with decorum in a way that will make her people proud." Lilibet pushed gently on Susan's fluffy bottom until the puppy sat, then she was quick to hand over a bite of biscuit and plenty of praise.

Susan crunched loudly on the treat, sniffing wildly at Lilibet's fingers for more.

"Shall we go down to breakfast?" Mummy asked.

"I'm starving," Margot declared.

"A princess is never starving," Mummy replied as the two of them made for the door.

"Are you pleased?" her father asked as Lilibet scooped Susan up. He looked a little nervous, but Lilibet couldn't figure out why he would be. "I wanted to surprise you, else I would have let you pick her out yourself."

"She's perfect, Papa. Thank you so much." Lilibet kissed him on the cheek, smelling the faint hint of shaving cream on his skin.

"You mean"—Papa's voice broke off in the middle and he swallowed, his eyes growing a little misty—"the world to me, darling. I do hope you know that."

"I do." Lilibet's chest filled with emotion, and she was grateful for the comfort of the puppy in her arms. "I think it safe to say I've the best father in all the world."

A small sound escaped his throat, and she thought he might say something, but instead he nodded, putting his arm around her shoulders, squeezing. Lilibet was certain in those brief moments, she was taking some of the weight of the world off his shoulders. How much he'd overcome, how hard he'd worked to be the king and emperor his realm deserved.

Susan wriggled in her arms, nipping at her hands, ready to get down and explore. Lilibet set her down, then grinned up at her father, the smartest and most kind man she knew. "Whenever we're not together, Papa, all I need do is look to Susan, your gift to me, and I'll hold a piece of you with me."

Papa's lips parted, and he inhaled, all signs he meant to speak, but his lips pressed together once more. Silent. The words might have abandoned themselves in his throat, but his face was full of deep emotion that spoke volumes, loudly enough that Lilibet's heart pinched in acknowledgment.

Whatever else happened today, it felt like a perfect eighteenth birthday.

CHAPTER THREE

HANNA PENWYCK

I swore I wouldn't come back to live here.

I'd always be the daughter of the gamekeeper, but that didn't mean I wanted to live that life as an adult.

The taxi drove slowly along the road as the familiar surroundings of my childhood took root. The forest I'd tramped through with my father, stalking deer, finding foxholes, and the one time he'd had me shimmy up a tree as he chased off a poacher. The fields I'd tramped as a Girl Guide, and the looming castle walls up on the hill, where I'd raced along in the dark helping the ARP wardens douse the lights and deliver messages.

Two years ago, in the summer of 1942, I'd marched down the Long Walk at Windsor Great Park to the village and registered at the Labour Exchange. I'd been biding my time, determined to do my part for the war—and more than I had as a Girl Guide helping the ARP wardens at the castle. I wanted to be part of the action. Of course, my father was adamant that I do no such thing and instead remain at Windsor.

It had just been him and me for so long, I knew he was afraid of losing me. Mum's unexpected death when I was eight had been devastating to both of us. Dad had not remarried. I think part of him felt a little betrayed that I wanted to flee.

Not to mention he was worried about what kind of influ-
ence women in the military might have on me. In fact, I'd once
heard him and some of the other gamekeepers at Windsor refer
to the Women's Auxiliary Territorial Service as the Auxiliary
Tart Service.

If he thought insults like that were going to turn me away,
well, then he'd forgotten just who I was.

And that was that.

The day I turned eighteen, I was shipped to No. 1 Mechanical Transport Training Centre near Camberley in Surrey, put
in a bunker with a bunch of other women my age, and set to
training. Unlike the other girls who huffed and puffed and
complained about the physical labor, or the complexities of a
truck's engine, I was thrilled by it. Being a gamekeeper's daughter and a Girl Guide for years was almost like training to be
in the ATS. I was more than prepared, and more than ready for
the responsibility. I ran circles around them all.

Until last week.

I stared down angrily at the cast on my arm, wincing as the
taxi went over a bump, jostling me. The ATS ambulance I'd
been driving had taken a hit from falling debris of a demol-
ished building, and as a result, I had a broken arm. We weren't
even on an emergency run, just sitting blocked by traffic when
the stone rained down. Injured, and not even in the line of
duty—it felt a bit like failure.

Well, I thought, looking out the taxi window again, *as soon
as I am recovered, it is back to service for me.* But in the meantime, the doctors said I needed a few months at home to con-
valesce.

A few *months.* I thought the medic had misspoken, but he
only laughed at me when I asked him to clarify.

Home was Windsor Great Park, the one place I'd wanted to say goodbye to forever. It wasn't as if I didn't love my father; on the contrary, to me he was a real hero. But I'd never held any affection for the place I was raised.

Part of that could be explained by the teasing. I was always taller than everyone, gangly and awkward. And I was motherless—a fact that should have inspired compassion but somehow failed to. Instead, others living on the estate called me Little Orphan Hanna—after the American comic strip *Little Orphan Annie*, which one of my peers had been collecting through the post via an aunt in New York City.

The teasing made me wary, prickly even, determined, and a bit of a loner. I'd grown up without the typical girlhood crew. No tea parties or dressing up for me. No practicing makeup or talking about boys with the daughters of other servants on the estate. I was, however, a member of the Girl Guides. I loved the uniforms and completing the challenges for badges. And by the time I'd left, I'd become a leader and enjoyed every minute of it, though it didn't help my popularity among my peers. At Windsor, the princesses were also Girl Guides. They were some of the few fellow guides who'd ever been genuinely kind to me, though I couldn't have a friendship with them outside of the guides. They were royals, off-limits.

And so, my childhood friends, the ones I felt most comfortable with, had been animals—mostly dogs—and the heroes I met in the books I devoured.

"Here we are, miss." The cabdriver pulled to a stop, and I dragged my eyes away from the castle, turning them to the cottage where I'd been born.

"Thank you," I murmured.

Leaping out of the car, he opened the door for me. I wriggled my way out, trying not to look as awkward as I felt. As I straightened up a small gust of warm wind brought me the fresh scents of grass and magnolias, a distinct aroma I wished I could bottle and carry with me always.

I held my breath for a fraction of a second, studying the old cottage that was as familiar to me as the stacked stone medieval castle at my back. Red shutters on either side of the windows matched the red door with its big iron knocker in the shape of a lion's head. Wooden flower boxes overflowing with weeds—gardening had never been Dad's strong suit—jutted from beneath the windows.

I glanced up at the triangular roofline, noting that there was a patch brighter than the rest, suggesting a recent repair. The grass on either side of the brick walkway was neatly trimmed, and the old oak in the front yard still had the swing on it that I'd used regularly as a child. I could remember bolting from its wooden seat and racing through woods and fields of the park whenever I heard the faint call of the piper on the march. It was in those occasional moments that I'd catch glimpses of the royals who came and went.

The wooden front door swung open, and Dad ducked out. "Hanna." His tone was relieved, smile bright, faltering only slightly when his eyes reached the cast on my arm. "Glad you've come home, my dear."

I rushed into his arms, inhaling his familiar scent of leather and the outdoors.

The cabdriver cleared his throat as he set down my suitcase beside me.

"Oh, sorry." I pulled out the fare. "Thank you."

He departed with a tip of his hat, the gravel crunching beneath the cab's tires. Then suddenly there was a screech of the brakes. I whirled around as two corgis darted from out in front of the cab. My heart leaped to my throat, and I took off at a run, worried one of them had been injured. I'd heard just a couple of months ago that royal corgi Jane had been accidentally run over by one of the estate workers. Dad had written me that the poor chap was devastated by what he'd done, and the only thing that made him feel better was the kind letter he'd received from Princess Elizabeth, telling him he was forgiven and that it wasn't his fault since Jane often darted in front of vehicles.

Thankfully, both of the stubby-legged pups were all right. Dad tapped the hood of the cab to let him know he was good to go. Were these royal corgis? Glancing down I recognized one as Crackers, but I couldn't identify the other who was still not full-grown.

"We've a couple extra houseguests," Dad said. "I think you'll be pleased." There was a hint of teasing in his gaze.

I crouched down, careful not to disturb my arm as I attempted to stroke the wiggling dogs with my free hand. The corgis, however, did not seem to understand that a cast was meant to protect an injury, and the younger one clamped its jaws on the plaster for a game of tug. I teetered forward, nearly falling, but managed to brace myself just in time.

"Let go, you little dervish." I couldn't help laughing at the pup's exuberance. I tapped its nose, hoping to be released. But instead, its playful growls intensified. Crackers had thankfully gone off to chase a squirrel. Dad, seeing I was trapped, picked up a stick and waved it temptingly. When he tossed it, the young corgi released my broken arm at last and gave chase.

"You all right?" he asked.

I nodded, standing up and finding my mouth had gone dry

with nerves. The sight of the dogs and the screech of the cab brakes took me back a decade, to a day I'd been playing chase with my dog, Hank, in the castle park, and he'd taken off after a squirrel. That chase, and his life, had ended beneath the tires of our king's father's front wheels.

The king had apologized profusely, even offered to buy me a new dog. But Dad had refused, despite me wanting my dog replaced. Dad told me he didn't feel right about taking a new puppy when it was Hank's fault for running after the squirrel. I'd replied it wasn't Hank's fault . . . it was the squirrel's for taunting him.

I truly believed those cunning wood rats plotted the whole thing. My gaze scanned the yard for the corgis where they gathered around a tree, paws up on the trunk as they yapped at the squirrel, their little fluffy behinds wiggling in excitement. The squirrel stared down at them almost in comical thought.

"I'm fine, Dad. Just catching my breath." I flashed him what I hoped was a calm smile but felt more like my lips were peeling painfully away from my teeth.

"Let's get your bag inside."

As we walked toward the door, I asked, "I take it the corgis are our houseguests?"

As soon as the cottage door was opened, and before Dad could answer, the royal corgis darted inside, confirming my suspicion. Our black Newfoundland, Roger, lay at the hearth, watching with resigned irritation as they raced around him as if they owned the place.

The collar on the littler corgi caught the light streaming through the window. A royal crest, and beneath it, *SUSAN*, in bold. "Is this new pup a royal corgi?"

"She is indeed. Susan there is a bit of a nuisance during the day to the household staff. The princesses are off doing Girl Guide and Sea Ranger challenges today on the estate. So when I was at the castle this morning, I mentioned you'd be home . . . and of course everyone knows how well you get on with dogs."

"Da! You volunteered me for dog duty? With a broken arm?" I waggled my wounded limb for emphasis, grateful it no longer ached as much as it had a few days ago.

"Well . . . when you put it that way." Dad had the decency to look sheepish. "The little demons are a bit much. If you want, I can run them back to the castle."

"*Demons* is somewhat harsh," I insisted, my stubbornness kicking in. I almost reconsidered my defense of the dogs as Crackers leaped toward me, clamping down on the heel of my shoe. "But I see what you mean."

"Crackers, no," Dad ordered, but the little fellow didn't let go.

I knelt down, rubbing my hand along Crackers's overexcited head. "Will you let go of me, you little devil?"

Crackers stopped tugging, released my heel, and then peeked up at me and sat.

Susan stopped tearing around the cottage and approached, head down and sniffing. She couldn't be more than four or five months old, I thought, as she flopped down beside Crackers.

"I would only have to watch them for a day?" I asked.

Dad nodded. "Princess Elizabeth is quite fond of her dogs, especially her new puppy, Susan. She makes a point to feed them herself. So she'll want them back up at the castle when she returns."

Lilibet. It had been ages since I'd seen her. A lingering part of me wanted to rush off to wherever the Girl Guides were and join them. Some of my favorite memories were of the princesses rolling up their sleeves, not afraid to get their hands dirty. Not because I wanted to see them a mess, but because when we were all digging in the garden, building something, or cooking over an open fire we were all just people. I'd felt more accepted when they were there, maybe because then I wasn't the focus of my fellow guides' attention anymore. They were.

If watching her dogs helped the princess, how could I refuse?

"They're fine where they are." I stooped and gave each a pat on the head.

My father looked at the corgis—their attention fixed on me as if they were waiting for a treat. "I'll say despite all that time driving ambulances through the city, you still have a way with dogs." He clucked his tongue and shook his head in amusement.

"Have any biscuits?" I asked.

"Mm-hmm." Dad popped the lid of what used to be my mother's biscuit jar. When I was a girl it had been filled with a different confection every week.

My favorite were the shortbreads with jam centers. But Dad loved her crunchy creams, and Mummy loved her gingersnaps. The only way to go about it, she saw, was to make a different one every week.

Dad pulled out two square dog biscuits that looked homemade.

"Better the jar be filled with treats for them than me," he said, patting his stomach when I raised an eyebrow.

"When did you start baking?" I grinned, taking the biscuits, holding them out for the corgis to see, then tucking the treats into my skirt pocket. "If you want one, you'll have to be polite." I wagged a finger at the pups.

Dad laughed. "I didn't bake them."

"Who did?"

Crouching once more, I held out my empty right hand to Crackers, who sniffed it, then looked at me as if to say, *Where's my biscuit?*

I lifted his little paw, shook it, and then set it down. When I held out my empty hand again, Crackers put his paw on my upturned palm.

"That's it, good boy." I rubbed his head, then gave him a biscuit, and the dog trotted off in triumph.

"Mrs. Seymour baked the dog biscuits. She's been doing it for a few years now. She gave me a little sack when I brought the dogs down this morning."

Mrs. Seymour, a neighbor, had always been kind. "I heard about her husband." He'd been killed on the front.

"Indeed. Sad business." Dad stuffed his hands into his jacket pockets and shifted on his feet.

What is that about?

I momentarily forgot the question as Susan approached me. I repeated the steps I'd just taken with Crackers and was pleased to find this little one was swift to catch on. As with people, intelligence was an asset in dogs. I looked toward Roger, our own family dog, thinking he might play the game next. His head was up, ears pricked, but he didn't rise or approach me.

"Hips bothering him again?" I asked Dad.

My father nodded. "Best bloody hunting dog I've ever had."

Taking another biscuit from the jar I went to Roger, kneeling on the floor to give him a cuddle. He munched on the treat, then lay his head in my lap.

The corgis went back to hopping onto the furniture, with Crackers picking up a sofa pillow and shaking the life out of it.

Giving Roger a final rub between the ears and then gently setting his head down on his bed, I stood. "I suppose I ought to change and take them on a walk. Perhaps they'll have mercy on the furnishings once I've tired them out a bit."

"Do you think that wise?"

"I've broken my arm, not my leg. The only reason they sent me home was because they didn't think it safe for me to drive with the use of only one arm or fix an engine with the plaster making it awkward. So long as I don't need to fish them out of a foxhole, I'll be fine."

"Better steer clear of the forest, then. Plenty of foxholes there. Though fortunately it's not breeding time, so you'll not have to worry about the dogs catching the scent of a new den."

I held back the knowing smile that was trying to push through.

Dad was always reminding me of things I already knew. As a girl, that'd made me bristle. But I was older and wiser now, so I let him do it—seeing it for what it was: a sign of his love. "We'll stick to the plains of the park." I kissed him on the cheek. "I'll just get changed out of this uniform."

Dad picked up my bag, carrying it up the stairs to my childhood bedroom. It was strange to be back to the same bed I'd slept on when I was three, after becoming used, as a twenty-year-old, to sleeping in a barracks full of women. My cot with the ATS was smaller, and there were all the sounds of dozens of women every night. But at the barracks, I typically fell exhausted into bed and went right to sleep.

Here at home, I suspected I'd lie awake, counting the days until I'd be back in service.

I leaned against the wall, looking out the window toward the castle high on the hill. Nostalgia prickled at the edge of my brain where I tried often to keep it at bay. Not all my memories were bad; in fact, there were a lot that were amazing.

Dad dropped the suitcase on my bed, flipping up the latches and opening the lid for me.

"I'll meet you downstairs. Let me know if you need anything."

His footsteps faded down the stairs, and for a second I thought I heard the faint voice of my dead mother greeting him the way she had when I'd been little. The ghost of memories past.

Shutting the door, I tackled the cumbersome task of unbuckling my belt and unbuttoning my ATS jacket with one fully functioning hand.

I was lucky the fracture had been clean across the small bones of my forearm. From what I'd seen in my two years of service, the upper arm took a lot longer to heal, and so did nasty breaks that split the skin; I had neither.

I tugged off my skirt, unlaced and toed off my shoes, then stood in my shirt and tie, slip, stockings, and drawers, nearly depleted of energy. Taking care, I loosened the tie only enough to tug it over my head, as I'd learned to do for ease of dressing before I'd broken my arm—tying a tie was damned complicated, after all. Off came the shirt, slip, and the worn stockings I'd darned more than once.

I didn't even bother rummaging in my suitcase. What I was looking for I'd not taken with me.

Swinging open the doors to my wardrobe, I searched for my old pair of hiking trousers and wellies. I grabbed a suitable pair of socks and a cotton shirt. I just needed a scarf to tie around my head to hold my hair out of my face, so I'd be able to keep a sharp eye on my canine charges. As I pulled the scarf out, an old diary tumbled with it.

I picked up the leatherbound journal, complete with a lock. Most of the girls in our troop had received the same diary after Lilibet had showed us hers one night while we camped. They'd been gifts from the princesses; and though I'd thought myself too old for one—I'd been sixteen, after all, and one of the lead guides—the gift meant something.

I'd known from observation that Princess Lilibet wrote in hers every night. So I'd taken to doing the same myself.

I sat on the bed and opened the diary to the first page. I didn't need to unlock it, thanks to a pair of pruning shears I'd used on it after losing the key. It seemed like ages since I'd been given the diary, but in reality, it had only been four years. Strange how I felt so much more grown-up now than back then. I turned my eyes to the first entry:

Dear Mummy,

Up until recently, none of us really thought this war business was real. But we've been hearing lots of warnings from the Guards and dashing down to hide in the cellar. Last night a bomb fell near the lake. We went in the morning with the dogs to look at the crater. One of the dogs tried to make off with a piece of shrapnel and was only persuaded to drop it when a squirrel ran across his path . . .

Every one of my entries was addressed to my mum, already dead eight years when I'd received the diary. Tears pricked as I scanned the entries commemorating awards, picnics, a successful shoot with Dad. I'd missed her so much then and I did still. The pain was never dulled: it lodged like the ache of a perpetually pulled muscle, right in the center of my chest. If there were times I didn't notice it, that was not because it wasn't there, but because I'd gotten used to suffering its uncomfortableness.

"Hanna, everything all right?" Dad called from the bottom of the stairs.

"Yes, be right down," I called through the door, before tucking the diary back into the wardrobe.

Pulling the pins from my tight bun, I awkwardly braided my hair, then glanced in the mirror. What a mess. I was glad the scarf I tied on next covered most of it up. I looked at myself again, the transformation from military servicewoman to gamekeeper's daughter—one I'd sworn I'd never make—was complete. With a sigh of resignation, I headed downstairs.

"You going to be all right alone?" Dad asked when I found him in the den. "I've got a few pesky moles I need to go take care of. Their holes on the green are dangerous to horses."

"I'll be perfectly fine. The royal gamekeeper's job is never done, and I certainly will not be the one to keep you from it."

Dad studied me for a beat, and I could tell in that long-held look that he was worried about me, but he knew better than to try to argue with my plans.

With a perfunctory nod, he said, "I'll be back in time for tea, Han. Mrs. Seymour sent us down some scones and clotted cream when she heard of your arrival."

"What a treat," I exclaimed. I'd not had a scone in months. They weren't part of the ration at the barracks. We subsisted mostly on oatmeal. And clotted cream was unheard of in my daily life. "Her scones are divine."

"Never had better." Again, my senses prickled . . . There was a note of something almost sentimental in Dad's voice.

"Mrs. Seymour is showing you a lot of attention. Dog biscuits and now scones."

Dad took his hat from the hook by the door and settled it on his head. "She's a good neighbor. Looking out for us."

Clearly, I wasn't going to get anything more out of Dad about Mrs. Seymour. But now I knew to keep an eye and ear out. He hoisted his Winchester to his shoulder and headed out, whistling for his hunting hounds.

I closed the door, waiting until Dad and his horde disappeared into one of the trucks, knowing if I tried to set off now, my wee charges would try to go after Dad instead of taking direction from me.

"Come on, doggies." I snapped my fingers when the coast was clear. The corgis perked up, but Roger closed his eyes, pretending he'd not heard me. "We'll be back, Roger."

The older dog sighed heavily as if he hoped I was lying. I laughed, opening the door and watching the corgis trot out before shutting it again.

"Which way shall we go?" I asked as the corgis darted in every direction, sniffing the ground, no doubt to catch the scent of Dad and his hounds. "How about this way?"

I set off without thinking much about which direction, whistling for the dogs to follow, and mildly surprised when they did. Though I was acquainted with Crackers, Susan didn't know me; I wondered what she'd think of me as leader of their pack.

With Windsor Castle looming behind us, we meandered down the Long Walk—a road that led from the castle and the park—a path I'd walked more times than I could count. The Copper Horse statue of George III perched on Snow Hill was a favorite spot from my childhood, holding a nostalgic element that couldn't be cleansed away by rain or war.

Snow Hill was one of the places where Mum's presence was the strongest on the estate. Even after all these years it felt like a warm hug that I wanted to sink into forever. Our favorite time to visit had been on clear days when we could see all the way to London. Sometimes we'd even take a torch and hike the hill at night to see lights of the city on the horizon. But if I went tonight there'd be no lights. London had been dark for years on account of the blackouts.

I picked up a stick and chucked it in the direction we were moving. Crackers and Susan took off, their dark eyes following the stick as it sailed through the air. Their tongues flapped as they sensed the landing point. Their too-short legs raced at a speed that would surprise most. The wind ruffled the reddish fur on their backs as they both barked their claim.

As Crackers sank his teeth into the prized branch, Susan snuffled around the green grass for her own trophy. The hair on the back of my neck prickled, and I stifled a shudder as an air raid warning split the air.

The familiar buzz of an enemy bomber's engine sounded in the distance, a sound that chilled me—even after almost five years of war. The only time I was immune to the fear of it was when I was on duty, pushing an ambulance gas pedal to the floor—whizzing through London's streets.

Rushing headlong into danger with only myself and my willing crew was one thing; looking out for the corgis, with their tender, trusting eyes, was another. As if sensing my fear, they abandoned the stick and trotted closer, panting.

I snapped my fingers. "Come." My tone was clipped, urgent, and I patted my pocket, empty of treats, in hopes it would suffice as bribery. For a second time I was surprised by their obedience, and we rushed back to the cottage, certain the Luft-waffe was hot on our tails.

I wrenched open the cellar door, shooing the dogs down into the darkness. The buzzing grew louder, the air pulsing around my ears a sure sign that the bomber was nearly atop us. I looked back once at the clear sky, then pulled the cellar door shut.

·᠆ᢁᢀᢁᡠ᠂

CHAPTER FOUR

SUSAN

I remember this smell.

I've been to this place a few times now.

There's a loud wailing noise that's duller down here. The light of the sun is reduced to only a crack once the girl pulls the door shut.

She sits on the steps that lead to the only way out. She's not my girl, and yet I sense we're supposed to look out for each other. Crackers is comforting her by sitting in her lap. He's panting, and the cyclic breaths are making me edgy. But I'm too curious to fall into fear. I want to keep sniffing. What is that smell?

A few more snuffles and I realize the smell is coming from the girl. I move close to her, and her soft hand strokes my face. I can smell it in her palm. It's not pleasant. It makes me . . .

I whimper.

"It's all right, Susan. It'll pass," she says.

Crackers nudges my ear with his snout, and I lay my head on top of his, my paws planted on the girl's knees. She lifts me up, and I snuggle against her, side by side with Crackers. There's something different about her arm than my Lilibet's. She has something hard like bone on the outside of it. I put my teeth on it for a taste, confused by the flavor. Not bone. Not a stick.

"No, no, pup," the girl says, tapping my nose until I let go.

It didn't taste that good anyway.

I don't know much about time. My schedule runs on just a few markers—when to eat, when to nap, and when I need to find a spot outside to relieve myself. So I don't know how long it is until a shout sounds from above. It's the man, and he's calling out, "Hanna! Hanna!"

The girl's smell changes from the scent that made me nervous to one of excitement.

"Dad! I'm in here."

The door above us flies open, and light, nearly blinding, shatters the darkness of the cellar.

"Thank God. You all right?" The man's voice softens, fills with relief.

"Yes, we're fine."

The girl sets us down, and I follow Crackers who's bolting for the light. The man pulls the girl against him, the way I've seen Lilibet and her father the king embrace. I sniff at the girl and the man's ankles, realizing their scents are similar. He is her sire.

Crackers is running in a nervous zigzag, his nose pointing toward the sky. Then I catch it, a strange acrid scent.

"I heard over the radio it hit the dust destructor." The man shakes his head; his brow wrinkles.

What's a dust destructor?

"I hope everyone is all right." The girl—Hanna, yes, that's what the man called her—sounds worried, and they both look at a curl of black smoke rising through the sky toward the clouds.

That's where the smell is coming from, the scary smell. I quiver. Whatever it is—this monster with the black paw reaching into the sky—is it going to get us? I worry for Lilibet, Margot, the king, the queen, the man who cooks my food, and the ones who make my bed. Something is wrong, terribly wrong.

Crackers starts barking at the sky, and I run toward him, adding my own voice to the alarm. If we're to be the ones to keep these humans safe, we have to make sure they understand the danger.

The girl and her sire run toward us. The man scoops up Crackers, and the girl takes me in her non-hardened arm.

"Hush, pup," she says sweetly. "It will be okay. I've got a treat for you inside." She nuzzles my face with her petite snout, and I lick frantically at her chin.

Her voice is soothing, and I want to believe that she knows what to do.

We're carried inside, and when the door closes, that scary scent dissipates, and I'm distracted because Hanna is reaching into a jar and pulling out some of the yummy biscuits she gave us before.

"Treat?" she says.

I nod and open my mouth.

The delicious confection melts on my tongue, and I wag my tail in appreciation. This girl really does care for us.

Hanna's sire leaves. When he comes back a short time later, he's not alone.

Lilibet rushes in and scoops me into her arms. She smells like sweat and flowers all at once. I snuggle into her neck and give her a lick on her chin.

"Oh, my sweet Sus," she says with a kiss on my nose. I kiss her back, my tail wagging furiously. Lilibet glances at Hanna. "Thank you so much for keeping her safe."

"It was a pleasure. She's a fine corgi, Your Royal Highness."

Crackers barks and puts his paws on Lilibet's skirt, scratching.

"And you too, Crackers," Lilibet says, bending down to give his head a good rub. "You are a very fine corgi. Did you both like Hanna?"

I yip and wag my tail. I especially like her biscuits.

"I think they'll have a good time with you this summer," Lilibet says, smiling at Hanna.

"I am honored, ma'am." There is something sad in Hanna's voice as she says it, and I cock my head, studying her.

Lilibet smiles, nods, not seeming to notice the sadness. Then she's leaving, and I don't want to be left behind. We exit the cottage and pile into the waiting car to go back to the castle. I watch out the window as Hanna and her sire wave goodbye. In the distance the black smoke has thinned.

Relaxing into the car seat my anxiety fades. I have Lilibet back in my care. I know she is safe. But I can't relax completely. I worry about the girl. What does her sadness mean? Maybe I'll find out tomorrow when Lilibet leaves again for her duties with the guides.

Snuggling against Lilibet's leg I think I would be very happy never to experience one of those sky monsters again, even if it meant extra biscuits.

·⊷⧫⊶·

CHAPTER FIVE

ᏚᏢᎡᏆNCESS ᏞᏆᏞᏆBET

March 23, 1945

$\mathscr{F}$rom the outside, she hoped no one could tell she was nervous. After being ushered from the royal Rolls and into No. 1 Mechanical Transport Training Centre in Camberley, Lilibet stood, shoulders squared and expression serious.

As she straightened the ATS cap on her head and ran her fingers down the line of her uniform buttons she realized that she not only looked the part—she was starting to feel it too.

The air was crisp, cool, and she could pick up just the faintest hint of engine oil. At least a dozen military vehicles, including ATS ambulances, were parked outside the massive brick building and several other outbuildings.

The drive from Windsor had not been long, less than an hour. The worst part of the morning had been leaving poor Susan behind. Her corgi, a year old now, had whined and tried to hop into the car with Lilibet, only to be gently pulled back by Hanna, who'd agreed to be Susan's daily companion for the next six weeks while Lilibet trained at this facility.

Fortunately for Susan, Lilibet was going to return tonight, and every evening, to Windsor Castle, unlike the other cadets who stayed in the dormitory huts. Lilibet was torn about that.

She wanted the full experience of being a member of the Women's Auxiliary Territorial Service, but she doubted she'd be able to sneak Susan into the hut, and really, she'd not gone a day without her beloved corgi since she'd gotten her.

"Second Subaltern Elizabeth Windsor, registration number 230873, reporting for training, ma'am," she said to the officer awaiting her.

She might have been a royal princess, but Lilibet wanted to enter this training, to begin her service to her country, exactly as she intended to live her life: with dedication to duty and a dependability that her officers, peers, and people could respect. Which meant forgoing her title of princess in this situation.

"I am Major Violet Wellesley. You'll be reporting to me." The uniformed woman standing before her nodded, her countenance stoic, and Lilibet immediately respected her.

Here of all places, she wanted to be seen as one of her fellow ATS trainee drivers. A lot of people thought her presence silly. But she was taking it seriously. Princess Lilibet was not simply going to sit in her castle and watch everyone else do whatever they could to provide stability and safety to the country—no, she was now Second Subaltern Windsor, doing her bit. A part of the greater good, like any monarch worth their salt. Just like her father.

"Yes, ma'am." Lilibet touched her fingers to her forehead in salute.

Her commanding officer raised a brow, studying Lilibet a little harder, and then returned the salute.

"Lessons are this way." Major Wellesley turned for Lilibet to follow, and she did.

Hanna had given her some pointers, warned her that some of the cadets might look at her funny, given she was a royal. She wasn't wrong. Heads poked out of various doors in almost comical fashion as she followed Major Wellesley down the corridor. Lilibet kept a small smile on her face and nodded at those she passed.

"Your first lesson will be in practical mechanics," Wellesley said. "You'll need to change into your mechanic's overalls. Dressing rooms are just there."

A second uniformed woman handed Lilibet a folded stack of clothing, and Lilibet went into the empty dressing room and found the locker with her registration number on it. Seeing herself as just those digits was a sobering moment but also an exhilarating one. It was the first time in her life she'd felt like an ordinary girl. The feeling, that idea, made her smile.

Finished changing, Lilibet exited the dressing room to find Major Wellesley waiting. "This way," the officer said in her clipped tone, matching the perfunctory click of her heels on the tile floor.

They went outside, to what looked like a large barn, the massive doors flung wide. A dozen trainees stood around a truck with its hood lifted. Lilibet knew this was no random group and that each of them had been sworn to secrecy about her presence.

Lilibet nodded to the other cadets as she joined them. She sensed they were wary and hoped they'd warm up as they got to know her, just as the members of her Girl Guide and Sea Ranger troops eventually had.

Wellesley, who was also their instructor, began the lesson, holding up a metal tool with what looked like claws on either end. "Second Subaltern Windsor, have you ever handled a spanner?"

Lilibet was startled to be addressed. She suspected the other girls had already begun learning and had assumed today would be more of an observational day for her. Eventually she'd be learning how to fix a vehicle, and even drive one—this latter part she was most excited about—of course. But to be asked a question within moments of arriving. She'd not expected that.

Nervous laughter escaped her as everyone stared in Lilibet's direction. "No, never," she said. "But I'm willing to do so now."

Wellesley grinned. "Good. Here."

Lilibet accepted the offered tool, feeling the weight of it in her gloved hand.

"The spanner is used to loosen the bolts in the engine. Over the course of your training, you'll learn—you'll all learn—how to take an engine apart and put it back together. How to fix a stalled engine and drive over rough terrain." Major Wellesley's eyes traveled around the circle.

Lilibet passed the spanner to the next girl, paying attention as Wellesley pointed out the various places where bolts were to be loosened. A thrill went through her. At last, here she was, the first female in the royal line to actively serve her country. It wasn't a dream; it was a reality.

And she was going to do a good job at it too.

The morning raced by. All of it fascinating. At lunch, she was offered a place in the officers' mess, which felt odd, given she was supposed to be enlisted like everyone else, but Wellesley explained it—insisting that, as the king's daughter, she should be conversing with those in superior positions. Someday, she told Lilibet, if the war kept on, she too would be a major. This last argument persuaded the princess to join the female officers in their smoky mess hall.

At the end of her shift, Lilibet's brain felt full of moving engine parts as she climbed into the waiting Rolls. There wasn't a time she could remember being this exhausted, and she struggled to stay awake on her way back to Windsor.

Hanna was waiting with Susan and Margot too, outside the castle.

"Lilibet." Margot rushed forward, tugged her sister in for a hug, and then grabbed hold of Lilibet's hands, inspecting them. "Well, you aren't nearly as soiled as I'd hoped." Margot frowned slightly.

Lilibet raised a brow. "You expected me to be soiled?"

"Of course. You're digging in with the engines, aren't you?"

Lilibet laughed. "We wear gloves."

Margot rolled her eyes. "Oh, how boring you are."

Lilibet crouched down to rub Susan behind her ears. During the past year Susan had not spent any significant time away from Lilibet, so now she was yipping and nipping like a younger pup—clearly wanting to make sure Lilibet knew she'd been worried her mistress would never return.

"You sweet thing," Lilibet said. "I would never abandon you. I'll be home every night." She kissed her pup on the red-gold fur of her head. "And I'll tell you everything, I promise."

Lilibet glanced up at Hanna. "How did she do?"

"Quite well, Your Highness. We romped around the castle, and she helped me with my Red Cross duties. She's quite adept at tending to patients."

Lilibet chuckled and gave Susan a good scratch. "I never had a doubt."

Susan was a professional icebreaker if there ever was one. Often when Lilibet was getting nervous, Susan just needed to give her a little nudge and a lick and the jitters would pass. Sometimes when Lilibet looked into the deep brown eyes of her pup, she thought Susan could see right into her soul and that Susan knew the ins and outs of her brain better than she did herself.

"I am exhausted," Lilibet exclaimed, then finding her old governess, she added, "Crawfie, I should like to take supper in my sitting room tonight."

"Can I join you?" Margot asked, pouting as if she expected Lilibet to say no.

"Of course. I'll tell you all about spanners."

Margot wrinkled her brow and rolled her eyes humorously. "Sounds riveting."

Susan lay on Lilibet's feet as she dined with her sister and told her everything. And, when dinner was finished, the pup climbed into Lilibet's lap as she had a telephone call with her father at Buckingham Palace and recounted the day's events.

The following morning, when the royal car pulled into the training facility, the mood seemed to have shifted—and not in a positive direction. Some of the cadets openly glared when Lilibet didn't join them in the mess and instead ate with the officers. Lilibet understood their resentment over her special treatment. Her father had demanded it. But Lilibet hadn't wanted it and now she was certain that her instinct had been correct.

That night, with Susan curled in her lap, Lilibet contemplated asking her father to rethink his demands, but she worried if she told him why, there was a chance he'd yank her from service. That was a risk she wasn't willing to take. She hoped, perhaps, the resentment of the other cadets would blow over.

But the following day, the *Daily Mail* published an article claiming the "Princess Auto Mechanic" wasn't getting her hands properly dirty and that the other cadets were complaining. Lilibet was mortified. The situation was appalling on many fronts—including the fact that the other cadets had been sworn to secrecy. Nothing in her life was private, nothing at all. But what bothered her the most wasn't that fact—a lack of privacy had been the norm for years. It was that the press and her fellow trainees were seeing her as exerting her elite status.

After her engine lesson that afternoon, as they were all breaking up for lunch, Lilibet took Major Wellesley aside and asked to dine with the other cadets.

Wellesley pinched her mouth into a frown. "That is not what was agreed upon."

"They are resentful of my"—Lilibet's gaze followed the cadets from the garage, a few of them turning back and whispering behind their now-greasy gloves—"my neglect of them."

Wellesley frowned harder.

"They recognize that I am getting special treatment when it comes to lunch, and it is likely they believe that treatment extends further. I wouldn't want them thinking—or the English people believing—that my performance reviews are going to be affected by who my father is, or that any promotion I eventually receive is given rather than earned."

The expression of distaste on Wellesley's face softened. "I see."

"So I should like to have lunch with them."

"But the king—"

"I will speak to my father and let him know that I've insisted. He will understand." Lilibet said it with a confidence that wasn't entirely genuine. Not genuine, perhaps, but necessary. It might have started with the *Daily Mail*, but she had little doubt that soon all the rag mags would be speculating as to whether or not she'd even learned anything in training, or if her signing up was merely a piece of propaganda.

Wellesley hesitated, still looking concerned, and Lilibet was fairly certain that she was about to be denied. "All right," she said at last. "But you'll need an escort."

Progress. But Lilibet still suppressed a groan. "Is that necessary?"

"The king requires you have an escort at all times. If I defy his order as to where you're eating—even if you explain—I will surely still face a reprimand for leaving you alone."

She must have sensed Lilibet was on the verge of responding, because she straightened up and her eyes became as focused as two car headlamps on a dark night. "Second Subaltern Windsor. You were placed under my command, and as your superior officer, I will not entertain further objection. That would be insubordination."

Though Wellesley's words were harsh, Lilibet knew they were more bark than bite. But she didn't want to get her superior in trouble. So, keeping a straight face, Lilibet replied, "Yes, ma'am." And gave a forehead-touching salute.

Major Wellesley followed Lilibet to the cadets' mess hall. As the princess entered, the chatter, which had been deafening, dropped so low, she might have heard the passing of a lorry a mile away.

Lilibet swallowed, offered the assembled cadets a smile, and then joined the mess line to retrieve her meal, with Wellesley close behind. Full tray in hand, she made her way through the mess until she found a table with a single seat open between two girls, ensuring that Wellesley would have to sit at another table. Lilibet wanted the cadets to talk to her, to not be afraid of what they might say in front of their superior officer.

"Do you mind if I sit here?" Lilibet placed her tray on the table but did not sit.

The replies of "not at all" and "please do" were nearly universal, with only a few girls remaining silent.

"Thank you." Lilibet sat down, conscious that all eyes were on her. "I don't know about you, but I'm starved." She took up her fork and loaded it with mash.

As she put it in her mouth, timid laughs rose up from some of her companions, but they followed suit, loading their own forks.

The food was bland at best—the potatoes had been overboiled and undersalted, the peas weren't much better, and the fish was briny—but Lilibet ate heartily and without complaint.

Lilibet kept the conversation light, even interjecting with a joke or two, and by the end she felt the other cadets had warmed considerably to her. To capitalize on her progress, she invited Margot to join her for a day. Margot was the outgoing one and charmed everyone.

The first week gave way to the second and then the third. The more comfortable Lilibet became with both her training and the other cadets, the more time seemed to speed up. Still, the days were long; when Lilibet returned to Windsor each night, she could barely keep her eyes open. Crawling into bed, cuddling Susan close, and whispering to her about the day became the princess's bedtime ritual.

Susan gave her a sense of calm and really seemed to be listening.

"I almost ran someone over," Lilibet whispered one evening as she explained her driving lesson for the day to her corgi. "Major Wellesley nearly had my head." Instead of being mortified Lilibet laughed a little, causing Susan to lick her face. "Can I tell you something, Susan? Something I've learned that's more important than how to use a spanner? I've discovered I am more than just a title, *just* a princess."

It might have seemed a silly thing to say, especially to a dog, given how many girls dreamed of being a princess and that Susan wasn't likely to reply. But Lilibet had set out to prove to the other cadets and to herself that she was more than a figurehead—she was a woman, and a woman who was willing to learn and do whatever it took to keep her country safe.

If only Philip were here to see her progress, Lilibet thought as she gave Susan one last kiss on the nose and closed her eyes, prepared to sleep. He'd been so encouraging over the last six weeks in his letters. If he could see her in uniform, working on an engine, she knew he'd enjoy it. But she had another reason for wanting him there. His recent letters were vague about what he was doing; and the less he talked about his exploits, the more she knew he was in danger. *At least as long as they keep coming I know he is alive. And surely he will come to Windsor on leave soon.* It was her last thought before dozing off.

* * *

A MONTH AND a half into her training, Lilibet was ready to give her parents the surprise she'd been planning from the moment she arrived in uniform at the training facility. She climbed behind the driver's wheel of the ATS truck and put the vehicle into gear. Her palms were sweaty, and her hands shook slightly as she gripped the wheel.

"Just like we've practiced," Major Wellesley said beside her.

Several cameras flashed to catch her in action as she headed out for the long drive from the training facility all the way to Buckingham Palace. A drive made during the blackout.

"If the press is waiting at the palace, they're likely to get the place incinerated by the Luftwaffe." Concern made Lilibet's voice higher pitched.

"There won't be an attack," Wellesley assured. "You know that."

The news was still a state secret—that very day, in Reims, the German army had signed a document indicating their surrender. Tomorrow the announcement would be made to the rest of the world, and Lilibet would be at Buckingham Palace to hear it firsthand. After years of fearing the sky, there was no longer a reason to—but it was hard to believe or remember that.

Lilibet took her foot off the ATS truck's brake and let the vehicle slide forward as she steered them out onto the road.

As they approached Buckingham Palace, Lilibet made her way around the half circle as carefully as she could, but missed the first turn and ended up circling it again.

"I did that on purpose," she said.

"Of course you did." Wellesley laughed.

At the gates to Buckingham Palace, they were asked to show their IDs, and when she handed hers over, the guard looked stricken. "Your Highness, my apologies." He bowed low.

But Lilibet only chuckled. "I am Second Subaltern Windsor today, and there is no need to apologize for doing your duty, sir."

They drove into the courtyard and pulled to a stop in front of the palace entrance.

"You did a fine job, Windsor," Wellesley said.

"I had a great instructor."

Mummy, Papa, and Margot filed out, clapping with excitement, dogs surrounding them. Lilibet saluted her father, grinning with pride.

* * *

LIKE CLOCKWORK, AT three the following afternoon, the eighth of May, Prime Minister Churchill announced on the BBC radio that Germany had surrendered and the war against Herr Hitler was over.

Lilibet and Margot were in the drawing room with their parents and grandmother listening as Churchill recorded from the room in the palace where the radio station had been set up.

"Thank God," Queen Elizabeth said, sitting beside Queen Mary, both of them releasing their held breaths at nearly the same moment.

"The Blitz is over," the king said, turning eyes that shimmered with tears toward Lilibet and Margot. "The war in Europe is over."

"Us four can be us four again," Margot exclaimed, leaping up from her spot and throwing herself into her father's arms.

Lilibet was a little more stoic, sitting in her ATS uniform, Susan napping on her lap. "I am so grateful we are still four." There had been terrifying moments when she wasn't certain that would be the case, especially when the palace had been bombed with her mother and father in residence.

CHAPTER SIX

SUSAN

*T*he thing with dogs is we can smell your feelings.

Sometimes we care, and sometimes we don't. It really depends on what has our attention. And what our human is feeling.

For example, when Hanna calls me back after I've run off chasing a car or squirrel—something I admit I do often—I can always smell her panic, sense her fear. But I don't run back, because there's nothing to be worried about. And also because I really like to bite tires and squirrel tails.

Lilibet is full of smells. She smells happy when she holds paper with squiggles on it. And she smells much the same when she picks up the strange black handle and holds it to her ear. I can hear a voice on the other end—she calls it Philip.

When my Lilibet is on the black handle, I can smell Margot's jealousy as she skulks about.

And, on a daily basis, I can smell the irritation among the footmen who shoo me away as I do my rounds through the castle halls. They don't seem to understand that you never know when a rogue chair might come to life, and I am just doing my best to keep the furniture in its place.

I can smell the king's pride as well as his affection when he is with his family. I can also smell the rage when he yells either at men in the palace or at voices down another one of the black handles. And I can smell the queen's worry when she soothes him after a bout of anger.

Today's smells are a jumble of different types of happy—*jubilation*, that's the word. People are running back and forth, and when I put my paws on the windowsill to look out, I can see hundreds of people marching toward the palace.

Their cheers thunder on the wind and make me a little nervous. Loud booms rattle the window glass, vibrating under my paws. But not the kind that used to shake the world and smell like smoke. These are different. And no one is afraid of them.

"Papa, please," Lilibet begs. She stands in her uniform, the one that smells like wool and oil. Pinned on the pockets and lapels are shiny treats, which feel cold and wonderful between my teeth.

"No one will recognize us," Margot adds.

They want something. Maybe a biscuit? I like biscuits. I trot forward and add my own begging to the mix, certain the king is hiding the treats somewhere.

The set of the king's shoulders changes. I smell resignation. "All right," he says, and I anticipate the drop. I check for the other dogs, but they don't seem to notice that the king is about to toss us a delicious, well-deserved treat.

Now is good. Give us the treat, my king.

Instead, he keeps on talking, moving his hands as he does so, but his palms are empty. What kind of trickery is this?

"You have to take an entourage with you." The king looks at his daughters sternly, and now I'm confused. Are we not getting a treat?

"Oh, Papa, that will defeat the purpose," Lilibet says, pouting. She is as disappointed as I am at the lack of deliciousness.

"They'll be inconspicuous," the king says.

The princesses exchange a conspiratorial look I've seen before, usually right at the start of a game. I wag my tail. I want to play a game too.

I follow them to the balcony doors, swung wide, letting in the cacophony of the streets.

"The war is finally over," Lilibet says. "Philip will come home."

"It's always about Philip," Margot mutters.

One of the footmen tries to push me back inside, but I wiggle away from him, determined to be at Lilibet's side. She and the others—the family—wave, and the shouts from the people outside the gates of Buckingham Palace grow louder. I tremble, nervous, and Lilibet leans down, lifting me to see the thousands of heads.

"Not to worry, Sus." Her voice is soothing, and she smells sweet.

I want to tell her as long as I'm with her, I never worry.

But then she's putting me down and she and Margot are running through the halls, giggling. I chase after them, but Hanna, who's come to the palace, swoops in, lifting me up in her arms that are always surprisingly stronger than I remember.

"Not this time, my sweet." Hanna watches the princesses run and holds me tight as I strain to go after them.

They are running into the loudness. The cheers and booms and music.

I shudder, but Hanna nuzzles me close, her familiar scent calming.

"She'll be back," she whispers.

Will she? Sometimes people walk into the loudness and don't return. What if my Lilibet gets lost? What if she is taken?

I bark, letting Hanna know that there is a real possibility my Lilibet could be in trouble.

Hanna rubs my nose and coos. Her fingers smell like the biscuits she's put in her pocket, and I lick them.

"Nothing a biscuit can't fix, eh, Susan?"

Biscuits are my favorite smell.

* * *

LATER THAT NIGHT, Lilibet snuggles with me in her bed, whispering about the celebration. She and Margot had slipped unnoticed through the celebrating crowds in the street to enjoy the festivities, singing, dancing, and twirling each other as their entourage of sixteen followed. While she shares the story, I feel the thrum of glee pounding in Lilibet's veins. I imagine the princesses following the crowd toward the Ritz and leaping into an impromptu conga line—shuffling their feet and swinging their arms wildly and with abandon, the way that always makes me want to dance, too.

My princess fell asleep with hope and joy for the future, and I cuddled close feeling the same.

·⊸∾⊷·

CHAPTER SEVEN

HANNA

I watched through the small kitchen window as my father bid Mrs. Seymour good morning. Our neighbor had stopped by, and Dad had run outside, meeting her before she was halfway up the path to our door. I pretended to wash up the breakfast dishes, though with my eyes pointed outside, I wasn't doing a very good job of it. Mrs. Seymour was smiling up at him in a way that spoke of them being more than friends. This wasn't entirely news to me. Although my father had not said as much, his body language had given it away.

Dad's features softened whenever he spoke to Mrs. Seymour, and his whole body relaxed, the same way it had in my childhood in the presence of my mum. For the last year, Dad had kept his feelings about Mrs. Seymour a not-so-subtle secret. Seeing him like that brought on a host of mixed feelings. I wanted him to be happy. And his eyes sparkled as he replied to whatever Mrs. Seymour was telling him. But I didn't want him to forget Mum either.

All we had of her were memories. Pieces of her had seemed to fade away each day over the last thirteen years, and yet the slightest scent of her perfume on another woman or a rhubarb pie baking brought back a flood of images: the two of us dancing around the kitchen; the flour fight we'd had when Dad had walked in to find us covered in dust—even Roger had had a few patches of white on his dark fur.

Mrs. Seymour leaned closer to Dad, and my hands hung suspended, soapy and wet, over the sink. They reminded me of characters on a stage or in the cinema, falling in love. Seeing them like that through the window struck a chord somewhere inside me. Despite our country having just gone through some of its harshest times, flickers of hope had been ignited. I needed to feed that hope, not crush it—or at least I needed to try.

A scratch at my ankle had me looking down. Susan sat stoically peering up at me. She and Crackers had arrived over an hour or so ago, about the same time they did every morning since I'd taken up my duty as Princess Lilibet's dog watcher.

"Tell me, Susan, what do you think of love?"

Susan cocked her head, her little pink tongue coming out in a pant, and then she scratched my ankle again.

"Love is a biscuit, eh?" I wrung out the dishcloth, placing it over the tap to dry. I wiped my hands on a dish towel, then bent to scratch the corgi's head. "Mrs. Seymour seems to think so too."

I reached into my pocket, producing a small treat, and Crackers appeared from nowhere. I wasn't sure whether he smelled the treats or heard me pulling them out, but he never missed the chance to get one.

"Sit." I pointed to each dog in turn, a nonverbal command I was trying to get them to master. "Only those who show manners get treats."

Both corgis dutifully sat, their sweet brown eyes imploring me to relinquish the biscuits.

I stood, hands on my hips, watching them devour their goodies. "Care to take a walk?" I asked as they finished.

Both corgis stood, tails wagging.

"What about you?" I poked my head from the kitchen to stare at Roger, lying by the hearth. He raised his head, tail thumping on the floor, but made no move to stand. "Come on, old pal," I urged.

Reluctantly, Roger lifted his heavy body and trundled over.

I reached for my coat and scarf, which I was busy wrapping around my neck as the door opened and Dad came back inside.

"From Mrs. Seymour." He handed me a shiny blue tin. "Baked apples, freshly picked."

The scent of cinnamon and apples wafted toward me, and though I'd already breakfasted, my mouth watered.

"Is she buttering me up?" I raised an eyebrow, ready to start a conversation about what I'd already observed.

Dad grinned in a way that made him look years younger. "She certainly would if butter weren't still being rationed."

I laughed. "You're happy." It wasn't a question.

Dad nodded, his gaze meeting mine—his eyes asking, *Are you okay with that?*

I set the tin on the counter, breaking eye contact for a split second. "I'm glad for you, Dad, I really am. Now, I've got to get these fur balls out for some exercise."

Dad cleared his throat. "Good idea. I don't think our couch can take another round with Crackers."

I laughed, staring at the furniture missing two pillows that the corgi had massacred the day before.

"Before you go," Dad said, and I paused to stare at him, seeing his eyes squinted the way they normally were when he was concerned about something. "I've been doing some thinking."

I waited. The way he was hesitating made me nervous.

"Given your extended stay, and of course your work with the corgis, which is ever so helpful to the princess, what do you think about requesting a permanent position at Windsor? With the war over, they'll be in need of assistance."

I cringed—and the princess wouldn't need help with the corgis. I loved working on the engines as much as Dad loved to stalk a stag, but after my cast had been removed, they noted some nerve damage in my hand that didn't allow me to grip properly anymore. That had meant no more ATS, but fortunately I'd been able to volunteer with the Red Cross at the castle. With the war over, what was I going to do?

"Dad . . ." I bit my lip, knowing he'd missed me and that what he requested came from a good place. "I'll think about it." Though I didn't plan to. There had to be something else I could do that didn't involve staying at Windsor.

Dad nodded, and I walked around him, snapping my fingers at the dogs and in sudden need of autumn air.

The dogs and I took our usual route along the Long Walk, with me tossing sticks. When Roger got tired, I dropped him back at the cottage, wiping off the long streams of slobber hanging from his jaw. Back outside again, my gaze found its way to the castle, turrets jutting above the trees. It was a sight I'd seen thousands of times, and yet it still seemed unreal, and brought with it so many memories: running with the Girl Guides around the grounds, hiking through the woods, roasting sausages over a campfire, and learning to dress a wound. I glanced at my arm, the scars still visible, recollecting one of our lessons. We'd all been in the woods, and Princess Margaret had to pretend to have a broken leg. We'd fashioned a stretcher from two long branches and a blanket, then with sticks and bindings made from torn fabric we secured Margaret's leg. Princess Elizabeth and I had been at the head of the stretcher, carrying her sister back to the camp.

I followed the path of a tiny white butterfly flying in a little loop, and then up and up until it landed on our kitchen window. I had a flash of Mum smiling at me through the wavy glass of the same window years ago as I rushed off somewhere.

I suppose there had been a lot of good memories here too.

I called to the corgis, and we made our way toward the castle. Though I did not mean to join the Windsor staff, I felt obligated to at least inquire. After all, I'd given Dad my word.

We walked through the gate—with me having no idea where I was going, and the corgis taking off after every person that passed, excited to be back on their own ground.

A small black automobile passed us slowly. Once it was clear of us, the driver speeded up. The rev of the engine was all the encouragement the corgis needed. Their short legs spurred them forward as they went tearing after the car, their barks fusing with the sound of the engine. Panic overwhelmed me as I rushed after them.

"Come back! Crackers! Susan!" I shouted, my voice catching the wind and slapping me back in the face.

A liveried helper, hearing my shouts, passed the reins of the horse he was working with to another helper and joined my pursuit of the pups, his long legs gaining ground faster than my own.

Oh, please, get to them.

Oh, please, don't get run over.

The driver seemed oblivious to the dogs chasing behind as he rounded a curve in the road. If we didn't catch them soon, they'd run through the gates into town traffic.

"Susan! Crackers!" I shouted as the corgis too rounded the curve and were out of sight.

My heart pounded, my lungs desperately sought air, and my limbs screamed from exertion but as I rounded the bend in the road, there stood the liveried helper, holding one wriggling dog body under each arm.

Slowing to a stop, I doubled over, hands on my knees, trying to catch my breath. From now on I needed to keep these little monsters on a leash! Having caught sufficient breath to thank him, I straightened and looked the man in the face. My God, it was Forrest Darling—my childhood nemesis. Despite his sweet name, when we were children, he'd been anything but kind to me.

Forrest carried the dogs over to me. He was irritatingly handsome for an arse. Still, he had helped keep the corgis from harm. "Thanks," I said as I relieved him of Susan's wriggling body.

"Hanna?" Forrest seemed stunned. "What are you doing back here?" Crackers stopped squirming in Forrest's arms, apparently momentarily distracted by his voice.

"You can put that one down now," I said. "I think it's safe." I ignored his question; honestly, I wasn't interested in conversation.

"So you're the wonderful corgi keeper we've been hearing about."

Wonderful? I tried to smile, though I suspected I only managed a pinched look. "Yes. That's me. Thanks again, but we've got to get back."

"Let me help you." Forrest's tone was decidedly friendly, but I hadn't forgotten the chewing gum he'd put in my hair or how he'd convinced the other kids in our class to taunt me.

"We'll manage." I patted my pocket and realized I'd forgotten the leashes. Crackers was still at our ankles, momentarily tired from the car chase. But I had no desire to risk another on the walk back. I looked down. It was going to be hard enough to snag Crackers, but with Susan in my one good arm, how could I carry two dogs?

Forrest must have taken note of my hesitation. "I don't mind, Hanna. I've a break now anyway." There was just a touch of laughter in his voice, particularly in the way he said my name.

His tone brought back the taunts of our youth. "Forrest Darling, I wouldn't ask you for help if you were the last person on earth." My words were childish, and my tone churlish, but I didn't regret it. One should never regret being honest. That was what Mum had always said. I wasn't that little girl anymore who was too scared to say anything back. I was a grown woman who could repair an automobile engine as well as most people could boil water for tea. Forrest wasn't going to intimidate me anymore.

Forrest looked taken aback, a tinge of color on his cheeks. "Have I offended you in some way?"

"Surely you're joking." How in the world could he have forgotten the torment he'd put me through? People forgot where they put their bifocals or their keys. They forgot if they turned off the lights when they left the house, or if they'd put out the empty milk bottle for a refill. They did not forget destroying someone else's life.

"Not at all." The sincerity in his voice was shocking and, frankly, offensive.

"Were you asleep during primary school?" I asked in a cutting tone.

"What?" He frowned, his eyes twitching as though he were trying to see through space and time.

"Shall I remind you?" Completely exasperated, I was finding it difficult to keep the last of my temper in check. Susan sensed my distress and started to frantically lick me.

I was about to recount some of his offenses, but he gave me an apologetic smile and it froze the words on my tongue. Then he stooped and recaptured Crackers, giving the dog a rock in his arms.

"I am very sorry for whatever I did in school to cause offense, Hanna. Truly. I've put those days mostly out of mind."

"Why's that?" I couldn't help being curious.

"My mum was heavy-handed with her wooden spoon. My father was fond of giving me a good beating. Those aren't years I like to dwell on." He touched his left ear with his free hand. "One of them left me permanently deaf in this ear. It's why I worked here during the war instead of being at the front."

"Oh." Where a moment ago I'd felt vengeful anger, now I felt sad. And a bit guilty for the way I'd gone off. "I'm so sorry."

"I wasn't nice to a lot of people back then. I'm guessing you were one of them. I was angry at the world. And jealous of kids in situations better than my own. I know that's no excuse—not really. But please, accept an overdue apology. I wish I'd been nicer."

"And what about now? Are you nicer, Forrest Darling?"

He grinned, a flash of teeth and a dimple in the side of his cheek that seemed almost cliché with a surname like Darling. "I admit to having a bit of a reputation when I first took this job, but I've managed to prove to folks I'm not an utter arse. Pardon my language."

I laughed. "You were an utter arse."

It was his turn to chuckle. Then he indicated Crackers and Susan. "Shall we?"

As we walked, he confessed that as a child he'd been jealous of the close relationship I had with my father, and that I was such a good shot.

"My father never took me shooting," he said. "Which was probably a good thing, because I might have shot him."

"Sounds like maybe he deserved it." I'd been thinking it, but had not planned on saying it. "Sorry."

"You're not wrong. He was a real bastard. Gone now, heart attack." There was a somber pause, and then Forrest shook his head slightly and a small smile replaced the grim look that had preceded it. "Remember that one competition, where you whipped all of us in the targets?"

"I made a lot of lads angry that day." I shifted Susan in my arms.

Reaching the cottage, I opened the door, shooing Susan inside and then taking Crackers from Forrest and setting him down inside as well. I shut the door so they couldn't come running back out and then faced my childhood nemesis. "Thank you, Forrest, for helping with the dogs and for your apology."

"My pleasure, Hanna. Good to see you again."

That evening when Princess Lilibet arrived to collect her corgis, there was a twinkle in her eye, and I half wondered if someone had told her about my run-in with Forrest. "Hanna, you do so well with them."

"It has been a pleasure, ma'am."

The princess smiled. "What do you have planned now that the war is over?"

"I'm not quite sure yet," I answered honestly.

Princess Lilibet's blue eyes locked on mine. "I hope that does not mean we will lose you. I'd like it very much if you'd stay."

"Pardon?"

"To care for the corgis. I don't want to entrust them to anyone else. And with my royal duties, I'm going to need someone to help."

I shifted my gaze to Dad who had just come to join me in the front hallway, wondering if our conversation from earlier that day had been prompted by the princess or the other way around. "That is very kind of you, Your Highness—"

Dad cleared his throat, and Lilibet cocked her head, watching me. There was an intensity there, mingling with a genuineness, a goodness, that made one want to say yes.

I realized it would be a lost cause to fight. I thought of my mum . . . of the sacrifices she'd made in giving up her position as a nurse to marry my father and move to Windsor. Every generation of women, it seemed, was asked to give up some part of themselves for someone else. But Mum had been happy. And really, I didn't have anywhere else to go. Maybe I could be happy too.

"It would be my honor to stay." Even as I said it, I felt myself letting go of my dreams of a life away from Windsor for a couple of dogs and a princess I used to call friend. I knew plenty of people who would jump at the chance I'd just been given. But behind my acquiescence I felt more than a touch of sadness.

Lilibet smiled brightly. "It seems life at Windsor runs in the family."

"It certainly does." My throat constricted, feeling the trap close around me.

The only thing that made this any better was that at least I would be able to play with the dogs.

·❧·

CHAPTER EIGHT

𝒫RINCESS ℒILIBET

March 1946

𝒴 ou don't always have to be so reserved." Maggie had taken on a new nickname now that she was "more mature." At least that's what she claimed, but Lilibet suspected it was because Prince Philip had adorably taken to calling her sister "Maggie" in his letters, and she liked the sound of it.

"I'm not always reserved." Lilibet paced to the window, taking in the darkening sky. London was lit up like a million torches pointed toward the heavens. Even though it had been nearly a year since Germany's surrender, she was still surprised at dusk that the city didn't stay dark. How long would it be before she was used to the night being illuminated again? How long, as well, until the palace stopped smelling like paint? After the Luftwaffe bombing, there'd been walls and floors to repair, and smoke damage too. "I play games quite often."

Lilibet glanced in Maggie's direction, where she was arranging the settings on the white-clothed table that had been set for three in what used to be the old nursery but was now Maggie's sitting room.

Maggie tossed her a sure-you-do look before straightening a drooping tulip in the center porcelain vase. The flowers had been chosen to match Maggie's new yellow dress printed with tiny white tulips. Made of a soft fabric, it buttoned up the middle and cinched at the waist.

"Just yesterday, you and I raced at Windsor," Lilibet pointed out. There was nothing better than taking a good long gallop down the Long Walk on one of her prized horses—wind rustling in her hair, and adrenaline pumping through her veins. It was a sensation she was certain never to grow tired of.

"True." Maggie pursed her lips, a teasing twinkle lighting up her eyes. "And you were a very good loser."

Lilibet stifled a laugh. "And you were such a modest winner."

Maggie shrugged with a smirk as they both recalled how she'd tossed her hat and shouted loud enough that a few of the groundskeepers came running, thinking something was wrong.

A flash of car lights outside caught Lilibet's attention. She squinted to see if it was a red MG sports car or one of the royal vehicles. A streak of red zoomed into the courtyard, illuminated by the lamps along the circle.

He's here.

Lilibet's heart turned over. She stood, a hand pressed to the cool glass, as Prince Philip climbed from his vehicle, placing a shiny leather shoe on the graveled drive. Her stomach lay somewhere on the floral French Savonnerie carpet beneath her own sensible heels. Ages had passed since they'd seen each other, not since Easter in 1944, nearly two years ago. They'd communicated through letters. But letters weren't the same and a lot had changed in that time. Lilibet had gone from being a fresh-faced teenager to a woman of nearly twenty. Had Philip changed as well . . . changed toward her?

When VE Day had been declared, as she and Maggie had

danced in the street, she'd assumed Philip would return quickly. But his ship had been off the coast of Okinawa, and Japan had not yet surrendered. So the fighting continued, and any talk of a return date was met with uncertainty.

When the atomic bombs had detonated over Hiroshima and Nagasaki the prior summer, Lilibet had suddenly feared he'd never return. The devastation had been catastrophic, and the war had ended. But the victory felt more like defeat in light of the overwhelming civilian casualties and the horrible pictures of the total destruction that had emerged. Philip had been assigned to the decommissioning of his ship when it came to shore—a process that took time.

But now, finally, he was here.

"What's got you so—" Maggie pressed her face to the window, her words cut off as she spotted Philip sauntering over and chatting casually with the guards. "My," Maggie breathed, capturing in that one exhaled word precisely how Lilibet felt on the inside.

She felt as if her body had turned to vapor and she could blow away with the slightest breath. War had not ravaged Philip's good looks, nor, it appeared, had it dampened his spirits. Watching him joke with the guards, Lilibet couldn't help thinking Prince Philip was just as he'd been the first time she'd met him—full of life and so striking he rivaled Michelangelo's marble sculptures.

"Breathe, Lilibet." Maggie flashed her a smile as she gently patted her on the back. The gesture reminded Lilibet of years before, when she'd been Maggie's age and she'd done much the same while they camped out in the bowels of Windsor as the Blitz in London reigned.

"How do I look?" Lilibet smoothed the seashell-patterned

dress she'd chosen for the night, a choice born of something Philip had written in a letter about her being the lone sparkling shell, still intact on a beach of broken rocks.

In her typical cheeky fashion, Maggie said, "You look like my sister."

Lilibet rolled her eyes. "Maggie," she emphasized. "Please." All through the war, their clothing had been extremely limited, rationed like the rest of the country's. Even now, they were restricted to their coupon book, but at least they'd been able to update their wardrobes a bit.

Maggie fluttered her hands around her face, and then folded them over her heart, giving a twirl like those she'd done onstage during their pantomimes. "You look, dear sister, like a royal life raft that will save a prince who's been lost at sea."

"You do have a flare for the dramatic." Lilibet adjusted her pearls, her ears straining for the sounds of Philip's boisterous voice.

Maggie gave a deep curtsy. "I know."

A few beats later, Susan perked up. Lilibet's faithful corgi companion, who'd been standing next to her, cocked her head, her large, upright, triangular ears picking up sounds her human couldn't yet discern.

"What is it, Susan?" Lilibet bent, stroking a hand over Susan's soft head. Her dog looked up, brown eyes round with excitement, and she licked her snout. "Can you hear my prince?"

Lilibet glanced furtively at Maggie, who pretended to be fixing the napkins on the table, wondering if she had heard the possessive declaration, and glad no one else was present. When her father had been a duke and they'd never had any thoughts of becoming monarchs, life had been much simpler. But since he had become king and Lilibet heir presumptive, even the smallest things had to be kept quiet. She'd taught herself to rarely show emotion when she was in public. And even at home private matters were not spoken of because the walls had ears and newspapers were happy to take advantage of that.

Susan's little tail started to wag, setting her whole fluffy behind waggling, and Lilibet couldn't help but give the corgi's back a scratch.

A sharp rap sounded at the door, and then it was swung open by a footman. "His Royal Highness, Prince Philip of Greece, first lieutenant in His Majesty's Royal Navy."

Philip swept in, bending low at the waist. "Just Philip, Your Highnesses."

Lilibet bit her lip, restraining herself although every bone in her body longed to leap forward into his arms. Philip straightened, his blue eyes piercing hers, a small smile playing on his lips. While the servant was in the room, she kept still, determined to keep her face from giving away her feelings.

When the footman backed out and the door closed behind him, she let her stoic expression fall, smiling so broadly that she might have lit up London in the dark.

"Welcome, Just Philip," she teased.

"Princesses, you are a sight for sore eyes." Philip smiled at Maggie, and then returned his gaze to Lilibet, taking her in with an appreciative glance from head to foot that made her happy she'd carefully chosen her dress.

Maggie squealed in delight, offering the prince the reaction that Lilibet desperately wanted to. But she was nearly twenty, and adult women did not squeal. No, her smile was as far as she'd let herself go.

"I am so glad you've come," Lilibet said quietly.

"There's nowhere in the world I'd rather be." As he approached, her hand rose and he took it, kissing the air above her knuckles as he stroked her palm.

Lilibet's heart fluttered as though a thousand butterflies had been released between her ribs. Susan, not to be left out, rose on her hind legs, planting her front paws on Philip's knee, scratching away and giving a yip in welcome.

"And you must be Susan." Philip crouched down in reaction to the eager corgi, rubbing his large, Viking-like hand indulgently over Susan's head. Susan licked his palm.

"She likes you," Lilibet mused, her heart melting. She was glad that her pup approved of the man she adored. "Susan is very discerning in who she accepts." She said it with a chuckle, thinking of the hard time Susan gave some of the guards her father invited to the dances over the last few months—but she meant it. And that was why the dog's enthusiasm for Philip mattered.

Poor Roddy Macleod—a six-foot-four soldier whom she'd had a very slight crush on when she'd gone to the ghillies' ball last summer—hadn't fared so well. He'd taught Lilibet a Scottish reel, but had not passed muster with Susan, who'd poked several holes in his boots as she attempted to attack his feet.

"I am flattered to have met with her approval." Philip gave Susan one last scratch behind the ear as he glanced up at Lilibet. "She's got a sweet disposition—like her princess."

Lilibet could have stared into his eyes all day long. There was so much emotion in them, so much that didn't need to be said, because the princess understood it. So much that *couldn't* be said . . . at least not yet. The prince was an outrageous flirt, and she hung on his every word, wishing she could be half as clever. But she felt, or at least she hoped, there was something more to what his eyes said than idle flirtation.

"Would you like a tour of our newly painted quarters before we dine?" Lilibet indicated the table set for three. Her sister filled the role of chaperone this evening.

"For you, princesses, I will show an interest in paint," Philip said.

Offering an arm to each of them, Philip strolled with the princesses through the renovated wing of the castle, including Lilibet's new rooms. Lilibet found herself blushing as Philip stared at her canopied bed. She was glad that, from where he stood beside her, Philip couldn't tell—or at least she hoped he couldn't.

"What's this?" Philip let out a startled chuckle, lifting a framed photograph of himself in his seaman's beard from her mantelpiece.

Lilibet grinned. "That picture was a cause of scandal."

He smiled down at the photo before placing it back. "Surely not." He winked at her.

"Lilibet is telling the truth," Maggie said. "Someone told the papers and they wrote about it. They can't get enough of the two of you."

"I confess, neither can I," Philip said, taking his place between them again. "The three musketeers. I think we should go dancing at Ciro's. I've not been to a good club in a while."

"Can we? Please?" Maggie pleaded, clapping her hands.

"We should," Lilibet said. "But we'll need to make arrangements first. You know how Papa is."

"I'll ask him about it myself," Philip said confidently. "But first—about that dinner."

Back in Maggie's sitting room, Philip held out a chair for Lilibet, tucking her against the table, before doing the same for her sister. Ever the gentleman, he never ceased to impress Lilibet with his impeccable manners. The interesting thing about Philip was that he knew exactly what he was supposed to do but made everything seem playful in the end, unlike some of the stiff boards she'd had to put up with on more than one unfortunate occasion.

"I say, Maggie, we ought to remove the plaque on the outside of this door that says Nursery and replace it with Maggie's Playroom," Philip quipped, as if proving Lilibet's point.

The princesses laughed.

"You think I'm joking," Philip said. "I'm perfectly serious."

While they were served their simple fare of fish and greens, Lilibet's and Philip's eyes met frequently, so much spoken in the silence. "Tell us of your exploits," she said.

Philip's forehead wrinkled as he raised his eyebrows and let out a breath. "The exploits of a sailor?"

Lilibet grinned. "Well, you are a lieutenant now. You ought not to diminish what you've earned."

"The exploits of a lieutenant, then." He wiped his mouth, drawing her attention to his lips, raising thoughts of how much she wanted to kiss him.

Of course, it wasn't at all proper. And if her mother, or Crawfie, knew that she couldn't stop imagining what kissing him would be like, they'd probably try to wash her brain with a bar of carbolic soap.

"Commanding the men of the *Whelp* was the greatest honor of my life. The endless sea, with the blanket of stars above us, quickly came to feel like home. When we weren't actively engaged in our duties, we played cards and chess. Some of my shipmates were musical and they'd strum or drum."

"Sounds like a floating gentleman's club," Maggie teased.

"Something very like—at least when we weren't fighting." Philip took a long sip of his orangeade.

"We heard a rumor that in Sicily you foiled the Luftwaffe." Lilibet wiped the corner of her mouth with her napkin.

Philip gave a tiny laugh—he was always, Lilibet thought, modest, and that was commendable, despite what she'd said earlier about not diminishing his achievements. "That was in forty-three, when I was second-in-command of the *Wallace*. It was a fight, to be sure, but I have it to thank for my getting my own ship, at least in part. The Luftwaffe was bombing the hell out of us and the ships around us, pardon my language."

Lilibet nodded, understanding he'd spent the better part of his twenties on a ship and there was a reason people said *cursed like a sailor.* Maggie bit her lip, trying not to laugh.

"I had the men toss some rafts overboard, filled with bits and bobs. Before we pushed them away, we lit their contents on fire. Then we turned off all the ship's lights. From the sky the floating flames made it look like we'd been hit. But meanwhile we sailed right out of danger."

"How clever!" Lilibet was not surprised. Philip had been first in his cadet class. But even before that—in fact ever since she'd known him—she thought him one of the cleverest people she'd ever met.

Philip told a few more purely entertaining stories of his time on the *Whelp* as they finished their meal. But then his face changed. "I think the most memorable part of this last deploy-ment, besides reading your lovely letters, was after the Japanese surrender, escorting English prisoners of war from Tokyo Bay." His voice grew heavy. "Tears poured down their faces as they sat among us, and we just kept giving them tea . . . listening to their stories."

Lilibet could imagine it. The swaying of the ship. The salt spray on their skin as their countrymen, still in awe of being rescued at last, relayed their harrowing tales. And Philip's heart aching for those who'd suffered—Lilibet believed he had such a heart even if he was often one to jest—trying to make them comfortable with a cup of tea. "That must have been very moving," she said gently.

"I'll never forget it. And now we've got peace at last." He stared at her, and their eyes locked. Was it her imagination or did his seem to say she was where he'd found his peace?

"And homecomings," Maggie interjected, breaking the spell.

Philip flicked his gaze to Maggie, nodding as he straightened his back against the chair. "Although there are so many who will never return."

They were silent for a moment, reflecting on that sad thought—on the mourning of the world over more than half a decade of death and destruction. The world would never be the same.

All the more reason you must remain informed of the goings-on beyond the palace walls. One day you will be queen. She looked at him again. When the time came to rule, she'd need a man like Philip at her side—someone from whom she could take advice. If their metaphorical ship was ever being bombed, his quick, ingenious thinking might just save them— country and family—from disaster.

Dessert was served. As Lilibet took a small bite of her Victoria sponge, Philip said, "Tell me about what you've been up to."

Maggie's fork clattered against her plate. "Father's been

throwing us a lot of parties, and you know how much we like dancing. Now that you're back, you'll have to join in the fun."

"Parties?" Philip gave a lopsided grin.

"Yes." Lilibet tried for neutral, but she was certain a blush colored her cheeks. She didn't want Philip questioning her about her dancing partners or the men who'd tried to court her. So she went for a diversion. "And it seems, with the end of war, Papa's decided to let off a bit of steam. He even led a conga line out into the corridor."

"How I wish I could have seen that." Philip did a seated conga, one hand on his belly, the other in the air, making Susan, who'd been dutifully quiet beneath the table, yip.

"You may still," Lilibet teased. "I hardly think his dancing days have come to an end."

Cake finished, Philip pushed back from the table. "Let's dance now, shall we?"

Maggie leaped up, pulling out a record and putting it on her gramophone, while Lilibet and Philip rolled back the rug. A jazzy tune played with Noël Coward's voice crooning. Without further discussion the three of them cut loose right there in the center of the sitting room.

Perhaps drawn by the noise, Crawfie ducked her head in to check on them, but she left as quickly as she came, to Lilibet's relief. Crawfie had taken good care of them through the war, but Lilibet was too old for a governess now—a fact acknowledged by all since Crawfie was mostly in charge of Maggie's education now—and found the presence of this woman she'd grown up with stifling.

"Did you dance on the ship?" Maggie asked in the moment of silence as she moved the needle over the record to her next favorite song.

Philip ran his hand through his blond hair, which had dampened near his temples from their antics. "No. If I danced, it was when we pulled into port if I was invited off with some of the other officers." He glanced at Lilibet. "But no one I met in any of those places dances as well as you do." He took her hand and twirled her around.

"Me next!" Maggie leaped between them for a twirl.

After an hour or more of dancing, Lilibet was certain her hair was a fright, and sweat was making her dress cling to her back.

Philip joined her as she stood gulping a glass of water and catching her breath. His chest, she noticed, seemed to be heaving only half as much as hers.

Maggie put her cup down on the table with a decisive thunk. "Let's play hide-and-seek."

"I've not played that since Gordonstoun." Philip gave a rueful shake of his head, no doubt filled with memories from his boyhood school days.

"Are you saying you're too old for a little hiding in the dark?" Lilibet teased.

"Do you think we'll find you too easily since you're as tall as the ceiling?" Maggie added.

"That's it! You're on." Philip went to a lamp and switched off that light, casting one corner of the sitting room into shadows.

"That's not dark enough." Maggie flung open the door, calling out to the nearest footman, "We're playing hide-and-seek—turn off the lights, please."

Within minutes the entire wing of the castle was cast in shadows, and the three of them were laughing.

"Lilibet and I are going to hide, Philip. You have to find us first," Maggie commanded. Then she grabbed hold of Lilibet's hand and tugged her out into the corridor. "Count to one hundred before you come searching," she called over her shoulder.

"You go that way and I'll go this way," Lilibet whispered. Maggie let go of her hand and took off in the opposite direction.

Lilibet ran softly down the corridor, and then ducked into a curtained alcove. The window there looked out over the courtyard, and she could see Philip's little red sports car. Her heart was pounding so hard, she was certain he'd be able to follow the beats to find her. Realizing the lights outside illuminated her, she stepped onto the bench, her heels sinking into the cushion, so her feet wouldn't be visible from the corridor.

Every creak made her jump as she waited. Tendrils of shadows marked the curtain separating her from the corridor, then disappeared. She let out the breath she'd been holding, certain Philip had gone on.

But then a hand slid around the edge of the velvet, catching her forearm. "I've got you," Philip whispered, ducking into the alcove, letting the curtain fall behind him.

Lilibet could just make out his smile in the light from the courtyard. The same light made twin diamonds sparkle in his eyes.

"And so you have," she murmured.

He didn't let go of her arm, and she didn't try to pull away, enjoying the heat of his palm on her skin. A breath later, he did let go, only for both his hands to wrap around her waist as he lifted her down from where she perched on the bench.

Her head tilted back to look at him. The tips of her shoes touched the tips of his, and the hem of her dress swished like a kiss against her calves. She'd dreamed of a moment alone like this. A quiet, private snatch of time where they might share a kiss.

Philip touched the side of her face fleetingly, his brief caress sending a thrill through her limbs. "Lilibet," he whispered, his voice deeper than it had been a moment before. "I wonder if you might give me permission to kiss you."

Lilibet pressed her lips together to hold in a gasp of surprise. Not because he'd read her mind or wanted the same thing as she did, but because he'd asked for permission. If she'd just been a normal girl, would he have simply leaned in?

Oh, what did it matter? The very thing she'd been wishing for was about to come true.

"Yes." The word came out without hesitation.

Philip bent, his lips brushing hers. As she looped her arms around his shoulders, rising on her tiptoes and breathing in the salty, spicy scent of him, there came a little growl, followed by a bark and more growls. Philip jerked back, their kiss ending abruptly.

"She's got my trousers," he exclaimed with a laugh.

"No, Susan!" Lilibet bent, trying to pry her dog away from Philip's trouser leg. But Susan had gotten it into her head that this was now a game of tug-of-war. With her hind end rising and her forelegs down low, she jerked her head back and forth with vigor. "You naughty dog." Lilibet could barely keep amusement from her voice as she admonished her beloved corgi.

Philip, recognizing the humor in the situation as well, laughed as he bent to join her in trying to pry his trousers from between the corgi's teeth. Thrown off-balance by their efforts, the pair tumbled out into the corridor, hooting as they went. When Susan finally did let go, she barked, wagging the nub of her tail as if she were the queen of the game.

"Did she rip them?" Lilibet squinted in the dark, her fingers brushing over the place where Susan had clamped down.

"Nothing that can't be mended." Philip offered Susan a spirited head rub and a little playful growl.

Maggie came running, her footfalls echoing in the still partially unfurnished corridor. "What's happened?"

Lilibet laughed as Philip stood and then helped her to her feet. "Susan decided she wanted Philip's trousers."

"Naughty dog." Maggie shook her head, hands on her hips. "It's a good thing she didn't get them off. I don't know how we'd explain that to Papa."

Philip reached out and tapped Maggie on the shoulder. "You're it."

"Oh, but you found Lilibet first," Maggie retorted, crossing her arms over her chest.

"Actually, Susan found Philip." Lilibet giggled, then she took off running down the corridor with Susan nipping at her heels.

Tonight she'd had her first kiss with Philip. It might have been brief, but it had been wonderful. She was as certain as she'd ever been that, despite the dukes and earls her father had introduced her to over the last six months, there was and had only ever been one man she wanted to marry—Prince Philip of Greece, the sailor she'd fallen in love with at thirteen.

And tonight, after their kiss, Lilibet felt a sudden wonderful certainty that her dream of Philip as her husband was going to come true.

CHAPTER NINE

HANNA

The end of the week could not come soon enough.

My feet ached, and I longed to wear anything besides the formal, stiff wool uniform I wore daily to work. I'm not certain I'd ever understand how one could think two-inch pinching heels, a wool skirt, and a jacket with a blouse was at all appropriate attire for a keeper of the royal dogs. I spent most of my day walking and running. What I needed was a good pair of trousers and boots.

Of course, I'd been honored to be asked to join the princess—and Susan and Crackers—at Buckingham Palace. It was a job, and I needed one now that the war had ended. And I had a renewed sense of purpose, one beyond convincing the firm to let me wear something more dog practical.

At first, the idea of the position had made me feel stuck, like I wasn't ever going to escape a life I didn't want. But as each day passed, the more I enjoyed it. After all, my days were spent caring for dogs, which I love, and it certainly beat any sort of secretarial job.

Though this position got me away from Windsor, which is what I thought I wanted, as it turned out, I missed it. Or at least I missed my dad. The dynamics among the staff at Buckingham Palace were miserable. So many of them were like toddlers grappling for toys and treats. There were temper tan-trums, snide comments, rude gestures. Just this week someone had taken the left shoes from the pairs of work shoes lined up in the staff area. Oh, heaven help whoever that was when that box of lefties was found.

There was a smug hierarchy in the palace, despite the fact that surely—after working the last few years to stay alive and keep the royal family safe—there should have been a sense of pulling together on the same team. At Windsor we'd had that camaraderie—we'd felt more like we were all a family around a bountiful table with plenty to share.

I moved briskly through the halls of Buckingham Palace. Renovations had been going on for weeks now, repairing the damage from the bombs—accompanied by the smell of paint and a constant echoing of hammers. At first all the noise had irritated the dogs, but they seemed to have gotten used to it now.

With the corgis' leashes on, something I'd never forgotten to do after that day at Windsor, I approached the door leading to the mews. While the click of the corgis' nails had been muted on the carpet, they pranced now on the marble tile with little tinkling pings.

A butler passed, his chin held high as if he could sniff the ceiling. His black suit was as crisp and as stiff as his posture. I could see the point of his chin reflected in the shine on his shoes. I'm not sure he even knew what the carpet looked like, he spent so much time with his neck bent back.

"Excuse me. Are there any carriages out?" I asked.

I couldn't tell if Susan loved the horses or felt the need to corral them—but she certainly got agitated around them. Whenever they were out, she'd bark her head off and run this way and that, stressing herself, the horses, and me.

By the way she was prancing now, it was evident if I didn't take Susan out this minute there would be an accident on the floor. There wasn't time to get her out another door. So it would help to know if we faced an equine menace on the other side of this one, but the butler walked right past me, as if I didn't exist. Not even a twitch on his face to show he'd heard me.

"Excuse me!" I called after him.

His pace didn't slow even a fraction. My goodness but this was going to take a lot of getting used to. And how could he think he was any better than me? Because he didn't walk dogs, that made him superior?

I snorted to myself and stuck my tongue out at his back, not caring who saw, then proceeded to the door, where a footman momentarily lost his stoic face and was trying not to laugh.

"Is he always like that?" I gestured at the retreating butler.

The footman nodded. "Always," he assured me as he held the door open.

Susan snagged the poor fellow's ankle in a little nip as she passed.

"No, Sus, stop that," I admonished, and Susan let go, listening for once.

Fortunately, there were no carriages or horses out to distract her from the task at hand, so we hurried to the first spot of grass we could find. As Susan planted her feet, Crackers started to pull me in the opposite direction, leaving me to stand, in my pressed skirt and shirt, with my arms stretched out to the left and right.

"You'd make a delightful scarecrow."

I turned to find Forrest Darling approaching. The corner of his mouth was hitched up in a grin, showing the dimple in his cheek that was almost endearing. The fact that everything about him came off so charming was irksome, to say the least.

"What are you doing here?" I ignored both his joke and his attempt to be charming by it.

Forrest shrugged his broad shoulders, looking so comfortable that it made me want to shove him a little off-balance.

"Same as you, I suspect," he said.

"Waiting for a dog to finish her business?"

Forrest laughed, wagging a gloved finger at me. "My four-legged charges are much larger."

"So you've been transferred to Buckingham Palace as well?" I tried to keep the surprise from my voice.

"Sort of."

I cocked my head, my expression conveying he should explain.

"We go where the princesses go, do we not?" His reply wasn't really a reply at all.

"So you'll be going to Windsor this weekend as well, then?" I pressed. That was what those of us who worked in the royal household did. Weekdays at the palace, weekends at Windsor. How had I not known he was part of the household before? I thought he was simply attached castle staff. There was a difference.

Forrest nodded.

Well, isn't this bloody rich? I decided to change the subject. "Susan has it out for the horses."

Forrest glanced down to where Susan looked as if she was seriously contemplating a go at his ankle. "I think she just needs to get to know them better."

"I doubt it. She thinks she's the boss of everything."

"Well, she needs to stop pestering them—for her sake as well as theirs. What if one kicks her?"

"Don't let the princess hear you calling her a pest," I said, more in an attempt at levity than a warning because everyone knew how much Lilibet adored her dogs. In fact, it was a running joke with the downstairs folks that speaking out against a corgi could get one dismissed.

As if to prove to Forrest that she was anything but a pest, Susan gave a sharp bark and jumped up on her hind legs, doing a little dance for him.

"At least she's cute," Forrest said, chuckling.

I couldn't help smiling. Susan was as adorable as they came. "True. And a sweetheart."

I knelt down, giving Susan a pat on the head and a treat from my pocket, which immediately brought Crackers to my side.

"Is it true they have their own chef?" Forrest asked.

I glanced up at him, the sun beaming down around his head. I squinted. "Yes. Don't the horses?"

"Not unless you count the farmers who prepare the hay and oats."

I laughed and straightened back up. "Susan and Crackers here get a steady diet that is probably better than what we ate growing up. But from what I've heard, their chef is none too pleased. He'd been hired thinking he was going to serve the princesses."

"Which he is technically—he's in Princess Elizabeth's service." There was a hint of laughter in Forrest's tone, and I was suddenly glad to have a familiar face in these new surroundings.

"I'll remind him of that the next time he gets snippy with me." A horn blared somewhere beyond the gates, and I glanced over. A steady stream of people passed by; and nearly half of them paused at least momentarily to gaze between the thick black wrought iron bars of the palace gates in hopes of glimpsing one of the royals.

A little girl squealed and pointed to the corgis, and I waved, understanding the delight at seeing a cute dog—and in this case a royal one. There'd been plenty of times throughout my life that a little fur ball had stopped me in my tracks.

"Happen a lot?" Forrest asked, bringing me back to our conversation.

"The chef getting snippy? You wouldn't believe." I rolled my eyes. "The way he holds his head you'd think he was the head butler."

Forrest let out a groan. "It's the same in the mews. Since I transferred in, they've done plenty to try and 'teach me my place.' Doesn't matter that I worked in the mews at Windsor for nearly a decade."

"Teach you your place how?" I asked.

"Dumping muck in a stall I've just cleaned." Forrest shook his head.

"That's so . . . shitty." I smirked and bit my lip. I didn't usually use such language, but I just couldn't help myself.

Forrest let out a roar of a laugh. "It bloody well is."

Crackers and Susan tugged at their leashes, tired of standing still. I meandered slowly across the lawn and Forrest kept pace with me. "What did you do in response?" I asked.

He grinned and wiggled his brows. "Dumped it back."

I gasped in mock astonishment. "Oh my, I bet that didn't go well."

"Well, they didn't do it again. And I call that a win."

I stopped, thinking about what he'd said. "Perhaps I should give the staff downstairs a taste of their own medicine?"

Forrest shrugged. "Couldn't hurt."

I thought about the stuffy butler, how he'd just walked past me as if I were not more than a speck of dirt on his over polished shoe. How, when he could have helped avoid a corgi disaster, he chose to snub me instead. What an arse. If he was willing to act that way when it came to helping the princess's dogs, what would happen if I made a move at revenge? "I think I'd be flayed alive."

My statement seemed to amuse Forrest, as he chuckled softly. "Oh, I don't think so. I bet they're giving you a hard time because they know how much Princess Elizabeth respects you. They are jealous."

"You think so?" I raised a brow, looking back toward the palace, the light from the sun reflecting off dozens of windows. I wondered how many people stared through the glass, how many, if any, were watching me now, judging me. Then I glanced back at Forrest, realizing I'd found an ally in an old enemy.

He tugged off his gloves, stuffing them in a pocket, and then ran a hand through his hair. "The royal animals are family to the household, more so than the staff is. You are personally in charge of the royal dogs. Your father is the gamekeeper at Windsor—a position that commands respect. You grew up with the princesses. The king and queen know your name." Forrest hooked a thumb over his shoulder toward the palace. "Trust me, it's jealousy."

I hadn't thought about it like that before. "Maybe so. But he treats the others the same way. The poor scullery maids—I don't think they are ever allowed to even look in the butler's direction."

"Probably not. The hierarchy is what keeps people in line, right? Without it, where would those in charge be?"

"I think they should take the behavior of their majesties into account and emulate them. The king does not look down his nose at the scullery maids, and the queen does not pass me by without at least a smile."

"Perhaps the old guard did." Forrest pulled his gloves from his pocket, putting them back on. "Well, I've got to return, else they may change their minds and shovel that muck right back."

"It was nice talking with you," I said, surprised at the genuineness of my statement.

He glanced over at me then, a little smile tugging at his mouth. "You too, Hanna."

The way he said my name, as if we were old friends, sent a warmth tunneling through me that was not altogether unwelcome, even if it was unnerving.

"And when Susan is ready," he continued, "I can try to give her a gentle introduction to the horses. Won't do for them to not get along; the princess needs to be able to take her dogs on carriage rides."

"That would be a good idea," I said, giving a small wave as he moved away.

After walking the corgis about the palace grounds, the sounds of the city in the background, honking horns, and the clock tower chiming the hour, I returned to the kitchen, determined to begin making friends with my fellow staff members. Surely that was better than engaging in a tit for tat.

I found the dog's chef chopping mushrooms beside a pile of diced raw chicken.

"For Princess Susan's dinner?" I kept my tone jovial and an inviting smile on my face, praying my new attitude served me well.

He glanced up, eyes narrowed for a minute, and then gave a small laugh. "I never thought, when I went to culinary school, I'd use my training to make dog food."

"I should think not, but imagine how jealous some of your former mates will be when they find out you are personally in charge of the feeding of the most beloved fur-covered royals in the house?"

He paused in his chopping, eyeing me up and down. I could tell by his skeptical expression that he thought I was making fun of him, and what I'd hoped would be a friendly interaction was in danger of going southward.

"You please the princess when you feed her dogs," I said sincerely. "And when the princess is pleased, so are their majesties."

The chef's expression softened, and he nodded slowly in tandem with his chopping. "I'll endeavor to look at it that way. And perhaps I'll add a flourish of parsley to their dishes, if only to remind myself it's still art."

I tapped the table. "And I will point out how much Crackers and Susan enjoy their meals when I speak with Princess Elizabeth this evening."

That brought a true smile to his face, and then to my dismay, Susan latched on to the poor man's ankle and gave a powerful shake.

"Susan, no!" I cried.

Crackers, not one to be left out, grabbed hold of the chef's other cuff, and they shook their heads in tandem with growls of delight, tails wagging.

"My God, woman! Get a hold of your charges," bellowed the chef.

I couldn't help laughing as I tempted them with treats. We'd been making such good headway a moment ago, only to end like this.

"This is not what I signed up for," he shouted, yanking on his trousers, which tore in the grip of tiny, sharp teeth.

"Please don't quit," I said over my shoulder as we rushed from the kitchen. "You're a wonderful chef."

PART II

ℭHE
ℬRIDE

ROYAL REPORT

TRUSTED NEWS OF ALL THINGS ROYAL

Well, we knew Prince Philip was a royal flirt, but we had no idea he would soon be called the Naked Waiter. What, you ask? Where can we make a reservation? You can't, unless you belong to the Thursday Club, where apparently the naughty prince served his men's-only group in nothing but a mask. We wonder what our beloved princess thinks of this? It's one thing for a prince to have many society girlfriends, but to be naked in public? Do tell . . .

CHAPTER TEN

SUSAN

A rush of air ruffles the fur on my back, and I stick my nose toward the sky, breathing in the scents of this magnificent place Lilibet calls the Scottish Highlands.

It's my favorite place, and it's hers too.

All the sounds and smells of London are a distant memory here. The overwhelmingness of a big city is erased from my soul by the quiet moors and swaying trees in the forest. From hers too, I think, looking up along the smooth wall of white cloth to find my princess sitting, fork in hand, at the table it cascades from, having her dinner.

The squirrels are my nemesis in London, but I have so many more here. Birds, foxes, groundhogs . . . So much more living to do. So much more excitement.

Last week I got stuck in a foxhole. I thought I was going to die with my hind end up in the air, my legs wiggling for purchase and finding nothing. But Lilibet pulled me out, wiped the dirt from my nose. I'd gotten nearly all the way in, the scent of the foxes strong, and all I wanted to do was scare them away, to tell them who was boss.

We spend every day outside, even when it rains. Lilibet is in her element here. At suppertime, we head back inside. And every night, like tonight, despite the king's protestations, I am fed dinner with Lilibet. She doesn't like to be apart from me for too long, which suits me just fine. I dine on deliciousness at her feet. I turn my attention back to my silver dishes—tonight's meal is rabbit! Oh, the delights of having my own chef.

When the food is gone, and the chatter dies down, I follow Lilibet through to the drawing room and she lifts me into her arms. We lounge before the fire where she and Maggie often play cards. They slap the deck and shout "Snap!"

Tonight, there is no shouting, and the game seems half-hearted. I prick up my furry ears.

"Do you think they will allow it?" Lilibet whispers to Maggie. I raise my head from her lap and nudge her to pet me.

"I should hope so. Everyone thinks you're going to get married."

"The papers do, but Mummy and Papa seem to think otherwise." Lilibet rubs behind my ears. There's nothing like a good ear scratch.

"They can't now."

Lilibet sighs. "They do, trust me."

I cock my head, studying Lilibet. She is biting her lip and Maggie is looking confused. Hmm.

Maggie lays down her hand of cards, completely forgetting the game. "You've done all they asked, and still chose Philip."

"He is my one and only."

They speak in hushed tones, which is good. Because often I hear everything that they say louder repeated by one servant after another, and then all those same servants balk at its being in the papers. It is one of the times I wish I could speak human—so I could tell their majesties who is gossiping. But instead, I must content myself with occasionally narrowing my eyes and barking at the offenders.

"Then ask. The worst that can happen is they say no, but I'm betting after all this time, they will finally recognize he is what you want, and you deserve that."

Lilibet sighs and lifts me up to give me a kiss on the head. "I'm going to do it."

"Do what?" Papa enters the room, looking curiously from one to the other.

Lilibet stiffens, and I nuzzle closer, sensing she is nervous. I lick her hand, giving her courage.

"I should like to invite Philip to join us at Balmoral, Papa."

Philip. He always gives me the best treats and tosses the ball as far as he can. When I chase after it, he pulls Lilibet in his arms if no one is looking, and then there is a different kind of smell. One that makes me wrinkle my nose in curiosity. The smell of courtship. Love. Feral. I'm not sure I like it.

The king frowns. Maybe he doesn't like it either. "He would have to request leave."

Lilibet's heart thumps in her chest and I think she may be holding her breath. *Breathe, dear one.*

"He can request leave as he's done in the past when he wintered with us at Windsor," Maggie says nonchalantly, as if it is no big deal that they are considering inviting the man courting Lilibet to their Scottish castle.

"I suppose he could." Papa nods.

Lilibet sits a little taller and smiles. I yip in response to the king's reply and my princess's happiness.

"Thank you, Papa. I will write to him now." Lilibet sets me down and makes her way to a writing desk.

I know she doesn't want to wait, because she doesn't want the king to change his mind.

Is it wrong that part of me wishes he would? I don't want to share my Lilibet with Philip at my favorite place. So instead of following Lilibet to the writing desk, I go to the king, put my paws up on his leg, and he rubs my head.

I bark, and he lifts me up. If only I could make my tongue form words. I'd tell him to reconsider. But alas, I am silenced by a good belly rub.

·ᴏᴄᴇ᧞·

CHAPTER ELEVEN

ᴇLIZABETH

August 1946

Dearest Philip,

I should like to invite you to Balmoral for part of the summer season, if you would be able to obtain leave from Corsham and your duties there. Certainly, the cadets can make do without you as their instructor for a time, though no one is your equal.

There's to be grouse shooting and deer stalking, which I know you will enjoy. I propose we make a wager that I down the first stag. I do hope to see your red sports car through the trees as you approach, though Papa will probably say you're scaring away the game.

Maggie says to tell you that she's got a new record for us to play and awaits many evenings of dancing. While I try to steer clear of most of my sister's antics, this is one I most heartily look forward to.

With much anticipation,
Elizabeth

*D*ressed in tweed, her boots laced tight, and a beige scarf covering her head, Elizabeth walked beside her father over the Scottish grounds of their summer retreat. A light wind rustled through the trees, and their boots crunched on fallen leaves and pine needles. It was a walk she'd done countless times before, but breathing in the Highland air, the earthy scents of wet bark from a morning drizzle, moss, and pine sap, never got old.

Birds sang, welcoming in the morning. The only interruption to their greeting was the occasional squirrel running for his life from Susan.

They headed for the River Dee, climbing into a waiting rowboat, Susan, ever the explorer, hopping in as well.

"I . . . believe your visitor is . . . coming today," Papa said, swishing away a few midges that fought for space around his face. Since he'd been working with Mr. Logue, his speech had become much more fluid. Though it had always been better when speaking with family in private.

"Yes." She tried to keep her voice steady, but the truth was, she was entirely too excited. Elizabeth dipped an oar in the water, watching the ripples cascade out as they were propelled forward.

Susan put her paws on the gunwale, lapping at the river water as it splashed up with each stroke of the oars. If only life could be as simple and joyful as Susan made it seem. Elizabeth watched her dog for a few minutes, then caught her father's eye. He was staring at her with a very thoughtful expression.

Elizabeth was grateful for her father's invitation for an early morning trip before breakfast. But she suspected it was to get her alone and speak with her about Philip. And the look on his face suggested now was the moment. Her stomach did a little flip, and she pressed a hand to her middle, hoping to settle her nerves.

"You and Philip have been . . . seeing a lot of each other," Papa said, confirming her suspicions.

"We have." But not in the way she wanted. Not alone. True, they'd laid eyes on each other quite a lot. On the weekends, now that he was within a reasonable distance of London, Philip drove in from his base at Corsham to stay with his uncle Dickie Mountbatten at his house on Chester Street.

They'd coordinated their arrivals at parties, clubs, and races so they didn't show up too close together and start rumors. When they danced, Elizabeth had to pay just as much attention to the other gentlemen, though she longed for only Philip as her partner. It was a delicate balance that required so much forethought. And a whole lot of frustration.

The few times Philip had escorted her and Maggie about, the reporters' cameras had been flashing in their faces, the newspapers and rag mags filled with speculation, so much so that when she had an outing on her own, the pesky journalists were shouting, "Where's Philip?"

It made the entire idea of a courtship out in the open impossible, and miserable.

Tongues were apt to wag at the idea of a royal marriage. And when the potential groom was an exiled, penniless prince, the ensuing drama printed in the rags was enough to make Elizabeth consider going it solo. But only for a split second.

There were so many rules about who an heir could and couldn't marry. Of course, the major one was permission from the reigning monarch and approval from Parliament. Added to that, a title was necessary, no divorces, no Catholics either. Fortunately, Philip was a prince, he wasn't divorced, and he'd converted from Greek Orthodox to Anglican. The biggest barrier happened to just be gaining permission; the hesitation from her father was enough to make Elizabeth's head spin. Philip might have been a prince without a home, but he was a descendant of Queen Victoria, just as she was.

"You're very young," her father started, dragging her from her continued mental debate. He dropped his oars inside the boat and pulled out his silver cigarette case, opening it up to a neat line of identically rolled white papers filled with tobacco. He lit a cigarette with a match, the smoke puffing between them before the breeze took it away. He blew out the match, dipped it in the water with a sizzle, then tucked it in his pocket. "You've much to do . . . still. No need to . . . settle down just yet."

The peace of the water in the early hours of the morning warred with the very loudness of her mind. She too let her oars down and settled in more comfortably, tugging Susan on her lap. There was never an end to the comfort Susan provided, and Elizabeth stroked her dog, who panted from her exertion with the water droplets.

"Papa, I may be young, but—" Elizabeth cut short her rebuttal, taking note of her father's ashen pallor. "Are you feeling well?"

Her father gave a mighty cough into his handkerchief and then nodded with a rusty laugh. "Just . . . fine, darling. Now, what were you saying?"

Elizabeth narrowed her eyes, trying to see past the reassuring smile. Papa had been coughing a lot more lately. And sometimes his handkerchief came away from his mouth red. Though he tried to hide the evidence that not all was well, Elizabeth knew she wasn't the only one to have seen it. But no one said anything, as if the king's bleeding lungs were a secret to be kept under lock and key inside a vault with ten-foot-thick walls.

Her mother was worried, and often lamented his smoking.

Even the staff were growing more concerned, their side glances and creased brows quickly smoothed when they saw her looking. But her father kept on as if there was nothing to be concerned over.

"I am not so young, Papa. You proposed to Mummy when she was only a little bit older than me."

"Ah . . . the first time." Her father laughed, taking a long drag of his cigarette. "It took several more proposals . . . a visit from the queen mother . . . and two years before she agreed." The king let out a rattling cough as he gazed off into the distance as if seeing those memories of a young, obstinate Elizabeth Bowes-Lyon in his mind's eye. "Your mother worries that with Philip's . . . disposition he'll have a hard time following in your footsteps . . . bending the knee, as it were."

Elizabeth had heard the story about her mother and father's courtship a dozen times before, and it always made her smile. Mummy had said something to the effect of being afraid that if she married, she'd never be free to think, speak, or act as she wanted. But that needn't be something they had to worry over with Elizabeth and Philip.

"With Philip, I feel that I will have a true partner. Someone who will stand by my side when it comes time for me to take my place—in the very distant future. I'm confident that I am free to think, to speak, to act without his prejudice. He understands me in a way that I think most people do not. And he respects lines of succession. I think he'd do well as my consort."

Susan licked Elizabeth's chin, as if to let her know she agreed and approved.

Philip was her opposite in many ways. He complemented her personality and brought out the best in her. Where she was reserved, he was outspoken. But all it took was one wink from him and she opened up, a side of her emerging that was rarely seen. Elizabeth smiled just thinking about him.

"I do like Philip, Lilibet." The king pointed his cigarette at her, the ash reaching a length that made her itch to tap it. "I like him quite a lot more than I let on."

"What is the reason for your opposition, then, Papa? Is it his sisters?" Unfortunately for Philip, and for enough others in England, several of his sisters had Nazi ties. Though the war was over, the Nuremberg trials were not. Nazi officials were going to be held accountable for the atrocities of war and the crimes they committed against humanity. Any association with the regime, no matter how small, was a permanent stain that marked even those who were only collaterally adjacent, rather than involved themselves.

"That is a mark against him for certain . . . but one that is easily overcome, considering his wartime military record."

"He's served Britain well. Think of how much he did during the war. He took down German ships. He saved British sailors. He is a hero." He was *her* hero.

"Indeed. A hero and a brilliant lieutenant." Her father drew on his cigarette and coughed yet again—a terrible racking cough that shook his shoulders and left him gasping and wheezing. Elizabeth's stomach plummeted and she wished she could pluck the cigarette from his fingers. "I think . . . where a lot of the opposition comes from is . . . that he's a titled prince, but he's got no land. No money. People worry he's . . . only interested in you for how it will improve his circumstances."

Elizabeth bristled. It was a rumor she'd heard before, and it was an insult. As if Philip wouldn't want to be with her *for her*. They'd not read his letters. Seen how he cared for her. How he made her feel safe and fun. She didn't often feel fun, not since her father had become king. But around Philip . . . he brought her to life. She loved him. But more, Philip had told her more than once that when he was with her, he felt like he had a home. No matter where they were, there was something about her steady presence that made him feel grounded in a world where so much of his life was in upheaval, unsettled, and with no permanent place to lay anchor. They were good for each other.

"Philip is not a leech, Papa."

Her father smiled and took a last drag on his cigarette, putting the ember out on the bottom of his shoe. "I know. But there is also the question of his Greek nationality and the current political climate there . . ."

This was a conversation they'd had before. According to the Home Office, from whom her father was obliged to take advice, marrying Philip while he was still a Greek citizen would be dangerous politically, given the current upheaval there. And yet, Philip couldn't seek British naturalization without the consent of his cousin, the Greek king, who needed time to sort out his own situation, and so it wouldn't look to the Greek people like Philip was running away, further weakening the Greek king's political standing.

"He is practically British, Papa." Elizabeth nuzzled the top of Susan's head, smelling the oatmeal bath she'd been given the day before. "Why does everyone forget that? He's been exiled from Greece since he was an infant, and he's been in England all that time. His great-great-grandmother, just like mine, is Queen Victoria, and his mother was born at Windsor. I'd say he's more British than most."

Her father chuckled, which led to another coughing fit. He brought out his handkerchief and while most times Elizabeth looked away, this time she met her father's eyes. "Perhaps you should follow Mummy's advice and quit smoking?"

"Oh, there's nothing wrong with my smokes." Her father picked up his oars and started to row them leisurely back to shore.

"Perhaps I'll argue my case for marriage before Parliament." She was only half serious, and hoped it didn't come to that. After all, she'd yet to even receive a proposal, but it was very much on her mind, and Philip had hinted as much.

"Any marriage between the two of you, should it come to pass, will be much more easily explained if he were a naturalized citizen," the king said. "So I think that is something we should work on as soon as the political matter in Greece is settled."

"In circles we go." Elizabeth tried to hide her irritation. "Sometimes I wish I was back to being a regular girl."

The king loosened his grip on one of the oars and gave her a splash, the cold droplets landing on her face, which startled Susan and made Elizabeth laugh.

"You were never a regular girl, Lilibet."

* * *

ULTIMATELY, IT WASN'T the flash of a red sports car that alerted Elizabeth to Philip's arrival but the sharp, excited barks from Susan. Moments earlier the corgi had been lying, perfectly relaxed, on Elizabeth's lap as the princess sat on the wool couch in the sitting room. Now she was on her feet yapping, her two forepaws tapping enthusiastically on Elizabeth's thigh as she did a little corgi dance.

"Has he arrived, Susan?" Elizabeth had been waiting all morning, reading the same page in her book over and over again in anticipation. "Tell me it's Philip and not Cook with your lunch."

Susan looked her in the eye, barked, and then pranced to the other end of the couch and back. Moments later, Philip's familiar laugh filtered from somewhere below. The sound never ceased to thrill Elizabeth.

She closed *The King's General*, marking her spot in the Daphne du Maurier novel, and leaped from her chair, following Susan, whose little behind wiggled excitedly as she scratched at the paneled wood of the sitting room door.

"Shall we go and greet him, then?" Elizabeth cocked her head at Susan, whose pink tongue rested just outside her mouth as she panted eagerly and then gave a yip in answer. Elizabeth had nearly reached the door when it began to open.

Elizabeth held her breath, imagining Philip on the other side, sweeping in with all his Viking glory. But it was only Bobo's familiar head popping around the door's edge. Bobo, Elizabeth's dresser, had become increasingly the princess's confidante, where it used to be Crawfie, whose duties were now mostly involved with Maggie's education.

With a conspiratorial wink, Bobo said, "I believe we've a new houseguest, Princess. Make haste before Maggie gets there first."

Elizabeth laughed softly. Energetic Maggie was quite possessive of her attention from Philip. Elizabeth didn't blame her sister. They'd been sort of the three musketeers for years with Maggie playing chaperone so that she and Philip could spend time together. And honestly, it was endearing that her sister admired Philip so much. Especially since Elizabeth hoped to bring him permanently into the family fold sooner rather than later.

Not waiting for Elizabeth to make up her mind about seeking the prince, Susan dodged around Bobo's legs and took off in the direction of Philip's voice.

Elizabeth wished she could do the same, but that would hardly be decorous. So she proceeded at a more sedate pace. Rounding the corner of the corridor and arriving at the top of the stairs leading to the grand entrance of the castle, she saw Philip standing below. His shirtsleeves were rolled up, revealing golden, well-toned skin. Her father and mother had beaten Elizabeth to greeting him, but Maggie had yet to appear.

Susan barreled down the stairs, drawing Philip's attention. He knew where the corgi went, Elizabeth likely followed, so his eyes rose to the top of the stairs where they found the princess and he offered her a caught-you-staring smile.

Elizabeth descended the staircase in Susan's wake. Too cute to resist, the corgi was now collecting pats from everyone standing there.

When Elizabeth reached the foyer, she smiled but was careful not to beam. Similarly, she tried to keep her voice calm. One must always appear unaffected, that was what her grandmother Queen Mary advised.

"Philip, delighted you could join us," Elizabeth said.

Philip's eyes danced, making Elizabeth's heart do the same.

"I'm grateful for the invitation, Princess. Your family has been nothing but generous over the years." He turned to her father. "I am in your debt."

"Nonsense," the king interjected. "You've given much of yourself to this family and to our country."

"And thus far, unscathed," Philip said with a chuckle and a nonchalant shrug.

He was always so confident. If only Elizabeth could bottle

some of his assuredness, she'd feel like she was on top of the world.

"Well, I need to get back to my correspondence," the queen said. "Bertie, don't you have some matters to attend to?" She glanced from Philip to Elizabeth. "We'll see you at tea."

A moment later Elizabeth and Philip were standing in the vestibule alone. Or almost so. And to make sure Susan didn't go for the cuff of his trousers, Philip quickly produced a bone from one of his pockets and stooped to offer it to the corgi.

"I should let you freshen up," Elizabeth said. "Shall I have one of the footmen show you to your room?" She sincerely hoped the answer was no.

"I require no refreshing." Philip studied the lines of her face, his eyes shifting from one place to another as if he was memorizing, or perhaps checking that nothing had changed.

After all, he'd told her once her face looked like home to him, and didn't one always examine home after arriving?

"How about a walk?" Philip nodded toward the door. "I've been cramped up on a train and then in the car. My legs could use a stretch."

"The train? You didn't drive?" Elizabeth had gotten so used to seeing him in his sports car that the idea of him leaving it behind had never crossed her mind.

"I love the MG, but it's a bit of a hike from Corsham."

"Yes, I suppose it could have gotten uncomfortable." She gave him a smile. "Fresh air sounds lovely." Then, glancing down at her dress and realizing she was not exactly appropriately attired for a jaunt, she added, "I'd best change." She hesitated, unwilling to leave Philip even for a brief time. "Or perhaps just some wellies."

Philip grinned. "You're living on the edge."

Elizabeth laughed lightly. "Blame yourself. You do challenge me to be more spontaneous."

"Let's find you some wellies, then."

Wellies acquired, Elizabeth called for Susan to follow, for the first time having to encourage her dog out of the house. "I think she's a bit distracted with your gift."

Philip chuckled. "If I'd only known the way to win her heart before, I'd have spared a few trouser legs the repairs."

"Better late than never. Your future trousers thank you." Elizabeth took the arm Philip offered.

Outside, the sky overhead was blue, and the sun—far more visible than in London with its constant smog—glowed splendidly at its center. A cool breeze wafted over the grass and through the trees, lifting the hem of Elizabeth's skirt. Suddenly a pheasant flew quite close to Elizabeth's head, causing her to duck as it settled with a loud squawk on the ground only a few feet farther on. The bird was enough to get Susan going. She launched into a run after the bird, yapping happily.

They walked through the grass, following a path the household had been using since before Elizabeth could remember—a path that made a six-mile circle, winding and wooded. Elizabeth's favorite landmark along the way was the pyramid Queen Victoria had built in remembrance of her beloved Albert. The castle had seen several generations and monarchs since Albert bought the property in 1852 for his queen. And knowing they tread the same pine needle–laden footfalls as her ancestors always made Elizabeth smile.

They crested a hill where the trees broke open enough to make the tops of the castle battlements visible.

Susan came snuffling forward, a stick so large in her mouth that it was making her head tilt to the side. Elizabeth picked up the stick and tossed it, watching the tiny legs of her corgi take off at a pace most people would be surprised to see.

"Corgis were bred for speed and hunting," Elizabeth said. "A wonder when you look at them—they are so entirely goofy."

She smiled as Susan snatched up the large stick again.

"And full of personality," Philip added. This time he tossed the stick as they continued on the path toward Albert's pyramid.

Then there it was on the top of a hill in a Scottish forest. Though it wasn't as large as the ones in Egypt, it was still an incredible feat to imagine men carrying the chiseled rocks the mile and a half from the castle. Elizabeth liked to imagine that one day a hundred years before, Victoria and Albert had stood in this very spot. That had to be the reason she chose this clearing, because of the memories it gave her.

"She really loved him," Elizabeth said as they emerged into the clearing surrounding the pyramid. Every time she came here her eyes were drawn to the monument's epitaph. Today she read it aloud. "'To the beloved memory of Albert, the great and good prince consort, erected by his broken-hearted widow Victoria R.'"

Elizabeth couldn't imagine the pain her great-great-grandmother must have felt in losing the man she'd loved. Looking up at the prince beside her she couldn't imagine a world in which he didn't exist—she didn't want to imagine one.

"Lilibet." Philip took her hand.

Elizabeth glanced down where he held her fingers against his palm, lost entirely in the sensation and in the moment.

"When I was young, all I wanted was a home." His voice drew Elizabeth's eyes back to his face where Philip's gaze locked on hers, the blue of his irises battling the sky for which was truer. "I survived in exile and grew up in one household or another, never really finding a place to belong. To call my own. Still, I've been blessed. I am a prince. I've seen victory in war and been spared the injuries so many men endured." He paused, bringing her hand to his mouth and kissing the backs of her fingers.

"Blessed, but you've worked hard too," Elizabeth said. "You forged your path forward with a strong will and hard work."

"I've had a bit of fun too," he replied with a chuckle. "And now I've found a home. You, *mon petit chou*, are that home."

"Your little cabbage?" Elizabeth smiled, squeezing his hand.

"Indeed, my little beautiful cabbage." Philip got down on one knee and pulled a small blue velvet box from his pocket. He opened it to reveal a large round diamond, surrounded by many more, set in platinum. "I've fallen in love with you. Wholly and absolutely, Elizabeth. And, if you'll have me, I wish to devote the rest of my life to you, as your husband."

She'd been waiting for this moment, wishing for it. And, truth be told, hoping for it as she'd drawn Philip to this special spot—because to have it happen in a place she loved, surrounded by the beauty of a countryside she'd someday reign over as queen, made it perfect. Overwhelmed with emotion, Elizabeth could barely catch her breath. She was standing on the threshold of a life of happiness and love. A life spent with a man she admired and adored.

"Say yes," Philip urged, his head tipped up toward her, eyes filled with the same swirling emotion she felt.

Without hesitation, Elizabeth let out the secret she'd been holding. "I'm in love with you too, Philip. I will gladly be your wife." These were words they'd not expressed openly before. Hearing them and saying them was beautiful—transformative. Elizabeth's chest swelled with unreserved emotion.

Philip slipped the ring on her finger and then stood, tugging her against him in a way that was so much more intimate than in a dance. This was a lover's embrace. His lips brushed the top of her head as she listened to the steady thump of his heart, breathed in the subtle scent of his soap. Then she leaned back, suddenly wary. "Do their majesties know?"

Philip grinned. "Of course, I asked your father's permission. And he gave his blessing . . . with one reservation."

Elizabeth's heart fell slightly, having just one guess at what that would be. "That we wait?"

Philip nodded. "He has valid reasons." Then he offered her a glowing smile. "You are worth the wait, and I hope you think I am."

"Of course you are." After the conversation she'd had with her father, she knew what was coming—things in Greece needed to settle down and in the wake of that Philip needed to become a British citizen. Once these obstacles were cleared from their path, she would walk down the aisle on her father's arm, say her vows, and move out of the church and into the rest of her life with Philip at her side. Staring down at the ring on her finger she was overwhelmed by what it symbolized.

"It's beautiful."

Philip brushed his thumb over the knuckle of her ring finger. "I had it made with diamonds taken from my mother's tiara."

Elizabeth glanced up at him in surprise. "Your mother's tiara?"

He nodded, a smile of pride on his face. "She gave it to me last year when she thought I might ask you to be my wife. What better way to present to you my promise than with the ring made from the diamonds of my own royal family?"

Elizabeth's heart swelled. "You're a romantic at heart, Philip."

He winked with a conspiratorial grin. "Don't tell."

"I promise I won't." She reached up to touch his face, then said, "I can't believe I'll have you all to myself." Even as she said it, she recognized the falsity of the statement. Neither one of them would ever truly belong solely to each other. Surely Philip realized that as well. One day she'd be queen of the United Kingdom of Great Britain, Northern Ireland, and other realms. Defender of the Faith. When that day came, she'd belong to the people. But before that they'd have each other as a primary focus. And surely by the time she had to put her people first she'd be gray and wrinkled.

"You already have me." Philip brushed his lips over hers. "My one bright spot in the sea of darkness while we were at war. My true home. Nowhere and no one else matters as you do."

Throughout their friendship, Elizabeth had heard rumors of his other girlfriends. Women like Osla Benning, a Canadian socialite who'd remained in Britain during the war working at Bletchley Park. She'd also heard rumors of the women he'd danced with and entertained abroad. But the lascivious tales were printed because they sold papers. What was left out and never mentioned was how Philip pretended to be asleep at a number of parties to get out of driving interested women home.

What about his past was vile gossip and what was fact . . . the truth was, none of that mattered to Elizabeth. Not at this moment. This was the beginning of something new. Standing on the hills of Balmoral where their great-great-grandmother might have once stood with her beloved, they were making a pledge to each other. A pledge of life and love. Of fidelity and honor. Elizabeth was choosing this man to stand by her side, always and forever. And he was, she believed, choosing her in the same way. Choosing to keep himself loyal to her until death parted them.

"I want to kiss you." His gaze flicked down to her lips.

Elizabeth stared up into his blue eyes that mirrored the Scottish sky. "We're engaged." The words came out a whisper, as she could barely catch her breath. "You need never ask again."

Philip lowered his mouth to hers, sealing their troth in the very same way generations of men and women had before them—with a kiss.

CHAPTER TWELVE

SUSAN

*M*y paws rest on the stones warmed by the sun; there is a bird perched at the top of this strange structure in my favorite place of all, the Scottish Highlands where the wind always smells sweet.

I need the bird.

Want it.

Can taste it.

I'd once nearly caught one of these strange creatures that soar through the sky. The flap of its wings brushed wind against my face. The tip of a tail feather clenched between my teeth. I'd held tight, but the thing flew off, leaving me to spit out the fluff it left behind, along with a rather unflattering, smelly goop on my nose.

I bark up at this bird, whose head shifts to look at me in jerking movements, and it squawks back in a language I don't understand. A squeal comes from the other side of the stacked stones and simultaneously scares away my prey as a burst of adrenaline rushes through me.

The voice is my Lilibet's. I've never heard her make a noise like that before. Is she hurt?

I rush around the stones to see her and Philip holding each

other in a way that makes me jealous. They are laughing and nuzzling, and there is that smell again.

I wrinkle my nose, sneeze.

It's the same smell I sniffed when my keeper Hanna and I rode from the train station with that man who loves the horses. I sneeze again. Maybe I'm allergic to this smell—whatever it is. Looking at my Lilibet standing with Philip's arms around her I forget my itchy nose. Why can't I be involved in the cuddle? I love cuddles.

Barking, I race to them, squishing my way between their legs.

"I can't believe we're getting married." Lilibet takes the barest step backward, allowing me to stand over their feet, only inches apart.

My princess looks down at her hand where something sparkles. I want to bite it. To snatch it off her hand and run with it. Something about the way Philip stands—his posture is possessive. And the ring, the ring is like the collar they put around my neck. Is that how Philip is claiming her, my Lilibet? How he plans to take her away from me?

Not today.

I give his ankle a nip to let him know I'm displeased, and then I lift my paws up to her knees. They are trembling. Is she all right? She doesn't look scared, and yet her body vibrates the way mine did when the loud booms were firing during what the humans referred to as "the war."

Does she want me to get rid of Philip?

"Oh, Philip," the princess says. He leans down and puts his mouth to hers.

It's unfair he is allowed to do that. Whenever I try to lick her mouth, Lilibet puts a hand on my snout and kisses me between the eyes instead. It always makes me dizzy.

I look up at Philip, pondering what all this means.

"Don't you worry, Sus." His brow lifts as he gives me a look that says *Can we call a truce?* "I won't take her away from you . . . at least not for too long. But you won't be coming on our honeymoon, and we certainly won't be sharing a bed, the three of us."

I sneeze again, this time the way I do when I dissent. *We'll see about that, Prince Philip, just you wait.*

·⁓ઝ⁓·

CHAPTER THIRTEEN

ℰLIZABETH

February 17, 1947

Dearest Philip,

There is a high probability that Papa insisted I go on this
cruise to South Africa with him and Mummy because they
hoped all the time away from you will cause me to change
my mind. If their only concern was your citizenship, surely
your uncle Dickie's coup, achieving your naturalization so
quickly and directly from the Home Secretary, would have
assuaged that. Why, then, am I sailing around the world
on this four-month tour?

But my parents' hopes of dissuading me are futile. I've
not changed my mind, dear Philip. If anything, no matter how clichéd, I've come to learn that absence truly does
make the heart grow fonder. I am counting down the days
until I can return to England and set eyes on you again.
I will not be compliant the next time someone schemes to
put us out of each other's sight.

This morning we are to arrive in Cape Town. Do stay
warm; we've heard word that, while we've left for sunny
climes, England is having the worst winter anyone can re-

member. Peter Townsend has even said his wife is having
trouble heating the house, as there seems to be a shortage
of fuel.

Much love,
Your Cabbage

July 1947

𝒯he diamonds twinkled on her finger, a signal to everyone
that she was engaged, as she took Philip's arm where they stood
on the balcony of Buckingham Palace, waving to onlookers.

This was their first official appearance as an engaged couple,
and all the photographers and newspaper people were here for
the occasion. Philip was dapper in his naval uniform, and Elizabeth had chosen a daffodil-yellow silk dress, a double strand
of pearls, a floral brooch, and her favorite pair of white heels.

Susan must have escaped from Hanna—which seemed to
be the corgi's new trick—because she squeezed between Elizabeth and Philip, poking her head between the marble balusters
of the balcony, wagging the small nub of her tail as she took in
the crowd.

It had been nearly a year since Philip asked her to marry
him on the hill beside Prince Albert's pyramid, and from that
day to this it had felt as if they'd been fighting their first battle
as a couple—the battle to actually get married.

But now, all the obstacles seemed a thing of the past. Elizabeth had finally turned twenty-one, which seemed to be the
magic number her parents had been looking for. Philip had been
naturalized as a British citizen, which seemed to be the thing
the British government wanted. And thanks to the intervention

of clever Uncle Dickie Mountbatten, the papers reported favorably on the match, making the English people insatiable for it. Outside the palace gates, traffic was being diverted to provide space for the enormous number of people who had turned out to cheer the royal couple's engagement, their shouts a deafening chorus of unintelligible words.

Philip leaned down and murmured, "Look how they cheer for you."

Elizabeth glanced at him. "For us, darling."

"Perhaps they are cheering for the fairy tale."

Elizabeth smiled at him, the curve of her lips neatly mirroring that of his own as if they shared a secret. *Fairy tale* was a very good way of describing their relationship.

"They will love you as I love you," Elizabeth said.

"I do hope you love me more, my little cabbage." Philip gave her a wink that had her knees weakening.

They waved to the crowd, both of them giddy to finally share the news they'd been keeping secret since last summer at Balmoral. No more would she have to pay equal attention to all the male dancers at a ball. No more would she have to leave the gorgeous engagement ring locked in her bedroom when she went out in public. No more would she have to play coy when asked if there was an engagement forthcoming.

The freedom to shout to the world that Philip was to be her husband lifted a massive weight from Elizabeth's shoulders.

* * *

THE NEXT FEW months were a flurry of wedding planning and royal duties. Philip moved into Kensington Palace with his grandmother the Dowager Marchioness of Milford-Haven and began to set up his household staff. Whenever Elizabeth stopped at Kensington Palace or Philip visited her family at Buckingham Palace, they would sneak away and Philip would steal a kiss. And now when they went to parties or clubs, they needn't worry about anyone getting the wrong idea. They danced every number in each other's arms. Of course, Maggie still tagged along to keep things appropriate, her excitement at Philip becoming her brother loud enough for all of London to hear.

All this whirlwind of things done publicly and together was wonderful, but it was the times they attended races or traveled up to Scotland for hunting that Elizabeth enjoyed the most. The outdoors was where she was truly in her element, where she felt most free to be herself—and it was the same for Philip.

Philip continued his career in the navy, and now there was some talk of his being stationed in Malta. The idea of living as a naval wife in Malta, out of the limelight of London's expectations, triggered a longing in Elizabeth that was hard to even describe. Of course, they'd had no official word of the posting yet, but they whispered about it and luxuriated in making plans for their life away from the palace. And Elizabeth allowed herself to imagine a time when she'd be able to live as a regular woman, a wife free from royal entanglements, at least until duty called.

"Darling." Mummy entered the drawing room where Elizabeth had been reading an Agatha Christie. "The wedding invitations are being prepared for the post."

Elizabeth marked her place in the novel and smiled. "Wonderful."

"Might you have a word with Philip about his sisters?"

Elizabeth's stomach soured. It had seemed obvious within her own family that Philip's sisters who were married to Nazis would not be given invitations, but she had yet to speak with him about the matter. The idea of having to tell him they couldn't come was unsavory—because however vile their allegiances, they were still his siblings.

Elizabeth pushed the words through her lips: "Of course."

"I do hope he understands." Mummy busied herself at her writing desk, and Elizabeth was glad her mother couldn't see her face, which she was certain had paled.

Elizabeth stood, needing to get some air, and to think about how she would phrase the rejection. "I have no doubt he will."

That evening, as Philip's red MG pulled into the palace courtyard, Elizabeth met him outside with Susan at her heels.

"A sailor could get used to this." Philip unfolded himself from the MG and bent to kiss her cheek.

"I thought we'd take a walk. You know how much Susan likes to lead us around."

Susan sat at Philip's feet, looking up expectantly.

He fished a treat from one of his pockets and held it down to her. "Of course she does."

Susan greedily grasped the treat between her teeth and took off running.

"You've something on your mind, cabbage."

Elizabeth glanced at Philip, a little surprised. Apparently, she'd not done as good a job as she'd wanted to in hiding her nerves.

"How did you know?" she asked.

"You've a slight crease to your brow, love. It's the same crease you always get before you say something you've been mulling over for a while. Or when you have to say something you think might be controversial."

She touched her forehead, feeling the crease. "I suppose I ought to work on keeping a straight face."

Philip shrugged. "Only if you plan on betting in card games."

"I might." She laughed. "Isn't that sort of what it's like for monarchs when they stand before Parliament?"

"Touché." Philip glanced at her with amusement. "Though it will be many years before you have to worry over that."

"Which leaves me plenty of time to practice."

"Tell me, cabbage, what is on your mind?"

This was a conversation she never wanted to have. But if she couldn't tell the ones she loved what she was thinking, or what was important, even if it might hurt, then how would she be able to one day say with confidence she was ready to be a queen?

"It's about your sisters," she hedged, her fingers fidgeting with the belt at her waist.

"Ah," Philip drawled without an ounce of animosity. "I think I know where this is going."

Elizabeth was hopeful that was the case, so she wouldn't have to say it aloud.

Philip slid her a wry smile. "You've not invited my sisters."

Elizabeth stopped walking. Facing Philip, she reached for his hand and squeezed it lightly, not caring in those brief moments that someone might see them and snap a picture. She locked her gaze on his, hoping he could see the depth of her feeling in that one look.

"Are you upset?" she asked.

Philip shook his head without hesitation. "No, I understand the politics, darling. And I want nothing to spoil our day."

"I'm so sorry, Philip." And she genuinely was. Elizabeth couldn't imagine what she would do if Maggie had decided to fall in love with a Nazi; it was bad enough she'd set her sights on a married man in her father's service. Drat Peter Townsend.

"You've nothing to be sorry for. They made their beds and are happily lying in them. If there's one thing I learned, it's that you can't feel guilt for the actions of others. You don't control them. And if you shoulder the guilt for what they do, you'll be miserable forever."

Philip always made sense. Elizabeth had to resist the urge to lean into him and press her head to his chest, if only to hear the steady, rhythmic beat of his heart and know that all was going to be well in the end. "You're too good to me."

"We're good to each other." Philip glanced from side to side, then he leaned forward and pressed a quick kiss to her forehead. "No one saw, I swear."

Elizabeth laughed, and pointed at Susan, who was sitting with her head cocked to the side, one ear perked particularly high. "Someone did."

Philip chuckled. "I should like to know her thoughts."

"Perhaps not. I think she's jealous."

Philip picked up a stick from the ground. Susan didn't hesitate, beginning to run before the limb had even left his hand.

With Philip in a jovial mood, and the conversation having gone much better than she expected, Elizabeth decided to broach another topic—one she was certain was going to give rise to resistance. "Philip, I have a request for a wedding gift."

"Anything for you, darling."

Elizabeth bit her lip. "It's not a possession, but rather a . . . pledge."

"Oh?" He raised a brow, a playful smile on his mouth.

Whatever thoughts were going through his mind, they were certainly not what she had to request. "I would like you to give up smoking."

Philip's eyes widened; for a moment he was speechless, then he asked, "Why?"

Elizabeth had prepared and practiced what she'd say. "Papa . . . he smokes quite a lot, and it's caused him a lot of health problems. I know it's a source of constant stress for Mummy, and I—" She paused, swallowing a mix of grief over the blood on her father's handkerchiefs and fear over how Philip would react to her request.

"Consider it done, darling," Philip said, taking her hand in his and giving it a gentle squeeze. "By the time I walk into Westminster Abbey to say my vows to my most amazing bride, I will have smoked my last."

Elizabeth wished she could fold herself into his arms right there, in the open. Her heart swelled; she hadn't imagined she could love him more than she did when they set out for this walk. And she'd been wrong.

"Thank you, Philip."

"I shan't say I won't miss it"—he chuckled—"but for you I'd do anything."

Elizabeth couldn't help herself; she rose on her toes and planted a quick kiss on his lips.

·⚬⧽⚬·

CHAPTER FOURTEEN

SUSAN

Humans have lots of traditions. Lots of rules.

For dogs, there is one basic rule: follow the leader.

And that means paying attention to the leader. What does their body language show? What is their smell—are they happy, sad, angry, afraid? What does their body language suggest about whether they are about to move and where? Followers in a pack have to be constantly on the lookout for what's to happen next. It won't do for one of them to fall out of line.

Lilibet is the leader of my pack, such as it is. So when she is standing at the center of a bunch of women who are cooing and oohing, naturally I'm curious. They are fussing over her, and I can tell by the way her lips are pinched at the side that her smile is not genuine. She's irritated by their fawning.

I muzzle my way forward, wishing I could nip an ankle or two to get these women out of my way. But then I'd be shooed from the room, which is the last thing I want. Queen Elizabeth is here—the mother of the bride, they keep calling her—and she's quite adamant I'm not to bite.

The queen doesn't understand. But sometimes Lilibet does. Sometimes she whispers, "I would have bitten him too" about whoever my latest morsel is. She understands that some people need a bit of herding.

"Oh," says one of the older women as I push through. "What is that mutt doing in here?"

Mutt? Who is she calling a mutt? I turn around, glancing behind me for any tramp that might have wandered in. She certainly can't be referring to me.

"Susan is not a mutt," Lilibet says. She turns away from the looking glass, and crouches to pull me in for a snuggle despite the women scolding her for wrinkling her gown. I lick her palm and gaze into her beautiful blue eyes. "She's a darling princess. A queen among corgis."

Yes, a queen, I yip in my own language.

"Well, she needs to go outside, before she ruins your beautiful gown."

"I daresay a smear of dog saliva might ruin the duchesse silk."

I'm tempted to lick the silk to prove the woman wrong, but my eyes are caught on the hundreds of embroidered flowers and glistening pearls. I want to bite, to taste, to wrangle them free. I want my Lilibet to put on her practical clothes—as she calls them—and come outside with me for a long walk. I want us to be back at Windsor and not in this stuffy palace where there are too many rules.

"What will poor Susan do without you when you're on your honeymoon for three weeks?" Lilibet's mother asks, her voice warm with pity.

Weeks? Lilibet wouldn't leave me for weeks to go off with Philip alone—not to the moon, not anywhere. Would she? I glance up at her, watching her face soften as she stares at herself in the mirror and wondering just what changes are about to occur. The air around us vibrates a little as if she is trembling but hiding it so well no one will notice. And they don't. But I can tell. I can always tell.

My Lilibet is nervous . . . excited and, I cock my head . . . nervous. That's it.

"I won't be leaving Susan behind," Lilibet says matter-of-factly.

"What?" several women say at once—all their voices either exasperated or surprised.

"How does Philip feel about that?"

I glance at Lilibet, wondering the same thing. Sometimes he likes me and sometimes he doesn't. But he's never cruel—not like some of the footmen I've had to put in their place.

"Philip adores Susan," Lilibet replies, taking on the air of authority that makes most people stop questioning her.

I edge a little closer to Lilibet and I pant, my heart racing a little at the thought of being left behind. Of being dependent on Philip's goodwill when he is the one encroaching on my time with my princess. He was asking me to share her with him, so shouldn't it be the other way around? Shouldn't he be dependent on my goodwill?

A knock interrupts before any of the ladies-in-waiting or the queen can contradict Lilibet. I hope they forget the conversation completely and that no one has the time to inform Philip of Lilibet's plan. He's very persuasive when he talks to her, and she respects him a great deal. When Philip is there, I feel like there are two alphas, and I get confused about who I should follow. But my loyalty is forever with Lilibet.

"Enter," Lilibet calls, and Hanna opens the door, dipping into a curtsy.

Hanna's gaze parts the crowd until she sees me. "I've come to fetch my charge, ma'am," she says. Her voice often sounds like she's got a laugh behind it she can barely contain.

Lilibet gives Hanna a special glance, as though that one look expresses a list of directions.

Hanna nods at my princess before snapping her fingers and drawing my attention to her feet. She begins to briskly walk toward the door, expecting me to follow. I wish more than ever I could tell her in words that she'd understand that I don't want to leave. I'm not ready to let Lilibet go.

I bark in protest, which only earns me a few sharp words from some duchesses I care nothing about. In the corridor, with the door to Lilibet's suite closed, Hanna kneels before me.

"I have a secret to tell you, Susan, but only if you promise to behave." Hanna smells excited.

I sit to show her I know how to behave, and I love to know secrets. I have so many, but even if I could figure out how to speak like a human, I'd keep them all locked up.

"Good girl." Hanna strokes a hand over my head. "You're going on a trip, after Princess Elizabeth is married."

I sigh, though it comes out a pant. I was worried ever since the stuffy ladies said I shouldn't. The thought of being separated from Lilibet for weeks, and possibly forever, makes me want to claw through the thick palace walls and burrow into her overwhelming gown.

"But you'll need to behave. Do you think you can handle being hidden under blankets?"

Hidden under blankets? I cock my head to the side, confused and intrigued.

"I think you can. And if you want to be with them—Princess Elizabeth and Prince Philip—you will need to hide and be quiet."

I bark, because I do want to be with them. I need to keep an eye on Philip. I need to be there for Lilibet to soothe any fears she might have or to give her a cuddle when she needs to talk— like I do every day. I am her faithful companion always. I lick Hanna's hand so she knows I understand.

"Here's a biscuit, and there will be even more when you complete this mission."

I like the sound of that. I take the biscuit, crunching on the sweetness of it. It is good, but not as good as Mrs. Seymour's at Windsor.

I follow Hanna about as she gathers things into a bag, and then takes that bag out to the coach, looking around as if she doesn't want to be seen. Forrest pokes his head out of the mews, stinking of horses. I curl my lip in his direction.

"Give it here," he whispers, hand outstretched.

"I hope we can make this happen as the princess requested," Hanna says, worry tinging her words as she passes him the bag.

Forrest's movements are steady, but from the scent of him I can tell he is nervous. "Me too, or else it's our heads."

Hanna looks down at me, and I stare up into her eyes, seeing so many different emotions that it makes me nervous. "I wish I could make her promise."

You can, I want to say. *I promise.*

But instead, I shoot forward and nuzzle her leg.

"Sometimes I think she can read my mind," Hanna says.

Forrest nods. "I wouldn't put it past her. She's a smart dog."

·᭣ɔℓℯᴐ·

CHAPTER FIFTEEN

Ɛ LIZABETH

November 20, 1947

*T*oday was her wedding day.

When Elizabeth had awakened that morning, she'd pinched herself, to make completely sure she wasn't still sleeping and dreaming. Afraid she'd discover yet another day, yet another thing stood between her and this marvelous day. But nothing did. She ate toast and a poached egg with tea, and listened to Maggie prattle on about something, but she couldn't say what. Her mind was entirely on the day ahead as her stomach rolled around like the sea in a storm.

Elizabeth had let the women fawn over her as they admired the wedding gown she'd saved her ration coupons to purchase. Though the war was over, there were many commodities that still were in short supply, and the royal family had made the decision to show respect for their people by living by the rationing rules. And the British people loved that. In the post Elizabeth had received hundreds of clothing coupons offered by the people who were thrilled at the prospect of the wedding, and though she'd been grateful for the generous donations, she'd returned each one as it was against the rules to share coupons.

Inspired by Botticelli's *Primavera* and designed by Norman

Hartnell and his head embroideress Flora Ballard, Elizabeth's duchesse satin gown was embroidered in a floral design highlighted with pearls. A dramatic and lengthy silk and tulle train fell from her shoulders.

With slips and stockings in place, Elizabeth had stood as the gown was carefully lifted over her head. She'd yet to try it on and felt a moment of panic that it wouldn't fit. It was bad luck to try on a dress before the wedding, and so meticulous measurements had been taken over and over to ensure it fit her body perfectly.

Elizabeth's lungs burned from holding her breath.

They'd buttoned up the back, a task that took so long she could hardly bear it. When at last they'd finished, and Elizabeth hesitated to view herself in the full-length mirror, Susan had appeared to calm her nerves.

Grounded by just one last corgi cuddle before sending her off with Hanna, Elizabeth faced the mirror once more. Seeing the silken confection on a hanger was entirely different from seeing it following the curves of her body in a flawless fit. It was absolutely stunning, a work of art, and Elizabeth felt herself awash in gratitude for the hundreds of women who'd worked on the gown for nearly two months. She fingered the creamy fabric that brought out the brightness of her eyes and even made her hair, which she'd always considered to be a little dull, shine.

"Darling, you are stunning." Mummy pressed a kiss to her cheek, then swiped away a tear.

"Goodness," Maggie breathed. "Philip may have to fight off a wave of men when they see you in this."

"Oh, Margot," Mummy said with a click of her tongue, but Elizabeth giggled.

Papa entered the dressing room, wearing his crisp uniform, a smile on his face. "A present for you from the groom."

He placed a slim rectangular blue velvet box into her palm. Elizabeth flipped open the lid to reveal a diamond bracelet that caught the light of the sun, creating dancing, sparkling prisms on the ceiling.

"The diamonds are from what remained of his mother's tiara after he had your engagement ring made," the king said.

Elizabeth's throat tightened with emotion. "It's beautiful. Would you, Papa?" She held out her wrist and her father clasped the diamonds around it. The bracelet was cool and heavy against her skin.

"I know the path to get to this day wasn't exactly as you would have chosen." Her father's voice was solemn. "But I'm grateful we're here."

Elizabeth melted into a smile and blinked to hold back tears. "So am I."

It was as if the entire room breathed out a collective sigh of satisfaction. This marriage they'd been worrying about, mulling over, and even arguing about, was finally on the verge of happening. Mummy and Maggie filed out with the rest of the staff and bridal party to board the coach that would take them from the palace through the streets of London to Westminster Abbey.

The room was quiet, and Elizabeth relaxed into the comforting familiarity of being with her beloved father.

"Before we go," Papa said, "I just wanted to tell you how very proud I am of you."

"Oh, don't make me cry."

"It's the truth, darling. You are a wonder. It's hard for me to give you away today, but Philip is a worthy man." Her father's eyes glistened with unspent emotion.

"You're not giving me away," Elizabeth said. "I'll always be your Lilibet."

The king smiled softly, a touch of wistfulness on his face. "It's true—no one can take you away completely. Besides, you're my heir, and I forbid it." This last part he said with a chuckle.

As they glided out of the room, Elizabeth spied Hanna down the corridor, kneeling before Susan. She nodded at her corgi keeper, pleased they'd had a chance to talk—to plan—the day before, and further reassured by Hanna's nod when she'd come to collect Susan.

Elizabeth might be riding off to her honeymoon in a few hours, but not without her darling corgi.

Outside the palace, the four horse–drawn Irish State Coach awaited. Elizabeth's gaze passed over it, from its gilt top to the blue and black exterior with gilded paint and royal crests. Lamps were fitted at the four corners above the wide, red-painted wheels. A driver and footmen stood stoically by.

Once Elizabeth was arranged in the blue damask interior, the horses pulled onto the square and the deafening roar of the crowd began.

"My goodness, has all of London come out to see me off?" Elizabeth said, marveling, as she waved.

"Maybe more. People have traveled from far and wide *to* London for the occasion." Papa's tone was full of pride, and it caused Elizabeth's chest to swell with a sudden choking emotion.

For many months the public obsession with the courtship and the question of would they or wouldn't they be married had been more of an annoyance to Elizabeth than a pleasure. But suddenly she realized there was another way to look at the British fascination with her and Philip—the people were invested in them.

Philip had understood that all along. He'd convinced her, along with the palace powers that be, that their wedding should be filmed and televised for the world to watch and celebrate with them.

And now, gazing gratefully at the onlookers as they cheered her on her way, Elizabeth understood as well. The sight of her countrymen and -women waving and smiling made her forget the nerves roiling in her belly at the prospect of walking down the long, red-carpeted aisle of Westminster Abbey. Made her stop worrying about tripping over her own feet along the way.

Alighting from the carriage at the abbey, she paused. From the time she was a girl of thirteen, she'd been waiting for this day. And now it was finally here. She was happy, yes, but suddenly she was gripped by something more profound—a feeling that made it hard to draw a breath.

"Are you all right?" Papa whispered, arriving at her side.

"I'm . . ." She licked her dry lips. "Overwhelmed."

"Take my arm, darling. I've got you." Thank goodness for Papa's strength.

Elizabeth pressed her lips together for a moment, trying not to cry. Today was the start of something new, the first day of the rest of her life; and yet, despite the excitement of it, she was also leaving her old life behind. "Us four" would now be "us two."

As she entered the abbey, the sea of guests' faces was a blur. All she could do was stare at the handsome naval lieutenant at the end of the aisle. Philip stood tall in his uniform, proud, and, if she wasn't mistaken, with a mist of incipient tears in his eyes that matched her own.

She flashed him a nervous smile, and he returned it, his smile full of confidence and unwavering love.

Elizabeth straightened her back, and marched forward on her father's arm, fully ready to join Philip in the next adventure of their lives.

"I'm ready," she said, just above a whisper.

* * *

HAND IN HAND, Elizabeth and Philip emerged from their wedding reception into the piercing din of a crowd cheering and a shower of rose petals that floated over them, landing at their feet. Elizabeth wore a mist-blue dress and matching coat. A blue beret topped with a pom-pom of ostrich feathers perched on her head. They waved to the onlookers. Both of them grinned from ear to ear as they climbed into the open carriage that would take them through London to the train station.

As they settled into their seats, Elizabeth found Hanna in the crowd of servants waving them off, and her loyal dog watcher gave a slight nod. A moment later she felt Susan's cold nose snuffling her wrist.

"Susan, my darling girl." She gave her a scratch behind her ears as the corgi poked her head from beneath some blankets where she'd been hidden.

"Susan?" Philip looked down, amusement and surprise on his handsome face. He let out a laugh. "How did she get in here?"

"Surprise," Elizabeth said, waving to the crowds of people, their carriage moving smoothly along their route.

Her husband raised a brow. "I thought our honeymoon would just be us . . ."

"I believe you knew when you married me that Susan was

part of the package." Elizabeth kept her tone light, teasing, though she meant every word.

"True." Philip stroked a hand over Susan's head. "Just as long as she knows she's to have her own bed tonight."

Elizabeth's face heated at the thought of what would happen tonight once they'd reached Broadlands in Hampshire where they would pass their wedding night before going on to Birkhall, one of the houses at Balmoral. Uncle Dickie, who owned Broadlands, had promised not to be there, and none of her family would be at Balmoral, so they could enjoy true privacy on their honeymoon. The one thing they'd lacked since the beginning of their courtship was the luxury of time to enjoy each other without interruption.

"She's got her own bed." Elizabeth glanced up at him. "I'll not let her interrupt . . . our sleep."

"Good." He leaned over and gave her cheek a kiss, making some in the surrounding crowd go wild.

* * *

ON THE TRAIN, Susan slept in a chair across from them. They had the entire carriage to themselves, except for a few staff, including Hanna, and guards who meandered through to make sure they were all right.

The train stopped in Hampshire, where a car waited to take them to the Broadlands. When the car rolled up in front of the magnificent house, they didn't go inside right away. Instead, they strolled, enjoying the autumn air and stretching their legs. Elizabeth loved that Philip was every bit as active as she was.

Susan ran in circles around them, her tongue flapping, as joyous as either one of them. Inspired by her corgi's sheer exuberance, Elizabeth began to run, her hands out to the side as if she might take off in flight. When she spun around to smile at her husband, she found him right behind her. They nearly collided, but instead he pulled up short, tugging her into his arms and swinging her about before kissing her.

"I've never felt so free," Elizabeth said, her fingers curling into his hair. "It's absolute heaven to finally be alone."

"We'd best enjoy it. As soon as the locals realize we've come, someone will tell the press and they'll send their photographers to sneak a few shots."

Elizabeth frowned, realizing the truth of his words. No matter how the royal family tried to be discreet, people had a way of finding things out. That had been the story of her girlhood since her father's ascension to the throne and doubtless it would be the story of her married life as well.

Not this evening perhaps, but soon they would be swarmed. Disappointment filled her and she tried not to let it sour her mood. "Perhaps we should offer them a few moments in exchange for a promise to leave us in solitude?"

Philip nodded thoughtfully. "As unfortunate a compromise as that would be, it would be better than dodging them over the next few weeks."

"Indeed, it would." Elizabeth let out a great sigh. "It is the one thing I have hated the most since Papa took his place as king. The constant barrage. I think people forget we are people too."

Philip stroked her cheek. "Maybe we can make some changes one day."

"I don't even know if that is possible." They walked onward, hand in hand, planning their media strategy instead of what they should have been doing, which was kissing and sharing secrets, alone.

Still dressed in their going-away clothes, they had their staff inform the local media that it was now or never. And the press jumped at their offer. The newlyweds allowed themselves to be filmed walking around the grounds, sitting on a bench, tossing a stick to Susan. They posed holding hands, glancing lovingly. They gave the press exactly what it wanted—an illustrated story of a newly married princess and prince that would sell papers and assuage the curiosity of readers. In exchange for a promise that they'd be left alone.

And true to their word, the journalists and photographers disappeared.

The newlyweds dined in the small sitting room off their bedroom. A simple meal of fish and potatoes, followed by apple cake. And when dinner was over, Philip shooed everyone out of their suite—even Susan, who reluctantly went off with Hanna—and closed the door.

"I want my wife to myself," Philip said with a smile on his lips.

"Promise me that for the rest of our days together we'll steal moments like this," she demanded.

"I promise."

Philip flipped through some records, putting on a soft jazz tune, and then took her in his arms. Their bodies were flush as they danced—closer than they'd ever been before—and he nuzzled her neck. Gooseflesh rose along the length of her limbs.

"Imagine what people would have thought and said if we'd danced like this at the Four Hundred." Elizabeth stroked the back of his neck.

Philip chuckled, before giving her a kiss that lingered and grew deeper. "That might have even made headlines in Canada."

"And what about this? This would have caused a scandal."

She took the pins from her hair, tossing them onto the floor as she shook out her curls.

"You're stunning. They would have all swooned." Philip ran his hands through her hair, curling a tendril around his finger and stooping to inhale the scent of her. "You don't know how long I've been wanting to do this."

A lump formed in her throat. "Now you can do it every day, husband."

"I am a lucky man."

Elizabeth plucked at the buttons on her dress, feeling suddenly emboldened. "I think we're both about to be lucky."

Philip's eyes widened and he whistled low and long. "Who knew my shy, stoic princess had a wild side?"

It was a side of herself she'd never let come out—one she hadn't known for certain was there either. But she realized it was a side that would be hard to put back. "You bring it out in me."

"As long as it's only me." He reached for his tie, tugging at the knot.

"Only you." Elizabeth took his hand in hers and led him to their bed.

·◦∾◦·

CHAPTER SIXTEEN

SUSAN

*T*oday might be the best day of my life.

My feet are pressed to the dash of the Jeep, and we're bouncing over the moors of Broadlands. Philip is driving on my right, and the princess is perched to my left. They both have the widest smiles on their faces, and if I could curve my lips like theirs, I too would be smiling just as broadly.

I can hear their hearts pounding, but not in a nervous way or the way that brings that funny smell before Philip licks her face. No, this is a euphoric beating, and its rhythm matches my own.

The windows are down, and wind from the unkempt wilds blows into the vehicle, seeming to bring with it a new and captivating smell every minute.

Lilibet rubs my back, her hand gloved as it strokes my fur. "You like this, Sus, don't you?"

I bark at her, then face forward again, watching birds in the sky and animals that dash into the thick grass and the cover of the trees to get away from us. I never want this ride to end, though at the same time, I wish we'd stop, and they'd let me give chase.

Lilibet's hand slides from my back, reaches for Philip, holding his hand, their fingers threading together, her leather gloves a soft beige and his dark brown. I stare at my paws, wondering how hard it would be for her to hold my paw like that.

And then we go over another big bump and Lilibet and Philip are laughing and shouting for joy. I wag my tail and bark, certain I have never been this happy before.

It's just been us three out here, enjoying life as if the rest of the world didn't exist. And I like that just fine.

CHAPTER SEVENTEEN

ℋANNA

No one informed me that being invisible was a requirement for the job as keeper of the corgis—though I suppose as a servant of a royal I probably should have surmised that on my own. Fortunately, I'd perfected that skill over the years and so, while I'd needed to learn the politics of Buckingham Palace, I did not need to acquire an ability to go unnoticed.

I cracked open the door to the bedroom designated for Susan's use and found her still asleep in her raised wicker bed. An utterly shocking occurrence, considering that, by the time I stuck my head in every other morning this week, she'd been busy killing various pillows placed in her bed to keep her comfortable.

Susan's adorable head popped up and cocked to the side, her golden ears twitching. The expression on her face was one of sleepy surprise, and I couldn't help laughing.

"Waking up late, I see," I cooed.

Susan leaped over the side of the bed and bounded toward me, yipping as she came.

I'd been arriving earlier each morning to collect her. Hoping to find the sweet spot before she started to tear up pillows and generally make a racket, requiring a footman to dash outside with her before she woke the honeymooning royals. Well,

I thought, looking at my watch, just before sunrise appeared to be the winning hour.

I shushed Susan with kisses as I attached her leash, then led her outside as quietly as I could. Princess Elizabeth and Prince Philip were honeymooning on the Balmoral estate, after having passed their wedding night at Broadlands. I'd offered to keep the pup with me in the servants' quarters, but Elizabeth didn't want to be without Susan.

The unbreakable bond between the two of them was undeniable and fascinating. Susan sensed Elizabeth was near even before the servants were aware of her approach. And the faces of the princess and the pup lit up at nearly the same moment they spotted each other. It felt, strange as that might seem, as if they shared a soul.

Honeymooning meant a lot of adjustments for Susan. She couldn't sleep with the princess. And beyond that she had to adjust to sleeping entirely alone. At Buckingham Palace and Windsor, she always had canine company in the form of Crackers and the other family dogs. And when she stayed with me at Windsor, I let her sneak up to my room when Dad wasn't paying attention and crawl into bed with me.

I actually felt sorry for the sweet thing. There were so many changes in her life, it was a wonder she hadn't dug a hole through the floor to escape.

The sun was barely starting to rise in the east over the River Dee as we emerged from the house, and though it wasn't yet winter, autumn in the Highlands meant the dew had turned to crystals on the grass overnight. Susan pranced, her paws bouncing higher than normal as she trotted. She looked down warily at her little paws as if she were surprised by the difference between Scotland and London—although we'd been here for days.

"A bit cold, eh?"

The voice from behind startled me, and I whipped around the find Forrest standing there, a jacket wrapped around him, his scarf blowing in the wind. He raised his hand to his hat as a gust of Scottish air jostled it.

"What are you doing out here?" I frowned, then realizing that might have come off a bit rude, worked to put a smile on my face. "I mean, good morning."

I'd been trying harder to be more cordial to Forrest. Our time together at Buckingham Palace had convinced me that he was nothing like the cruel child I'd known. He'd apologized, and he'd more than made up for our past. These days more often than not he was my partner in crime—if you could call my moments of subterfuge on the princess's behalf crime. Without his help I'd never have been able to sneak Susan into the honeymoon carriage.

Forrest grinned. "Guess I'd better bring you tea next time I sneak up on you in the morning. Might warm the spirit."

I smiled, this time genuinely, and unfastened Susan's leash. "That would be very welcome."

"You're very loyal to her," Forrest said thoughtfully.

Straightening a little, wondering if he was commending or questioning my loyalty, I replied, "Well, she will one day be our queen."

Forrest chuckled, then, nodding toward Susan who'd finished her business and was trotting after some scent she'd caught, said, "I meant the dog."

"Oh." I smiled, then started after my canine charge before

she got too far ahead of me. Already here at Balmoral, Susan had established a certain path for her morning walks. She seemed to think of herself as a guard of the estate and duly made her rounds.

"She's a special pup, that's for certain," I called over my shoulder as I headed off in pursuit.

"Quite the personality." Forrest caught up with me, then adjusted his pace to match mine.

Susan turned, one front paw lifted, watching us. Had she heard what he said?

"That she is. Go on, Susan," I called. "Show us the way."

Susan let out a low bark and moved off again.

"The way she loves the outdoors you'd never guess she'd spent the night in a custom-made bed," I teased.

"Or that the chef got up before dawn to make her breakfast," Forrest added.

"Her breakfast will be better prepared than mine." Susan was by far the most spoiled dog in all the world, I was certain.

Forrest grinned. "I had a bowl of oats, about the same as what I'll feed the horses, if that makes you feel any better."

I couldn't help but laugh. "You'd best get about your morning rounds, then, before the horses complain."

"I can go a little way yet. We don't start in the stables this early."

"Lucky you. But then why are you awake?" I found myself thinking that if only Susan would sleep a little longer, I'd spend that time in bed myself. As we passed under a stand of trees another Highland gust whipped the chill morning air around us and I reached up to rub my shoulders.

"You're cold. Here." Forrest started tugging off his jacket and held it out.

"Oh, no, I couldn't. I'm fine in my own. Besides, I wouldn't want you to freeze."

"I've a warm heart. I insist." Forrest wrapped the jacket around my shoulders. It smelled of him and I found that rather more pleasant than I expected.

"Thank you," I said, unable to look at him, sure my face was redder than a cherry. "But if you start to shiver, I am giving it back."

"Deal." He took off at a run, chasing Susan, who picked up her pace, delighted that she'd enticed a human into playing her favorite game.

As the pair disappeared from sight into the dense trees, a smile melted over my face, and a sudden thought sliced into my half-awake brain—what if this was our life, our dog, and Forrest and I were on our own honeymoon?

It was a crazy enough thought that I tripped over a tree root and nearly fell flat on my face. Righting myself, I stared into the trees ahead, listening to Susan's barks and Forrest's answering calls.

"You're crazy," I said to myself. "Absolutely crazy."

But the seed had been planted, and even running after them—wind whipping at my face, the steady incline of the trail making my legs burn—didn't erase the idea or that warmth I was suffused with on account of it.

As I came over the rise in the forest where the pyramid to Prince Albert loomed into view, jutting into the sky, I nearly ran into Forrest, who'd stopped dead in his tracks. The look on his face was one of utter surprise and shock. My gaze searched frantically for Susan, worried she'd gone flying over the edge of the cliff or been otherwise injured.

Then I spotted her wagging tail where she stood just to the

left side of the pyramid. Beside her, two pairs of snuggling feet stuck out from beneath a tartan blanket.

"Oh, dear God . . ." I whispered, meeting Forrest's eyes. If the princess hadn't roused from Susan's antics, it would be a miracle. Still, I erred on the side of discretion and snapped my fingers at my charge. "Susan," I hissed. "Come back."

Susan turned, tongue flapping out of her mouth as she ran back toward us, excited over what she'd found—the princess and her groom snuggled out in the forest where they'd obviously spent the night.

As soon as the dog reached us, Forrest scooped her up and we turned, hurrying back in the direction we'd come from.

"Not a word about this to anyone," I said.

"Agreed," Forrest replied, his eyes still looking rather wild.

When we were a safe distance away my heart rate came down a notch or two. I stopped walking and started to laugh. Quietly at first, but before long I was positively guffawing—I couldn't help myself. And Forrest joined me.

Susan struggled in his arms, desperate to be let down. But he held tight. There was no way we were going to chase her back to the snuggling honeymooners.

"Could you imagine if the press got the glimpse we just did?" My face flushed at the thought of the headlines.

Honeymooning Royals Caught Canoodling at Great-Great-Grandfather's Monument . . .

"Somebody'd be sacked, no doubt," Forrest said.

That sobered me up a bit. "Well, there are no reporters to be dismissed on a word from the royal family. But . . . I might be." I imagined a red-faced Princess Elizabeth telling me to pack my things. "They must know I know."

"Because of Susan?"

"Yes." I nodded solemnly. Would her highness dismiss me over the incident . . . even though it obviously wasn't my fault? I mean I couldn't possibly have known the royal couple had spent the night out-of-doors—let alone on Susan's customary route.

"Could have been a footman with the dog," Forrest offered.

"I called out to Susan; the princess certainly would have recognized my voice."

"Perhaps a footman with a throat ache." Forrest shrugged.

Now that was funny, and I let out a sharp laugh. "Well, this may be my last morning here, and, if so, it has been lovely knowing you."

"I hope you're not dismissed, Hanna." He paused to swallow. "But even if you are, I hope to still see you."

"I hope to keep seeing you too."

In the safety and privacy of the woods, Forrest gripped my hand with his free one, and tugged me toward him. I leaned in, the magic of the morning filling my blood. When he kissed me, I sighed, feeling as though this were the most right thing in the world.

Susan didn't agree. She nipped me on the chin.

CHAPTER EIGHTEEN

ℰLIZABETH

December 24, 1947

*T*his was not the first Christmas holiday Elizabeth and Philip had spent together, but this Christmas Eve at Sandringham felt distinctly different because they were now married. Their bellies were full of parsnip soup, beef Wellington, and sticky toffee pudding; the presents had been opened; and now they returned to the drawing room.

Elizabeth stood at the piano, singing as her father and Maggie played a duet, their fingers sliding over the keys. Mummy, her grandmother, and Philip watched from the gold-fringed upholstered sofas that had graced the drawing room since Elizabeth was a child. They'd finished decorating the rest of the Christmas tree, a Norfolk spruce cut from somewhere on the property the day before.

As she sang, Elizabeth kept her eyes on her husband, offering him a smile that he returned—his own being more broad because he was not taxed with singing. All his life, Philip had been searching for a place to belong; and in the short time they'd been married he'd started to relax into her family. So perhaps he'd found one—Elizabeth certainly hoped he had.

It had been a crash course in living with the extended family. Clarence House in London, which was to be their permanent residence, had been undergoing a complete renovation. To avoid the chaos of construction, Elizabeth and Philip lived at Buckingham Palace in the meantime. Philip seemed to have a little trouble with that.

But attending the various social events mandated by being a part of the royal family was a different matter. At times Elizabeth could tell Philip was getting frustrated with the long list of duties. He went along with all that was required of him, though, and *mostly* without balking.

Even in any difficulty, she had a way of assuaging him, and Elizabeth felt pleased and blessed with how well Philip was handling his new royal role. And now, as he looked into her eyes with his baby blues, she was reminded of how much she loved him. He was her prince among princes and made her the luckiest princess in the world.

"Bravo, bravo," Philip called, clapping as the song drew to an end. Susan, who'd been resting near his feet, stood to bark in her own great happiness, hurrying forward, her tiny tail wagging with delight as she danced around the piano until she found Elizabeth.

Elizabeth knelt to stroke her dog's head, locking eyes with Susan and whispering, "I've a gift for you."

Susan's mouth dropped open a little, her lips peeling back in what Elizabeth swore was a smile. Anyone who thought dogs didn't smile hadn't looked hard enough.

"Another," the king called out, and Maggie confirmed with a clap and an "Oh, yes."

"You go on," Elizabeth said, glancing at her mother. "I need to get something for Susan."

"Oh, you do spoil that dog," her mother teased affectionately.

"Just as you taught me." Elizabeth snapped her fingers at Susan and winked at Philip as she drew her dog toward where the stockings hung by the large hearth.

Susan sat obediently, watching every one of Elizabeth's movements, the tip of her pink tongue out.

"A gift for my dearest," Elizabeth said, plucking the stocking from the hook that said *Susan* on it.

Elizabeth laid it on the floor, watching Susan sniff around the opening. Philip came up beside her, his hand resting on the small of her back.

"If you dote this much on your dog, I can't wait to see how you'll dote on our children." Philip leaned in and pressed his lips to her temple.

Elizabeth glanced up at him, with a light laugh. "Wouldn't it be wonderful if by next Christmas we had a little Philip?"

"Or a wee Lilibet."

She leaned against him, her head resting on his shoulder. They'd yet to conceive, but that didn't weigh too heavily on her. They'd only been married a few weeks, and they didn't even have their own house yet.

Though she had moved to the palace as a young child when her father was forced to ascend the throne, Elizabeth had enjoyed growing up before that weighty moment in her parents' private home. It was her hope that her own children would have the same opportunity—and for longer. After all, Papa was still relatively young. So perhaps she'd be able to raise her children completely away from the spotlight before taking up the throne herself.

Elizabeth wrapped her arm around Philip's waist.

"I'm so happy," she whispered, her eyes dampening.

"As am I." Philip offered her a smile so full of pure love that it made her chest swell.

Susan was now tearing into the stocking, pulling out, in rapid succession, a rubber ball, a stuffed fox, and a biscuit made for her by Hanna's stepmother.

"Which will you choose?" Elizabeth teased as Susan picked up one thing and then set it down in favor of another.

Susan glanced up, tail wagging furiously, before returning to her bounty.

Behind them the king played a jovial song and Maggie's voice rang out. Susan finally settled on the biscuit, trotting off to hide behind the Christmas tree and feast. Elizabeth retrieved the other toys, tucking them back into the stocking and re-hanging it so that Susan's gifts couldn't be pilfered by one of the other family dogs, namely Crackers who fancied himself something of a king in his old age.

"Shall we dance?" Philip asked, holding out his hand.

"Have you ever known me to turn away a dance?" She took his hand.

"Never."

Philip twirled her where they stood, and pure joy rushed through Elizabeth. Surrounded by her family and music, dancing in the arms of her handsome husband while the ground outside Sandringham was covered in sparkling white snow—it was a fairy-tale Christmas Eve.

Everything felt perfect, and so right. Gone were the worries of war, the drama of a new role in life. Elizabeth felt as if with Philip, they could conquer anything that might be thrown at them, because look how much they'd already triumphed over.

"Have you ever thought about breaking tradition?" Philip asked, interrupting her train of thought.

"Why would I think about that? Traditions were made for a reason. They are important."

"All right then, have you ever thought about creating new traditions?"

Elizabeth cocked her head, staring into Philip's eyes as they danced, and looked at him questioningly.

"For example, when we've a residence of our own, and children, we could celebrate Christmas at our own home rather than Sandringham?"

Elizabeth frowned, glancing around the drawing room of Sandringham where she'd spent more Christmases in her life than not. "But Christmas is always at Sandringham, ever since our great-great-grandmother Queen Victoria first celebrated here."

"But don't you find excitement in new things?" Philip gave her a twirl.

"Quite the opposite mostly," she confessed.

And it was true. Elizabeth loved tradition, and not only for herself but for what it meant to others watching and surrounding the royal family. "The people here at Sandringham look forward to our visit," she continued, trying to explain the wider ripples of what might seem like a stodgy tradition to her dashing, daring husband. "And while Christmas is a family and religious holiday that I cherish, I am not just a wife and someday, hopefully, a mother. I mustn't forget my duty as the daughter of the head of the Church of England—a duty that will only become more solemn when it is my turn to rule. The people of England expect certain things from their leaders."

Elizabeth felt the tug inside her between a desire, a duty,

to remain constant to royal traditions and the spirit of change that had allowed her to marry the man now holding her in his arms. "What would changing Christmas celebrations achieve?"

Philip leaned close, whispering next to her ear. "Think about it, please, for me."

"Oh, Philip. I will think about it. And I am willing to make new traditions with you. But . . ." She hesitated, not wanting to give him too much hope on the issue of Christmas. "Well, if we were not who we are, then I would say absolutely we should have Christmas at our own home. But the thing is, my love, we are Princess Elizabeth and Philip, the Duke of Edinburgh. We cannot lightly set aside the Christmas traditions that generations before us have cherished."

Undeterred, her husband put on his most persuasive expression and said smoothly, "I am not suggesting we do it lightly. But sometimes change is a good thing. It's progress."

"Progress for the sake of the greater good is something I am eager to embrace. But progress merely for the sake of saying we—or anyone, for that matter—did something different doesn't make sense."

Philip frowned, his expression becoming guarded. Elizabeth could feel his disappointment; and behind her ribs, her heart stuttered. She wanted to make him feel better—to say they could do whatever he wished—but she knew that would be only her heart speaking and not her head. That was a luxury she did not have as heir to the throne.

"Listen, darling." Elizabeth smoothed her hands over his shoulders. "Why don't we take it one Christmas at a time? Perhaps the opportunity for change and new traditions will present itself in ways we can't predict."

His face lit back up, and she was pleased to have made him

happy for the moment. She knew better than most how hard it was for him to walk two steps behind. Traditionally a man led his wife, but for them—at least in the larger sphere—it was the opposite. She wanted him to feel secure that within their own private relationship she very much wished him to be in charge, even if the rules of law made her position higher than his everywhere else.

"You know, Philip, I often wish it was just us and not the kingdom that we had to think of," she said.

"I appreciate that, my little cabbage," he said with a smile.

"Good, because I do hate to see you disappointed."

He pulled her in for another discreet kiss. "And I never want to see you feel that way either."

"If you two lovebirds would like to join us, we're thinking of a game of cards." Maggie rolled her eyes. "And if you don't hurry, Papa has threatened to form another conga line."

Elizabeth laughed, her memory harkening back to the reception after her wedding where her father had led a long line of people dancing through the corridors of Buckingham Palace.

"I wouldn't mind a conga line," Philip said with a laugh.

"Oh, heavens, Philip! What about a game of charades instead?" Charades was one of Elizabeth's favorite games.

Maggie clapped. "Oh yes, I do love charades."

The king smiled, rising from the piano bench to join his wife on the sofa. "You go first, Lilibet."

Elizabeth hurried to the center of the drawing room. It took only a moment to figure out what she wanted to do. She pantomimed pulling up a velvet curtain to let the family know she'd chosen a play, then indicated one word, three syllables. Going to her knees on the Aubusson rug, she lifted the fringed edge, bending this way and that, pretending to be soaring.

"*Aladdin!*" Maggie and Philip shouted in unison. It was the play Philip had come to see them in one Christmas, a happy memory for Elizabeth and one she wanted to remind Philip of at that moment.

"Yes!" Elizabeth laughed and stood. "You'll both have to go since you said it at the same time."

Maggie and Philip withdrew to a corner where they conferred in excited whispers.

Returning to the center of the room they stood, hands on their hips to signal they were people. Then they broke out into a Charleston reminiscent of the many nights the three had gone out dancing when she and Philip were supposed to be pretending he wasn't courting her.

"Nightclub dancers!" Elizabeth shouted.

"Bright young things," called their mother.

Philip and Maggie shook their heads, then stuck out their tongues and wiggled their fingers with their thumbs on their noses before dancing some more.

Papa let out a roar of a laugh. "Fred and Adele Astaire!"

Philip and Maggie both stopped dancing and pointed at the king.

"You got it!" Maggie shouted.

"I adored their shows. Do you remember when Lilibet was an infant and Adele came to meet her?" the queen asked.

The king laughed again. "Yes. Poor Miss Astaire, she looked like she was going to faint."

"My goodness could she dance, though," the queen said nostalgically.

Elizabeth had heard the stories of how before she was born her father and uncles used to dance with Fred and Adele Astaire at the nightclubs after one of their performances. She'd even heard rumors that all three of them tried to court Miss Astaire at one time, but that she'd chosen Uncle David as her beau. That always made Elizabeth question her taste, but Adele had broken it off with him, so she had to have some sense.

"Your turn, Papa," Elizabeth said.

The king took a few minutes before holding out one finger to indicate one word and then signing two syllables. Then he got down on all fours, stuck out his tongue as if he were panting, and started to trot back and forth.

"Crackers," Maggie shouted.

"Dookie," the queen tried.

"I think she knows the answer." Philip laughed and pointed as Susan began making circles around his majesty where he mimed—yipping and wagging her tail.

"Susan?" Elizabeth said with a giggle.

The king picked up the dog, rubbing his nose to hers. "None other."

"Now, Susan," Elizabeth said, "you know the rules of the game, right?"

Everyone broke into laughs as Susan barked and ran from person to person, licking them as if she did indeed know the rules.

"Sometimes I think she understands everything we say." Maggie tilted her head to look at the corgi.

"No doubt. She is very wise," Papa offered. "I knew that from the moment I picked her out of the litter."

"She's certainly tried to put me in my place." Philip chuckled. And as if responding, Susan came up to him and gave his shoe a little nip. "See what I mean?"

"Susan, stop it," Elizabeth said. "We can't buy him new shoes every time you want to tell him what to do." Susan ran to the princess and put her paws on Elizabeth's knees. "I know: you want your toy fox, don't you?"

Susan barked in response, and Elizabeth rose to fetch it. When she returned to the group, Philip remarked about how their children would likely be just as spoiled as Susan.

"Well, as long as they don't take to biting your shoes and nipping your ankles, it should all be fine," Elizabeth interrupted, assuming an air of seriousness, though it was hard to keep a straight face.

"She has a point," the king said. "Maggie went through a biting phase. Drew blood from me once or twice."

"Papa!" Maggie's mouth fell open in exasperation and disbelief.

"It's true," their mum said, looking as serious as one of the palace guards. "But at least the wounds didn't require stitching."

Elizabeth could remain serious no longer. And she wasn't the only one. The entire family laughed until their stomachs cramped and tears filled their eyes. As Elizabeth glanced around at the people she loved most dearly in the world, she wanted to savor this moment of familial bliss forever, locked in a special place in her heart so she could pull it out and relive it over again for the rest of her days.

·⊶⊱·

CHAPTER NINETEEN

*H*ANNA

I sat beside Forrest at the servants' table, the center filled with delicious food Cook had prepared for the Christmas Eve celebration. A roast goose, plum pudding, potatoes, and stewed greens.

The evening's chatter had run the usual gamut from pleasantries to rumors, with the latter being tutted by Mrs. Burke, Sandringham's housekeeper.

"We don't need to be spreading rumors." Mrs. Burke stared from one end of the table to the other, in a matron-of-the-schoolhouse sort of glance, which had every one of us sitting up a little taller. "Leave that to the press."

"Ah, it's all in good fun," one of the maids grumbled.

Mrs. Burke swiveled to stare at the girl. I swear steam curled from her ears as she said, "There's no such thing as fun at the expense of another" in a way likely to put a fear of ever saying another word into not only the shrinking maid but all the rest of us at the table.

Forrest and I exchanged a glance.

I wanted to escape with him outside for an evening stroll in the snow. It was a white Christmas and, though the sun had already set, we could enjoy the way the stars reflected on the snow-covered grounds. Mrs. Burke always frowned at us when we walked off together, then she cornered me when I returned, letting me know she was girlhood friends with my stepmother and that she needed to be sure I was keeping things on the up-and-up.

Of course I was, though it wasn't any of her business. Nor did I think it was fair she was threatening to tell Mrs. Seymour, who had only just married my father.

The royal family had already eaten, and the king was playing the piano, the notes of the music and the family's singing trickling down to the bowels of the servants' hall, providing a backdrop to our meal.

With our places cleared at last, and Mrs. Burke's attention focused elsewhere, Forrest and I slipped away. I retrieved Susan from her dinner and then the three of us headed out into the snow. It wasn't deep enough for Susan to sink under, so she took off at a run—her tiny pawprints scattering here and there.

I'd barely finished buttoning my jacket when Forrest kissed me. If Mrs. Burke was looking out the window, she'd certainly seen us. But as our relationship accelerated, we'd become accustomed to tempting fate.

"I've a gift for you." I reached into my pocket, at the same time Forrest reached into his.

"And I have one for you."

"Me first. It's just a little something," I said, handing over the gift wrapped in burlap and tied with twine.

Forrest unwound the twine and pulled out a tiny wooden recorder; with a smile he pressed it to his lips and gave a few notes.

"You're always whistling while you work. When I was young, I used to whistle a lot. Mum got me a recorder. She told me I had a good rhythm, and I ought to give it a whirl. I hope you'll enjoy it. In any event I certainly hope you'll be better at it than me."

"I love it." He blew a few more notes, surprisingly talented at it for having just played for the first time. "And now it's time for you to open yours."

I accepted the similarly wrapped gift, carefully untying the twine. Inside was a worn strip of leather. My name had been carved onto one side, and on the other it said: *Love, Forrest.*

"It's a bookmark I made from one of the reins used on the horses that pulled Princess Elizabeth's wedding carriage. I hope it reminds you of one of our first coups—getting Susan secretly on board."

I laughed, hugging the strip of leather to my chest. "Oh, thank you. It's wonderful. I will never read another book without it."

Forrest gripped my hand in his, giving a little squeeze, his eyes locked on mine. Susan seemed to sense the affection in our moment, because she came jealously running up to us, snowflakes flying in her wake.

"She doesn't want to miss out on the fun." I laughed, stooping to give her a pat before finding a stick to toss.

"Hanna." Forrest's feet shifted back and forth, and he seemed suddenly nervous.

"Are you all right?" I peered at him more closely, and he seemed to have gone a little pale. "Was it dinner?"

"No, no, nothing like that," he said, his voice quivering just a touch. "It's just that I've got something else for you."

"Oh?" I paused, watching as he took a deep breath.

Forrest pulled a small box from his pocket and knelt on one

knee. Susan darted from where she'd been digging in the snow and put her paws on his thigh, licking the box as if it were a treat. And in that moment, I realized exactly what was happening.

Susan barked and tried to snatch the box, and I pressed my hands to my mouth to stifle a gasp of surprise mingled with a shocked laugh. Those reactions seemed unfair to Forrest, who was already feeling overwhelmed.

"I've got something better for you, pup." Forrest pulled a piece of biscuit from his other pocket and tossed it into the snow. Susan bounded after it, leaving him free to turn his attention back to me. My heart swelled with emotion.

"What are you doing down there?" I asked, a nervous flutter in my belly. I'm not sure why I asked. I was perfectly aware of what such a stance would mean, especially when it was accompanied by the presentation of a small box. But still, my own nerves were apparently getting the better of me.

Forrest opened the box, and the moonlight sparkled on a diamond set in a gold band.

"Hanna, from the moment I saw you chasing those dogs at Windsor, your hair flying wild, and a look of determination on your face, I knew I wanted to run after whatever it was you were chasing. And nothing's changed. I love you, and I'm hoping you'll do me the honor of becoming my wife."

A sob escaped me as emotion filled my lungs and stole away all my words. Tears pricked my eyes, and a lump filled my throat.

When I didn't speak, Susan rushed forward, barked at me, barked at Forrest, and then licked the ring, as if to say, *If you aren't going to say yes, I will.*

Both Forrest and I began to laugh, and I dropped to my knees in the snow, petting Susan and holding out my hand to Forrest. Then realizing I was still wearing gloves, I peeled them off with trembling fingers.

"Yes," I finally said with a laugh bordering on a happy cry. "Yes, yes."

PART III

THE
MOTHER

ROYAL REPORT

TRUSTED NEWS OF ALL THINGS ROYAL

We have been delighted by all the letters pouring in for beloved Susan, a most royal corgi, with words of advice as the royal family expands. Here we've shared a couple.

Dear Susan,

You will always be Princess Elizabeth's beloved corgi, but now you have a new charge. A wee prince or princess to care for. The new baby is probably going to be loud, maybe a little scary. But that's how it communicates, just like you bark. I'm sure you've met a baby before and if you haven't, then you likely will soon to prepare you.

With love,
The Smythe family

Dear Susan,

For so long you've been the baby in the family, and now you will be a "big sister." Your princess will likely be very tired after delivering the baby, and your walks with her may be few and far between. Try to have patience, and show her that you love her even if her time with you is cut short.

And if you need a dog walker, I'm always available!

Sally

·｡⤸⤷｡·

CHAPTER TWENTY

ℰLIZABETH

October 1948

𝒯he cool breeze did little to cure the boiling heat Elizabeth felt all over. And her legs were especially heavy today. With only Susan for company—just as she arranged it—Elizabeth sank to the grass-carpeted land and tapped the dull wool skirt covering her thighs for Susan to come cuddle.

Dutifully, Susan approached, being gentler than she usually was as she climbed into the slowly disappearing space she used to occupy. Susan licked Elizabeth's belly, as if she understood there was a wee one in there, due in just a month's time.

"Oh, Susan, sometimes I wish I were a regular woman."

Susan stared into her eyes, and Elizabeth held her gaze, knowing her pup was truly listening to her every word, was feeling every emotion along with her.

"You have always been such a faithful companion."

Susan blinked as if to say, *Of course.*

It had been a hard morning. Elizabeth and Philip had had a row—a noisy, obstreperous one. She'd thrown a newspaper at him: a paper with his face splashed on the front page and a headline proclaiming him a philanderer. There was an entire exposé on his supposed date with a stage star. How he'd taken her out to dinner and then they'd gone dancing all night long, ending in a torrid tumble.

Now Elizabeth was feeling guilty. It was true Philip often enjoyed the company of stage stars, but so did she. Going to dinner with someone glamorous and famous wasn't a big deal; they did it all the time. *Just because I am sentenced to nine months of feeling miserable doesn't mean Philip has to be.*

Philip had sworn the affair part of the article wasn't true, that the reporter was only out to cast him in a bad light. He'd declared himself offended that she'd fallen for it. Had she fallen for press nonsense? Or was there something more?

"Am I a fool?" Elizabeth asked Susan.

Susan sniffed at Elizabeth's belly once again and then rose to lick her on the chin.

"You're right. He loves me. He'd never do anything to hurt me."

Elizabeth lay back, staring up at the sky, where swaths of blue tried to poke through the clouds and the sun was covered by a thick gray haze. Susan climbed off her and curled up at the princess's side.

Absently, Elizabeth stroked her corgi's head. "I don't know if I'm ready to be a mother," she confessed.

Lately she'd been wondering how she was going to handle being someone else's mother when she still needed the advice of her own. But ready or not, a mother she would soon become. All she could do was take one step at a time.

"With Philip's help, the help of our household staff, and the support of my family, surely my own new little family with thrive," she said to Susan.

Women had been becoming mothers for millennia. This was no different. But even as the last thought was fresh in her mind, she knew that for her it was. Her child was going to be heir to the throne. He or she would be talked about in the papers, as she had been ever since her father ascended to the throne. As Philip made headlines now. She and Philip were always on display. And the wee prince or princess would be too—the public would be mad for coverage of her child. How was she going to give that child a normal childhood? How were she, the baby, and Philip ever going to get away from the constant spotlight? The constant scrutiny?

It seemed impossible.

Elizabeth rolled to her side, looking at Susan and stroking the corgi's soft belly. If someone took a photograph of her now, Elizabeth thought, the headlines would doubtless say something like: *Devasted Princess Collapses on Palace Lawn After Learning About Husband's Affair.*

They'd be wrong. She wasn't one to collapse at bad news. Never had been. Elizabeth was a doer, a woman of action and planning. When a conflict presented itself, she found a solution.

So what was her solution going to be with this?

The king and queen wanted her and Philip to hide away. To go somewhere until the ravenous rumors died down. But Elizabeth had a better idea.

They should go out, be spotted dancing in clubs like they used to. People needed to see that though they were married, though she was heir to the throne, though she was pregnant, they were still in love.

Elizabeth felt a sudden surge of energy. Instead of letting the rumors grow bigger, she and Philip would undermine them. She'd heard that some gossipmongers were even reporting she wasn't cutting it as a wife and that was why Philip had allegedly stepped out of their marriage. But she knew better.

Unless he'd somehow managed to sneak in a lover between

brushing his teeth at night and having his tea in the morning, the vicious snakes were crazy.

This was just a hungry, beastly media who wanted to throw a rift in a good thing. They wanted to play on Philip's past as a royal playboy, the man who used to be teasingly known as the Naked Waiter.

Everyone knows that sex and scandal sold more papers.

Elizabeth sat up then, as did Susan, who looked at her expectantly. "Enough thinking. It's time for action."

"Who are you talking to? And what are you doing out here?" Maggie's voice came from behind, and Elizabeth turned slightly to see her sister.

"Wishing I was back in Paris."

Maggie grinned and flopped down on the ground beside Elizabeth, not caring at all that her soft yellow dress was likely to be grass stained. "We did have a wonderful time, didn't we?"

It'd only been a few months since they'd returned from Paris, where—while she'd been secretly harboring the news of her pregnancy from the rest of the world—she, Maggie, and Philip had enjoyed the City of Light with all its fantastic clubs and dancing. Their official purpose for being in Paris had been a state visit to open the exhibit on British life. And that event had been a success as well, described by some French papers, rather hilariously, as "the Norman Conquest in reverse."

It'd been Elizabeth's first time leaving the Commonwealth, and it'd been fascinating to be a foreign dignitary. She'd placed a wreath on the tomb of the unknown soldier at the base of the Arc de Triomphe and been decorated with the Grand Cross of the Legion of Honor by the French president, Vincent Auriol, while Philip had received a Croix de Guerre. They'd had an official dinner at the Élysée Palace, and visited Versailles, walking in the footsteps of Queen Victoria, who had visited the palace almost one hundred years before. It was powerful to know that generations past had taken a similar journey. Elizabeth believed wholeheartedly in the importance of tradition.

Elizabeth had been careful to conceal her pregnancy. It wouldn't do for the French press to break the story before she gave it officially to the British press. She'd shied away from actually sipping any delicious French champagne as the smell made her quite nauseated, although she'd taken every glass she was handed, knowing that making it obvious she wasn't imbibing might set tongues wagging. Even so, she'd caught plenty of people trying to get a look at her waist to see if it was thickening. Thank goodness none of them had been in her suite, or they would have seen her being sick every morning after her egg and toast.

Though given the press's obsession with her, she was a little surprised not to see them hanging from her balcony in the hopes of one good snapshot. The leeches.

"The most marvelous time," she replied to Maggie. "I think the races might have been my favorite bit of all." No holiday abroad felt complete to Elizabeth without a trip to a racecourse. In France they'd sat in a presidential box and watched three intense horse races.

"Mine was dancing at Chez Carrere." Maggie's arms went up and she swayed them back and forth as if she were back at the nightclub, listening to the crooning notes of Edith Piaf. "You caused quite a stir, sister mine, by attending horse races and nightclub dancing. Oh, the tut-tutting!"

Though Maggie teased, some of the more conservative British papers had indeed been disappointed in Elizabeth's behavior, believing she was setting a poor example.

"As if having a little fun is immoral." Elizabeth rolled her eyes and gave Susan a good scratch on the chin.

"Of course it is," Maggie teased. "At least for that sort."

Elizabeth rubbed a hand over her belly. "If they'd known I had the future heir on board while I was dancing, they would have torched me."

"They tried. But you, Princess Elizabeth, are a force to be reckoned with."

"Am I?"

Maggie snorted. "I've never heard you ask that."

"What do you mean?"

"You don't doubt yourself. You were born to greatness." Maggie shrugged. "Leave all the self-doubt and shameful, scandalous partying to me."

"I do doubt," Elizabeth said softly. It felt good to say it, even if it sobered the moment.

They stared together up at the sky, their minds thick with memory—much of it shared.

"Do you think Papa will be all right?" Maggie broke the silence, her voice so soft it almost didn't carry.

Recently their father had been complaining so much about pain in his legs, and his temper seemed shorter than usual. He'd even snapped at himself, and at inanimate objects, like whatever chair he was getting out of.

"I am sure." Elizabeth projected much more confidence than she felt. In fact, in the pit of her stomach there was a lingering fear that was increasingly becoming a conviction that the king was not going to be all right at all. But to put voice to her worries would make them more real, and that was not something she was ready to contend with. "He's under a lot of stress. That's all."

"Yes." Maggie's voice lacked conviction. "You are probably right. You always are. All it is is stress."

* * *

BUT THAT *WASN'T* all it was. Elizabeth found that out two days after she gave birth to her son, Charles, on the fourteenth of November at Buckingham Palace via cesarean section, when her father canceled his engagements for the foreseeable future.

She lay in bed, exhausted, Charles asleep in her mother's arms, and she lifted the offending medical bulletin and seethed that she'd not been told in person.

She was both hurt and angry that her parents had been keeping this massive secret from her. Canceling appointments and issuing a medical bulletin in regard to the circumstances wasn't trivial.

"I can't believe you didn't tell me," Elizabeth said in a hushed, irritated tone to her mother, who'd come to visit. Elizabeth didn't want to wake the sleeping baby, who looked so pink and tiny held by her mother. "Tell me everything now."

Queen Elizabeth hesitated, already having dug her heels in for months, no doubt, and that only increased Elizabeth's irritation.

"His Buerger's disease has inflamed the blood vessels in his legs. He's been suffering greatly. At one point"—her mother hesitated again, swallowed hard—"your father was in so much pain that it made him cry out aloud.

"Gangrene nearly set in, and the doctors were so worried about saving your father's legs that they temporarily forgot to fuss about his cirrhosis of the liver and his continuing lung problems." Queen Elizabeth softly stroked baby Charles's chin.

"Lilibet, we didn't want to worry you. Especially in your delicate condition. Didn't want to risk your health or this little fellow's."

Choked with emotion, Elizabeth couldn't speak. It had gotten that bad, and no one had said a damned word to her. And she hadn't even noticed. If only she'd paid more attention . . . maybe she would have detected something, anything, even if they were trying to hide it from her. She understood they were showing parental care, but she wasn't just their child—she was next in line to the throne. As such, she should have been one of the first people notified.

Finally, she managed to ask, "Will he lose his legs?"

"We hope not." The queen pressed a kiss to Prince Charles's downy head. "We've been told if he rests as his doctors have instructed, he will likely keep them and may even be well enough to attend Charles's christening in December."

Elizabeth breathed a sigh of relief at that. "We should hold the baptism here at the palace, rather than the abbey. That way Papa won't have too far to go."

Her mother looked up at her, a sadness about her eyes that Elizabeth hadn't seen before. Witnessing that raw display of emotion from a woman who generally kept her feelings locked up tighter than the crown jewels was more terrifying to Elizabeth than having been kept in the dark about the king's health.

"You're a good daughter, Lilibet. And you'll be a great mother too."

CHAPTER TWENTY-ONE

SUSAN

Can preparation for change really make you ready for it?

Lilibet had read me letters from our adoring public—letters warning me of what to expect when the royal baby arrived. These kind folks tried to assuage me with bits of advice that mostly didn't make any sense at all. I am a dog, after all. We understand breath, heartbeats, movement. We have a limited vocabulary and *baby* was definitely one of the words I'd not been able to accurately decipher or define until now.

My princess had taken me to the park to meet babies, ones that tugged my ears with sticky fingers. Those in the palace who had miniature humans brought them around for me to meet on the lawn, where the strange little hairless things wiggled, crawled, and attempted to run, generally falling over. And all these babies, however bewildering, had one thing in common, an annoying thing—they cried, screeched, really.

I knew Lilibet subjected me to all this to help prepare me for when her own child was born. And I made a valiant effort, because I love her, to not bite the ankles of the wee things. This was especially hard for me because all of them seemed determined to torture me: trying to steal my stick or the balls she threw to me, grabbing my fur instead of stroking it, even stepping on me occasionally.

So I might have been able to survive such things when our baby arrived. But what Lilibet hadn't really prepared me for was being displaced . . . *replaced.*

This thought occurs to me the minute I realize my spot on her lap is gone. I run up to her knees, expecting to take my place, but a swaddled thing lies there, in my spot, drooling.

A prince they say he is.

After more time spent in this baby's presence, I am convinced that Prince Philip's left shoe is more princely than the thing that squirms in Lilibet's arms. I approach it often, sniffing. It tends to smell faintly of milk and of what comes out of its hind end. There are moments that recall me to my puppyhood—faint reminders of being huddled in a group with my siblings when I was born. The squeaking, squirming, suckling is all just a little bit the same.

I am curious about this wriggling being. On this occasion I inch forward, tail tucked, head bowed. I don't want them to shoo me away. As soon as I'm beside the sofa, Lilibet pats a place next to her, and I leap carefully onto the cushion, not wanting to disturb what for the moment seems to be a peaceful infant.

"Do you love your new brother?" Lilibet whispers the question because if Philip hears her referring to this thing as my brother, he gets irritated and reminds her I am a dog.

Love it? That's yet to be determined. But I still love Lilibet, so I probably need to try and make peace with the prince. I sneak a look at the tiny pink face, the dark fringe of hair, the squinted blue eyes that have suddenly opened to take me in. His fingers jerk out from his blanket, flailing in the air with no purpose other than movement. I remember being so vulnerable. So unused to moving.

I lick the small thing's hand, noticing it tastes faintly of Lilibet and Philip combined. Interesting.

I pull my head back again and cock it. I am supposed to like it, this thing they call Prince Charles. I'm supposed to look after it, protect it like I do my Lilibet. She told me that. I am supposed to love it, as I do her. But how can I when I want to be in her lap? When he's taking my place?

Frustrated, I bark, and Lilibet shushes me.

"Where's Hanna?" Philip asks. I dread what's coming next.

I will be whisked out of the room. I'm not supposed to bark anymore. But barking is how I talk, and Lilibet used to love when I talked. Now they want me silent.

I back away from the squirming little monster, jealous. Missing my Lilibet even before I am taken away.

A moment later, Hanna swoops into the room, greeting the royals with deference before cooing at the wee prince and then turning her kind face to me.

"Come, Susan. I've a treat for you."

Who am I to resist a treat? They are the only thing that hasn't changed in the palace since the arrival of the baby. I wag my tail as I trot forward, momentarily forgetting my feelings of loss. Until the little prince wails, and I find myself feeling both irritated and sad again.

Then Lilibet shushes him too.

I stop chewing my treat for a moment, struck by a thought. This Charles and I have something in common: we are both too loud for each other.

·❧·

CHAPTER TWENTY-TWO

ℋANNA

Susan was always a dog up for adventure. Ever since she was a wee pup.

It was easy to get her into the automobile for transfer to Thelma Gray's Rozavel kennels, where Rozavel Lucky Strike was waiting—a champion stud the queen had picked for Susan. Mrs. Gray's was where Dookie, the royal family's first corgi, had been bred, whereas Susan had been bred in Cambridgeshire at the Hickathrift kennel by Mr. Taylor.

We all—me, Princess Elizabeth, Prince Philip, the king— agreed it was a good time for Susan to be bred. The corgi was an appropriate age, and now that the princess had a baby, she thought perhaps Susan might like to have one too. I wasn't sure how Susan felt about that. In fact, I suspected she'd rather just have Elizabeth back to herself. But who was I to argue with her royal highness?

The drive north wasn't long. Susan spent most of the time with her paws on the side of the car, her head out the window, smelling the air as we passed through London on our way to the country.

When we turned onto the drive, she sniffed frantically, letting out some yips as she hopped down and circled the back seat before hopping up again. Likely she could smell the other dogs.

"You're going to meet your beau," I said, feeling a little hypo-critical, since really, she wasn't being courted but rather impregnated. "I hope he's a true gentleman." He probably wouldn't be. Male dogs usually weren't exactly . . . flirtatious as they went about this business.

I'd watched plenty of it happen, having been the daughter of the gamekeeper at Windsor. But Susan seemed eager to meet the new dogs she could smell; and when we pulled to a stop, she scratched at the door to get out.

However, Thelma had given strict instructions not to let Susan roam, lest one of the other studs get a hold of her. Multiple dogs were howling inside their kennels. I wondered if they'd caught Susan's scent and that had them going nuts, or if it was simply that they were alerting Thelma to an intrusion.

The breeder emerged from her house, hurrying toward us with a wave and a friendly smile.

"You made good time," Thelma said, peering into the car to where Susan scrambled to get out, her claws clicking against the window. "My, she's feisty."

I smiled, proud of Susan and the bit of independent streak she'd managed for herself. "The queen spoils her, and so do I."

"As you both should." Thelma smiled. "Have you a leash and collar?"

"Yes." I held up the matching leather leash to her collar with Susan's name embroidered on it.

"Perfect. I'll take her inside then to meet Lucky Strike. He's my pride and joy. What an honor for him and for me, to have him sire a royal corgi."

"Princess Elizabeth is so very pleased you agreed," I said.

Elizabeth had been going on for weeks about Lucky Strike; his sire, Red Dragon; the quality of their bones; and Lucky

Strike's disposition. She certainly had the makings of a proud doggie grandmother. But I suspected it wasn't just her interest in corgis and her love for Susan that had led to her extreme engagement in the breeding process. I thought it likely she'd also been trying to distract herself from the king's declining health.

His majesty was currently recovering from spinal surgery, intended to help with the vascular issue in his legs. Besides obsessing over Susan's breeding, Elizabeth had gone out on the town dancing for her birthday the month before, which was a little cause for stir, given she was a new mother. But of course, even new mothers needed to have fun, didn't they? And to be honest, it really seemed like Elizabeth was trying to send a message as she danced on her husband's arm until the wee hours of the morning.

"Of course, we're honored," Thelma gushed.

We leashed Susan, who wriggled so much I feared she'd break free. Thelma and I hovered over her, as if she were a royal and we her bodyguards, until she was safely in the breeding room.

"Could we have a moment alone?" I asked Thelma.

"Of course." Thankfully Thelma didn't look the least surprised at my asking, probably because she too was a dog person and understood the special bond.

As soon as the door closed, I squatted down to floor level. Susan ran to me, panting, and I rubbed my hand over her head. She wasn't really paying attention to me. There were so many smells that she was too busy sniffing. Looking down at her more closely I noticed the tiny wet pawprints on the wood floor in the direction she'd come from, indicating her paws were damp. She was nervous. "Susan," I said, scooping her into my arms, "this is going to be scary. Things often are that we don't know anything about. I'm hoping animal instinct helps."

Susan cocked her head, one of her ears swiveling as she listened. I hoped, however irrationally, that she understood at least some of what I was saying. She so often seemed to.

"I've never had a baby, so I'm probably not the most perfect person to discuss this with you. But this thing that happens next—that's where it leads, to motherhood. I *know* you, Susan. I know you've got heart. When the time comes, you'll make a great mum to all the wee ones Lucky Strike is going to give you."

I could feel myself beginning to choke up. So I glanced away from the dog, up at the ceiling, and concentrated on the spider in the corner that had woven a web and waited eagerly for its prey.

Sensing my unease, Susan nuzzled my hand, bopping under my palm with her nose until I was rubbing dutifully behind her ears.

"Well," I said perfunctorily, hearing the sounds of Thelma returning. "Just remember, this part won't take long."

* * *

MY WEDDING TO Forrest was a whirlwind affair. I barely remembered walking down the small aisle or greeting the guests, who included our close friends from Windsor and Buckingham Palace and of course my father and the former Mrs. Seymour, or Jane, as I had now been instructed to call her since she was my stepmother.

Princess Elizabeth had the palace staff arrange a suite of rooms in the servants' quarters for us at the palace and gave us a small cottage close to Windsor so I could be near my father. The spot was also close to her own country house, Windlesham Moor, so it would be a convenient place for me to live while caring for Susan when the princess and Philip were in residence at Windlesham. There wasn't exactly a precedent for this arrangement, but with Elizabeth, when it came to her dogs, she did not seem to feel the need for one.

When I told her our double marital living arrangements were too much, Elizabeth said, in a no-nonsense voice, that they were not at all. She pointed out we'd each had our own rooms at both locations before.

Once our wedding celebrations were over, and I'd changed into my traveling suit, there was someone waiting to accompany us on our honeymoon. Susan, now pregnant, was to accompany us for our short stay in Bath. She was, after all, my charge.

Soon it was time to return to work, and because of Susan's delicate condition, Elizabeth asked me to keep the corgi with me at the cottage and care for her there rather than at Buckingham Palace. Our time in the country wouldn't be too long. Corgis took only about sixty days from conception to whelping. After that, Forrest and I would keep the new mother and her pups with us at the cottage until the wee ones were weaned.

While Susan waited to give birth, Elizabeth came to visit whenever the royal family was at Windsor. Susan adored their time together. I could tell they were both missing each other, and I was only a slight comfort to either of them.

Two months into our stay at Windsor I noticed Susan acting strange after supper. She was walking in so many circles that she surely must have been dizzy, and she was even making me so. When she lay down on the floor, panting, I knelt beside her and rubbed my hand over her thick belly.

"I think her time has come," I said to Forrest.

"How can you tell?"

"Instinct?" I'd been there plenty when Dad had to aid with a whelping or the birth of other animals on the estate. I knew the signs. "Did I ever tell you about a time that I helped my mum birth some foxes?"

Forrest knelt beside me, watching Susan, his gaze flicking over to mine with interest. "You have not. But I've a faint memory of it, just from things I heard in primary."

I nodded, a small grin on my face. "All of Windsor talked about Mum and her pet foxes."

"I bet your dad wasn't too pleased." Forrest chuckled.

I nodded. "But he loved her so much, he was willing to indulge her in pretty much anything."

"How did she get the fox?"

"We were on a walk, the three of us, and we came across a fox with her foot caught in one of the traps. But she was very much alive. And rather than acting frantic, as they usually do, this poor creature looked right into my mum's eyes, so sad, as if she were begging her for help."

"I've seen that look before."

"Susan's mastered it," I replied, and we both laughed, setting Susan's ears twitching. "Well, we got the fox out of the trap and Dad said, 'Bloody hell, she's knocked up.'"

Forrest let out a burst of a laugh. "You sound just like him."

"Can you picture my mum giving him a dressing-down for speaking that way in front of me?"

He grinned. "Aye, I can."

"Well, Mum said Dad could make it up to her if they brought the fox home and he helped her nurse it back to health. Which he did, and then she did. They delivered the fox kits some weeks later.

"We let them all go back to the wild once the pups were a few weeks old. And for years, when we'd go on our walks, doing the rounds, we'd search for Mum's fox. I saw her more than once."

"That's adorable."

"It was." I paused, feeling emotion well in my throat as tears stung my eyes.

"What's wrong?" Forrest asked.

"After my mum died, I didn't see the fox anymore. It's like she knew Mum was gone, so she left too." I wiped a tear that trickled down the side of my face. "Animals can have a special bond with humans. I think that fox had vowed to keep a watch on my mum as a thank-you to her for saving her. And . . . when Mum was gone, the vow was fulfilled."

Forrest put his arm around me, hugging me close. "Your mum was special. And passed a lot of that specialness to you, my love. I'm certain she's looking down on you now with pride."

Susan gave a little pain-filled yelp, her body tensing, drawing us both back into the immediacy of the moment.

From then on, my focus stayed on my furry charge.

While Susan labored, I let Elizabeth know what was happening. The princess promised to come as soon as she could.

Six puppies, plump and alive. Their tiny, red, furry bodies reminded me so much of the foxes. Their eyes were closed, their little snorts and squeals so adorable and memorable I got choked up over and over.

Susan cleaned her pups, then lay in her exhausted state and let them nurse. As she did, she stared at me. Her large eyes filled with something that looked like contentment.

"Good job, Susan. You're a good dog," I whispered.

* * *

THE FOLLOWING MORNING when Elizabeth arrived from Clarence House—her London house, the renovations now complete—Susan practically trampled her own children to rush into her princess's arms.

"Oh, my darling Sus," Elizabeth said, wrapping the corgi in her arms and kissing her. "You're a mother now . . . just like me."

Susan barked and leaped down, running toward her litter in the box lined with blankets. She clearly wanted to show off her babies.

"They are gorgeous." Elizabeth peered into the makeshift pen. "I had told Philip I would only take one, but I think I need two. Two of the females."

"Are you planning to sell them, ma'am?" I asked. "Should I ask Thelma to find buyers?"

"Oh, no." Elizabeth waved the thought away. "I'll never sell. They will be gifts. Windsor corgis." She glanced up at me with pride. "Every royal corgi from now on will be descended from Susan." She turned back to her beloved dog, beaming with pride. "You're a queen, Susan. A matriarch of your own royal line."

"I can think of no greater gift to anyone than a Windsor corgi." I glanced down at the sweet litter, so cherubic with their little squirms and grunts.

"I shall give this one to Charles," she said, pointing to a female. "Sugar. And this one will be Honey, and I think Mummy will like her very much."

"I am certain they will both be pleased."

"Would you like one?" Elizabeth asked, taking me by surprise.

I'd never had a dog of my own; they'd always belonged to my dad or the royal family. My days were already filled with

Princess Elizabeth's corgis, two pups of which she was going to keep. To take on one of my own might be too much. Then again, they were so sweet, and it had been hard to do anything but stare at them and cuddle them since they arrived. In fact, the very idea of parting with them made me feel as if I were having to give up my own children.

I opened my mouth to say no when Forrest answered. "She'd love one."

"I would?" I blinked, trying to think as I looked at my husband. He was nodding, his expression confident. He was right, and before I could even argue with myself, I said again, "I would." Only this time more definitively.

"Name her Biscuit," Forrest said with a meaningful smile. "After all, that's Susan's favorite."

I laughed.

"Biscuit." I pointed to the female pup who was cuddled closest to Susan.

"A perfect name." Elizabeth lifted Biscuit from her bedding and rubbed her nose on the puppy's head. "So sweet."

Then she handed Biscuit to me, and I held her close, breathing in the sweet puppy smell.

"We'll give the two males back to Thelma," Elizabeth said. "As for the final pup, well, I shall have to see who is most deserving."

"What about to Philip's mother, Princess Alice?" I suggested.

"A perfect idea. I think she would adore one."

Susan sniffed and licked at her puppies, then settled down on her side, gifting their ravenous appetites with her hardworking body.

·᠊ঙ৯৯᠊·

CHAPTER TWENTY-THREE

ℰLIZABETH

November 1949

𝓑oarding the plane to Malta was bittersweet for Elizabeth.

She was headed to the beautiful island off the coast of Sicily and North Africa where Philip had taken up his new post for the Royal Navy on the HMS *Chequers*. She was leaving one-year-old Charles behind in the care of his nannies to do so.

Guilt riddled Elizabeth for saying goodbye to her child. Had she not been heir to the throne, Charles might have traveled with her. But royal children, and most especially those directly in line for the crown, were not allowed. So Charles had to remain in the utter safety of the palace walls rather than traveling abroad, even with his parents.

As she stepped off the plane into the warm, salty air, and spied the blue-green coast and rocky cliffside, the sandstone dome-topped buildings, some of Elizabeth's guilt ebbed. After all, she'd lived her entire life in the service of the crown, and now she was being given this one short span of time when she and Philip could live like a regular navy couple. It was not wrong to savor that—to enjoy it.

Philip was waiting, standing handsome in his uniform as she got off the plane with Bobo and Lady Pamela Hicks (her lady-in-waiting, and Philip's cousin), and a guard to ensure her security. Elizabeth held Susan's leash, having relieved Hanna of her Susan duties for the duration of this trip. Hanna still had her hands full, however; she'd be taking care of Susan's puppies in England.

Elizabeth longed to rush into Philip's arms. She wanted to feel him lift her in the air and swirl her around the way romantic couples did in the cinema when they were reunited. And the way he sometimes did when they were alone. But they were not alone. They were on display, so she needed to be reserved, ladylike—proper. Looking past her husband and their people, she expected to see the press. They were not there! Philip and the royal staff had managed to keep her arrival quiet.

What was appropriate changed in an instant. Elizabeth quickened her steps into a subdued run of sorts. When she reached Philip, she embraced him, and he closed his arms around her. My goodness, she'd nearly forgotten how solid he was, how good it felt to be in his arms. And the scent of him was sea salt and spice, a tantalizing mixture she'd recognize anywhere. Philip smiled down at her, then kissed her briefly—too briefly—but still it was more of a kiss than they could have had if the press or scads of people had been present.

They were soon in public again, and the news of her arrival spread. Thousands lined the streets as they wove their way toward their lodgings—the summer palace, Villa Guardamangia, an eighteenth-century limestone villa owned by Philip's uncle Lord Louis Mountbatten. Elizabeth waved at the women in hats and sundresses and men in summer suits. Beyond those at the roadside, yet more people jovially raised their hands to wave either from tables and chairs set up outside cafés or as they walked along.

Elizabeth quickly fell in love with Malta. The weather, the views, and the freedom she and Philip enjoyed on the island made it feel like they were on holiday. There were moments when she felt as if they were living in the way non-royals lived their married lives. Philip went off to his ship each morning leaving Elizabeth to go shopping—driving herself in the Daimler. She had lunch with the other naval wives and hosted women for tea. In just those few first days she lived more freely than she ever had before.

Elizabeth woke on the one-week anniversary of her arrival to Philip stroking a path from the base of her spine to her shoulders and kissing her neck. Flipping onto her back she stared into his eyes—eyes as blue as the Maltese waters. "Good morning, husband."

"It is indeed a good morning, wife. I have a surprise for you."

"A surprise? How shocking that I didn't receive a bulletin informing me of your surprise beforehand," she teased. Everything in Malta, at the villa, felt so much more relaxed than it did in London.

"I was able to bribe them all to keep you in the dark."

"Naughty prince."

Philip chuckled. "I want to take you out on the *Eden*."

"Sailing!" Elizabeth sat up, smiling. She loved to be out on the ocean, though not as much as Maggie, who'd recently discovered she loved water-skiing on a trip with friends.

"There are some beautiful coves and inlets along the bays, and I want to show you. I was thinking a picnic." Philip drew circles on her bare shoulder as if he were marking the pathway of the water on her skin.

"I love picnics."

"Perfect."

"You're perfect."

"I try my best to please you."

"And you succeed." Elizabeth ran her fingers through his blond hair, settling her palm against his cheek. "I missed you."

"I missed you too."

Elizabeth flopped back on the bed. "The days are passing too quickly."

"If I could command time to stop, I would."

She smiled up at him, then leaned back up to kiss him.

* * *

AN HOUR LATER, they took the picnic the cook had packed for them and made their way to the *Eden*. Just off the tiny island of Comino, Philip maneuvered them through the Blue Lagoon and dropped the anchor.

"Want to swim before we eat?" he asked. "I packed our suits."

Elizabeth grinned, her eyes feasting on the gorgeous water. "Yes."

Philip jumped off the boat first, his strong and able body barely making a splash as he dove in. When he came back up to the surface, he shook his head, flicking his wet hair from his forehead. She gave a deep and satisfied sigh.

Whenever she was with Philip, he made her feel so young, so carefree. Looking at his glistening face, Elizabeth let go of the worries surrounding her father's illness, as well as the stress of all her royal responsibilities. With arms spread wide, she leaped into the water to join him. She held perfectly still, letting herself sink into the salty depths before stirring herself to rise to the surface.

On the deck of the boat, Susan barked, her body wiggling with excitement, then she too leaped into the water. Elizabeth squeaked, fearing Susan would injure herself, given the length of the fall. But the resourceful corgi swam toward them as though ocean swimming were second nature.

Philip came up behind Elizabeth, his arms going around her waist. "I can't believe we haven't done this before," he said.

Elizabeth turned in his embrace, her arms slipping around his shoulders, fingers threading into his wet hair.

"Feels like we're just two ordinary people," she said.

"Two ordinary people who own a boat and can sail across the bays of a glorious Maltese island," Philip teased.

Elizabeth giggled. "Well, not royal—how about that?"

Philip kissed her, the taste of the sea on his lips. "I don't think you could not be royal if you tried."

"I *could* try."

"But it's so much a part of your charm."

"And being a Grecian god is part of yours." She leaned in for another kiss.

"Being a sailor is also a huge part of my appeal."

Elizabeth laughed in delight, then splashed him before swimming after Susan, who was paddling as fast as her legs would take her after a bird that kept diving into the water.

Once they were back on the boat, Philip laid out a blanket on the deck, and they sat wrapped in their towels, dining on sandwiches and fruit, accompanied by glasses of champagne. Nearby Susan tucked into her own meal of chicken, carrots, and rice.

Elizabeth adjusted her hat, then leaned back on her elbows, enjoying the feel of the sun on her skin. The sun here was different, not just from the sun in London. Even when they visited the British coast, the sun was never this warm.

"I can already tell that returning to London is going to be hard. I don't want to leave," Elizabeth said.

"I wish you never had to." Philip tossed a grape into the air and caught it in his mouth, grinning as he pressed his teeth into the fruit and let the juice pop.

"You rascal," she said, wiping the droplets that had landed on her cheeks.

Philip tickled her ribs and she began to tickle him back. Their movement and laughter attracted Susan's attention and she rushed to them. Body wriggling with excitement, she clamped her teeth on Philip's hat.

"Susan, no," Elizabeth called, laughing.

"Let her go," Philip said. "If it makes her happy, it makes you happy, and that makes me happy."

He leaned in to kiss her, and Elizabeth forgot all about the hat.

That night, Philip took Elizabeth to the Phoenicia hotel, so they could dance. The band played one of her favorite songs, "People Will Say We're in Love," from *Oklahoma!*, and when Philip dipped her backward at the end, the crowd, which had gathered to watch them, cheered.

As November rolled into December, and Christmas loomed, Elizabeth couldn't help but stare at the blue sky and think about how dreary and freezing it must be in London. She was going to get to spend Christmas here, alone with Philip—no family to entertain, no dignitaries to make polite conversation with. Just the two of them, existing in this place. It was a beautiful thought, but often it was followed by a less pleasant one—sweet Charles would spend his second Christmas at Sandringham without his parents. When guilt over that darkened her mood, Elizabeth tried to remember he wouldn't remember this Christmas. He was still too young.

There were other dark moments as well. Reminders that this

Maltese bliss, however marvelous, was not to be forever. And that while she enjoyed it, her father continued to struggle with his health.

One morning after a call with her mother—a call in which the queen had refused to relay anything negative about the king's health, saying instead he was just the very image of perfection—Elizabeth had phoned someone who would be honest with her: Maggie.

Her sister's voice on the telephone was rough and sleep filled.

"What on earth has possessed you to call me so early?" Elizabeth could practically see Maggie's pout through the telephone line.

"It's nearly lunchtime."

Maggie groaned.

"Late night out with Charmin' Sharman?" Elizabeth asked. Sharman Douglas was the daughter of the American ambassador. She'd been in London a couple of years now and had a reputation for tearing up the town with her friends. Maggie often joined them and drew all sorts of criticism from her parents and the public for it.

"She won't be here much longer and then I don't know what I'll do. She's just the most fun." Maggie let out an exaggerated sigh and Elizabeth could hear her flop down on her bed or sofa.

"You've a million other friends."

"True."

"How is Papa?"

There was a silence on the other end that made Elizabeth nervous. "Tell me the truth, Mags. Mummy won't. You know how she is: when she wants to believe something, she insists it is true. I've just hung up with her and her description of Papa sounded like a commercial for an indestructible male specimen."

Maggie's laugh was tight. "Well, that would be false advertising. Though he's better than when you left."

"Good."

"Quite cranky, mind you. I think his legs still pain him. And he still hasn't quit smoking, even though Mummy begged him and despite the doctors constantly droning on about how it's only making his lung complaint worse."

"Oh dear."

"Perhaps when you come home, you can convince him to quit. He listens more to you than anyone else."

"He hasn't listened to me about this in the past. But I'll try again. How about you quit too?" Elizabeth urged.

Maggie had taken up a habit of smoking cigarettes in a long gold filter—a fashion she'd made extremely popular in London. She puffed excessively and nonstop.

"Oh, Lilibet, I'm young. Don't douse my fire."

Elizabeth sensed the tension and resentment in Maggie's voice. Pushing Maggie away was the last thing she wanted— they were sisters, allies. "I won't. I'll save all the dousing for Papa, a torrential downpour, though I'm sure he'll say a little rain never bothered him and keep right on smoking."

Maggie laughed. "He'll be so happy when you're home. So will I. I've missed you."

"I've missed you too," Elizabeth said. But even as the words came out, she stared out the window at the villa's stunning water view. "If only we could all transplant ourselves here."

"I've never known you to be a believer in fairy tales."

"I've never been to Malta before."

Maggie sighed. "Take me with you next time."

"Let's not talk about next time. I am still here, and I am not eager for it to end."

* * *

BUT END IT did, and shortly after the new year Elizabeth returned to England. She brought back more than a few gifts from Malta to share with her family as they gathered at Sandringham—she was pregnant again.

Staring at herself in the mirror before Bobo came to help her dress, Elizabeth ran her hand over the puckered scar left by the birth of her first child. Beneath it, she was harboring another heir. A product of love and abandon.

This pregnancy would be different. Less frightening and new. And this time she'd be able to spend most of it in Malta. Would that make her feel any better? she wondered as, overcome with sudden nausea, she rushed into the bathroom to be sick just as Bobo arrived . . .

"Oh dear," Bobo called from outside the bathroom door. "Was it the oysters?"

Elizabeth rinsed her mouth. "I don't think so," she called through the door. "I think I need to set up an appointment with the royal physician."

"Oh." Bobo's voice was full of knowing and a hint of pride. "I'd best get on the telephone, then."

"Thank you."

Later that afternoon the doctor confirmed what her body had already told her—she was indeed pregnant.

With Philip somewhere in the Red Sea, it was impossible for Elizabeth to share the good news. Her feet tapped impatiently against the floor until Susan lay on top of them, making her still. Elizabeth smiled and wiggled her toes, causing the corgi to lick her ankle.

"Elizabeth, I'd like you to come with me this afternoon to look through the boxes," her father said as they finished the last dregs of their tea at luncheon. It had been a light fare of whitefish and salad.

The red boxes—full of state papers and correspondence—always made her wary. She only ever looked at them when he'd been too ill to do so himself. Why was he asking her to join him now?

"Is something amiss?" she asked quietly.

"Not at all. You've just been . . . gone for weeks and I thought doing the boxes . . . together would give us some time to catch up."

Elizabeth smiled. Papa had some color back in his cheeks, and his disposition since she'd arrived back in England had been cheerful and animated.

"I would love to spend the afternoon with you."

Elizabeth followed her father into his office. The scent of cigarettes and leather permeated the room. He cleared his throat as he walked toward his desk, the seat creaking as he sat for the thousandth time where kings and queens before him had sat for generations to work on their bulletins and cor-respondence.

Elizabeth sat opposite him, and when he opened his ciga-rette case, she couldn't help saying, "Oh, Papa, do put that away."

"Not you too, Lilibet."

"It's not that—I mean it is that—but really the reason is . . ." She bit her lip. She hated the scent of cigarettes, especially when she was pregnant. "I'm going to have another baby, and the smell makes me ill."

"Another baby?" Papa broke into a grin and came around the desk to hug her, his affection returned as she hugged him tightly back. His grip was firm, but beneath the layers of his suit she could feel bones where before there had been muscle.

"Philip doesn't know. I've only just confirmed with the doctor today, so please don't say anything to anyone yet."

"Of course not. There will have to be an . . . official announcement . . . but that can wait."

Elizabeth sighed slightly, missing the less formal environment of Malta—a place where she'd been blessedly unburdened by "official announcements." Then she reminded herself that Malta didn't have Papa, and she loved him.

"You make me so proud," Papa said, taking his seat again. "You have grown into . . . a wonderful woman, Lilibet . . . And when I'm gone—"

"Let's not talk about that. I am counting on you being here for a long time." Even the thought of a world where her father didn't exist brought tears prickling to the corners of her eyes.

The king's face softened, and he reached across the desk to give her hand a little squeeze. "As heir, my dear, my death is . . . always something you must be prepared for . . . So let me just finish."

She nodded.

"When I'm gone—which will not be, God willing, for . . . a very long time," he said with a gentle smile that told her he was looking out for her feelings, "you will make a remarkable . . . queen. You've always had . . . a good head on your shoulders . . . A level head is what the . . . crown requires, but also intelligence . . . And you, my dear, have that in spades. You're decisive in your reasoning . . . and practical in your . . . assessments."

"I can only hope—a very long time from now—that the British people will feel the same about me as you do. But I will have huge shoes to fill. You've been an incredible leader, Papa. Thrust into a position you were never trained for, you led our people through the upheaval of your brother's abdication, a world war, and the ensuing economic fallout. They trust you, Papa. You are beloved. You are a man, and monarch, to admire."

Papa's eyes moistened. "If I am beloved . . . of the people of the United Kingdom, you are . . . beloved to me." His voice cracked as he spoke the words. "Never forget that. And believe that the people will . . . one day see in you . . . all that I do."

"I will never forget." Elizabeth fanned her face with her free hand and blinked, trying to hold back the dam itching to break. "Now, on with the correspondence before we ruin all the papers with our waterworks."

Papa laughed and slapped the stack. "Fair enough. I don't . . . suppose the House of Lords would . . . appreciate smeared responses."

"Are you sure you're all right, Papa? You would tell me?" She didn't want to come right out and accuse him of hiding the diagnosis he'd kept hidden from her before.

"I would. I'm sorry that . . . I didn't before. I am well, darling. Feeling haler . . . and heartier than I look, I assure you."

He was thinner than when he'd taken the throne. Grayer. More wrinkled. The toll being a monarch had taken on him was not kind, and the illnesses that plagued him left him looking frail enough to blow away with the wind. Yet there was a robustness in his countenance, a fierceness in his eyes, and so she decided to believe him.

They laughed together and then got to work. Elizabeth found herself wishing and hoping that there really were going to be so many more days and years like this ahead.

* * *

JUST AS SHE'D hoped, Elizabeth spent the rest of her pregnancy in Malta, relaxing on the *Eden*, with a sack of *galletti* every time she sailed because the crackers helped with the seasickness exacerbated by her pregnancy. She watched Philip play rousing games of polo with his uncle and his shipmates. The pair danced and attended an array of parties. Elizabeth shopped and had tea with other naval wives. And all the while Elizabeth watched her belly swell with a mixture of excitement and sadness—sadness because she knew at some point, she would have to leave her lovely and relatively normal life in Malta and return to England to give birth. No heir could be born out of the country, that was the law. Her life as a naval wife was coming to an end.

On the day of her departure, as the plane raced down the tarmac and then rose into the air, Elizabeth pressed her hands to the window and wondered if this would be her last vision of paradise. At very least it would be months before she could return, and even if she did, leaving behind two children would double the guilt. Perhaps guilt too crippling to allow her to return to the simpler existence she'd been enjoying.

After arriving in London she got to both celebrate her mother's fiftieth birthday party and welcome Princess Anne to the world. She was born at Clarence House on August 15.

"Isn't she so precious?" she said to Maggie when her sister came to visit.

Throughout her pregnancy Elizabeth had wondered if it would be possible to love another child as much as she loved Charles. But as soon as Anne was born, she knew that the answer was yes.

"She's absolutely an angel." Maggie stroked her niece's soft downy head. "And speaking of angels, you've another visitor."

Maggie snapped her fingers and Susan leaped onto the bed, standing timid as she looked at Elizabeth and the tiny infant swaddled in white.

"Oh, my darling Sus, will you look? Another little one for you to love."

Susan edged forward, her little nub tail still, her ears down. She looked nervous and panted.

"Come, it's all right." Elizabeth held out her hand, stroking Susan's head and ears. "Come see."

Susan sat gingerly beside her, looking down at Anne, who slept much more peacefully than her brother had.

"What do you think?"

"I think she thinks you should give her a treat," Maggie answered in Susan's place.

Elizabeth laughed and baby Anne's face screwed up as though she would cry but quickly softened again into peaceful sleep. "You're probably right."

Susan looked into Elizabeth's eyes, and the princess felt like her dog could see straight into her soul. Then the corgi dropped her head in a little, rather solemn nod, as if she were conveying her love, her admiration, her promises.

Elizabeth gave Susan's chin a scratch. "You're a good dog, Susan. Don't let anyone ever tell you otherwise."

A few weeks later, Philip, back in England for the birth of Anne, was promoted to lieutenant commander and given command of his own frigate, the HMS *Magpie*. Elizabeth couldn't have been prouder. He was moving up in his naval career. They had two beautiful children, a prince and princess. Her father's health seemed on the rise. Everyone was happy. And the world was still spinning.

After Anne's christening, Philip broke the news that he would have to return to Malta, and Elizabeth collapsed in her grief.

But it wasn't just her grief that made her feel awful. Anne's birth had been more difficult than Charles's, and she was taking a while to recover. She was exhausted, still in pain, and the doctor recommended she wait another month before returning to her royal duties.

Elizabeth blew her nose into a tissue, feeling utterly drained. She'd contracted a terrible cold on top of everything else. She knew she was lucky to have the help of nannies and staff, but she still felt utterly wilted. Anne was a voracious eater who fed nonstop and slept little. Charles was demanding much attention, throwing tantrums at having his place as the only child taken away. And Philip had gone back to Malta to assume his command of the HMS *Magpie*.

She closed her eyes, and the blue wallpaper of her private sitting room faded. In her mind she saw the blue waters of Malta—the ones in the bay where she and Philip had swum together on her first trip. All she wanted was another afternoon on the *Eden*, soaking up the sun, with none of the other irritations. Was it wrong to want to run away? To escape her own stubborn body?

A knock interrupted a sneeze, and she tried to sit up straight when she wanted to collapse. "Come in."

Mummy entered, with her face pinched in the stern way she had when she was about to issue orders.

"After Charles's second birthday celebration, you should return to Malta for Christmas with Philip." The queen stood there, hands folded neatly in front of her but shoulders and back so straight she might have been a commander in the army. "Alone," her mother added. "The children will come with us to Sandringham."

Elizabeth swallowed hard. She'd already known she'd never be allowed to take Charles and Anne with her, but another

Christmas without them sounded like misery. So she hesitated to agree to her mother's suggestion.

The queen must have sensed that. She softened her voice a bit and said, "Lilibet, you've just had a difficult birth and you have been mothering alone. You need this break."

Her mother walked to where Anne slept in a little bassinet with Susan curled beneath her. She took a long look at her granddaughter and then turned back to Elizabeth. "I know you're too young to remember, but when you and your sister were Charles's and Anne's age, I had your father to help me—at very least to hold my hand. Being a parent is a difficult job and it's harder when you're alone. You need to take some time to recover."

"I've been recovering for nearly three months."

Queen Elizabeth squared her shoulders. "No, you haven't. Not really. In any event, this is not a suggestion, Lilibet. I've already begun planning."

"An order? From the queen?" she couldn't help but tease, though her tone suggested a bit of a bite to it. "I do hope you don't send me to the gallows."

"I might," her mother teased back, "if you decide to fight me on this."

"I will consider your proposal."

"Good. And perhaps after Christmas, your sister can join you in Malta."

Elizabeth's heart soared. She and Maggie had often talked about how much fun it would be to spend time in Malta together. They'd spent much of their youth together, and the last few years they'd been so far apart. "I would very much like that."

"It's settled, then. We'll celebrate Charles's birthday next week and then you will get on a plane."

Elizabeth looked at baby Anne again, just shy of three months old. "I want to." Elizabeth bit her lip. "But I don't know if I can."

"You can," her mother said. "You must. You can't take the children, but you should be with your husband."

Elizabeth rose to stand on legs that didn't feel nearly as strong as they always had, and knew her mother was right, even as she went to the cradle and gazed down at Anne, her pink, chubby cheeks the perfect place to kiss.

"I'll have to wean her."

"She'll survive, Lilibet. It is an unfortunate fact but sometimes a princess must sacrifice the thing she desires for the greater good."

It seemed an odd thing to say about an infant. She wrinkled her nose at her mother. "But she's just a baby." Elizabeth shook her head sadly.

"I'm talking about you, darling. In some instances, you sacrifice your time with your husband to be with your children; in others, sacrifice your time with your children to be with your husband. And there are occasions when you will be forced to sacrifice things that cannot even be predicted to do what is required as an heir to the throne. There are no easy choices for the heads that wear the crown. Your father is proof of that. There are only checks and balances and an attempt to keep the scales even as best one can."

Elizabeth nodded, knowing she was right. And, after the door had fallen shut behind the queen, she sat down next to the bassinet with one arm around Susan and cried, for the very same reason.

·ലൈം·

CHAPTER TWENTY-FOUR

SUSAN

The king smells funny.

There's a dark scent that wafts from his mouth and nose and makes me uneasy.

When I'm close to him, I smell it on his skin, oozing from his pores. Something is inside him that shouldn't be. It makes me sneeze, and my heart speeds up. If I could dig inside his skin, I would take it all out and bury it in the yard.

This is the man who found me. The one who gave me to Lilibet. Something is wrong with him. And everyone around him seems on edge. They look at him funny, exaggerating the tones of their voices, walking on eggshells, like if they aren't careful, he, rather than they, might fall and crack. Are they worried he might just split open and spill out the bad stuff? I am.

I'm nervous around him. Weaving about his legs and looking up at him, I want to know what the darkness is. It doesn't show on the outside, unless he coughs up the bright red spray that he tries to conceal whenever it comes from his mouth. The smell is . . . scary.

There's a gray tinge to his face. The once ruddy cheeks that pinkened further with the wind when we went for walks only turn slightly less gray when we are outside. Unless we are going uphill, then they seem to turn white, as does the outline of his lips. I don't stray too far from him when we are outside. Afraid that if I do, he'll disappear.

His breathing is labored.

Today Lilibet is particularly on edge. We're supposed to pack up and head back to Malta. I love it there, the sea salt air, the endless birds to chase, all the fascinating smells. My princess is happiest there. Always smiling. The weight of the world lifted from her shoulders.

Every other time we've left the palace for our return to Malta, she is excited. She smiles broadly as she wishes everyone well, and we run out to the car that will take us on our way to board the giant metal bus that shoots up into the sky. Philip is happiest too. When we all go up into the air together, he takes Lilibet's hand. I think he is happy because in Malta, he doesn't have to compete for her attention—at least not with anyone other than me.

In England, he has Maggie, the king, the queen, the servants, the world to contend with. But in Malta, they call themselves "us two" and it seems perfect.

"I'm not sure we should go," Lilibet whispers to Philip as they walk to the breakfast room at Buckingham Palace. He's only just come home to escort Lilibet back to Malta, so she doesn't have to travel alone.

I've been allowed to join them, while poor Sugar and Honey had to go with Hanna and Biscuit to the corgi room for their breakfast. Crackers is more often than not at his age with the queen. My invitation to breakfast makes me feel that once again I am Lilibet's favorite, which I consider my rightful place.

I rush ahead to check the dining room for intruders, since it's my job to protect the princess. I know this. The king has told me often. And I take my job extremely seriously.

The footmen move out of my way as I weave around them, lifting their feet and cursing under their breath as they lose their balance in surprise. A rogue chair leg leaps out at me, and I clamp my teeth on it to make sure it's not going to get my princess, but it remains steady and dead as I shake it.

Good.

Lilibet and Philip are the first of the family to arrive for breakfast. The children are with their nanny. Maggie is next, rushing in with her sunny disposition always now in a cloud of stinky smoke. I greet her as happily as she greets me, though, because I love her.

Next come the king and the queen.

He smells worse today. I try hard not to recoil. The queen fidgets more than she normally does. She is worried—very worried. That puts me on edge. Have I missed a threat? Frantically I check each window. Nothing other than the guards with their furry black hats. I wonder, do they wear those hats to ward off any other dogs or cats? I wonder too who had to die to make those hats.

"Good morning, darling." The king's voice is scratchy and draws my attention back to my family. Even from here I can smell the darkness on his breath, and it makes me pant.

"How are you this morning?" Lilibet asks, her keen eyes, which usually miss nothing, focused on her father.

"Well." He smiles, though it's tight and his lips are particularly white, as are his gums. "I've not felt this well in so long."

"That's good to hear." I sense the beat of Lilibet's heart receding slightly. She believes his easy lie, though I can hear his heart speeding up as he relays it. If only humans could sense each other's pulses as I can sense them.

"Come, darling." Philip pulls out a chair for his wife before a footman can, and when Lilibet sits, I lie at her feet, waiting for my breakfast to be served.

"So you return today to Malta," the king says.

"I'm not sure we should," Lilibet says.

I notice Philip's legs stiffen beneath the table. The only reason he came back was to retrieve us.

"Perhaps we should stay here a little longer?" Lilibet's voice is gentle and questioning. She is an adult woman, but with her father some childlike deference always creeps back.

"Nonsense." The king taps a foot, making me want to lie on top of his shoes, to offer him some comfort.

The queen's legs beneath the table are pressed firmly together, as if they would meld into one. Tense, she is so tense. I inch closer to the king where he sits at the head of the table. The closer I get, the more terrible the smell. Can the others sense it? The sickness that grows within him. Can they smell the rotting?

"Philip has his duties to attend to, and you've yours," the king says.

"Quite right," the queen replies. "Winter in Malta is beautiful."

"And hot," Lilibet says, but there is a tinge of wistfulness in her answer.

The king laughs, which only makes him start to cough, his body heaving against the table and making the dishes clatter. I hop to my feet, wanting to help, but there is nothing I can do beyond offering comfort.

As the queen jumps to pound on his back, Lilibet hands him a glass of water. The footmen exchange hidden glances.

I bark, and bark again. I wish they could understand what I'm saying. He's sick. He's got something inside him that grows bigger by the day. Latching on to the parts of him that make him live—and leaking out whenever he breathes.

"I'm fine," he wheezes, slamming his hand on the table. "Good God, woman, stop pounding on me," he shouts.

The queen backs away, and I can sense her hurt at his outburst. Philip shifts awkwardly on his feet.

"Papa," Lilibet hedges. "Drink this."

The king growls in a way that makes me back up, but he takes the glass of water and drinks. I stand next to Lilibet, leaning a little against her leg so she feels my strength.

"Go to Malta," he orders.

And then the scents of breakfast distract everyone from what's just happened, including me, because I really do like a bit of sautéed rabbit and cabbage.

◦⦁◦

CHAPTER TWENTY-FIVE

*ℋ*ANNA

I tied my scarf around my head as Susan pranced at the
door with Sugar, Honey, and Biscuit close behind her. As my
hand touched the brass knob, hurried footsteps approached.
I turned to see Princess Elizabeth speeding toward me. Her
hands were twisting unconsciously in front of her. I dipped into
a curtsy.

"Might I join you?"

I found it funny that a royal princess would ask me, her servant, if she could join me while I walked her dogs.

"It would be a pleasure to have you, ma'am," I said, hoping it
was the right reply. It was certainly a sincere one. Glancing at
her hands and the pinch between her brows, I wanted to ask if
she was all right, what was worrying her. But that would have
been inappropriate—very.

"I need to get out." Elizabeth bent down, cooing at her "girls,"
as she called them.

Susan's three puppies had grown leaps and bounds and were
now the same size as their mother. I'd used the tricks learned
from my father's training of hunting dogs to help me school
them. So they were mostly well-behaved unless they were jealous over a stick, a treat, or some attention. They remained with

the princess most of the time, Honey with the queen, and Biscuit with us, unless we were deployed to one of the many estates owned by the royal family, such as Sandringham where we were now.

Elizabeth marched out into the yard with vigor. Her health since giving birth to Princess Anne was at last renewed. The dogs—used to listening to the princess when she was around—ignored me completely, except my own girl, Biscuit.

My sweet Biscuit glanced up at me, a question in her eyes, and I could see she was confused, trying to decide if she should follow Elizabeth or me. To follow me would mean not following the pack. And yet not following me would mean betraying the one who fed her. I, quite frankly, didn't mind either way.

I chuckled under my breath, and waved her off, watching her happily trot to stay in line with Susan and the other corgis.

"How are things?" Elizabeth's question took me a bit by surprise. Princesses didn't normally ask such things of their servants, and in so casual a manner. It was rather alarming.

We had a history of chatting—but we talked about dogs: breeding, food, the care of their coats. Outside those parameters we didn't have casual conversations—or at least we hadn't since the days when we'd both been Girl Guides and the other children had accused me of being a toady for helping the princesses.

I cleared my throat, glancing toward Elizabeth, who looked at me expectantly. "Going well. And you, Your Highness? The little princess appears to be thriving and is so sweet."

Elizabeth smiled, looking nostalgic almost as we marched across the grass on a familiar path.

"She is. I'm so happy to have had two healthy, well-mannered babies. Her majesty says they remind her of me. I thought for certain at least one of them would have Philip's or Maggie's disposition."

"They may prove you right yet," I teased before I realized what I'd said, clamping my mouth closed and holding my breath. This is why we didn't speak casually, because it was easy to fall back into friendly terms. I had to remember that.

But Elizabeth just laughed. "Very true."

We walked in companionable silence for a few more moments before the princess cleared her throat. I had a feeling she wanted to say something or ask me a question but that she was hedging, and I'd never known her to be one to hesitate. She always seemed to know what to do, how to say the right thing, stand the right way, project the image of a royal while making people like her—just like her father.

I didn't want to push—that wouldn't be appropriate. But I cared about this woman . . . my future queen, and I did want to support her if I could. Rather than looking at her and perhaps making her nervous I concentrated on my feet, putting one in front of the other, as the entire conversation made me feel a little off-balance. I kept quiet so she could fill the space if she wanted to.

"I worry about my father," she said at last, an edge to her voice that I'd never heard before.

"I am sorry to hear that you are concerned."

"You . . . haven't heard anything? You know, belowstairs," she asked.

"Nothing," I said honestly. I wondered if she was solely trying to find out if there had been any rumors regarding the king's health. I looked up at the sky for a moment; maybe Elizabeth was actually worried that his majesty's health was worse than she was being told. That was a terrible and sobering thought.

"You'll tell me if you do hear anything, won't you, Hanna?" Elizabeth stopped walking, forcing me to stop and meet her eyes.

"Of course, ma'am."

"Thank you." She broke eye contact, picking up a stick, stripping off its leaves, and then throwing it. The corgis dashed away, barking. Reaching the stick, they grabbed its various parts, tugging, until it snapped in half. "Oh dear, we'd best find another before a brawl starts."

She laughed and I joined in as we looked for three more sticks. And when each dog was holding her own prize we continued on our walk, our conversation focused entirely on the mundane. But something had changed. That moment of candor on Elizabeth's part, her asking me to keep an ear out for discussion of the king's health, had altered things. Now as we walked it almost felt like she was a friend. Not that I would have dared say that aloud.

There were class distinctions to be respected—having grown up on a royal estate, I knew that beyond those were the very strict lines between royals and staff. I mean, for heaven's sake, there was even a hierarchy within the world of servants— one the butlers never hesitated to make certain we remembered. And I certainly wasn't going to take after the traitorous Crawfie, who'd sold her memoir to make a few pounds. I was shocked, given it had been Crawfie who admonished us as children not to say anything to anyone about the time we spent with the princesses as Girl Guides. And if I was shocked, the princess must have felt entirely betrayed.

"Same time tomorrow?" Elizabeth asked, expectation in her eyes and drawing me back to the present.

"I'd be honored, ma'am."

Elizabeth smiled. "I'll take these three with me, shall I? Please have Chef Smythe send up their bowls."

I nodded, attaching a leash to Biscuit so she'd return with me. She fussed a bit at seeing the rest of her family off, but as soon as we started on our way toward the kitchen she perked up.

Chef Smythe smiled at the sight of her. He had a special attachment to Biscuit and always gave her an extra treat.

After passing Elizabeth's message to the chef, I took Biscuit's portion along with me and retreated to my room, where I found Forrest brushing his teeth at the basin. As he stood in only his underwear and socks, I couldn't help staring at the exposed skin of his muscular arms and the knot of muscle above his knees. My husband was beautifully made. Enough that it made me sigh.

Forrest gave me a knowing look, one that promised he'd disrobe all the way if only I asked.

"Getting a late start today?" I glanced at my watch, pretending that I didn't want him to do just that. Normally he was out the door by now, eager to get to his shift with the horses earlier than expected.

He glanced at me, foam around his mouth, and winked. "Someone kept me up later than I'm used to."

I blushed, recalling the very . . . energetic night we'd had.

Setting down Biscuit's food bowl, I picked up a hand towel and passed it to him so he could wipe the water from his face.

Forrest finished that task, then tugged me into his arms for a kiss. "How did I get so lucky?" he asked, eyes gazing into mine.

"I'm honestly not sure. I suppose me giving you a second chance helped?" I raised a teasing brow and grinned.

"And me not being a little prig too."

I laughed. "That is probably the biggest thing that's changed."

Forrest chuckled, and Biscuit started to bark at us. "Someone is jealous."

"I fear her feelings were hurt when the princess whisked her mother and sisters away to feed them breakfast herself. Poor Biscuit is in desperate need of attention to assuage her ego."

"Ah." He bent down and tugged her up against him. Biscuit licked his face as though he still needed a cleaning.

"Can I ask you something?" I pursed my lips, trying to figure out exactly what to say that wouldn't come across as odd.

"Of course. What is it?"

I busied myself putting his toothpaste cap back on and wiping away the droplets of water from the sink. "Have you heard any rumors about the king's health?"

Forrest straightened, leaving Biscuit behind on the floor, and his brow wrinkled. "Actually, I heard something yesterday."

My eyes widened. This was not what I'd expected. I'd expected, or maybe hoped, the princess was worried for nothing and there'd be nothing to discover. "What?" I asked softly. "What did you hear?"

"It was when they came back from hunting. I was returning the horses to the stables. The king had already headed into the house but a few of the other hunters remained. I heard them whispering about him coughing up blood. They stopped when they saw me."

"Blood?" I blanched, feeling my own blood drain from my face.

Forrest nodded. "They said when he coughed and wiped his mouth, they saw red on his handkerchief."

I frowned, picturing the king wiping his mouth as I had seen him do dozens of times. I'd never seen blood, though I tried not to stare when he was doing that. It was entirely possible I missed it. "Maybe they saw wrong?" I pushed back largely out of fear.

Forrest shrugged. "Could've." He rubbed my shoulder. "Why do you ask?"

"Something Princess Elizabeth said on our walk." I hung up Forrest's towel on the small hook beside the sink, then leaned against the cool porcelain.

"Your walk?" Forrest raised a brow.

I nodded. "She joined the dogs and me for our walk. Talked to me like we were two ordinary people."

Forrest looked me up and down. "You are definitely not an ordinary person."

I laughed, waving away his flirtation. "Seriously, Forrest, maybe I should have said like she was a regular human."

Forrest ran a comb through his hair. "She was a human last time I saw her."

"Yes, but a royal. And she treated me as an equal . . . that's the word I should have used in the first place."

"I love to tease you. But I'm pretty sure it all works the same on her insides as it does ours."

I poked his ribs through his white undershirt. "You could get sacked for saying that."

"Could I?"

"I don't know, but I wouldn't be surprised."

Forrest gave a low whistle. "All right, so she talked to you on your walk. About his majesty?"

"Yes, and she asked if I'd heard anything about the king's health. I haven't—not since the whole debacle with the blood clot in his leg."

"I wonder if they could be related?" Forrest put his chin in his hand, pondering.

"I have no idea. I know dogs. I know stag. I know foxes. I've not yet had any of them treated for blood clots."

"Nor have I with horses."

I let out an exaggerated sigh, flapping my hands up and then down. "We're of no use diagnosing a king."

"None at all." Forrest moved to our small wardrobe, pulling out his freshly pressed uniform. He put on his shirt, buttoning from the top down.

"If you hear anything else, you will tell me, won't you? Princess Elizabeth's asked me to keep an ear out." I handed him his trousers, disappointed that I was helping him to dress when I really wanted us both to climb back beneath the covers.

"Is she trying to squash rumors?"

I shrugged. "I had that thought. But then"—I lowered my voice even though we were alone—"I wondered, does the princess fear she's being kept in the dark?"

Forrest mulled that over a moment as he tucked in his shirt and snapped his suspenders into place. "I wouldn't be surprised if she was. Parents protect their children. And beyond that everything royal tends to be very hush-hush."

I nodded. "Seems like the only royal thing that nobody tries to keep private is the birthing of heirs. And that's something, if you ask me, that ought to be private. Thank heavens King George put a stop to the archaic tradition of the government officials watching the births before Elizabeth had Charles or Anne."

"Sounds ghastly."

"I know I wouldn't stand for it."

Forrest sat on the edge of their bed, putting on his boots. "I'd love to keep chatting, Mrs. Darling, but I'm expected at the stables. But I will keep a sharp eye and ear out."

"Thank you. Until tonight, then." I smoothed a hand over his shoulder, the wool of his jacket soft but itchy beneath my palm.

He grinned. "A sweet promise."

By the time he'd left, Biscuit had finished her breakfast and, uncertain of whether Susan, Sugar, and Honey had finished theirs, I leashed Biscuit and headed in the direction of the princess's suite to take them back outside to conduct their business once more.

Philip passed me on the way, a genuine smile of greeting on his noble face. "Good morning, Mrs. Darling."

"Your Highness, a lovely morning."

His gaze dropped to Biscuit. "Why do you keep the dog on a leash?"

The question seemed obvious, given the rest of the royal corgis had a run of the household. "To keep her in her place."

The prince looked puzzled a moment. "Ah, well, I wonder if we should do the same with the others."

"If you wish it, Your Highness."

"Oh, no." He chuckled. "It is never if I wish it. Only my darling wife." At that he kept on going down the hall, leaving me to try and hide my smile.

CHAPTER TWENTY-SIX

ℰLIZABETH

Dear Lilibet,

This summer at Balmoral has been dismal, and I do wish I was back with you in Malta, the sun beating down on us as the sea sprayed up over the rails of the Eden. *It was glorious and makes me long for sunnier times. It is bleak here. Not only in weather, but . . . I do hate to write this in a letter, but I haven't been able to get in touch with you otherwise.*

It's Papa. His health seems to be taking a turn for the worse. We thought he was getting better after that bout of influenza—and I still blame the treachery of Uncle David and Crawfie for his illness. He was so stressed to find out that coincidentally they had both published books about their times with royals. And Crawfie after Mummy told her not to write it, that it went against confidentiality! Scandalous!

Every time I watch Papa have to pause to catch his breath after walking only a few steps, his cough incessant, I think of the undue torment those two put him under.

Mummy has tried to get him to call the doctors so many times, but he simply refuses. Even Peter Townsend has tried his hand at convincing him. Oh, Lil, I'm so afraid.

Your loving sister,
Maggie

September 23, 1951

Elizabeth paced the halls of Buckingham Palace, Susan parading beside her. They'd gotten the news of her father's operation that morning when they'd been at Clarence House and had come over swiftly.

Just a short time ago they'd gone to Lambeth Palace, the residence of the Archbishop of Canterbury, who had conducted a service for them as the entire country lifted prayers for the king's health and well-being.

None of them knew exactly what was happening, or where, but it had been said that he was undergoing surgery for a lung complaint. When Elizabeth had returned from Malta after receiving her sister's letter, she came to find her father in a worse state than when she'd left him in June after conducting the trooping of the color for him.

Behind the closed doors of the Buhl Room—where Elizabeth had given birth to Prince Charles—the sun shone through stained glass windows, and the lit chandeliers were a stark contrast to the light of the medical lamps that hovered over her father's unconscious form since the entire chamber had been converted into an operating room. It had been so strange to see the gurney where her father would be put to sleep, his body opened up to the elements to remove the abnormalities that lay within. Strange to think that behind those wooden doors, surgeons had their hands inside his chest cavity.

The images her thoughts provoked made her feel light-headed and she had to sit down, putting her head between her knees before she fainted or threw up.

Somewhere in the castle, her children were laughing and playing together. Little Anne, one year old and toddling about while a nearly three-year-old Charles ran ahead of her, encouraging her unsteady steps.

Susan whimpered at her feet, and Elizabeth looked down to see the concern in her longtime companion's eyes. For weeks now, Susan had been fretting over the king, whimpering when she went near him, sniffing him as though he had meat in his pockets. Was it strange to think that maybe Susan knew something was wrong before the doctors did?

Elizabeth stroked a hand over her corgi's head, and then heard the assured, steady steps of Philip as he approached.

"Have you heard anything?" Elizabeth studied his face, which he kept noticeably blank.

He shook his head, placed his hand on her shoulder, and gave a little squeeze. "Could be hours more, darling, but he's in excellent hands."

Hours later as they all huddled in the drawing room, Elizabeth's eyes were wide, her head on Philip's shoulder. Maggie had curled up in a chair and was dozing, and Mummy was staring blankly into the flames lit in the hearth.

The doctors came, their faces somber. Elizabeth looked for signs of blood, what one would expect from surgery, but they'd cleaned up before presenting themselves to the queen and heir to the throne.

"How is he?" Mummy asked, leaping from her place on the

sofa. All of them followed, coming to stand in a line before the doctors, willing them to give them good news as they tried to hide their trembling.

"He is recovering. We found structural abnormalities in his left lung—tumors. More than we thought originally. We weren't able to save the lung and had to remove it. He should recover, though he will likely not be as active as he once was. He can survive with only one lung."

One lung. Elizabeth drew in a breath to her two healthy lungs and imagined what it would be like if she could only draw in half as much air. Tears pricked her eyes, but a princess could not cry, at least not in front of her people. Still, her heart ached to know her father would be limited. And yet, she was extremely grateful the operation had been a success and her father was going to live.

"How long for his recovery?" The queen's voice was dull and flat, but it didn't fool Elizabeth. She knew that deep down her mother was just trying to hold it together.

"That depends on him." The doctor in charge gave a know-ing smile. "He is often thwarting our advice."

"I'll make sure he doesn't this time," Mummy said.

"I think it may help him recover, if perhaps he doesn't real-ize it was cancer we found, ma'am," the doctor said, wincing even as he uttered the words that would mean lying to the king. "Before he went under, he said if it was cancer we found to let it rest and let him go. Of course, we are duty bound to remove tumors. We've an oath to uphold."

"Of course." Mummy's face paled and she wouldn't look at Elizabeth, who stared at her, incredulous.

Papa needed to know how dire the situation was, or he'd not take it seriously. How could the doctor even suggest it, and her mother agree? Even all the years the king had been coughing up blood had not made him stop smoking. What would be the reason to cease if they simply said he was all better? If he were to know and understand that cancer filled his lung, that he had another chance, perhaps he'd do something about it.

Elizabeth glanced at Philip, who was frowning equally, and she was glad to know she wasn't the only one doubtful of this conversation.

But there was no argument from her mother, and when her father woke, he was told he was well on his way to recovery and would be fine.

* * *

TWO WEEKS LATER, Elizabeth was reluctantly climbing the stairs to a plane for a seventeen-hour flight to Canada with Philip—a trip they were supposed to have taken before her father's surgery. While the idea of traveling while her father was still recovering made her nervous, Elizabeth was also captivated by the chance to see another part of the world. She balanced daily on the edge, with her nerves on the left and her desire to go on the right.

Though she'd wanted to take Susan with her, it was impossible. Elizabeth was going to be so busy with all the engagements it really wouldn't have been fair to make Susan suffer a long trip just for her own comfort. And so she left her companion at home with strict instructions to take care of the king—and with her father promising to make sure Susan got any cuddles she needed.

"I don't think we should go," Elizabeth said to Philip as they took their seats, nerves winning out.

Elizabeth moved to stand, and Philip put a reassuring hand on her arm. "Your father said he was feeling much better. And the doctors have assured us that he'll make a good recovery if he follows their advice."

Elizabeth nodded, though she still didn't feel right about it. Papa wasn't necessarily following their advice to the letter, and he had a bad reputation for thwarting it altogether. To top that off, she was especially weary since they'd made her take a sealed envelope in her bag that was a draft of the Accession Declaration should her father take a turn for the worse while she was overseas. It almost felt like tempting fate to bring it on board this airplane.

Seventeen hours later, her hands sore from wringing them so much, they landed to a massive crush of people and flashing cameras as photographers jostled for the perfect position.

Elizabeth waved and smiled, though it felt forced. She shook hands with countless people and by the time they reached their accommodations her face hurt. She flopped onto the massive bed with the thick down coverlet, and Philip flopped beside her.

"That was an enormous crowd." Elizabeth rolled to the side.

"And all for you." Philip brushed a few strands of hair from her forehead.

"I don't know if I'll ever get used to so many people wanting to see me, touch me." She stared at her hands, having already washed them several times in the hopes of avoiding anyone's illnesses. The last thing she needed was to compromise her father's health when she returned home.

"I don't think I will either, but I do enjoy watching them fawn over my beautiful wife."

Elizabeth grinned, feeling beautiful simply by the way he looked at her. "I suppose I should be used to it by now. But it makes me so nervous, and it's also confusing. Why should they care about me?"

Philip shrugged. "You're a princess."

"So?" Being a princess her whole life she'd never really thought about what it would be like to meet one.

Philip laughed. "Well, here at least, you're their princess and they've never met you. There is something of a fascination in the unknown."

"That I can understand." She rolled onto her back, staring up at the plain white ceiling. "Do you think I've disappointed them?"

"How could you?"

"Perhaps I'm not clever enough, or animated enough? I do try to maintain dignity, but I've heard people complain before that it makes me seem aloof or uninterested."

"Everyone who knows you knows you're neither of those things. And I think there's nothing wrong with maintaining your dignity. You are a royal, after all. We must be dignified."

Elizabeth rolled her head to the side and smiled at her husband. "Philip, I do love you. You always know how to make me feel better."

He chuckled and gave her ribs a tiny tickle. "It is my royal duty to make sure you are always pleased."

Elizabeth laughed and gave him what she hoped was a bit of a naughty grin. "Is it?"

He nodded, his own lips curling with understanding.

"Then I think you should continue with this mission, sir."

"Starting now, ma'am?"

"Right now."

* * *

"MAMA!" CHARLES CALLED as he burst from the doors of Buckingham Palace with Anne toddling and babbling behind him.

Elizabeth knelt down and caught her children in her arms. She'd missed them the month they were in North America and was equally delighted that they hadn't seemed to have forgotten her. It was a constant worry with them being cared for by nannies that they might one day not remember she was their mother.

Susan was right on their heels, as were Sugar and Honey with Hanna coming along right after them. Susan's tiny pink tongue flopped out of the front of her mouth with each bound.

"My apologies, ma'am," Hanna said, awkwardly trying to curtsy and gather the dogs, who were leaping over Elizabeth and the children, yipping and licking.

"What a greeting I've returned to." Elizabeth chuckled as she patted and stroked the dogs one after another.

But the best greeting of all was once she was inside and saw her father walking toward her. His gait was slow, but his coloring much improved and he'd even gained a little weight.

Over tea, he spoke of wanting to go hunting and that his doctors had approved the activity as long as he used a light gun and didn't exert himself.

"I would go with you." Some of the best times they'd had together as father and daughter had been while alone on the moors, hunting a stag or shooting pigeons. Out there, their royal duties melted away, and they could be themselves, settled into nature and the thrill of the hunt. "Perhaps we can give it a try before Philip and I return to Malta."

"I could use a good hunt before I return," Philip added.

And so it was decided: they would all zip up to Sandringham for a hunt and stay on through the Christmas holiday before she and Philip returned to Malta.

The king talked quite animatedly about an upcoming world

tour he was planning for March the following year. Plans were being set into place to travel to South Africa, Australia, and New Zealand. Maggie was excited to be able to join him on the journey as she complained she never got to go anywhere, and especially since she'd get to spend more time with him. Elizabeth too wished she could go, but she had other duties that required her to remain behind in her father's absence, which would also mean in the spring that Philip would be in Malta and she in London. The idea of being separated from her husband again was never a pleasant one.

She hated the time they were apart. The rumors that inevitably swelled, but mostly the loneliness of not having her confidant with her. Maggie was a good counterpart, but if she was going to be gone with their parents, then Elizabeth would be even lonelier at Buckingham Palace.

At least she'd have the children, Susan, her puppies, and Hanna.

* * *

Sandringham
December 1951

Elizabeth's knuckles rapping on her father's door echoed oddly in the hallway, or perhaps it was only in her head. The sound seemed to reverberate as though the great house were already empty of everyone.

"Come in," her father called.

Elizabeth entered the room, which smelled faintly of cigarettes and her father's cologne.

The king sat behind his desk, the red box open, and he grinned as she entered. Elizabeth never tired of the delight in her father's eyes when he saw her, as if she were the most favorite part of his day.

"You wanted to see me?" She edged forward, taking in every line and angle of his face, searching for clues and answers that weren't easily available.

"Of course I did. I would . . . see you every day for . . . the rest of my life . . . if I could." Though his stutter had improved slightly over the years, he was now hampered with having to draw in more air to speak.

"Oh, Papa." Elizabeth laughed, taking the seat opposite him and swiping underneath her skirt so it wouldn't wrinkle. "I would see you too." She smiled at him, noting the way his eyes misted ever so slightly.

"I wanted to . . . discuss something . . . with you."

Elizabeth nodded, trying to breathe despite her lungs' sudden inability to do that very thing, as if her own body were emulating the difficulty he was having at that very moment. It made her heart ache.

"As you know . . . Group Captain Townsend has . . . gone to South . . . Africa on a . . . scouting mission for . . . my impending . . . travel there."

Elizabeth had heard nothing *but* that since Townsend's departure—Maggie seemed to have quite an affinity for the man who'd become her chaperone more often than not at nightclubs and dinners and dances. Elizabeth had the sneaking suspicion that her sister might have feelings for Townsend.

Wholly inappropriate, of course. He was nearly twice her age and had a wife and children to boot. But nobody seemed to think a crush was a matter to worry over, and so Elizabeth let Maggie vent day in and day out about missing her sparring partner.

"Yes, of course. I'm sure you're very excited to see what he's got to say."

Her father glanced out the window, staring for a while at the white landscape, the cloudy skies that threatened to drop more snow.

It was the first time Elizabeth, and Philip too, had been home for Christmas for some time, though she knew Philip was itching to get back to his command after having been gone for so long.

They'd all listened outside the door after breakfast as her father recorded his Christmas message that would go live to-morrow morning as everyone woke for the holiday.

Every word, every completed sentence had been exhausting even to listen to. Her father struggled to pull in his breath, and the anxiety of it made his stutter rear its ugly head. All the same, when he'd finished, she felt proud of him for having done it, and relieved too that he'd gotten through it without quitting or growing angry.

"Despite my feeling . . . better than I was . . . when you returned . . . from North America"—he drew in a deep breath that sounded more like a wheeze, and Elizabeth held back her wince—"I think it best . . . if you and Philip—"

"Papa, no." Elizabeth rarely, if ever, interrupted her father, but she knew where this was going, and she had to. She just had to.

At that moment Philip knocked, then entered the room.

"There you are," her father said, as if he'd been expecting Philip, which Elizabeth hadn't been aware of.

Philip nodded stoically, taking in the stricken look on her face. He came forward with his assured step and placed his

hand on her shoulder. The weight of it was a comforting anchor, without which she might have simply floated away.

"Sir," Philip said to her father. "You look well."

Her father grinned, and she knew the compliment landed
where it needed to, even if it was a lie.

"Papa has just made the most ludicrous suggestion. He
thinks we should go to Africa in his place."

"What?" Philip looked from Elizabeth to her father, and she
could see every thought running through his mind.

He'd only just come back from a trip abroad and was needed
at his post in Malta. It was hard to command a ship if you
weren't on board, or even in the vicinity. He'd lamented that
often when he'd gone with her to Canada. To delay his return
again would mean a great sacrifice to his career, which was not
something that either of them had anticipated. Or wanted. Or
were ready for.

"I think it best," her father said, not expanding on his health
or any other reason why he might suggest it, but Elizabeth knew.
If he couldn't make it through a simple Christmas speech, or
even a private conversation, then how was he going to travel
across the world and make speech after speech?

The very idea seemed impossible and devastating all at once.
The fantasy that they'd all been living in, where her father was
recovering and on his way back to health, was rapidly vanishing.

"Why don't you just postpone the trip, Papa? Everyone will
understand. You've only just had surgery a few months ago.
They wouldn't expect you to do so much so soon."

The king opened his mouth to respond and then shut it
again, his vision going to where his hands rested on the desk
over the correspondence he'd taken from the red box.

"I'm afraid . . ." He drew in a breath, and in that moment,

she could indeed see all of his fears. "I'm afraid it can't wait . . . and I find in my current . . . situation . . . that I can't postpone the trip."

Elizabeth's stomach plummeted. What wasn't he telling her? "Papa, are you well? Do you think the . . . abnormalities are coming back?"

He grinned at her, though it didn't quite reach his eyes. The brave face he was trying to put on for her held a crack in the middle. "I am perfectly . . . well, darling. I'm just taking . . . longer to heal . . . than I'd like."

The two of them stared at each other for several beats, Elizabeth trying to decode her father's words at the same time she tried to figure out just how she was going to disappoint her husband again. While her father seemed like he was trying to hold back a confession she feared hearing.

"What about Maggie? Can she come with us, then? And the children?" Elizabeth said at the same time Philip said, "So we're going?"

Taking in the crush of disappointment all over Philip's features flayed Elizabeth open wide. My goodness, but she hated that her duty superseded his, and that with her duty came his setbacks.

"I think it best . . . Maggie stay behind . . . along with your children," the king was saying, his tone indicating it wasn't up for discussion. Then he looked at Philip. Really looked at him, their eyes connected, her father's mouth a grim line of a man who was about to convey dismal, life-altering news. "And I'm afraid you'll . . . have to give up . . . your post in Malta . . . for the time being, Philip."

But the way he said it, the serious countenance of his stare at Philip, conveyed more than that; it said possibly permanently.

A block of something heavy and foreboding settled in her belly, and Elizabeth was fairly certain that nothing was ever going to be the same again. That when she stood up and walked out of this room, she was going to be crossing a different threshold and life would never return to the way it had been.

"I think Philip and I will need to discuss this," Elizabeth said, wanting Philip to feel as though he might have some say, even though from the look and sound of things, the decision had already been made.

"Of course." The king pushed to stand from his chair with some difficulty. "One other thing. You will be . . . going in January, not March."

"So soon?" Philip's tone was full of shock and distress. "I'd hoped to prepare my men for my departure."

"I'm afraid that won't be possible."

Elizabeth stood still, worried that if she tried to move to comfort her husband she'd falter in her steps. This was a blow Philip would feel deeply.

* * *

IN THEIR SUITE, Elizabeth stood in the center of the sitting room while Philip paced, running his hands through his hair. Everything was changing, and much quicker than either of them had anticipated. She could feel his discontent as it radiated from him, sinking into her own heart.

But at the same time, she felt the ache of her father's disappointment in his own body betraying him. His inability to stand well, his inability to speak. His inability to take command of his own position as king.

And all of it came crashing down on her shoulders. The weight of it so much she started to stoop. She, who'd wanted to be a simple naval wife, who'd spent the last two years doing just that, was inexplicably becoming more than just a princess. She was taking on the duties of a monarch, her father's duties, which could only mean that at some point, he expected not to be able to do them anymore.

Though he claimed he was fine, she still worried that he was, in fact, not fine at all. And that those duties were coming sooner than any of them ever anticipated.

CHAPTER TWENTY-SEVEN

$\mathcal{H}$ANNA

$\mathcal{I}$ stared down at the small, battered brown leather suitcase on my bed. My few meager possessions were packed inside, and yet I felt richer than ever.

From the drawer in my night table, I pulled out my old diary.

I ran my hand over the well-loved cover. With Forrest already having gone off to work, I opened the journal, starting a new entry in the same way I'd done before—addressing it to my mother.

Dear Mum,

I'm going on a world tour. Me. Who would have ever thought I'd leave Windsor, let alone the country? Our first stop is to be in Africa. I'm equally enthralled as I am terrified. What if Susan takes off after a lion or elephant? Thankfully, Honey, Sugar, Crackers, and Biscuit are remaining behind with Dad.

There's some grumbling downstairs at Forrest having been invited. His main job is in the stables, where he's been promoted to coachman, working with the horses and carriages, but now and then when the royal family travels, he's also been known to take up a position as a driver, and

this has only been because of me. There's some jealous ten-
sion about it, people thinking I have curried special favor
with Elizabeth. Maybe I have.

But I genuinely like her, and I think the feeling is mu-
tual.

My pen stilled on the paper, creating a fat blob of black ink. There was so much more I wanted to say, and yet it wasn't meant for writing down. The worries the princess had over her father. After his recent surgery, he was slow to recover and weaker than ever.

Though he tried to project a strong image, everyone could tell there was something very wrong before the surgery and even after. Though, from the rumors I'd heard, the king didn't even know how bad things were with his own health. In fact, he'd started smoking again, though the doctors had been adamant he quit.

The interesting thing was I think Susan knew then how bad it was, just like she knows now.

Normally quite a strong-willed, brave dog, she was skittish around the king, sniffing him too much and panting. It made me wonder if dogs could smell when people weren't well, when something wasn't right inside the body.

I'd noticed that Crackers too seemed to pant more around the king, to lean against him as if trying to shoulder some of the burden in his old self.

Dogs truly were our soulmates, our protectors in things that might harm us from the outside as much as the things that harmed us within.

I closed the journal and tucked it between the folded clothes in my suitcase, planning to take copious notes of our journey so I could remember forever what it was like to be abroad, likely the only time I would ever experience it.

Forrest, for my birthday, had given me a Leica IIIf camera so I could capture our moments on film. I tucked that in too, and then closed the suitcase.

* * *

SUSAN RAN WITH abandon in a field we'd been assured was safe. She stopped and sniffed, tasted, pawed nearly everything she passed. Then a beetle buzzed about, landing on the tip of her nose, and Susan stopped short, sitting, her eyes concentrating on the small bug and its brightly colored wings as if it were relaying a message.

She was a strange dog, more incredibly intelligent than any other I'd met. Able to express emotion and curiosity like a human. When she looked at me sometimes, with those sorrowful eyes, I imagined she was relaying her own messages. Imparting to me what the joys of life should be. That we should relish the little things like the wind in the grass, a small beetle, and so much more. The power of friendships and loyalty.

It made me wonder, what was the purpose of life, if not to live for every single moment and find those tiny pockets of joy we could relish forever? To forget past transgressions, to forgive? I glanced over at Forrest, knowing already that I'd done that with him, and I was better for it.

Of course, not every moment in life would yield such bounty as love, but what was the purpose of stewing? We couldn't let the pains of the past hold us back from where our futures intended to bring us.

In the end, we are the creators of our own stories: for what-

ever life presents before us, the path we choose is our choice
alone.

"What are you thinking about?" Forrest asked.

I pointed to Susan, who shook the beetle from her nose and
continued on, barking for us to follow and bounding farther in
the field. "What do you think she was thinking?"

Forrest laughed. "I think she was wondering whether or not
she could eat the beetle."

I grinned. "Maybe."

"What do *you* think she was thinking?"

"I wondered if they were somehow having a conversation." I
shrugged. Sometimes the thoughts I had on animals and nature went over other people's heads. I attributed my knowledge
to growing up walking through forests and searching for animals and tracking their paths. From having to guess what an
animal's decision would be before the animal made it. I'd been
taught by the best, my father, and I loved it.

"I love the way your mind works." Forrest put his arm around
my shoulders and tugged me against him, pressing a kiss to the
top of my head.

"My father would love it here." I breathed in a deep lungful
of air, and then exhaled, trying to memorize the various scents
so I could tell him everything.

"He would," Forrest agreed.

I lifted the binoculars Dad had given me, watching everything come into focus. He'd told me every time I looked through
those, he would be looking through my eyes. It was silly, but the
sentiment was powerful, and I planned to memorize every plain
blade of grass, the shapes of the trees, the curves of the rivers,
and every hoof or pawprint I saw, so our journey truly could

come alive for him, through my telling him of it and showing him the pictures I would take.

I scanned the horizon, my binoculars coming into focus on Elizabeth and Philip as they meandered. Susan had caught up to them, and Elizabeth bent to scratch her behind the ears, with Philip looking down lovingly.

I knew this trip was going to be good for them.

Here, without the children, without the daily strain of her father's illness, perhaps Elizabeth and Philip could rekindle some of what they'd lost over the last year.

The way Philip was looking at her now made me smile, and I was pretty sure that what I hoped for them would come to pass.

A whistle rent the air, and we turned to see that the guides in our caravan were signaling us all back.

I called for Susan, rounding her up even though she darted in circles, not ready to leave. With Forrest's help, I loaded her into the utility vehicle with us. Elizabeth and Philip jumped into the one ahead with a guide and a guard. The long line of cars took off then. As we passed the expansive plains, capturing pictures of the giraffes, gazelles, rhinos, and all manner of birds, all I could think about was how incredibly lucky I was to be on this journey of a lifetime.

With Susan vying for space on my lap in order to get a better view out the windows, I scooted closer to Forrest, giving her space to stand on the seat.

Forrest put his arm around my shoulders, glancing down at me, in very much the same way I'd just seen Philip looking at his wife.

"I love you," Forrest whispered, the sound of it almost drowned out by the engines roaring over the plains.

PART IV

T H E

Q U E E N

ROYAL REPORT

TRUSTED NEWS OF ALL THINGS ROYAL

It is with great sadness that we lay to rest our beloved King George VI, who passed away too soon. And may we offer our official homage to our Queen Elizabeth II.

Long live the queen.

Our beloved royal family must be as stunned as the rest of the world to learn of the passing of the king. We are a nation grieving, but they are a family mourning. Our condolences.

·❦·

CHAPTER TWENTY-EIGHT

ℰLIZABETH

Nairobi, Kenya
February 6, 1952

Dear Henry,

It is with great pleasure I send you these greetings from the
wild plains of Africa. You would not believe the scents I've
sniffed. Some sweet, some foul, but all of them delicious. I'd
bring you back some of my discoveries, but I don't believe
your keeper would enjoy the carcass of a mongoose or the
leg bone of a zebra. Alas, all I can leave you with is my
felicitations.

Do make sure the squirrel population is maintained un-
til my return. I'd hate for the palace grounds to get overrun
and of course I'd hate to return to nothing. Equal measure
in all things, Henry, remember that.

Cordially,
Susan

ℰlizabeth laughed as she put the final touches on the letter
to her equerry's dog back home in England. She'd made a joke

about having Susan keep in touch with the dogs of the palace servants, but Elizabeth was pretty sure no one had thought her to be in earnest. In all the serious nature of this trip, she was finding some pockets of joy and silliness.

The best was that she and Philip had grown closer. In the midst of her father's illness and having two babies, and the official royal duties piling up, Elizabeth had forgotten what it meant to be a wife, a woman in love. And here, away from mostly everything, they'd been able to recapture the romance and the reasons they wanted to be with each other. With a lifetime ahead of them to live, this was something she'd have to remember.

Philip was silly and joking, and romantic and charming. He was gazing at her the way she hadn't seen in so long. With love and longing. Gazes that she returned wholeheartedly.

"Elizabeth."

She put the letter down, turning at her desk to see Philip's figure blocking the sun shining through the doorway. The way his face was crestfallen, the slump of his shoulders, scared her and she leaped up from her chair, though her legs didn't feel strong enough to hold her. She swayed, heart pounding, and a whistling started in her ears.

All of the happy, silly feelings she'd had a moment ago evaporated, and instantly she was on edge.

"What is it?" she asked, trying to hide the wobble in her voice.

Philip cleared his throat but couldn't seem to find the words. Elizabeth worried there'd been an accident, one of their men injured. Not Susan; she was here beneath the desk.

She kept her hand braced on the back of the chair for balance. "Philip?"

Philip's face didn't change, his voice soft as he held out his hand. "I thought we might take a walk."

Elizabeth frowned but smoothed her skirts and took his out-stretched hand in hers. Normally warm, the skin of his palm felt cool to the touch. They meandered to the garden, filled with hibiscus and greens, with sunlight spilling on the shallow stream that trickled around them.

"Elizabeth," Philip said again, and she had the distinct impression her husband, who was never at a loss for words, struggled now. "There's no easy way to say this, darling. And I—" His voice cracked.

Fear rippled through her, and she looked at him wide-eyed, and then suddenly she knew. No accident of their people, no change of plans in their journey would have brought out such emotion in pragmatic Philip. This was catastrophic. This was the news she'd never wanted to hear.

She had almost felt the loss that morning as she'd stood watching the sun rise. A magnificent eagle had circled over-head, dipping its wings at her as if in salute before it flew high into the sky. She'd been mesmerized by it, thought about her father and how he would have loved to see a thing like that. How special it was to have seen such an important bird.

And how he never would.

"I'm so sorry," Philip said. "Your father, he has passed away."

Though she'd known what Philip was going to say, she still shook her head, the sting of tears blurring her vision. Perhaps if they could only rewind time, she could live forever in a mo-ment when her father was still on earth. She put her hand to her mouth to hold in the cry of agony climbing her throat. "What?" she managed to say, though it came out more of a hushed cough.

"He's gone, my love. I'm so sorry." And Philip tugged her against him, holding her tight to his strong body as anguish rippled through her.

Only a week ago, her father had come with them from Sandringham to London. They'd gone to Drury Lane and watched *South Pacific* at the Theatre Royal. The king had grinned at her the same way he had since she was a child and sung a few of the lyrics that she and Maggie had memorized and belted out more than once.

And then the next morning, he'd seen them off, ignoring the advice of his doctors and advisors and standing in the freezing January weather for nearly half an hour as they boarded the plane and took off. She'd watched him wave until he was a tiny speck, trying to memorize every bit of him until she couldn't see him any longer.

Now she'd never see him again. Those images of him, waving her off on this world tour, were the last she'd have. Oh, how it crippled her with pain.

"We need to go back," she said. "We never should have left."

Philip nodded, somber. "I've already told them to get the plane ready."

What would she have done without Philip?

As Elizabeth went into the lodge to prepare for their departure, people started to drop into bows, curtsies. All of it confused her until Philip's cousin Pamela Hicks, who'd traveled with her as a lady's maid, rushed over and gave her a hug, then gasped, let go, and dropped into a formal curtsy.

Elizabeth was queen.

Elizabeth waved everyone off, trying hard to put her feelings in a box. To recall the stoicism of her mother, of her grandmother. Of her father.

No one could see her sorrow, for she was now queen, and queens must remain strong. To show emotion was to show weakness, or at least to give any enemy a chance to take advantage. To know her weak points, and to exploit them.

Elizabeth straightened her shoulders and concentrated on remaining still, quiet.

She didn't remember getting onto the plane but realized as she did so that she'd not brought along anything black.

"I have nothing to wear."

"We'll have something sent to the airport when we land," her secretary, Martin Charteris, said.

"What will happen when we arrive?" she asked. She only half-heartedly listened to his answer. Thinking about her mother, her sister, and the nation in mourning. Oh, her poor mother. To lose her once vibrant husband. The man who'd wooed her, won her, lived through a war with her.

As she thought all these things, holding her tears at bay, everyone around her acted different. Even Philip to an extent, though his differences were more like he was trying to balance a delicate Fabergé egg on the tip of a sword.

Elizabeth had left the country a princess and was arriving home a queen.

Philip watched her steadily as they flew, offering her comfort often. And she took it, but then pushed him back, because every time he held her, she felt like the dam she was holding inside was going to burst. She had to rush to the bathroom more than once to cry.

The plane landed with a jolt, and moments later, Pamela collected a dress bag from someone who'd managed to climb aboard. She ushered Elizabeth, along with Bobo, into a private area to change her clothes, trading her white shoes for black and affixing a black velvet and lace hat to her hair.

"You're like ice," Pamela said, touching her hand.

Elizabeth nodded. "Better to be frozen than melting."

Pamela nodded, a mist showing in her eyes, and Elizabeth looked away. Out the window, she could see a line of black limousines, and remarked they looked like hearses.

Prime Minister Winston Churchill greeted her at the bottom of the airplane stairs, offering his condolences, the red rim of his eyes proof of his sincerity. The tarmac was a crush of people, as were the streets of London. Everyone they passed was dressed in black, a nation in mourning.

At least she wasn't alone in her grief.

But it wasn't until her grandmother Queen Mary arrived at Clarence House within an hour of Elizabeth's return and took her hand, kissed it, and said, "God save the queen" that Elizabeth felt the shift in her rise all the way from her toes to the top of her head. And it was overwhelming. Too tremendous.

It must have shown on her face, because her grandmother stood straight up in that moment, and said, "Lilibet, your skirts are much too short for mourning."

Elizabeth smiled at her grandmother's being a stickler for protocol. At least there were some things that wouldn't change— and would help her feel as normal as she possibly could.

Though she'd known for a long time now that being ordinary was something she would never be.

CHAPTER TWENTY-NINE

SUSAN

I've never known what death is.

I was born. I live.

Everyone else around me lives. Our days are filled with activity, food, rest. I listen to the conversations going on around me. Lilibet sobs, a gut-wrenching sound. I cuddle close to her, and she hugs me tighter than she ever has before. Sometimes so tight I think I might lose my breath. Nothing that a little bark doesn't remind her of.

The king is dead.

The man who found me. The man who gave me to her. He is gone now.

But what is gone?

Are we ever truly gone?

When he is not in the room, is he gone? When I am not with Lilibet, is she gone? Am I gone too?

It seems to me that if someone is gone from us at any moment, they might come back. But Lilibet has said he's never coming back.

So where is he?

Is he on another plane? Another place or time, where he is laughing and chasing a stag, rowing a boat on a lake, or playing the piano in some palace? Even when he is gone, his scent remains, lingering on his clothes and his pillow. Wafting through the air of the rooms wherever we go.

I can smell him. I follow his scent, but it always leads me nowhere. As if I just missed him, it disappears into the walls or carpet.

When we die, we leave pieces of us behind. The memories.

So again, I ask, are we ever truly gone?

If people remember we existed, then we must in fact still exist.

I snuggle closer to Lilibet and I lick the tears on her cheeks. *He's still here*, I want to say, but I don't know how to form the words.

"Oh, Sus," she says, through her tears. "What will I do without him?"

Keep on living, keep on doing the same things you're doing now.

"You always make me feel so much better," she says. "I'm so glad he gave you to me. I'll be able to remember him always through you, Crackers, Sugar, and Honey."

Yes, we live on through our memories.

Lilibet doesn't send me to the corgi room that night but keeps me in her bed between her and Philip. My favorite place. I lay my head on her pillow, stare into her red-rimmed eyes, and wish I could take away the pain. When she eventually falls asleep, her limp hand resting on my ribs, I let my own eyes fall closed.

We'll get through this together.

All of us.

Philip's hand slides over Lilibet's, squeezing gently, and in the crack of moonlight through the blinds I can see a tear slide down my princess's face. I resist licking it clean, because I don't want to wake her, and because I don't want to get kicked out of the most comfortable place in the world.

·⤙⥇·

CHAPTER THIRTY

*H*ANNA

*A*voiding the palace staff was easy when I was in my cottage at Windsor, surrounded by the dogs, a fire lit in the hearth, soft music playing. Outside we were surrounded by trees and grass, rather than busy streets and guards. Upon our initial landing in London from Africa, Elizabeth had asked me to take Susan while she attended official business.

I'd been able to escape the crush of people who wanted to know everything, from how the queen had found out about the death of her father to what it was like seeing an elephant up close.

They were a nosy bunch—strangers, servants, reporters—and sometimes came off as quite insensitive. More interested in the gossip than the pain a real human being was feeling.

I'd been summoned from Windsor to Clarence House by Elizabeth, who needed Susan's warmth as she navigated the new waters of ruling. As we pulled up the drive, I could barely contain the nerves that bubbled beneath the surface of my skin. We'd been at Windsor to give the new queen space and time to settle into her new duties, but that had not lasted long. As soon as I stepped out, with Susan, Sugar, and Honey on their leashes, Biscuit back at my father's cottage, it felt as if a thousand eyes were on me.

Through the fog of my breath, I could make out the curtains of the grand house twitching, and then the front door opened and the butler appeared, staring at me. He'd never made eye contact with me before like that, and I feared what he was going to ask.

"We're glad you've come," the man who'd never spoken to me in my life said.

I cocked my head to the side, a smart retort just begging to come out, but I kept my lips clamped closed and nodded instead.

"I'll just be a moment." I walked through the red-carpeted house, past the red and white damask walls adorned with paintings, to the side yard to let the dogs loose so they could do their business after the long car ride.

I know my relationship with the queen is unique, and it isn't just because of the corgis but because of our girlhoods, thrust together in the middle of a war. We cooked our dinners together in the forest; we camped out under the stars, whispering our dreams to the night sky. Without those few formative years as Girl Guides together at Windsor during the war, our friendship likely wouldn't be the way it was. If not for those years, I would simply be her dogs' caretaker, instead of the sometimes companion I'd become.

The moment I stepped back into Clarence House, I could hear Philip. He was speaking rather passionately about something, and between his boisterous laments, there was a silence that I could only assume was because Elizabeth, who never raised her voice, was responding.

The corgis started to run in circles, sniffing the butler and few servants who passed and taking a taste of the corner of the carpet and the legs of a few chairs. I snapped my fingers and ordered them to come. Susan complied first, while Sugar and Honey completely ignored me.

The raised voices seemed to have caught Susan's attention and she whimpered, looking for which direction they came from.

"They are discussing the Royal House name."

I glanced at the butler, who stared straight ahead; if I hadn't heard him speak, I could have imagined it, since he didn't look to be engaging with me at all.

"It's Windsor," I murmured, tossing Susan a treat as she waited patiently. Not to be left out, Sugar and Honey decided to finally obey and rushed forward, sitting excitedly as I hooked on their leashes and gave them each a biscuit.

"Indeed, it is." Had the butler's mouth not even moved that time?

Curiosity ate at me about the name. How could this even be an issue? "What does he wish it to be? Mountbatten?" I asked in a low tone.

The butler laughed, but so quickly that if I'd not caught the twitch of his mouth, I'd have missed it. "That's been bandied about, but truly, he is most adamant that it be Edinburgh-Windsor."

"Edinburgh-Windsor," I repeated, rolling the awkward hyphen around in my mouth.

"It's absurd," the butler said. "Philip thinks they should follow precedent of their great-great-grandmother, Victoria."

"Because she took Albert's surname as the Royal House name?"

"Precisely."

I smiled. "But our queen is no Victoria."

The butler slid me a sideways glance and a smile, both of us understanding that Elizabeth would prefer to stand on her own two feet. "Exactly."

Victoria had deferred to her husband in so many things, though she never did name him king. Elizabeth had not even named her husband prince consort. It was her father's wish that she remain in control of her own throne, something that had been relayed to Philip many times. Perhaps something he'd yet to grasp or had hoped would change.

A door opened abovestairs, and Philip's voice rang out clearly. "Am I to be the only man in all of Great Britain who can't give his children his own name? I'm nothing but a bloody amoeba."

I knew little of amoebas, but I was fairly certain no one thought of our prince as one. He stormed down the stairs, past the corgis who looked at him expectantly, until he disappeared. Moments later, Elizabeth appeared, not seeming the least bit harried by the argument.

I sank into a curtsy, and the dogs all remained seated as I'd taught them, though their little behinds bounced up and down on the carpet. It was only a matter of seconds before one of them broke ranks and the rest followed suit.

"Ah, Hanna, you've come. Susan." She hurried down the stairs and gathered her dog in her arms. "Oh, how I have missed you, darling." She placed kisses all over the corgi's face, then bent to give equal love to the others. "What would I do without you?"

The butler slunk away, leaving the two of us there in the corridor with the dogs.

"Shall we walk them?" Elizabeth glanced up, a slight sheen in her blue eyes the only sign she might have been bothered by what had transpired.

"If your majesty doesn't wish to do so alone." I wasn't sure what the protocol was now that she was queen. I didn't even think I was supposed to look at her, so I kept my gaze toward my shoes.

"Oh, Hanna, not you too," Elizabeth grumbled.

"Ma'am?" I asked, chancing a glance in her direction.

"Everyone keeps me at arm's length now. No more conversations or jokes, as if I might lash out and demand their heads. I kept my name, Elizabeth, because it is mine and because it reminds people of the golden age of the first queen of that name, not because I plan to execute everyone."

I nodded, feeling a little sad for our queen, who'd had so many unexpected changes of late.

"So shall we?" She took the leashes from my hand and marched ahead, and I had no choice but to follow her into the gardens or remain behind like an idiot in the foyer.

We walked in silence across the lawn, which I was used to. A lot of times we did this. Elizabeth loved to be outside. The sky above and the grass below, surrounded by her dogs, put her in her element. Outside, she wasn't a royal, a wife, a mother; she was simply herself. Before she was queen, we'd sometimes walk over to St. James's Park, blending in with everyone else out for some exercise. I guessed those days were over now. Every so often I caught her wistfully gazing in that direction. She must have been thinking the same thing.

"Dogs have it so easy," Elizabeth said.

"Mostly," I agreed.

"Mostly?" Elizabeth eyed me, and I bit my tongue for having contradicted her. "Do go on."

"Well, they've a job to do. Whether it's as a hunter or merely as a companion. They know what their job is, and I think they suffer disappointments in themselves when they don't do it well."

Elizabeth nodded, watching as Susan rushed after a squirrel who'd been brave enough to try to dig something out of the frozen ground.

"Take Susan, for example. She knows she's a companion to you, ma'am, and that her job is to be there for you. To listen and love you unconditionally. But she's a deeper responsibility too, and that's to show you how to enjoy life and the little things, like the pure joy of chasing down a squirrel."

Elizabeth laughed and looked after Susan. "She is quite adept at her job."

"And I think she takes pride in it."

Though the squirrel probably thought differently.

* * *

Down in the kitchen, I walked past the staring staff as I made my way to Cook to see about the dogs' dinner.

A bundle of tittering female staff whispered and then shoved one forward, their spokeswoman, I assumed.

"Hanna, a word if you don't mind."

I did mind. I turned and stared at the younger, neatly put-together woman, letting her know in my gaze that I was annoyed with what she was about to do. They were all going to be sorely disappointed that I wouldn't betray the queen's trust or spread gossip. It was one thing to chat with the butler when we were witnessing an event, but another to talk behind the queen's back.

"What is it?" I asked sharply.

The young woman winced, and I experienced a moment

of guilt for addressing her so harshly. "Have you heard about whether we'll be moving houses?"

"What do you mean?" I pretended not to know but was also secretly glad this wasn't a chat about something more personal. Of course they would want to know where they were going to be working.

"We've heard that the duke would like Clarence House to remain the royal residence, but tradition has been that the monarch resides in Buckingham Palace."

"The House of Windsor has always been one to follow tradition," I said, leaving it at that.

"So we will be moving houses, then?"

"I may walk the queen's dogs, but that does not mean I am privy to any sort of state decisions. I'm a dog walker, nothing more."

The woman scowled. "You're more than that and you know it. Why are you being so closemouthed?" she hissed. "You went to Africa with them."

Was the woman mad? I wasn't invited to go on a vacation with them. I was working. "Because she wanted Susan there with her. Again, I am the dog walker."

Behind the woman I could see a sea of frowning faces. "You just think you're too good for us, Hanna Darling." The way the woman said my surname came out more a sneer than anything else.

"I don't think that at all." This was feeling so much like when I'd been a child back at Windsor. I hated the sudden itch to my skin, like I wanted to crawl out of myself. I drew in a slow breath. I wasn't that girl anymore. I was a grown adult. A loyal servant. No matter what they said, I wasn't going to allow them to make me feel less than myself.

"You're a goody-goody."

I raised my brow and then I laughed. Apparently, she thought lobbing insults would make me change somehow. "So, because I won't give you what you want—information I'm not even privy to—you're going to resort to childish name-calling?"

The woman stuck her nose in the air.

"Well, in that case, I'd best share with you all I know." By the widening of the other woman's eyes in surprise and satisfaction, I gathered she didn't understand sarcasm.

I rolled my eyes, and turned my back on her, calling over my shoulder. "Actually, never mind."

My goodness, the vultures, to think I would gossip. And I wasn't lying about not knowing anything. It's not like on our walks Elizabeth laid out all of her royal plans. The confidences she shared with me were more personal than state matters.

We talked of dogs, family, love. Intimate things that even these classless wenches wouldn't understand. They wanted some juicy tidbit they could sell to the papers for a few shillings.

Friendship wasn't something that could be bought or sold, nor were intimacies.

In the kitchen, a new chef prepared the dogs' dinner.

"What happened to Mr. Smythe?"

"Decided he'd rather cook for people."

"And you?"

The new chef grinned as he put a flourish of parsley sprigs on top of chopped rabbit, carrots, peas, and potatoes. "I aim to please. No matter the mouth it enters, I want to know I've fed them a well-thought-out meal that will nourish as well as delight."

I couldn't help but laugh in surprise. "I like you."

He glanced up at me. "Let's hope the queen's girls do too."

With the last of the garnishes on the silver dishes, I lifted the tray to take it upstairs.

"Oh my," Elizabeth said, giddy when her eyes landed on the silver tray and individual bowls.

"They are going to be spoiled by the new chef," I said.

"That they are."

I set the tray on the sideboard, leaving the queen to feed the dogs herself as she loved to do.

I made my way to the corgi room, set on cleaning it up in preparation for their bedtime, but as I did, I passed the butler on the way.

"Good for you," he said, again managing not to move his mouth or his face.

"Pardon?"

He paused, glanced from side to side down the hall. "You're not a traitor."

I raised my brows, partly at his words and partly because this time he actually did speak like a normal human. "Of course not. What are you talking about?"

"The little birds are chattering."

"Oh." I rolled my eyes. "They are most displeased."

He grinned. "Most."

It was good to know, besides Forrest and the new chef, that I had an ally among the servants. Most people, when they thought of the palace and backstabbing, thought of the courtiers or politicians trying to curry favor. Bribing and lying their way to whatever resolution met their agenda. But it could be just as vicious among the staff. Most complained about being underpaid and overworked.

They were all sworn to secrecy, and there were a good number who remained loyal. But there were just as many willing to sell out.

It was a sad business. The queen, and those who'd come before her, had to trust the people who helped them run their lives and the country. What was there without trust?

The little corgi room was adorable. Raised wicker beds with embroidered cushions of fabrics I couldn't afford. But I wasn't jealous; it made me laugh. I picked up the balls that had been strewn about by the dogs, straightened their plush cushions, closed the curtains so the room would be dark when it was time for them to sleep. I checked their water bowls, refilling them to the exact measurement the queen preferred for nighttime thirst.

I made sure all their leashes were hung on the wall, smiling at the addition of new sweaters for each corgi to wear outside in the snow. They were knitted with love, probably by loyal, dog-loving subjects, and sent as gifts. The corgis were forever receiving toys, sweaters, leashes, bowls from the public. One of the tasks that Elizabeth had given to me was to write thank-you notes for the gifts—written as though I were one of the dogs myself. It was quite hysterical.

Everything set in place, I turned off the light. When the first corgi woke before dawn, it was a footman who took them out to do their business before me, which was the usual when they stayed the night with the queen. They'd want their breakfast immediately after going out, and it was my job to deliver it.

"There you are." Forrest approached me from the hallway.

"What are you doing here?" I asked. "Is everything all right?"

He grinned. "Yes. I thought you might want to go out for a bite to eat tonight, rather than dining downstairs."

I frowned. "That might make my situation worse."

Forrest shrugged. "Let them stew without you having to witness it. Besides, there's a new chippie nearby I wanted to try."

I smiled and linked my arm around his. "That does sound a lot nicer than having to dodge the hens' pecks."

Forrest laughed. "Incredibly nicer. And I promise I won't peck."

.⟨∾⟩.

CHAPTER THIRTY-ONE

ℰLIZABETH

Mid-February 1952

ℰlizabeth stood by the window of Clarence House, the place she and Philip had painstakingly remodeled to fit their every need, looking through the sheer curtain toward the lawn.

Since she'd returned, the area just beyond the gate was always filled with people—journalists mostly, snapping pictures of the house and any glimpses they might get of the new reigning royals.

A shift in the silence alerted her to Philip's presence. He stepped up behind her, placing his hand on her shoulder. There'd been so much tension between them lately. And not because they didn't love each other. Lying beneath the surface of their skins was resentment. Perhaps more so on his part than hers.

Philip had known from the first day he met her that she was the heir to the throne. The constant reminder of her being queen one day had not been ignored; if anything, it had been amplified by her parents, the media, Maggie, any of their friends and family.

But the truth was neither of them had been prepared for how fast it happened.

"How are you?" Philip asked, with a hint of hesitation in his voice. The last time they'd spoken had been the day before when they'd had a heated debate about moving to the palace.

The thing was, neither of them *wanted* to move households. But Elizabeth, having grown up with the palace directing her every step, was used to having her life dictated. Philip, on the other hand, had reminded her fiercely that she was the queen, and that *she* should be able to make the choices. But as much as she wanted to put her family first, to put Philip and his desires first, even to put her own wishes first, that wasn't a choice she could make.

Kingdom, family, self.

The prime minister had insisted they move to Buckingham Palace, reminding her that it was her responsibility to do so.

"I don't think I'm ready." She whispered the words that had been gnawing at her, clawing away at what little reserves she had left in her nervous system.

"You are."

Elizabeth turned from the window and looked up into the clear, confident eyes of her husband.

"How?" At least she managed to keep the tears at bay.

"You were born ready."

She shook her head, looking somewhere over his shoulder. "No, I wasn't."

Philip cupped the side of her face, and she flicked her gaze back up to his, trying to absorb the confidence he felt.

"Theoretically, you were," Philip continued. "Yes, your father wasn't born to be king, but he was next in line, and you were named a princess at birth, putting you in the path of succession. No matter how far away it was, you were always royal. It's in your blood. And beyond that, my dear and brilliant wife, you, above any other royal I know, take your job as seriously as the blood that runs in your veins. Remember that. There is no one else in this world who could rule the way you have and will."

Elizabeth ran her tongue over her lips, feeling their parched roughness. She nodded in understanding, even if she didn't one hundred percent believe him, because he was right. No matter which way she looked, the throne had always been there before her. And for the majority of her life, she'd known she would follow in her father's footsteps.

No amount of preparing, no infinitely perfect timing, would have made her feel equal to the task. There was a great loss that came with the great responsibility, the biggest of her life. Taking the throne, accepting the crown on coronation day meant also accepting that her father was not coming back.

No more would the halls resound with his loud, booming voice. No longer would she sit opposite him at the desk and read through the papers and ledgers that came in the daily red box. It would be a job that she would do alone. Just as she'd rule alone.

And perhaps that was what made her most fearful—that great, wide aloneness.

Philip would be there for her, certainly, as would the rest of her family, the prime minister and the House of Lords, and every single British subject. But, when it came to sitting on the throne, that was a task that no one else could or would shoulder for her.

It was as depressing as it was daunting as it was magnificent.

Philip pulled her gently against him, and for a moment, she leaned into his solid form, breathed in the scent of his aftershave, and closed her eyes. Behind shuttered lids she could pretend that they were back in Malta. She could almost smell the salt spray of the ocean and hear the caw of the seagulls as they swooped for fish in the gently rolling waves when they went sailing.

"Well, we might as well go now," she said. "Even if it pains us."

Philip nodded, resigned.

Straightening her shoulders, she prepared for the countless time to make an appearance for her people, and to move forward with what would be the honor of her life.

CHAPTER THIRTY-TWO

SUSAN

*B*eneath the table, my head resting on Lilibet's shining black leather pump, I can feel her nerves whistling through her body. Sense the rapid heartbeat, and see her hands wringing in her lap.

I long to jump up and rest there. To tell her all will be well, and give her a reassuring lick. But she's told me in no uncertain terms that I am to remain down here, out of sight.

It is Christmastime, and as has been done in years before, there will be a Christmas message to the people. Lilibet's told me she is going to be broadcasting it over the radio live and that she hopes everyone will like her message as much as they used to like her father's.

I stifle the tremor in my own body, her nerves working through me, as in front of the desk where she sits there are a dozen or so people with massive machinery that will supposedly do this broadcast.

I've listened to the radio before, mostly with Lilibet, and occasionally now with the children, Sugar and Honey joining us. The sounds are irritating but seem to elicit happy laughter from the tiny royals, my charges when Lilibet isn't around.

"Are you ready, ma'am?" one of the men asks, his heels clicking together in a way that draws me to look at him sharply.

Hanna does that with her heels when it's time for us to go somewhere. I hope he doesn't think I'll be going anywhere with him. Lilibet has said I can remain as long as I lie here at her feet. I wait for a call, just so I can let them know I won't be complying, but it never comes.

"I am." Lilibet's voice is firm and calm, nothing showing the way she truly feels, for I can still hear the pound of her heart and the rush of nerves as it washes through her, and then me.

I'm not certain why we dogs can sense those things. There's something in the human-dog connection that makes us fully aware of our people's feelings. It is a gift, for it tells us how to respond.

I nuzzle Lilibet's ankle, wishing I could form words and tell her she will be brilliant, that I love hearing everything she says so the people will too.

But as much as she smiles at me, at her children, there is a sadness to her eyes. It is loss. The loss of a beloved father, her mentor, the man who found me and brought me to her. I miss him too.

"And we're live." The man points at Lilibet, and she sits up a little straighter.

"Happy Christmas," Lilibet says. "Each Christmas, at this time, my beloved father broadcast a message to his people in all parts of the world. Today I am doing this to you, who are now my people."

I look up at her as she speaks. I can see her. I can hear her. And I love her so. Lilibet continues, and I can barely understand the things she says, only that she speaks of things that the people will find important, no doubt, of family and happiness and celebration. And laced through it all, her sorrow coats the words.

This is the first Christmas without King George, and it is a somber affair. Though everyone is trying to keep up their spirts, snatching happiness where they can, there are waves of sadness that I feel in my bones. Even Maggie's piano playing only seems to make smiles happen in little twitches.

Oh, my darling Lilibet, if only there were a way I could make you feel better. I start to stand, to put a paw on her knee, but she stays me without missing a beat in her speech and I lie back down, eager to obey her commands.

She is a queen, after all, and I her dutiful subject and admirer. Besides, there had been a promise of a long walk and a tasty treat if I behave. As in all things, I like to make good decisions for myself, especially when they involve treats and walks.

·⚬✺⚬·

CHAPTER THIRTY-THREE

ℰLIZABETH

June 1953

𝒯he tension in the room was palpable.

Elizabeth tried to keep her mood calm, stable, issuing smiles and small jokes as was her norm. But the tension was thick enough to cut with a knife.

Maggie was irritated with her—well, perhaps *irritated* wasn't the right word exactly for how her sister felt. Though the sideways glances, the stiff responses, the cold shoulder brushes, and the sometimes loudly muttered retorts were enough to give away that Elizabeth was not her sister's favorite person at the moment.

"Nearly twenty-four million views," Philip was saying as they rewatched the televised coronation.

At first, Elizabeth had been staunchly opposed to her coronation being televised. Her father had not thought it a good idea either. A coronation was a sacred event where a person became head of state and church. This was not something that should be streamed into televisions around the world but a private, solemn affair.

In the end, Elizabeth had been able to keep some of the rituals private, but the rest had been recorded.

She'd spent weeks walking up and down the White Drawing Room at Buckingham Palace with either the Imperial State Crown or a bag of flour on her head. She had to practice keeping her head steady—one tilt and everyone in the world would watch her drop the crown. She'd even worn sheets attached to her shoulders to simulate the cape.

All of those hours had made her feel surprisingly confident when the event came into play. Whatever nerves she had she simply willed away, knowing this was her duty and that somewhere above, her father was watching her with pride. Not even the downpour had put a damper on her special day.

"Such a gorgeous gown," Maggie whispered, briefly overcoming her sour mood; though, by the way her arms were crossed over her chest, she wasn't giving up her grudge completely.

Elizabeth watched herself on the television screen entering Westminster Abbey, wearing the silk embroidered gown designed by Norman Hartnell. It had been the ninth design he'd presented to her last October. Studded with pearls, crystals, and sequins, and embroidered in gold and silver thread and pastel silks, the gown was adorned with the national floral emblems of her dominions, which made it truly an incredible work of art and a political message of peace and prosperity.

The weight of the gown was immense, and the heaviness had helped her feel grounded as she'd walked down the aisle.

Elizabeth glanced toward her sister. Shadows marred the skin beneath Maggie's eyes. Sitting in a chair opposite her was Group Captain Townsend. Elizabeth had agreed to have him involved in more family affairs ever since Maggie had divulged their love for each other and wish to marry.

Of course, Elizabeth had spoken to their mother, who was devasted by the news and thought they should just placate the couple for now. A marriage between them was impossible for two specific reasons—the Royal Marriages Act, and then of course, Townsend was divorced. Royals didn't marry divorcés. They only had to look at Uncle David to see how that turned out. Right now, since Maggie was only twenty-two, she needed permission from the monarch—Elizabeth—to marry. Once she was twenty-five, she could make the choice on her own. However, because of the Marriages Act, if she married Peter, who was a commoner, she'd have to give up her titles, her place in the line of succession, and her annual stipend.

Was that something her sister was willing to do?

Perhaps she was. Love did funny things to the brain, didn't it? But for now, Elizabeth felt the need to protect her sister from the losses she was willing to give up in the name of her heart.

Elizabeth was not unfamiliar with the passionate feelings of love and romance. She glanced at Philip, who was looking at the television screen with a mixture of awe and adoration. He truly loved her, was proud of her; and knowing that made her smile. Peter Townsend often looked at Maggie the same way. And she wasn't unsympathetic to their plight. After all, her parents had tried to get her not to marry Philip. Had thought distance and time would allow their feelings to fizzle.

It only made them love each other more.

Perhaps it was silly for her to think that it would be any different for Maggie, but she didn't want to be the one to tell her sister she couldn't marry the man she loved. How angry she'd been when their parents had tried to tell her that. She might be the sovereign, but this was her sister. For now, it seemed easier to just let things lie with promises of looking into it, rather than outright denial.

On the screen, the crown was being lowered to her head. To avoid the gaffe of the Archbishop of Canterbury putting it on backward as he had with her father, Elizabeth had asked for two silver stars to be put on the front of the St. Edward's Crown. Elizabeth rubbed the back of her neck, even now feeling the weight of the extra nearly five pounds on her head, and how hard it had been to hold her neck straight.

One didn't realize the true weight of nearly five pounds until it sat on your head for over an hour. To get used to it and build up the muscles in her neck, she'd sat with her red boxes and a bag of flour on her head as she worked on correspondence. The children, when they'd come to see her in the afternoons for tea, had found the bag of flour on her head to be comical, and even dear Susan had barked at her whenever she wore it as if to let her know that there was something that didn't belong.

Susan jumped up on the couch, curling into her lap, as if she could sense Elizabeth had been thinking of her. Elizabeth stroked her fingers through the corgi's fur and over the softness of her adorable snout. What would she have done without her dog's companionship all these years? It was as if the moment Elizabeth touched Susan, a sense of calm filled her.

Perhaps in the next litter, Elizabeth should make sure Maggie got a corgi of her own. She would need it in the coming months and years, depending on what she decided to do with her future.

Giving up Townsend or giving up her place in the royal family. Either choice was one that would weigh heavily on Maggie, who had such a tender, sensitive heart.

"The television doesn't do the gown justice," Elizabeth said. "Nor the crown, but it is rather fascinating to see. I hardly remember the whole thing."

"You didn't seem nervous at all," Philip said, reaching over to give her knee a gentle squeeze before pulling back from showing such affection in front of others.

It was difficult to go from one way of acting in the privacy of their apartments in the palace to being with others and then to another mentality altogether when they were in public. "I don't think I was. But it was still entirely overwhelming, and I was filled with such emotion."

"Your papa would have been so proud," Mummy said, wiping a tear from the corner of her eye. Her mother was not one to be oversentimental, so the gesture made Elizabeth's heart do a double tap.

"He was with me in spirit," Elizabeth said, as were those in whose footsteps she'd followed.

She glanced toward the empty spot on the couch beside her where her grandmother Queen Mary might have sat if she hadn't passed away a few months before. She'd told them not to make a spectacle of her death, not wanting her passing to overshadow Elizabeth's triumph at her coronation. The same advice had been given by the cabinet and Winston Churchill about requesting an inquiry into whether or not a marriage between Maggie and Peter could be possible.

Nobody wanted to overshadow that day.

As much as Elizabeth smiled on camera, she deeply felt the weight of all those things she'd been told to brush aside.

* * *

AUTUMN HAD TURNED the leaves on the palace grounds and throughout London from lush green to deep auburn and gold. The sky was overcast as she and Philip had climbed the stairs on the airport tarmac and waved goodbye to Maggie as they boarded.

Her sister was going to take care of the children for six months at Balmoral, while she and Philip finished the six-month tour they'd started before her father had passed away.

Elizabeth wasn't too keen to finish it, not wanting to be away from her duties as a monarch for so long and also not wanting to be away from her children. Of concern was that both of them were sick right now, an ear infection and a cold, and no parent wanted to leave the country when their little ones were sick.

But, as Philip and Churchill and Alan Lascelles, her secretary, had reminded Elizabeth, traveling abroad was also part of her duty as queen. And duty came first, as much as she wished this time around she could change that.

And so she'd boarded the plane with only a minor complaint or two to Philip, which always made her feel a little guilty, given he'd had to relinquish all hope of a naval career in order to be on the plane with her and by her side as her husband and not even prince consort at that. Though she felt guilty sometimes at not making him her consort, she knew it was the right decision and the one her father had made her promise to keep.

Despite his disappointments, Philip was momentarily assuaged because she'd had put into law that if she was to pass early, he would be regent until Charles was of age. A role that had previously been Maggie's.

The papers had had a field day with that, believing that she'd taken the regency from her sister after the entire media scandal about Peter Townsend and his subsequent post abroad—which they all proclaimed an exile.

If only they would allow matters of the state to remain

matters of the state instead of making them into a media scandal, or trying to twist the narrative into something it wasn't.

Susan hopped up on Philip's seat before he could lower himself, looking pleased with herself at having beaten him to the punch.

"Your attempts to usurp me won't work," he teased, scooping Susan up and depositing her on the floor.

Elizabeth grinned. "You have to hand it to her: she's had a campaign against you for the longest time."

"I respect her tenacity." He chuckled.

Elizabeth patted her lap, and Susan leaped up, settling there with a glance at Philip as if to say, *Ha, this is even better.*

The ensuing trip was a whirlwind. When she could, Elizabeth took Susan with her on a leash to make her rounds, and Susan proved to be incredible at breaking the ice with strangers. She settled Elizabeth's nerves and those of who wanted to speak with her. Susan was an easy segue into conversation with questions like "Do you like dogs?" "Have you got a dog?" "Would you like to pet Susan?" and even "Susan is the famous matriarch of the Windsor corgi line. Oh no, we don't sell them."

Susan pranced as if she were the queen herself, and seemed to be completely in her element. Though when the crowds tended to converge too much, she got a bit agitated, and Elizabeth would have Hanna take her away.

Whenever they got the chance, Elizabeth and Susan walked on the grounds of whatever palace, villa, or estate they were housed in, finding peace and quiet together as they exercised. Sometimes with Hanna, sometimes without.

"No matter what duties are required of me," Elizabeth said, bending down to meet her corgi's eyes, "I shall always make time for our walks."

It was a promise she wasn't able to keep.

Duty seemed to be what ruled her life, and the simple pleasures of a walk in the park, a hike in the woods, or simply tossing a stick on the lawn always seemed to take last place. Whenever she was ready to put on her mac and wellies, someone was there with a list of things she needed to do. The life she'd dreamed of having seemed to slip further and further from her grasp. And the walks she used to take with Susan and Hanna turned into just Susan and Hanna.

It only made Elizabeth more resentful of the uncle she blamed for taking it all away. In fact, she wished she could cut off Uncle David's allowance. If he was going to abandon his royal duties—foisting them on her father, which had caused him the stress she believed led to his death, and then her having to don the crown instead of living the life of a Royal Navy wife—then he didn't need to roll around in the money the countrymen he'd abandoned worked themselves to the bone to make. Not to mention his Nazi leanings during the war.

In the six months they were abroad, she gave more than one hundred twenty speeches. So many that she didn't even speak some days to save the voice that was threatening to go.

Tea with honey and lemon helped, but by the end of the six months, Elizabeth was ready not to speak for an equal length of time. A reprieve she was certain not to get.

The stress of it all wasn't clear only in Elizabeth's pale face and sore throat but in Susan, who no longer liked to accompany her on visits and seemed more inclined to walk with her head down than jump and wiggle.

She'd even snapped at the porter taking their bags, and the only thing that calmed her was Elizabeth lifting her into her arms and rushing them both into the vehicle that would take them to the airport. Susan was even acting up with Hanna. The stress that Elizabeth was feeling was leaching into her darling corgi.

"Oh, Susan, I think perhaps this trip was too much for you. So many people, too many planes."

Philip raised a brow where he sat across from her in the limousine. "I can relate."

Elizabeth pursed her lips but said nothing, still smarting from the embarrassment of being caught by journalists throwing a tennis racket and her tennis shoes at Philip's back as he ran out of the house after a recent argument.

Lascelles had been able to retrieve the footage; and when she'd composed herself, Elizabeth had come out to apologize, making a joke about marriage.

"Needless to say, I may not be able to play tennis again for some time," she'd said to the press. And now, to her husband, "It isn't Susan's fault that you left your tennis balls out. If I were her, I'd have chewed them up too. It doesn't mean you can threaten to get rid of her. I still can't believe you called the local pound."

Philip smirked. "Perhaps she and I will come to an understanding one day."

"I doubt it." Elizabeth laughed, sliding to the opposite bench to sit beside him. "You two ought to kiss and make up."

Susan looked at Philip, and if Elizabeth wasn't mistaken, the little corgi's eyes looked like they were widening as she sneezed in protest.

·⌒◦ℰ◦⌒·

CHAPTER THIRTY-FOUR

HANNA

Crouching low, I offered Susan a biscuit from the tin that my stepmother, Jane, had sent just for the corgis. She prepared the biscuits especially for them once a week, and my charges never passed up an offer to taste.

But today, Susan sniffed the presented treat and turned away. Her eyes were downcast, shifting from me to the ground and back. Her ears weren't as perky, and the nub of her tail didn't even twitch. I was immediately concerned.

"What is it, Sus?" I sat back on my heels. "You love these biscuits. They're your favorite."

Susan licked her lips but didn't bite.

There'd been a distinct change in Susan's behavior that had started while we'd been on the whirlwind tour and had continued since we'd gotten home. She was less inclined to follow directions, had snapped at me and others a few times, and, in addition to not being interested in the biscuits, she was not eating as well as usual.

I set down the tin and rubbed a hand over Susan's head, which prompted just the slightest movement of her tail. "Are you sick, old girl?"

Susan lay down, her head resting on her paws, and she

looked up at me, then away again. Normally she would have curled herself into me, but she just seemed so sad now.

Prancing like they had ants crawling up their legs were the other corgis, waiting for the biscuits to be tested. With one last look at Susan, I offered them each a treat, and then we continued on our walk, with Susan reluctantly joining us.

She reminded me of myself after my mum had passed: sullen and not interested in anything anymore. A great sadness had claimed me back then, and even all the attention my father paid me couldn't pull me out of it. Was Susan in mourning?

Or was she just sick?

It was hard to tell with dogs. But I was worried about her. There was most definitely something wrong.

After we returned from our walk, I called the queen's secretary. "I need to speak with her majesty regarding Susan: she's not well."

"I'll put you through right away."

"Hanna? What's wrong?" Elizabeth asked almost immediately, her voice filled with worry.

"Sorry to interrupt, ma'am, but Susan's not eating well and has just refused Jane's biscuits."

There was a pause and I sensed Elizabeth was both relieved and worried at the same time. "That is not like her."

"Not at all, and she seems . . . sad. I think I should call the veterinarian just to make sure she's not sick."

"Yes, please do. I wish I could be there but it's impossible today. Please keep me informed." The regret in the queen's tone reached through the phone. If not for whatever duties she had to attend to today, she would have dropped everything, taken a car, and driven herself from London to Windsor.

"I will, of course, ma'am."

The veterinarian was quick to visit, knowing he'd be looking in on the queen's corgi. He listened to Susan's heartbeat and her breathing. Looked into her eyes and her ears. Felt around her tummy. Took her temperature.

Then he shook his head and gave me a puzzled look. "She appears to be in perfect health."

I glanced at Susan, who lay there, despondent almost. "But she's not herself."

He shrugged, giving the corgi a little pat on the back. "Perhaps she is simply slowing down. Dogs tend to do that with age, and she's ten."

I nodded, not liking his answer at all, and knowing Elizabeth would also not be pleased. Perhaps I should get a second opinion before I called her. Old age wasn't a good enough diagnosis for the marked change in Susan.

But even the second veterinarian claimed that Susan was in perfect health. With a frown, I called the queen's secretary once more, and again I was rushed through on the line.

"How is she?" Elizabeth's voice was filled with the same kind of tension I felt—like a worried mother far away from her child.

"They both said she was fine, ma'am." I explained about the first veterinarian and then the second. "I am as baffled as they are. I've known Susan since she was a puppy; I can tell when something's changed."

"I quite agree." A pause, a few breaths, then, "I think perhaps she needs me."

I nodded though Elizabeth couldn't see me. "Shall I have Forrest bring the car for me? I can deliver her to you this evening."

"Yes, Hanna. I think it best."

And so I bundled up all of Susan's things and we made our way to Buckingham Palace.

Elizabeth was occupied in her receiving room; and since it was close to Susan's suppertime, I led my charge toward the kitchen, where the chef had been alerted to our arrival. Susan seemed perked up now; perhaps it really was that she just missed Elizabeth. She pranced beside me with the usual spring in her step, glancing up, the pink tip of her tongue hanging out of her mouth.

"Ah, so good to see you again, Your Highness," the chef said with a laugh, bending to give Susan's head a scratch.

Susan sniffed his hand, giving it a lick, the first sign of affection she'd shown in some time. I'd be lying if I said I wasn't jealous. I'd been cajoling her for days with no results.

"Liver, cabbage, carrots, and rice at your service." The chef held up the silver dish, the aromas wafting toward me.

Without warning, my stomach roiled, threatening to turn over the remnants of my earlier tea. I swallowed it down with wide eyes, but the chef looked at me oddly.

"Are you unwell, Hanna? You've gone quite pale."

I shook my head, swallowing down my nausea again. "I don't know what's come over me." Another look at the greasy pile in the dog dish had me gagging once more. I thrust Susan's leather leash at Chef and took off for the nearest toilet.

Spent and empty, I leaned back on my heels, pulled the chain to flush away the evidence of teatime, and wiped my mouth on a tissue.

Maybe I was sick. Or maybe . . . I pressed my hand to my belly, still flat.

Forrest and I had not been trying to have a baby, but we'd not *not* been trying either.

I'd been so busy taking care of everyone else, I didn't have time to take care of myself. Or to realize that, for however long,

I'd been carrying around a child. It couldn't have been too long, considering my stomach had not swelled yet. But I couldn't remember the last time I'd had a period either.

How was I supposed to have a baby now? Susan needed me. Elizabeth needed me. The other corgis needed me.

But the real problem was that the world wasn't the same as it had been during the war, where the men were off at the front and the women took up the working positions. I was lucky to have this position as it was. But if I were to become a mother, that would all go away. We'd yet to have the discussion, but Forrest would likely assume I'd no longer work when we had a child. That I'd stay home to care for him or her.

Tears pricked my eyes. Of course I would love any child we had created together, but that didn't mean I wanted to lose my identity. I *wanted* to work. I wanted to be able to be a mother and the keeper of the queen's corgis. I wanted both.

Was that even a possibility?

Perhaps I was simply fooling myself into believing. But plenty of women worked and cared for their children out of necessity. Could I claim necessity? Was sanity even a good enough excuse or one that would be accepted?

I pushed myself up off the floor and exited the ladies', seeing in the corridor as I did the initials *ER* engraved over an archway. *Elizabeth Regina.* I really need look no further than my own queen, Elizabeth, to realize that the possibility was right there in front of me. For the queen, the woman I served, the woman who served an entire country, was a working mother.

CHAPTER THIRTY-FIVE

Susan

There comes a moment in every dog's time on earth when life gets the better of us.

Today is that day for me.

For an indeterminate number of days, I've been feeling as though my princess is lost to me. Dogs don't count days. We don't keep calendars, and we don't wear watches. For us, time is marked by meals, adventures, walks, and cuddles. We are creatures of habit. And we thrive on our routines.

To say my routine with Lilibet has been thrown off is an understatement. It has been forever since I felt as connected to her as I used to be.

And to top it off, I'm pretty sure Hanna has a litter growing inside her. Her belly is round, and she waddles when she walks, and she tells me to slow down so she can catch up. She smells funny. Like biscuits and milk, and I've already lost my princess to her litter; I can't stand the idea of losing another person dear to me.

It is purely coincidence—given I can't tell time, nor do I care for what a clock might say—that I choose the moment I pass the royal clock winder to bear down on his ankles and sink my teeth in.

The man yelps, and I just hang on. I want someone else to

feel the pain of loss I am feeling. The desire to be with Lilibet. Maybe she will come get me. Snap at me to release the man, like she used to when I bit Philip. If Philip were here right now, I'd bite him too.

But it is Forrest who comes to the clock winder's rescue, and fearing he'd put me in the stables with the horses, I take off in the other direction with him chasing me, and soon enough there comes Hanna. I run them in circles, and it's almost like a fun game we used to play.

Only this time when Hanna catches me, her face is not full of joy as it usually is. This time, she looks at me with her mouth turned down, her brows drawn together.

Oh no . . .

"What have you done?" she whispers. "My God." Hanna glances at Forrest and their exchanged expressions are fearful.

"It's the queen's dog," Forrest says, as if that makes any sense. Everyone knows who I bonded with.

"They won't put down the queen's dog, will they?" Hanna asks, the fear in her voice making me tremble.

Hanna's heart beats rapidly; her breathing increases too. She is worried, and that makes me worried.

Hanna makes direct eye contact with me then. "It's like she knows what I said."

I don't, but I can sense that what I've done is pretty bad; at least that they are contemplating my fate, whatever putting me down meant. Maybe it meant they'd never pick me up again. My punishment would be a lifetime without any more cuddles. Is that what happened to Crackers? Did someone put him down somewhere and forget to pick him back up? I miss Crackers.

"I need to tell Elizabeth what happened before she hears it

from someone else." Hanna's speaking low and glancing furtively toward the clock winder.

I pant with nerves, but also hope. Does this mean she's going to take me to see Lilibet too?

And she does. Hanna marches right past the mean butler, who is always telling her what to do, and then she begs an audience with the queen from one of the snotty secretaries who deserves to have his ankle bitten. I never cared to learn his name, because mostly I felt his job was to keep me away from my Lilibet. And why would I ever want to identify a man whose sole job was to keep me away from my girl?

"She is otherwise engaged with the boxes at the moment," he says, as if Hanna and I were nothing better than a couple of chewed-up sticks.

"Well, I think she would like to know that the clock winder was wounded today."

"Wounded?" The secretary's gaze flicks right to me, and I should be offended he automatically assumes it was me that did the wounding, except he's right.

The man picks up the black handle thing and moves his finger in a circle on the block it's attached to. "Ma'am, Mrs. Darling is here to see you. There's been an accident with the royal clock winder." There is a moment of silence and then, almost disappointed, he says without looking at Hanna, "She'll see you."

Hanna doesn't bother to wait for him to show her in; she just pushes around the desk and into the queen's office. And I stay as still as possible in her arms, hoping she'll forget I'm there in case she decides to put me down.

Lilibet is there in an instant, as if she'd replaced the black handle and rushed right to the door.

"Oh, Susan, what did you do?" she coos at me, taking me from Hanna's arms and cuddling me against her body, her familiar scent surrounding me with comfort.

Not enough to make her put me down, I should say.

"She's bitten the royal clock winder." Hanna bites her own lip. "Quite badly."

Lilibet stiffens. "Does he require stitches?"

"Yes."

"Oh no." Lilibet looks at me; her brow is wrinkled, her mouth turned down. Just like Hanna's. She's disappointed in me, but I don't sense any of the fear that Hanna had, and she is still holding me. I suppose that's a comfort. "What's gotten into you, girl?"

"Perhaps she's grown a little territorial," Hanna offers.

"That could be it."

I wish I could say I don't bite anyone else this week, but when Hanna disappears, I latch on to a Grenadier Guard and then a palace sentry, followed by the policeman who tries to help chase me.

It isn't that I've suddenly grown vicious, but I miss Lilibet; and every time I bite someone, I get to see her. I'm a dog. We're creatures of habit, as I've mentioned before, and we're also very well trained to seek our rewards.

"But look at her," Lilibet says as I lie calmly in her arms, content to be with her once more.

Philip, having heard the commotion, comes rushing in. He is growing frustrated as the servants demand my head, which sounds quite awful. I'd rather keep it right where it is.

"She's the very picture of innocence." Lilibet bends down and kisses my head.

Philip stands, his hands on his waist, both brows raised in a skeptical question. I get the sense he thinks Lilibet is a bit out of her mind. "And you expect me to relay that to the servants who are now afraid to even walk past her?"

Afraid? Who would be afraid of me? I perk up at this, my ears flicking, and I cock my head to stare at Philip. Perhaps he is the one out of his mind.

"Oh, Susan, why do you keep biting people?" Lilibet's eyes shimmer, and she trembles slightly. I lean up and lick her, as if to tell her everything will be all right. "I won't get rid of her, Philip. My father gave her to me for my eighteenth birthday. She's been with me for the last decade. She is part of my family, and all I have left of him."

Philip's determination seems to crack at that. His hands slip from his hips and his head bows slightly. Even his face falls into what looks momentarily like sadness or guilt. "Fine. But you need do something about her biting people. The papers are already talking about the vicious corgis in the palace."

Lilibet's hand smoothes over my head and I lean into her. I love these moments with her, when I have her attention and her love.

"I will," she says. Then she pulls my face toward hers, and stares me right in the eyes. "No more biting."

I wish I could tell her I agree, but I don't know how to form the words.

I'm sorry, I want to say. *I let my emotions get the best of me.* Even dogs aren't perfect.

·⟨ ୭∕୧ ⟩·

CHAPTER THIRTY-SIX

Elizabeth

Balmoral Castle
September 1954

Elizabeth stood outside in the fall weather, watching as the animal psychologist knelt in the grass before Susan, who was sitting perfectly still, watching the man.

The psychologist stared into Susan's eyes, and she stared back. It had already been several minutes. A silent conversation she wasn't part of. Tension prickled in Elizabeth's limbs. She was prepared at any moment to leap forward and wrench Susan away from the psychologist should her cranky girl decide it was time to take a chunk out of yet another person.

Surprisingly, since they'd had their conversation, Susan had not bitten anyone else. Elizabeth liked to think she'd gotten through to her, but the logical side of her said it was impossible for Susan to truly have understood her direct order. Yet here they were.

Because of Susan's behavior, they'd been forced to hang signs around the palace that said: Beware of Dog.

Ridiculous, really. Susan hadn't a savage bone in her body until recently, and Elizabeth was fairly certain it was her fault.

First, she didn't have enough time for her favorite corgi, and second, she'd forced Susan to become a mother when she'd sent her to the breeder.

Guilt riddled Elizabeth at all the emotional trauma she might have put Susan through, she who was supposed to be her constant companion.

The psychologist glanced up at Elizabeth. "You should be a part of this, ma'am. We're going to make vows now that we've had our chat."

The silent chat, Elizabeth wanted to add, but she didn't.

Instead, she nodded. She was still more than a little skeptical about this meeting, but letters had been pouring into the palace from all over the world, remarking on Susan's change of behavior and that an animal psychologist could help.

"Come kneel here in front of her and look into her eyes the way I have been."

Elizabeth did as she was instructed. Susan's eyes twinkled, and Elizabeth thought there was just a slight wink on Susan's left eye, as if the psychologist was playing into her hands—well, paws.

"That's it, ma'am, just gaze at her. When dogs and their humans look at each other, making eye contact like this, it is a sign of respect but also love. The longer you do it, the stronger your bond will become."

"I wish her to respect me as her queen," Elizabeth said, half teasing. "Susan, bend thy knee."

The psychologist looked surprised at first, and then he chuckled. "Susan respects you, ma'am, that is a certainty. I've never seen a dog who listens and follows their human so well."

"Is that so?" Elizabeth was a little surprised to hear it. She'd always had good relationships not only with Susan but with the other family dogs and the hunting dogs. Though more than once people had told her she had a special bond with animals.

"It's true, ma'am. You've a way with her. All your dogs, in fact. It's quite impressive."

Elizabeth smiled but didn't say what she was thinking: that she felt more of a connection with the dogs than with most people, most of the time.

"There've been a lot of changes lately, ma'am," the psychologist continued as Elizabeth stared into Susan's lovely brown eyes. "For you both."

"Yes."

"And in those changes, some routines have been disrupted."

"That's correct."

"Dogs are creatures of habit. Susan feels the disruption, perhaps even more keenly than you, ma'am, and so I think for Susan's benefit, it would be good if you spent more time with her on a regular schedule."

Elizabeth nodded. "Our walks. We used to do them every day at the same time, twice a day if I could. But lately . . . I just haven't even been able to walk myself. I'll do my best to resume them."

Susan blinked at her, her tiny mouth opening as she panted with what seemed like excitement.

"Have you missed that, girl?"

Susan gave a yip, her behind wiggling as she wagged her tail while sitting.

"You have an excellent rapport with Susan, ma'am. She pays attention when you're talking," the psychologist said. "Did you know that dogs can understand somewhere in the neighborhood of two hundred words in addition to hand signal commands and whistles?"

Now this was something Elizabeth did know. She'd grown up around dogs, always finding their company to be a pleasure but also their behavior to be interesting. "Yes. I think our dog Dookie could hear the word *rabbit* from clear across the estate." Elizabeth laughed.

"He just might have, ma'am; they have very good hearing. Now speaking of that, Susan here has heard us say her name and the word *walk* many times. Dogs do have the ability to put two and two together, but they also have reactions to what you might call their cue words. For your pretty girl here, *W-A-L-K* is a cue word that she's about to spend time with you. As are certain movements on your part. For example, if you put on your jacket, or even walk near the door you use to go outside at the same time every day."

"There is also Hanna, and the footmen too who take her." Susan's head cocked to the side at the pronouncement of her caretaker's name. "Hanna is my corgi keeper. She spends just as much time with Susan as I do." Even though Hanna was round with child, a decision had still not been made on whether she would continue in her position. Elizabeth had told her she was welcome to stay on if she could find childcare, and had been glad to hear that Hanna's husband supported whatever decision she chose to make.

"Ah, then I'll have to meet with her as well to make sure Susan is getting consistent care." Suddenly he looked nervous. "Pardon my saying so, ma'am. I'm certain you will make sure she knows what we've discussed."

"I will, of course, but it can't hurt if you speak with her as well."

The psychologist glanced back at Susan as he agreed to do

so, almost as if looking at the dog was easier than looking at his queen—not unlike the people she met on a daily basis, but also not unlike herself.

"You are wonderful with her," Elizabeth said, noting how Susan seemed captivated by the psychologist, as much as he was with her.

"It might sound silly, ma'am, but I believe that some people are born with a closer understanding of animals than others. A kindred spirit, or bond, if you will."

"That doesn't sound silly to me at all."

He smiled sheepishly with a little shrug.

"I've always been fond of animals, since I was a little girl. Dogs, horses, even chickens." She laughed. "I think if I'd not been ordained by God to be queen, I would have liked to be a veterinarian." Oddly enough, he was the first person she'd ever confessed that to.

"You would have excelled, ma'am."

"I appreciate the compliment."

"Shall we resume same time next week?" he asked.

Elizabeth opened her mouth, the reply of having to check with her secretary regarding her schedule on the tip of her tongue, but then she recalled the commitment she'd just made to Susan. "Yes, I will make certain we are available."

Thankfully, her schedule was free, and so she didn't have to worry about explaining to Sir Michael Adeane, her new secretary now that Lascelles had retired, why her dog came before her duties to the crown, which would not have gone over very well, especially because he was already up in arms about Maggie and Townsend.

Maggie had just turned twenty-four, and the journalists were practically banging down the door to find out if Townsend was going to propose. Elizabeth and Maggie spent the last couple of months at Balmoral out of sight of the public, for their usual summer holiday, and they'd decided just to stay through to the usual prime minister's weekend in mid-October. The added benefit of the long stay had been for Maggie to have time to think.

Though the hundreds of reporters and photographers that milled outside the gate, and a few daring idiots who'd attempted to sneak onto the estate, kept them virtually hostage.

Despite the upheaval, Elizabeth did manage to keep her promise of daily walks with Susan. It wasn't a chore. The both of them had needed to escape and find a way to breathe. Maggie had gotten thinner over the last couple months, smoking more and eating less, but Elizabeth hoped that soon the trouble would all be behind them.

She'd decided to support her sister in whatever way she could, and had advised her to write Prime Minister Churchill about her intent to see the marriage to Townsend through, and that Maggie planned to meet with him later this month.

Windswept and refreshed, by the time Elizabeth and Susan returned to the castle, Churchill had already arrived.

Maggie was waiting for her when she entered her private drawing room, outfitted in a soft wool plaid dress, her hair coiffed.

"Ma'am," Maggie said hastily with a short curtsy.

The formality of her own sister, her lifetime playmate, calling her *ma'am* and curtsying to her was not something Elizabeth was ever going to get used to. She wished she could tell her to stop, but tradition and formality were what had held the monarchy together for almost a thousand years, and she wasn't going to be the one to change that. At least Maggie was less formal when there was no one else around.

"I've been looking all over for you." Dark circles marred Maggie's eyes, and she was wringing her hands as she addressed Elizabeth.

"I wasn't far. Just a walk." Susan marched up to Maggie and demanded a kiss.

"He's here." The two words, strung together so heavily, lay against Elizabeth's shoulders like the determination Churchill brought with him. They'd been scouring the Marriages Act with legal aides and chancellors for months, and today they would be able to determine at last what needed to be done. What Elizabeth had been avoiding for months and months.

"You know, Maggie, that I would never stand in the way of your happiness."

"It is ridiculous we've had to wait this long. I'm practically a spinster."

Elizabeth approached her sister cautiously; reaching for her hand, she squeezed it, noting that Maggie's fingers were cold. Maggie's nervous brittleness made her feel as though she might flee at any moment.

"You're not a spinster," Elizabeth said with her usual calm, trying to impart some of it to Maggie, who looked ready to snap. "You're in the prime of your life, and I think about to begin a very happy season."

Maggie looked stricken for half a second before she ducked down to pull Susan into her arms. "What if I'm making a mistake?"

"What?" Elizabeth was taken aback. This was not at all what she expected Maggie to say. Of course, it was what she herself had been thinking, but she'd never tell her sister that.

"Townsend and I have been apart for so long—what if he's changed? What if I've changed? What if my feelings for him were simply stupid and girlish? I'm not sure I'm ready to give up everything for . . . for someone or something that seems to me an uncertainty at this point."

"Maggie." Elizabeth licked her lips, feeling a little at a loss for words. The entire country had been in an uproar for months, Mummy had a hard time even speaking to Maggie, all because of this relationship with Townsend, and she was having doubts? "I think it best that when he's on leave later this month the two of you meet so you can see for yourself before you make any decisions. Once made, it will be difficult to pull back."

Maggie nodded, nuzzling Susan some more before standing up and visibly letting out a breath as she swiped at her tears. "I'm just afraid that my fears will come true."

"Then you will find another man to love. You're beautiful, clever, and funny. You're—what do the papers say? The most eligible royal bachelorette?"

Maggie laughed. "They are odd, aren't they?"

Elizabeth smiled. "I don't think we'll ever understand them and their obsession with us."

"Probably not." Maggie hesitated a moment, clearly having something else to say. "Will you let me sit with you when Churchill relays the news?"

If not for the fact it was about her, the request would have been out of place, but Elizabeth couldn't see her sister barred from hearing from the prime minister himself just what the government had decided about her fate.

"Of course. We'll call you in so he can explain to you their findings."

But that evening after dinner, Churchill wanted to speak

with Elizabeth alone, to which she agreed, considering it wasn't only Maggie's fate that needed to be discussed, although that was a large part of it.

With Susan at Churchill's feet, he laid out the issues of the country, and then hedged toward Maggie.

"I'll be the first to tell you, ma'am, that the Royal Marriages Act is no longer appropriate to modern conditions."

"I tend to agree, given it was written almost two hundred years ago. However, there is something to be said for tradition and the rule of law in this country, and why our monarchy still stands."

"I agree. Which is why we've been working so hard to find a way to make a marriage between Princess Margaret and Group Captain Townsend possible. And while we do think that nearly seventy-five percent of the electorate will be in favor of allowing the marriage, it does not come without conditions."

Elizabeth nodded. "I would not have expected it to be freely given." Even if she wished that that were the case. "And I think those conditions should be discussed with Princess Margaret. I won't make the choice for her."

"I'm certain she is grateful for your consideration. They are much as you suspected, that she will need to renounce her succession to the throne, but they will allow her to keep her civil list allowance, as well as her duties and appellation of her royal highness."

Elizabeth nodded perfunctorily, slowly letting out the breath she'd been holding. The decision was fair. In fact, they were letting Maggie retain more than she had expected.

* * *

AFTER LUNCH THE following day, Elizabeth invited Philip and Maggie to join Churchill so that the situation might finally be discussed. Of course, she'd spilled everything to Philip the night before as she paced her bedroom. But she'd not been able to say a word to Maggie. She wanted her sister to hear it from Churchill himself, who could explain it all better if she had questions.

Maggie's face flushed as soon as he said the marriage to Townsend would be allowed. Her eyes shone with tears, though she kept herself together well and even managed a steady voice as she said, "Thank you for looking into the matter, Prime Minister. It is most appreciated by me and by my future husband."

Only Elizabeth noticed the slightly frightened flash in her sister's eyes. What she'd thought would be a certain decision seemed to still be frustratingly up in the air.

* * *

November 1955

Maggie flopped down on the sofa in Elizabeth's drawing room at Buckingham Palace and flung a pile of papers toward the marble top of the coffee table, missing the mark. The papers fluttered to the ground, all turned and folded to the various sections that talked about her and Townsend. The end of their love affair and how Elizabeth had forced two people to be apart.

"It never matters what we say—they always have their own opinions made up and printed." Maggie pouted. "I very specifically said in my radio address that the decision to part from Peter had been entirely my own."

Elizabeth nodded, taking the seat opposite her slumped sister.

Maggie's eyes were puffy from crying. It had been a tough

decision to make, and even tougher to have to address a public whose business it was not.

"I should be mourning the loss of love in private," Maggie went on.

"But you hate being in private," Elizabeth teased.

Maggie grinned. "Very true."

"I have an idea. There's an opera at the Royal Opera House called *The Bartered Bride*. A comedy about true love prevailing despite meddling parents. It would be entirely baffling to the journaling hounds if we dressed up and went to see it."

"It's too ironic."

"Precisely."

"Well then, shall I wear the strapless pink satin or the blue taffeta?" Maggie laughed shortly and waved away her question. "Who am I kidding—you've no sense of style."

Elizabeth rolled her eyes, taking her sister's insult in stride. Maggie had been contrary since the day she was born, and nothing was ever going to change that. "I have plenty of style, perhaps just not the kind you align with."

"No truer words have ever been uttered."

"Go away now, I've work to do."

Maggie stood, curtsied, and said, "Ma'am," in the way she sometimes did that showed she really held no deference for Elizabeth's position as queen, though she did respect her as her older sister.

"What was that about?" Philip asked, sauntering in with his usual air of confidence, his eyes twinkling as though he had some joke to tell.

Elizabeth waved her hand in the air, then stood up to give him a kiss. "Maggie being Maggie."

She tidied up the papers from where her sister had left them. Seeing the headlines, Philip frowned.

"My God, they just never leave us in peace, do they?"

"I'm afraid not. And Prime Minister Eden doesn't seem to have as much presence as Churchill did with the people."

"Well, if there's anyone who can turn the press, it's Richard," Philip said, speaking of Commander Richard Colville, who'd once been in the Royal Navy and then was asked by Elizabeth's father to be the royal household press secretary. He'd done such a good job, she'd asked him to stay on for her too.

"Perhaps I should have him work on a campaign, then."

"Couldn't hurt."

A knock on the drawing room door interrupted their plans for clearing the romance-gone-wrong news with Maggie and Townsend.

Hanna came in, giving a curtsy; then she jerked forward as a leashed Susan rushed in, taking a nipping swipe at Philip's trouser leg before greeting Elizabeth.

"Is it that hour already, you naughty girl?" Elizabeth said, bending down to scratch the corgi behind the ears.

Despite her eleven years, Susan was still full of energy when she saw Elizabeth.

"I'll leave the both of you to it," Philip said, backing out of the room as if he expected Susan to charge after him and finish the attack she'd started.

"You leave him be, Queen Bee," Elizabeth teased, then she glanced up to where Hanna stood. "How is Honey?"

"Doing better; the psychologist thinks it was merely a case of copycatting."

"Oh, Susan, you really must set a better example."

"He thinks that perhaps if Sugar were to be whelped, that

might give Honey something else to focus on. The two of them are so close, she's likely to nurture her and mother her."

"What a great idea. I'll give Thelma a call." Elizabeth picked up the end of Susan's leash. "Now, shall we walk and talk, sweet Sus?"

CHAPTER THIRTY-SEVEN

ℋANNA

ℐ should be dismissed," I said, finishing pinning the nappie in place on our son, Forrest Jr., Forr for short. As always, there was a pang of guilt that I was going to be leaving him for a few hours today to work. Was he going to remember me?

"Why? Because you had Forr?" Forrest asked, taking our son in his arms. He was an overinvolved father and I loved it. "Do you want to quit?"

I shook my head, wiping a bit of spit-up from Forr's lips. "No, of course not."

"You can if you want."

My heart lodged in my throat. I loved this man so much for his being willing to accept whatever decision I made, respecting me enough to make the right choice. But was I? What would my mother have done?

"No, I don't want to. And Jane is doing so well with the baby. It's just Susan's behavior, the biting and attacking half a dozen people." I paused a moment, my emotions getting the better of me. "The animal psychologist said it's partially my fault."

"He said that?" Forrest looked incredulous as we walked down the stairs toward the kitchen.

"Not in so many words, but he said that Susan was under a

lot of stress from Elizabeth's overscheduled days and felt abandoned by me when I went into labor, and then my maternity leave. And then Honey went on to follow the biting trend."

"Oh, no, no. It is not your fault at all. You can't blame their little bouts of anarchy on your having a baby." He shook his head with a chuckle. "Susan missed her mum, and she was acting out *before* you had Forr."

I nodded, emotion swelling my throat. I'd been with Susan as long as Elizabeth had, and we'd a strong bond too. If Elizabeth was her mum, then I was her auntie. Even if I didn't want to take the blame, in my heart I couldn't stop thinking that part of it lay on my shoulders.

"It feels an awful lot like I played a part. Dogs have feelings too, and are emotional, bonding creatures. Too much upset in their schedule and with their people can really be detrimental. I don't want to create any more disruption." What I didn't tell him was that I had changed my mind and thought of quitting my job, staying home to raise Forr after he was born. The moment our eyes had met, I felt a connection in my heart that I'd never anticipated. But after hearing what the animal psychologist had to say, I just couldn't bear the idea of disappointing Susan further. I loved that dog as if she were my own. I had to make it work.

Besides, I had a duty to the queen, and to Susan, as well as to my own family. And Forr was so young now; he wouldn't notice if I was gone a few hours a day. Not to mention that so many times caring for the dogs was done at our own cottage. I could, and did, have the best of both worlds.

A knock sounded on our door.

"Thank goodness for Jane," I said. Without her help I wouldn't have had another choice. Well, I could have found another sitter, I supposed, but it would have been costly, likely out of our budget, and Jane was willing to do it for free.

And I was lucky: when everyone was at Windsor on the weekends, I could bring little Forr with me to play with the dogs. The way he watched them all with keen eyes and reached for them, cooing and burbling, my father thought he was a gamekeeper in the making, which made Forrest always teasingly add that, no indeed, he would be a coachman like his father and maybe someday crown equerry.

I just rolled my eyes, because what they were both failing to see was that little Forr loved the dogs, and perhaps, he might just want to be a royal keeper of the corgis like his mother.

"I've just finished feeding and changing him," I said to Jane, "and he should be ready to go down for a nap soon." I gazed lovingly at Forr, who was pinching his grandmother's cheeks and giggling. "I'll be back in a few hours."

But a few hours turned into the rest of the day, as it seemed Honey's taste for policemen hadn't waned.

·✦·

CHAPTER THIRTY-EIGHT

SUSAN

When I was born, I could barely figure out how to use my short legs. But once I got the hang of walking, of running, there was no stopping me. I could run like the wind. Chase a squirrel, leap for a bird, run for miles without even thinking about stopping.

It's funny to look back and remember how well I moved, especially now when everything seems to be just a little slower. A little creakier.

But I'm not stopping.

Moving slower isn't a reason to quit.

Getting older isn't a reason to lie down forever.

At least that's what I tell myself when I think I can't go on.

Sometimes, I lie in the grass, panting from exertion, and stare at the sky, watching the clouds pass. I rest, and the world slows down enough for me to absorb everything that's going on around me. The things I missed when I was young and full of energy.

The way a bumblebee walks with its spiky legs on the yellow petals of a flower, or the way a bird hops with both feet and then pecks at the ground to pull up a worm.

Hanna is resting beside me, her baby crawling through the grass toward where Biscuit plays with Sugar and Honey. These are rare moments. Hanna's hand strokes my back and I turn to look at her, happy she's sitting here beside me. Happy she understands that I need more moments like this.

"Sus." I perk up, whipping around to the other side to see my Lilibet. She's met us here as she does most days, and now I'll get to go on a walk with her.

This is my favorite time.

I jump up and run to greet her. It feels like forever since I've seen her at breakfast. She's taken to letting me eat my meals with her and spend my days with her in her office while she works. It is a dream come true.

"How's my girl?" Lilibet asks as she scratches just the right spot behind my ears.

I wag my tail and give a little bark in answer.

"Are you ready?" she asks me.

I yip again and take off at a slower trot, but a trot all the same.

No matter how old this body gets, I'll still get it moving for her.

Lilibet hurries after me. The other corgis rush after us. I might have been jealous before about their interruptions, but not anymore. This is my time with Lilibet, but I need them to learn her habits too.

One day, they'll have to take over for me.

It's not something I ever thought of before. Even when the king went away to another place. But now I know, one day, not too soon, but one day, I will have to go away. And I don't want Lilibet to be lonely.

She is my everything.

·࿓·

CHAPTER THIRTY-NINE

ℰLIZABETH

February 1956

Not long after the royal family rang in the new year, Sugar birthed her litter of puppies. It seemed fitting to begin the new year with new life.

Elizabeth peered into the tiny pen where the little fur balls, no bigger than bread rolls, were squirming about one another and toward their mother in search of milk.

"Oh, they are so cute," seven-year-old Prince Charles said, and five-year-old Princess Anne copied him, peering over the edge. Their innocent faces were filled with wonder as they took in the pile of soft puppies.

They'd begged to come with Elizabeth when she went to Windsor to see the litter, and Elizabeth, wanting her children to have as much love for the breed as she, had agreed with enthusiasm.

"They are just too precious." Elizabeth stroked a finger over one of the silky, golden backs. "I had every intention of only choosing one, but perhaps a belated Christmas present for you both? What do you think?"

Her children looked up at her, doe-eyed and grinning. Then

Charles's brow wrinkled slightly, and his grin turned down. The lad could be so serious at times. "Will Papa let us?"

"We won't tell him just yet." Elizabeth winked. He'd made her promise she'd only pick one, but how could she when both her children wanted a puppy, and there were several to choose from? "Once he sees them, he will fall in love just as we have."

"Cross our hearts," Princess Anne said as she mimicked the move Charles made. It was adorable how she looked up to her big brother. That was, when she wasn't surpassing him in whatever pursuit it was. Anne was vibrant and active, quite a lot like her father, and loved a good challenge.

Elizabeth laughed. "Oh, do look what Susan has accomplished. Another generation of Windsor corgis." She lifted one of the tiny ones, its fur with a reddish-gold hint to it that almost reminded her of the whisky her father drank.

"I will call you Whisky," she said, kissing the puppy on its tiny pink nose. "And this one"—she lifted another—"will be Sherry."

"I want Whisky," Charles proclaimed, wiggling his hands toward her.

"But I want Whisky," Anne argued, giving her brother a little elbow in the ribs.

"Now, children, we'll not argue over who gets who. We'll let the pups decide." Elizabeth eyed them both until they nodded in unison.

Elizabeth set each puppy on the floor, and her children called to them while the tiny fur balls inched this way and that, but didn't make it very far in either direction.

"Well, I suppose we'll have to draw straws." Elizabeth chuckled.

"You're the queen: you decree who gets who." Charles's tone

was a little petulant as he crossed his arms over his chest and gave a wicked glance toward his sister. It had been hard for Charles of late. The poor lad needed a win.

"Well, fine, then." Elizabeth licked her lips, not wanting to cause conflict and for the dogs to be a bone of contention between the siblings. Heaven knew they didn't need any more of that. "Who was born first?" she asked Hanna.

"Sherry, ma'am."

"Well, then there you have it. By order of birth, Sherry shall be yours, Charles, and Whisky shall be yours, Anne."

Anne grinned as though she'd won, even though it had been a fair decision, which only made Charles pout more.

"Come now, pouting is not becoming of a prince, and neither is gloating, Anne."

Though both children had been reprimanded, they just grinned, any contention between the two of them gone now that they had a puppy each. They knelt down, Charles in his brown wool trousers and Anne in her thick stockings and plaid wool skirt, and started to pet their puppies, cooing at them the way Elizabeth had when she was a child meeting Dookie for the first time. It made her long for those moments when she'd been with her family, "us four" and no one else.

So much had changed since then, and the only thing she couldn't accept was her father's passing so much sooner than was his time. There was a tightening in her chest then, like her ribs were trying to squeeze tight enough to thread together. Elizabeth swallowed around the lump forming in her throat and commanded herself to relinquish the feelings of anguish before her children saw her fall apart. Those were moments that had to remain behind closed doors, when she was utterly alone.

"I think we'll need to hire two new footmen," Elizabeth said, bringing up a topic of conversation to take the feelings of loss away from her mind. "For the corgi room. There's just going to be too many of them for you to handle all on your own, Hanna. Besides, I need you to focus on the training and care of them, and not necessarily their bathroom needs."

"Doggie One and Doggie Two?" Hanna chuckled, referring to what they should name the footmen.

"Precisely, brilliant." Elizabeth joined in on the laughs. "What do you say, keeper of the queen's dogs? Can you handle the corgi staff?"

"It would be my pleasure, ma'am."

Elizabeth nodded, searching for just the right thing to say. "I appreciate it, Hanna. You've been indispensable to me all these years, and I do hope you're happy."

"I am, ma'am."

"Good." Elizabeth glanced down at the litter of puppies once more. "Then perhaps you'd like one too? Maybe for your son?"

Hanna's eyes widened, lighting up in a way Elizabeth had never seen before. "Yes, I would so very much, thank you." Hanna lifted up the pup with lighter hair, nuzzling the tiny body. "I have been partial to this sweet girl. I think I'll call her Ginny, Gin for short, keeping in line with your naming of this litter."

"'Tis the season for spirits." Elizabeth smiled down at the rest of the puppies. They'd give one to Thelma Gray again, and then find the right fit among the staff. She'd been serious when she said no Windsor corgi would ever be for sale. "Children, come along now. We must let Hanna work with the puppies; and when they are trained, they'll come live with us at the palace."

CHAPTER FORTY

ℋANNA

𝒯he snow-dusted yard of our little cottage at Windsor was dotted by five corgis. Susan and Honey were at Buckingham Palace, in the care of their footmen. Sugar was here with me and her puppies while I trained them before they were weaned.

Biscuit was attempting to corral the puppies, who knew nothing of order. A blur of reddish-gold fur as they ran this way and that. At eight weeks, they were rambunctious for spurts and then collapsed into hours-long naps.

Sugar was a good mama and cuddled and nursed her pups like the best of them, perhaps having learned from her own mother, Susan.

But today was the day to deliver Whisky and Sherry to the palace. They needed to be introduced to the other corgis in residence, and it was a careful process so that there wouldn't be any arguments or disagreements about the hierarchy of things.

"Mum-mum." Forr toddled around the yard with Biscuit egging him on. She was a good dog and loved to play with my son.

I never would have pegged a corgi for being a nanny dog, but Biscuit took the cake. In fact, Forr had taken his first steps in order to chase after her when she had a fit of the zoomies.

"Look how well you're walking, darling." I crouched, my arms wide, as I encouraged him to come closer.

Forr grinned, showing off two large teeth that had come in recently. "Doggie." He pointed at Biscuit.

"We have lots of them, don't we?"

"Doggie." He pointed to Gin.

"So many. Come here and pet them."

Forr trundled forward, collapsing into my arms and gazing up at me with the type of adoration I wasn't sure I deserved, given I was always gone—and today would be no different. His affection for me never seemed to wane, however.

"I love you," I said to him and gave him a big kiss on his warm cheek before he squirmed away to chase after Biscuit again.

Forrest helped me leash the pups and load them into the waiting car that would take us the hour's ride to London.

The other pups from the litter had been given away already, and one sent to Thelma in thanks for helping with the Windsor breeding program, which I was now fully in charge of. The program was an exciting new venture, the start of something new not only for the queen but for me too.

A familiar figure walking down the path drew the attention of the corgis and Forr. Jane always arrived fifteen minutes early, which I appreciated, as it gave me enough time to chat with her before I had to run out of the house. Fortunately, my son adored Jane, and never complained when I left him with her. A blessing for us both, but it also made me a little sad. It seemed silly for me to want him to miss me, and truthfully, I'm glad he didn't.

"I'll be back tonight," I said to Jane, who was tossing biscuits through the car window to every patiently, and not so patiently, waiting pup.

"Are you certain, dear?" Jane asked. "It's such a long drive."

"Positively. If I don't have to sleep away from Forr, I'd rather not. Will you be all right with Biscuit and Gin?"

"Fit as a fiddle. Especially with Forr to help." Jane gave Forr's chubby cheek a little squeeze that had him laughing.

"I don't know how much help he'll be."

"They will tire each other out." Jane winked. "And then they all crash hard for a nap."

She had a good point there. I kissed Forr goodbye, and thanked Jane again before climbing into the car that Forrest had pulled around.

The ride seemed longer than usual, only because Whisky and Sherry were bouncing around the car like a couple of furry balls, and one of them took a piddle on the floor, which in turn prompted the other to follow suit. Sugar lay on the leather seat and stared at them as if they were aliens and barked at them when they sank their teeth into the leather seats.

"Perhaps we should have crated them," I said as an afterthought to Forrest, who was driving.

"You'll know for next time." Forrest shook his head but chuckled all the same.

As much as he didn't seem to be worried about the damage they were causing, I was. This wasn't even our car.

"I do hope they don't dock the damages from our pay." I leaned over the seat to wipe the mess with one of the blankets I'd brought. "Oh, they do stink now."

"They won't dock our pay. They are the queen's babies. And surely, she knew they would cause some damage. Even Susan has been known to go to war with the dining room chairs."

"That's true, but I'm supposed to be keeping them in line."

I'd had this job for a decade, and I still worried it would be taken away. Especially now that I had a child. It might be easier for Elizabeth to simply let me go, thinking I had too many other obligations.

"I think she will forgive you for two rambunctious puppies taking a chunk out of the car seat. As I said, she doesn't seem to mind when they do the same in the dining room."

I drew in a breath and exhaled as I watched Whisky and Sherry wrestling on the back seat.

Elizabeth and the prince and princess met us outside when we arrived. Forrest and I made our bows, as the puppies and Sugar bounded out of the car.

Charles and Anne, dressed in matching sweaters and trousers, fawned over their puppies, which had changed quite a bit in the weeks since they'd seen them.

While the children and Elizabeth were playing with the puppies in the yard, I took Sugar to the corgi room to reintroduce her to Susan and Honey, given she'd been gone for a few months. There was something to be said about the hierarchy of dogs, and it was best to do the reintroduction without the puppies, who would be a distraction. Plus, I thought Sugar might enjoy having a wee break from the intense energy of her offspring.

As I walked down the corridor toward the corgi room, I heard a shout, and then another. I picked up my pace, rushing around the corner only to see one of the footmen kick Honey in the ribs and send her skittering across the floor.

"No!" I shouted at the man, my heart pounding and ribs aching as if I'd been the one kicked. "My God, how dare you?" I rushed toward Honey, who was cowering now in the corner, shivering, her ears back, nub of a tail tucked.

Sugar, as if to stick up for her sister, started barking like mad and yanking on the leash.

"She bloody bit me." The footman stabbed a white-gloved finger so violently toward Honey, it gave off the image of him trying to do it clear into the poor dog's heart. Then he pointed toward the toe of his shiny black shoe where two tiny pricks could be seen from Honey's teeth. There were no tears in his black trousers.

"Are you hurt?" I asked him.

He frowned and huffed a breath.

"Are you hurt?" I asked for a second time.

"No."

"So she grabbed hold of your shoe, and you kicked her?"

His face was red now. "She could have bloody well done some damage."

"You should be ashamed of yourself," I said to the man, soothing Honey, who was trembling now, likely both from pain and fear, as well as Sugar, who seemed irate. "Kicking a dog for biting your shoe. She was probably being playful, not vicious. And as you said, you weren't even hurt."

"*I* should be ashamed?" He smacked himself in the chest, spittle flying from his lips. "These dogs are a damned nuisance."

"Watch your language," I said sternly, standing and squaring my shoulders, Honey and Sugar behind me. "Why would you take a job as a footman for the corgis if you couldn't handle it?"

"Handle being attacked?" He was incredulous now, arms wide. His behavior was unnerving.

"This is clearly not the position for you. Nor, I daresay, are any positions within the palace."

He snarled and was about to say something else when a senior footman appeared.

"What seems to be the problem?" I recognized the man as Jerry.

"I was attacked," the junior footman replied.

"He kicked Honey clear across the corridor." If the idiot was going to feign innocence in this situation, I wasn't going to let him get away with it.

Jerry looked stricken, more at the idea of the servant kicking the queen's corgi than anything else. He'd surmised that the younger footman was not obviously hurt. But given that Honey had bitten a policeman before, it was important to at least understand the situation.

"Are you injured?" Jerry asked.

The footman glanced down at his liveried uniform, nothing out of place and only the two pinpricks in his shoe to indicate Honey's indiscretion.

"No."

"And still you kicked the dog?" Jerry's brow furrowed.

The footman glowered.

"You dared react in a violent manner against one of the queen's corgis? Why not simply remove your shoe? Or toss her a toy or treat?"

The man's hands fisted at his sides, and before things came to blows, I stepped in. "I think it best you leave, sir, before I tell the queen what has occurred here. Resign your position."

Elizabeth would be devasted to find out that one of her precious girls had been so viciously attacked by the very man meant to care for her.

The footmen had been hired by the palace managerial staff, and I would need to make sure that I was at the next interview. Another occurrence like this would be devastating.

With a vulgar retort, the footman stomped off.

"Horrible man," Jerry mumbled. "I'll make certain he's escorted off properly and with the usual contracts signed."

"Thank you." I picked up Honey, cuddling her close. "I'll see she's cared for."

PART V

CℋE
ℳONARCH

ROYAL REPORT

TRUSTED NEWS OF ALL THINGS ROYAL

Something is going on within the royal household. It appears our queen has banished her husband from the realm. Consigned to a yacht staffed by two hundred and forty, the Duke of Edinburgh will be sailing the world, even making a foray into Antarctica. What must he have done to be sent to the coldest place on earth to contemplate his sins?

꠱

CHAPTER FORTY-ONE

ℰLIZABETH

October 1956

Soon the HMY *Britannia* would blow its horn as it sailed out of port in Australia carrying Philip, along with a crew of nearly three hundred, on his four-month-long world tour.

Elizabeth's handsome husband stood on the tarmac, dressed smartly in a suit, waving goodbye to her where she stood with the children as he boarded the plane that would take him to Melbourne for the start of his adventure.

They'd been apart before; this was nothing new, really, except that he'd be gone over the holidays this time. That seemed an eternity to her.

Rumors swirled when news of his world tour were made public. Of course they did. Not even their press office could curb the waspish tongues of those who wanted to see drama where there wasn't any. And the media fed on that like the parasitic wasps who lay their nasty eggs in unsuspecting caterpillars.

People thought Elizabeth was punishing Philip for some reason, which was completely ridiculous, and no amount of explaining seemed to change their minds. They wanted there to be trouble within the royal family. Wanted the drama of an unhappy royal couple.

It had taken her a number of years to learn to look past those rumors, to not look for the threads of truth that people swore were woven into the fabrics of their lives when they weren't. Philip was an energetic, flirtatious, and charming man. Those qualities had drawn her to him when she'd been merely a girl. Drew her still. There wasn't any wonder that his nature might attract a critical eye, that if he chatted with anyone of the opposite sex, they might think it was leading to a bedroom. My God, but did they not have anything better to do than imagine her husband in some lurid and twisted tale?

Whether or not there was any truth to the rumors didn't matter. Rumors made money, and the media was a for-profit business.

The absolute fact was: Philip was devoted to her—and that was all she cared to know. He had given up his dreams of a naval career to be with her. Had given up his Greek citizenship, his ties to that throne, for her.

Oh, some might think he'd not had to give up much, maybe even thought he'd gained a lot by being named a duke, marrying a princess who was now a queen, living in palaces, and going on world tours.

However, if they truly knew him, they would have known that all Philip had ever wanted was to be an admiral in the navy, something he'd have no chance to be now. He'd wanted his children to have his family name—again, something he didn't have.

She was certain that until his dying breath, he would swear giving up those things didn't matter. But Elizabeth knew better. She saw Philip staring longingly at the sea, and the look of nostalgia that floated on his face as they boarded a boat on one of the lakes at Balmoral. The way he tenderly held the lines, stroked the rails, and looked out over the bow. The lake had become his ocean, and the rowboat his ship, the oars the engine.

The least she could do was let him live the life of a sailor for a few months. It was selfless of her to let him go and enjoy his time on the sea, as much as she selfishly wished he had said he didn't need it.

But she could look confidently upon the smiling face of her husband and know that this was the right move for him. When he'd been invited to open the Summer Olympic Games in Melbourne, Australia, there had never been any question that he shouldn't go, at least in her mind. And why not make it a wonderful sailing trip?

Philip had been instrumental in starting several athletic foundations in the United Kingdom and was an active athlete himself—something he'd passed on to little Anne. It only made sense that he should have the honor of opening the games. And if he was already going to be halfway around the world, he should make other state visits, and so they'd tacked on New Zealand, Ceylon, Gambia, the Galapagos Islands, and the Falkland Islands; and the icing on the cake was Antarctica.

Papers printed headlines about how she wanted to freeze him to death in the coldest place on earth, but if given the chance, wouldn't those very same people have strapped on their snowshoes and, bundled in layers, walked on the very icy grounds Philip was going to? Jealousy may have been at the root of some of the rumors.

If the unfortunate Suez crisis hadn't derailed his plans of going to Singapore where anti-British rallies made it unsafe, that too would have been on his agenda.

"Where's Papa's ship?" Anne asked, scrunching up her nose as she spun a massive globe in the drawing room at Windsor

when they were back from the airport. They'd spend the weekend here as planned before returning to London.

They'd been talking for days about how he was going to sail
on the massive yacht.

"He's going to board it in Australia after the games." Elizabeth spun the globe until the Australian continent came into
view.

"I wanted to go to the games." Anne pouted, stroking the
outline of the continent.

"I know, darling. Perhaps when you're a little older."

Charles said nothing, but Elizabeth knew he also had
wanted to go to the games. The idea of traveling the world
seemed much more exciting than starting school at Hill House
in Knightsbridge, where he'd been shuttled each morning and
returned to the palace each afternoon.

Hill House had been a bone of contention between her and
Philip. He believed their son should be given an education outside the palace, as he himself had. Besides that, he thought
sweet Charles was not developing socially quickly enough—
when the truth was that Charles took more after her. His disposition was not as competitive as Philip's—or Anne's, for that
matter. Anne had no qualms about riding roughshod over her
brother in order to get what she wanted.

Charles was a sensitive lad, and quiet. Philip had hopes that
an education outside the palace would toughen him up.

Elizabeth rubbed her son's back, smiling down at him.
"Would you like to go for a bicycle ride?"

Charles beamed up at her. "Yes."

"I want to go for a bicycle ride too," Anne said.

"Of course. We'll all go for a ride."

And so they made their way out to the Long Walk. Perched

on their bicycles, with their security guards on horseback and Susan strapped into the basket on Elizabeth's handlebars, they set off through the park, riding past other riders, walkers. People turned to wave, not unused to seeing them enjoying the grounds. The children gloried in the beautiful day, and so did Elizabeth. Happy for moments like this when she could spend time with them. The only damper was that Philip wasn't there.

The demands of being a queen often took precedent, and she felt as though her children were growing up in the blink of an eye. Thank goodness for Nanny Lightbody, Miss Anderson, and Miss Peebles, who helped to care for and educate the children, else they wouldn't be as sweet and bright as they were.

Susan's fur ruffled in the wind, and her tongue hung out of her mouth, flapping against her snout, which had become equal parts silver in the reddish-gold. There was no denying that her corgi was growing older. The last link to her father. But at least they had Sugar and Honey, Whisky and Sherry, and soon Honey would whelp.

The long line of Windsor corgis was Susan's legacy, and in a way, they were the legacy of the king, and of Elizabeth too.

Susan turned back to her, love and happiness in her brown eyes, and Elizabeth smiled, feeling wholly complete at that very moment.

* * *

October 29, 1956

"I want you to remember this night the next time you say I'm a naughty princess," Maggie teased, dressed in her gown and white gloves for the Royal Command Film Performance at the Empire Theatre.

"Oh, you are too much," Elizabeth said with a roll of her eyes as they exited the Rolls-Royce at the front of the theater.

Waiting inside was a receiving line of dozens of celebrities who'd come to greet them before the film, *The Battle of the River Plate*.

Elizabeth loved films and every year looked forward to the event. "Do behave yourself."

Maggie snickered. "I shall endeavor to be as charming as Philip would be if he were here, seeing as how I'm his replacement."

"You are never a replacement, darling. Can I not wish to see a movie with my sister?"

Maggie laughed at that. "As if we were two ordinary girls going to the cinema?"

Elizabeth grinned. "We are, only classier with our gloves." She wiggled her fingers.

Maggie hid her smile as they were greeted by the first in the receiving line, chatting with those they'd met before and being introduced to new ones.

About halfway through, Elizabeth stood before a stunning blond actress, Marilyn Monroe. She'd heard of Marilyn Monroe before and seen one of her films, *How to Marry a Millionaire*. The poor thing looked so nervous she'd licked off all her lipstick. Elizabeth could relate. It was one of the things that the press office had coached her on before every speech.

"Good evening, dear." Elizabeth held out her hand.

Marilyn gripped her hand, a slight tremble in her gloved fingers as she dipped into a curtsy.

"How do you like England?" Elizabeth asked.

"I like it very much. We've rented an adorable house in Englefield Green, Parkside House." Marilyn's voice was soft, almost too soft to be heard among the voices in the receiving line.

"Oh, so we're practically neighbors. Have you enjoyed Windsor?"

"Yes. As a matter of fact, I saw you when I was riding my bike. You had an adorable dog in your basket." Marilyn's blue eyes sparkled and her lips quivered slightly as she smiled.

Elizabeth laughed. "That's my Susan; she's a truly admirable dog and the very best companion."

"I love dogs. I have a basset hound back home, Hugo."

"I'm certain he's sweet. It was lovely to meet you."

"It was lovely to meet you as well." Despite the enjoyment Marilyn seemed to have in the moment, there was something sad about the actress that stuck with Elizabeth even as she continued down the line.

·࿐ೞಀೋ·

CHAPTER FORTY-TWO

SUSAN

The sun is warm on my back, and the grass soft beneath me. A beetle meanders over the blades as though trudging through a massive forest.

I pant, letting the heat roll off my tongue in tiny drips that slip and slide down the blades of grass, plopping onto the beetle, who is no doubt irritated by it.

Lilibet runs around the yard with the children and the new puppies, my grandpuppies.

I'm smiling, even if no one can tell, the corners of my wide mouth slightly tilted, my eyes squinted. Twelve years ago, the king lifted me from the litter, held me high, and declared me the one. Now here we are, three generations of me later, and the smile on Lilibet's face is just as full of joy as it was back then.

I wonder, is this the meaning of life? Watching future generations as they explore with gleeful curiosity?

Lilibet is still young for a human, though her mind has grown wiser, and I am nearing old age.

The young prince tosses a stick that sails through the air. The tiny pups chase after it, full of energy and joy. But they can't beat me.

I may be getting old, but this dog still has some tricks.

I rise and push my legs into a run, my claws digging into the earth for traction. I'll show these young ones how it's done.

I leap up, clamp my teeth around the center of the stick, chomp it tight, and then land on my feet. I turn with satisfaction toward Lilibet, who is clapping.

"I thought that might get you up," she says, as if it were her plan all along.

Not a second later, the stick that pokes out from both sides of my face is mauled by my granddaughters, who growl fiercely and shake their heads.

Inside I laugh, while outside I play along. There is a lightness in my heart to know that when my time comes, I will live on in these young ones. That Lilibet won't be without me, even if I'm not really here.

I shake my head, sending the pups flying, and then I run toward Lilibet, hoping she understands I want her to take the stick and toss it again before they catch me. And she does.

We do a few more runs like that, and then I lie back in the shade, panting from exertion, heart beating wildly from the game and from happiness.

Lilibet collapses beside me, running her hand over my back.

"Just look at them, Sus," she says.

And I do look at them all. The tiny prince and princess. The tiny corgis.

The peacefulness of the interlude is broken when Honey and Sugar come running to play with the puppies, possessing all the energy I just let out. A new, kinder footman chases them, as does the nanny for the children.

"Well, Susan, it's time we went back to work."

I know this word, *work*. It's what we do together. Lilibet sits at her desk, sorting papers and murmuring to herself; occasionally she picks up the shiny black handle and speaks into it. I tried barking at it once and nothing happened, so I've decided she does it to break up the tedium of stacking papers over and over again.

My job is to lie under her desk, my head on her foot that taps sometimes. I provide the calm the papers and the telephone seem to upset.

But mostly, my job is to remind Lilibet to smile.

CHAPTER FORTY-THREE

$\mathcal{H}$ANNA

Christmas and New Year's passed with the usual fanfare, though Elizabeth was more subdued, and it wasn't really surprising why. There'd been plenty of times the royal children spent Christmas without their parents, but in the many years that I'd served the queen I couldn't think of her spending it without her Philip. This past Christmas, he'd sent a message from his ship somewhere in the middle of the ocean and she'd responded with one of her own.

Rumors were still swirling not only in the papers and throughout the Commonwealth but within the servants' hall. I'd done my best to keep the rumormongers at bay, but people would be people. And those who served the royals loved nothing more than to spread a juicy bit that might get them five seconds of attention.

The very idea that Philip would be sent abroad as punishment by the queen was ridiculous to say the least. And the idea of him going on a nearly half-year stag party to spite her was even dumber. Did they actually think that Philip would betray her by sleeping his way around the world?

The rumors were like a badly scripted, and terribly portrayed, drama. Embarrassing, to say the least. There were still a couple of weeks left in Philip's tour, which meant that many more days of Elizabeth trying to ignore the papers.

And given what had transpired recently with Philip's private secretary, Mike Parker, the heat was on high. Prior to setting sail on the *Britannia* with Philip, Parker had evidently told his wife he'd had an affair. They'd agreed to separate and had tried to keep it hushed up, but her lawyer, greedy as he was for the money likely slipped to him, decided to tell everyone.

That had led to vicious articles in the press about Philip out partying and philandering with his soon-to-be-divorced best friend. Parker had resigned while they were docked in Gibraltar. On our walk, Elizabeth had briefly mentioned how upsetting the whole ordeal must have been for Philip, and the rumors were just becoming too much.

And I couldn't agree more. It was sickening, really. I couldn't imagine being in that position. As it was, sometimes Forrest and I would see a photographer camped outside our door, waiting for a glimpse of the corgis. Or on the windy tarmac where I greeted the queen when she returned from someplace.

Just the other day, Forrest had leaned over me in the car and rolled up my window as I shouted my opinions on their morals to the reporters who languished outside the Sandringham gates. Not my finest hour, I admit.

But today, I hoped to make up for it.

I was throwing a thirteenth birthday party for Susan. All the puppies were invited, and of course the queen and her children.

The staff had set up tables and chairs in an indoor area of the stables used to exercise the horses, cleared out for the occasion. The dogs were all to be served their own special cakes, baked by my stepmother, Jane, while the human guests dined on another.

We had games and relay races set up, and it should be an afternoon of delightful fun indoors, in contrast to the wintry weather.

There was something to be said about the celebration of life. We'd be celebrating Susan, yes, but everyone else too. I wanted to bring some joy to the queen, who'd been so stressed and lonely during Philip's absence.

And though I'd never say it aloud, and I'm sure she wouldn't admit it, Elizabeth had been a friend to me since we were children. Our roles in life, our places in society were quite a bit different—after all, she was my monarch—but that didn't mean on the inside I didn't consider her to be that special, constant person that one might name a friend.

And perhaps this party would become a tradition.

Doggie One and the new Doggie Two—thank goodness for him—were in attendance to help me corral the furry guests and the guest of honor.

As the queen, her children, the queen mother, and Princess Margaret arrived, the staff curtsied, and we handed each of the royals and guests a party hat that had been painted with Susan's face.

"This is adorable," Margaret exclaimed.

Queen Elizabeth grinned, looking a little more relaxed than she had of late, and she nodded in my direction.

"Welcome to Susan's birthday party," I said.

The children ran toward the tables, picking up the dog cakes and sniffing them.

"Put those down," their nanny admonished.

We'd corralled all the dogs inside one of the empty stalls,

and at my nod, the corgi footmen opened the door. A rush of reddish-gold and white fur flew out, their scarves in various colors of the rainbow flashing from around their necks.

Susan, despite her age, was first out; perhaps the others had let her in deference to her age and position within the pack. Though if placement were anything to be examined, Whisky, Sherry, and Gin had yet to realize they weren't to be first; and they quickly raced ahead, leaving Sugar, Honey, and Biscuit to take up the rear.

Their yips of excitement made everyone else coo and call out to them as the corgis circled the guests and licked their shoes. Fortunately, there'd been no more biting incidents, which led me to believe that the hateful footman had done something to cause Honey's reaction.

"Let's have our treats first," I said, knowing that at any second the dogs would catch the scent of the freshly baked goods and not be interested in the games. "Everyone, grab a corgi."

I laughed as I picked up Gin and put her on a chair, the others following suit. As soon as they were placed, their paws went up on the table and their snouts into the special dog cakes. It was a sight to remember, these dogs having a party. I recorded as much as I could with my Leica, taking photos of the dogs and the human guests. One of the queen with her children, one of her leaning down and Susan standing up to lick her on the nose.

While the dogs munched, the children grabbed their own cakes, and I led the group in singing happy birthday to Susan, whose ears swiveled when she heard her name. She lifted her head, cocking it to the side, cake crumbs stuck to the whiskers on her snout.

Elizabeth sang the loudest, standing behind Susan's chair,

a wide smile on her face and the faintest sheen of tears in her eyes.

The treats didn't last long, and the corgis jumped down from their perches to run around.

"What have you planned for us next?" Elizabeth asked.

"A dog relay, ma'am," I said. "We'll see how long it lasts."

We lined up in threes, separated by ten feet each, holding various toys. The footmen held the corgis leashed at the head of the two rows, and then let them go one by one as we all cheered and called out for the dogs to come take a toy. It was wonderful chaos.

Biscuit snatched the stuffed rabbit from my hands, the prince and princess in front of me, but rather than return to the footman, Biscuit rushed over to Susan, who promptly dropped her stuffed fox to try and snatch the rabbit. Whisky, Sherry, and Gin ran at the same time to snatch the fallen fox, and Sugar and Honey joined Biscuit and Susan in a game of tug-of-war.

"This is too delightful," Elizabeth said through a fit of laughter, clapping. "Why haven't we done doggie relays before?"

The prince and princess picked up discarded toys, shaking them in the air and trying to get the attention of the corgis for another round, but it would seem they were entirely too enamored with the toys they'd already snatched.

"We should make it a yearly tradition," Princess Margaret said as she lit another cigarette. "The Winter Windsor Corgi Relays."

"Perhaps spring would suit better," the queen mother said. "Then we could do it outside."

"Quite right," Elizabeth said. "The Annual Spring Windsor Corgi Relay Races. Not quite as good a ring to it as Winter

Windsor Corgi, but the idea of playing on the grounds sounds enticing."

"And hoops!" Prince Charles added. "They can run through hoops like at the dog shows."

Elizabeth smiled and patted her son on the head. "Indeed, they can."

I grinned at the group, pleased to see that my plan to bring some joy to the queen had worked, and even more pleased she liked it enough to keep it going. And, especially, the joy and added pep to Susan's step as she played was a gift in itself.

"What do you say, Hanna?" the queen asked me. "Can you manage it?"

"It would be my pleasure, as the keeper of the queen's corgis, ma'am."

·ᵒᵉˡᵉᵒ·

CHAPTER FORTY-FOUR

ℰLIZABETH

Lisbon, Portugal
Late February 1957

𝒯he pictures of Philip abroad with his wild ginger beard grown out—a bit of gray running through it where before there'd been none—had left many in the household laughing. Elizabeth had been particularly fond of those pictures as she remembered having the one from Philip on her mantel before they were engaged, back when she only had hopes of making him her husband.

He looked young, and happy, and full of life. Exactly what she'd hoped this trip would do for him. The beard represented Sailor Philip, the man who was in control of his own life and destiny and living where he wanted to be, which was at sea.

The days had been busy while he was gone, but the nights were lonely. Even the theater, dinner, and various other engagements couldn't replace the time the two of them spent in the evening with their shoes kicked off, their stockinged feet up on the couch or the coffee table, watching a television show or just chatting about what had happened throughout the day.

Those were the moments she missed, being able to spill everything out that needed spilling, and Philip helping her to clean it all up. The privacy of life behind closed doors where, though she was still a monarch, she was also a wife, a mother, a friend.

With their contacts in the theater world, Elizabeth collected a plethora of ginger whiskers for her and their staff to don upon greeting him.

Elizabeth twitched her nose, her face itching from the false whiskers, as she waited nervously inside her plane on the tarmac in Lisbon. Four months since she'd seen her husband. They'd decided to make their reunion into a state visit, and now here she was.

She wanted to launch herself into his arms, but as the queen and surrounded by people, she would need to be dignified, which irritated her. This wasn't the first time she'd felt this way, and it would certainly not be the last. Elizabeth tried to stand as still as possible; the only thing moving was her tongue as she ran it repeatedly over her now whisker-fringed lips.

Philip's voice sounded from the stairway leading up to the plane, and Elizabeth went rigid with excitement. He ducked under the doorway and looked up, surprise registering on his face at the sight of them all standing there dressed up to look like him, and then he burst into laughter. The sound was magic to her ears, and Elizabeth nearly leaped out of her skin with joy. His face was clean-shaven—Prince Philip returned and Sailor Philip put away.

"My God! What have you done," he said, laughing so hard tears gathered in his eyes.

Elizabeth laughed too and, forgoing propriety, rushed forward, pressing a kiss on his lips, deciding she didn't give a damn what anyone thought about it. This was her husband, and they'd been apart for months. Maybe in the end her show of affection would quash any rumors that might have still lingered.

Philip laughed and kissed her back, and then peeled off the fake beard from her face, flinging it behind him so he could kiss her properly.

"A jolly good prank, my queen," he said with another chuckle. "Jolly good."

"I've missed you," Elizabeth said. "I'm so glad you're back."

"Hale and hearty, my little cabbage." He squeezed her hand and brought it to his lips. "And excited for this time away from the palace with you."

She grinned. "We can pretend we're in Malta."

"I like the way you think."

"Now, let us go and show the world just how much of a rift actually exists between us."

"Precisely zero."

"Precisely." And she kissed him again, just for good measure.

No matter the distance, no matter the world's upheaval, not a person, place, or thing could come between Elizabeth and her prince. Susan took that moment to let out a bark from her seat on one of the airplane chairs. Not as agile as she was before, she leaped down in almost slow motion and approached the two of them with purpose.

Half-heartedly, Susan clamped her teeth on Philip's trouser leg, giving it a gentle shake.

"Somebody doesn't feel as though she got a proper greeting." Elizabeth bent down and scooped up Susan.

"I've brought you a treat, my little demon." Philip reached into his pocket and pulled out a tiny biscuit. "Perhaps we might call a truce today?"

Susan barked and gingerly took the treat, chomping on it with delight.

·ᨀᥣᨀ·

CHAPTER FORTY-FIVE

$\mathcal{S}$USAN

Sandringham
Christmas 1958

$\mathcal{I}$ pant beneath the Christmas tree in the drawing room, the toy from my Christmas stocking laid at my feet. It was tiring to pull it from within the red wool, and I need to take a rest.

Lots of things are harder now. When Lilibet and I take walks, I stop more often, lie down to rest my weary legs. She doesn't berate me but sits beside me, strokes my back. I yawn up at her, our eyes meeting. It's the best feeling in the world when we look at each other. I could stare into her eyes all day. Something inside me sparks when we do that, and happiness runs as rampant through my veins as blood.

"I don't want you to go," Lilibet says often.

I wish I could tell her that I'm not going anywhere, that I'm right here. But she seems to think me getting tired means I plan to go away. Like Crackers. Like her father and her grandmother.

Usually I roll over, let her rub my belly as I stare at the sky and contemplate life's secrets and how I can share everything I know with my princess.

"What are you doing over here?" Lilibet says now, sitting

beside me in the corner while the children play with their toys with their father, my nemesis to the end.

The queen mother and Princess Maggie are arguing over something, but I don't care to listen. They are always arguing over something; and most of the time I don't understand what it is, so why bother?

I lean against Lilibet's leg, and she lifts me gingerly onto her lap, running a hand over my back. I yawn and let my weight fall against her. It feels good to be in her lap, to know that in all the nearly fifteen years of my life, she's been by my side. My dearest friend, and I hers.

"Did you like your gift this year?" she asks, picking up the tiny stuffed . . . What is it?

Some things are harder to see now. It might be a fox, or it might be a cat. Either way, I definitely plan to shred it later, pretending that I found it on a hunt. But right now, I just want to lie here with her. To feel the warmth of her body beneath mine, the solidness of her that proves this wonderful life I've had is real.

When I'm in her arms, the aches in my bones go away. She does that to me. Brings me peace and comfort.

These moments have always been my happiest. When we are still and quiet together. Of course, I've loved the games, the hunts, the walks, the treats; but these particular snatches of time, when she is not rushing off or worried, when all her concentration is on me and I feel like she can almost hear me say *I love you* . . .

"I love you, girl," she whispers against my ear as she curls her body over mine and kisses the top of my head. "You have been the very best companion anyone could ever ask for."

I love you too, my girl. I love you too.

AUTHOR'S NOTE

*T*his book, while produced with a heavy dose of research and sticking true to much of Queen Elizabeth II and Susan's timeline, is a book of historical fiction. Because it is fiction, I used creative license in writing the story. The purpose of this author's note is to share with you what I learned and what I may have altered, as well as things that surprised me.

I come from a large family of humans and dogs. Until last year, we gathered at the family lodge for holidays. My parents had a climate-controlled kennel built for all the dogs my siblings and I brought so they could lounge in comfort, because fourteen dogs (a Newfie, a Newfie-Lab, German shepherds, a corgi, shorkies, a husky, and a terrier) in one house would have been madness! But it is these memories of long weekends, surrounded by family and pets, that I cherish and that also helped to contribute to some of the personalities in this book.

Most dog lovers I know, including myself, put a lot of thoughts and words into our dogs' mouths. We know them well and can decipher what they want, what they may need, and dare I say it, what they might be thinking.

Dogs do have facial expressions. It's easy to determine what they might be feeling based on those expressions, their barks and whines, and so on, just like you can determine a baby's needs and emotions from their various expressions and cries. Dogs can also learn words. Around my house, we have to spell out certain words because if the dogs hear, for instance, *walk* or *treat*, they go nuts. They know what those mean.

I'm not a dog expert and I don't pretend to be. But for this book I used not only my own personal experiences with my dogs and my friends' and family's experiences but also research. I read books and watched documentaries about dog behavior, and most of all, I researched Queen Elizabeth and her dogs to get an accurate picture of her relationship with them, as well as their lineage and life timelines. Of course, many of the scenes within the book are fictional, but there are also many that are based on fact. For example, Susan did accompany Queen Elizabeth and Prince Philip on their honeymoon, and she was hidden by staff in the blankets of the carriage. The corgis did have their own bedroom, footmen, and chefs. The corgis did have some biting issues—on both humans and furniture—and a lot of the staff did get annoyed by them.

Susan is the matriarch of fourteen generations of corgis. The queen never bred the dogs for sale, but simply for her love of the breed. And she stopped breeding her corgis in 2009, because she didn't want to leave any behind when she passed away.

The average litter for a corgi is five or six pups. Queen Elizabeth did not keep every puppy in a litter, and oftentimes the only ones recorded are those she did keep. Most of each litter were either given back to breeding kennels or gifted to family and friends. Also, because she did not breed them for sale, the queen did not register her dogs with the Kennel Club, though she was a patron, nor did she show them. An excellent, well-researched book that I adored and that I recommend for further reading on the royal corgis is *All the Queen's Corgis* by Penny Junor.

Hanna is a fictional character in the novel, as is her father.

They were inspired by Bill and Nancy Fenwick. Bill was a royal gamekeeper and was also known as the keeper of the queen's corgis, a position his wife shared with him. Nancy passed away in 2015—and the queen broke protocol to attend her funeral—and Bill in 2017. While Bill was sick, the queen would visit him on Sundays and walk his dogs. After he passed away, she adopted his corgi, Whisper.

Hanna's husband is also fictional. The role of liveried helpers is not really to travel from castle to castle. They are typically stationed at one palace's mews. But for the sake of this story, I fudged it a bit so that Forrest could travel with the princesses. Additionally, it is very unlikely that a royal coachman would also drive vehicles, as their job was to drive the carriages and oversee the livered helpers.

As for Queen Elizabeth's intimate relationships with her parents, her sister, her husband, and her children, the interactions and scenes within this novel are fictional, though many are based on true events and the research from many biographies, memoirs, articles, documentaries, videos and news coverage from the time period, and travel to London. My purpose in writing this book was to show that while she was a queen, Queen Elizabeth was also a woman and a dog lover, and I wanted to emphasize what a special bond she had with her corgis. On that note, the letters written between Queen Elizabeth and Prince Philip are fictional, as are the letters written to and by Susan.

Of course, there is so much that happened in Queen Elizabeth's long life that I was not able to include. And to be fair, this book is really about Susan and her Lilibet, and so it only takes place along the timeline of Susan's life. All my respect and love to them both.

.⸙.

ACKNOWLEDGMENTS

It's no secret that I love my dogs. They are my giant fur-babies. Lady Belle, a Newfoundland, has a very particular personality. She is intelligent, thoughtful, and opinionated. But she is also extremely sweet and adoring. Merida, a Newfie-Lab mix, is quirky and silly, and actually smiles when she's happy. A book that contains the story of a dog's life along with the lives of those who loved her could not have been completed without my own two faithful companions who provided constant support and research for this novel.

First, I must thank my incomparable agent, Kevan Lyon, who is also a major dog lover and supported the quirky idea of me writing a book with a dog's perspective. I am also grateful to my wonderful editors at William Morrow, Lucia Macro and Tessa Woodward, both of whom have been very supportive in bringing this corgi world to life, as well as associate editor Asanté Simons and editorial assistant Madelyn Blaney. Thank you to the hardworking people in the sales, marketing, publicity, art, and production departments. My gratitude to all the remarkable people of William Morrow, including our publisher, Liate Stehlik. Many thanks to my critique partner, Sophie Perinot, for helping me get this book into reading shape! I'm grateful to have had my princess crew, Madeline Martin, Brenna Ash, and Lori Ann Bailey, to help me plot, reading early pitches and talking me through scenes—you guys are the best! Thank you to Heather Webb for going with me to London to do some re-search for this book—what a blast! Thank you to my brilliant Lyonesses for their sisterhood and to the Tall Poppies for their enthusiastic support of this book.

Last, but never least, a special thank-you to my wonderful husband and daughters. You are my constant champions, my wonderful human companions, my fellow dog lovers, my fun dog-voice transcribers, my everything. I love you all so much.